SUSAN SHWARTZ
HERITAGE OF FLIGHT

TOR®

A TOM DOHERTY ASSOCIATES BOOK
NEW YORK

Author's Note

Several parts of *Heritage of Flight* have been modified from their original appearance in *Analog Science Fiction/Science Fact*. These are "Heritage of Flight," *Analog*, April 1983, and "Survivor Guilt," *Analog*, February 1986.

Copyright Acknowledgments

From *Wartime Writings 1939-1944* by Antoine de Saint-Exupéry, copyright © 1982 by Editions Gallimard; English translation copyright © 1986 by Harcourt Brace Jovanovich, Inc. Reprinted by permission of Harcourt Brace Jovanovich, Inc.

From "Ash Wednesday" in *Collected Poems 1909-1962* by T. S. Eliot, copyright 1936 by Harcourt Brace Jovanovich, Inc.; copyright © 1963, 1964 by T. S. Eliot. Reprinted by permission of the publisher.

HERITAGE OF FLIGHT

A TOR Book
Published by Tom Doherty Associates, Inc.
49 West 24 Street
New York, NY 10010

Cover art by Wayne Barlowe

ISBN: 0-812-55413-2   Can. ISBN: 0-812-55414-0

Library of Congress Catalog Card Number: 88-51628

First edition: April 1989

Printed in the United States of America

0 9 8 7 6 5 4 3 2 1

ACKNOWLEDGMENTS

I'd like to thank Dr. Dean Lambe, Robert Adams, and Sandra Miesel as well as the following organizations: the information offices of the United Nations, NASA, and the U.S. Army (with special thanks to Lieutenant Colonel Paul Knox); the Futurists II Workshop of 1985, Wright-Patterson Air Force Base; and the Schomburg Institute for Afro-American Studies.

. . . We have chosen to save peace. But in saving peace we have harmed our friends. And no doubt, many among us were ready to risk their lives in the interests of friendship and now feel a kind of shame. But if they had sacrificed peace, they would feel the same shame; because they would then have sacrificed humanity: they would have accepted the irretrievable destruction of the libraries, cathedrals, and laboratories of Europe. They would have accepted the ruin of its traditions and transformed the world into a cloud of ashes. And that is why we shifted from one opinion to the other. When peace seemed threatened, we discovered the shame of war. When it appeared that we were to be spared from war, we felt the shame of peace.

—ANTOINE DE SAINT-EXUPÉRY
"La Paix ou la Guerre,"
Paris-Soir, Oct. 2–4, 1938.

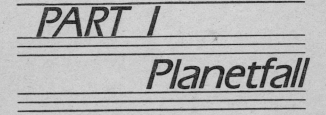

PART I

Planetfall

We go to gain a little patch of ground
That hath in it no profit but the name.

—WILLIAM SHAKESPEARE,
Hamlet, IV, iv, 18–19.

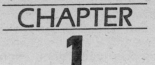

Realspace shimmered, elongated, then twanged back into existence, taking Pauli Yeager with it. The boards of her ridership, too painstakingly maintained to be new, blurred, then solidified once again. *Bad transit*, she judged. She shook herself mentally, then glanced at the chrono. It should have begun to move as soon as they entered realspace. Reality shimmered for a fearful "instant," then refocused. There: now the damned chrono had started up.

She put out a hand to touch the display, which gleamed ice-blue. Three seconds realtime had elapsed. *Very bad transit*. Jump was—or should be—instantaneous, however long it felt as space curved and light shifted about you. She swallowed hard, and blinked away a treacherous fog that would be the death of her if it hit when she was using armscomp. Despite lifesupport, which allegedly kept her suit at a comfortable temperature, she shivered and sweated simultaneously.

That actual time had passed . . . if Jump had been this bad for her fighter and its host, *Leonidas*, which had the best of a dying fleet's diminished store of matériel, what had it been like for the refugee ships *Daedalus* and *Sir Jeffrey Amherst*?

Before her transfer to *Leonidas* as a senior pilot—and that seniority was a laugh, if anything about this damned war qualified as laughable—she'd served aboard the *Amherst*. That had been temporary duty, another in the frustrating chain of TDYs that cheated Pauli of the advanced pilot training on New Patuxent she'd been wild for since the war had stepped up. New Pax gave pilots the best training, and increased their chances of surviving their first scramble. And if Exploration, the service she had wanted to enter, was no longer an option, the best training was barely good enough to keep her alive.

Wouldn't you just know that the instant *Amherst* was headed toward New Pax at long last, new orders would divert them to Wolf IV, one of the slagged worlds, half charnel and half rubble, to rescue and lift out as many survivors as possible for resettlement? She couldn't complain of her luck; it was better than any on Wolf IV.

Thereafter, it seemed, they were always on the run, retreating world by abandoned world, system by ravaged system in the Net of Worlds that had linked the Alliance with Manhome Earth, a Net the Secessionists had torn through, God only knew why.

This war made Alliance and Secess' maniacs even in retreat, fighting with the deadliness of scavengers forced against a cliff face to defend their last scrap of meat. This was not a war you could win, Pauli thought, remembering Wolf IV—the half-melted ruins, the fevered, feral survivors, and the factories stripped by raiders from both sides, desperate for components and supplies now that the production lines were gone, or going.

She glanced over her boards, which weeks of prayerful labor had raised to a semblance of their old speed. Like *Leonidas* itself, all the riderships had the best equipment they could scrounge, cajole, or steal. Why was it so important to protect refugees? Why, as the tiny convoy fled farther out and deep into the No Man's Worlds, had security intensified until the pilots rode out Jump in their fighters? At the last planetfall, Federal Security marshals had crammed onto the ships, and the pilots had hoped that they, at least, might offer some answers. But the marshals whose presence strained cramped ships' capacities to house and feed them were saying nothing. At least, not to the pilots, though they had summoned— by God, they had ordered as if they were cadets— Captains Borodin and Ver from their own ships onto *Leonidas* for a conference. When they emerged, the captains announced that the marshals would keep order on board and serve as consultants—that elastic, treacherous term for despots pro tem, as impossible to get rid of as to question.

After that meeting, the convoy altered course. It was hard to escape the conclusion that the marshals had ordered it. Too damned many marshals, eating supplies that the refugees needed, speaking officialese to no purpose but their own, issuing random orders, seemingly for the joy of turning line officers into flunkies.

Maliciously, Pauli hoped they enjoyed their new duties: mediating between the civs, who suspected anyone in uniform of some past or future atrocity, and their refugee charges, who feared anyone at all. Most of them were children, but they were children who had learned to claw for survival. Rescue parties had found battered adult skeletons in the rubble of Wolf IV; the medics had forbade anyone to question the evacuees.

Over in the *Amherst* and *Daedalus*, refugees slept two and three to a bunk. Even the riderbays emptied by crashes and firefights had been converted to makeshift barracks for the refugees, who crouched among emergency supplies they still did not dare touch as if they hid in caves. *Leonidas* would set the medics, techs, civs, and their charges down on whatever resettlement world the marshals intended, and then Pauli would transship for New Pax and the business of fighter training. Anything that would extend her life a little longer and give her the chance to strike back at the war that had ended any hope she ever had of growing up happy, or growing up at all.

Pauli activated communications, taking bleak comfort from the renewed chatter of a ship running in realspace. Comfort that they'd survived Jump. Satisfaction that they'd made it this far. Never mind happy. *Happy* was a word like *peace*: it had book definition, but no meaning. At least not for anyone she knew. The psychs had praised her flexibility; if flexibility meant that she could adapt to this, then it was another reason for satisfaction. Happy was a dream she had before she realized how long, and how final, this war looked to be. She had to adjust to it—or die; and the same damned psychs said she wasn't a quitter.

A klaxon brayed over the ship chatter, and red light pulsed in the gloom of her cockpit. Pauli checked her boards again and cursed. So much for careful maintenance! Her ship's alarm buzzer had failed. With luck, the weapons systems wouldn't fail too. She tightened her webs and braced for the launch that hurled her ship out into space. Gravity pressed, then slacked off as she banked into formation with the rest of the riderships. The port darkened to protect her from the actinic glare of the white dwarf that circled a much larger, cooler star. Scanners showed planets in this system, planets and a dense asteroid belt. The system was too crowded to be wholly safe.

Well, what would it be this time? Secessionist ships, or some Fed Sec marshal gone even more paranoid than usual? Ambush was impossible in Jump, but betrayal—that was feasible. Pauli activated internal security scan. After all, Secess' and Alliance had been one government once before the damned theories—expansion versus consolidation under human rule—blew apart the government, then started firestorms on the worlds themselves.

With the Net gone, patrolled by Secess', Earth was a dream of order and prosperity. Ironic, Pauli thought, that Manhome herself now had about as much meaning as the word *happy*.

Was it just the Secess', came a treacherous whisper, or had Terra chosen isolation, suspicious of friends who might, suddenly, transmogrify into enemies doubly vicious for the knowledge alliance and kinship had given them? She shivered. If she believed that—*let the Secess' show up soon*, she prayed, *so I can forget*.

She turned eyes back to her boards. The moments between system entry and attack were always tricky. You could betray a ship, especially as systems lost backups, and even some primaries were scrapped. A hidden transmitter, and there you were, vulnerable after Jump. Then the Secess' could emerge and strip down your ship, leaving you—if you were lucky and they were feeling kind—to limp back to whatever base might help you refit. There were fewer and fewer such bases on either side these days, Pauli thought.

She interfaced sensors with the other ships. They pressed forward, scanning, always scanning, so slowly that she felt no acceleration; on the newer riderships, you could feel G-forces build up only as you neared Jump speed. The navigation grids glowed with the patterns of ships on three axes. To her left and "up," one veered out of formation. A quick warning, and the light that represented it blinked back into its proper position: the shift of that light and the chrono's ordered clicks were the only movements Pauli perceived.

Her breath rasped in the tiny cockpit, threatening to cloud the visor of her helmet until she adjusted temperature controls downward. Recon felt motionless; it wore on the nerves until you wanted to blast something if only to see the light slash out to break the monotony and the tension.

Come on, if you're out there! Fire already! No pilot who actually wanted to get out and zero Secess' with virtuoso laserwork outlived his third battle . . . sometimes not even his first. But this damnable prowling, waiting for a strike that might come in a second, an hour, or never, made you want to scream or strike first, blindly, in an attempt to find some clear, safe way. She sweated with the need to see something, anything. It built up, as it always did, to a point where she didn't think she could bear it—and then the moment passed, as it always did; and the ships pressed forward, scanning for enemies.

Secess' out here didn't necessarily mean treachery. Attack could even be coincidence, as ships from both sides sought the No Man's Worlds, seeking to survive in these remote spacelanes by turning scavenger, even pirate. So far, she thought with a sort of chill pride, such scavengers only preyed on one another.

Quickly Pauli ran the armscomp test program again, as she had before Jump and would again, if they didn't suddenly engage the Secess' and she had to use her lasers for real. Testing was never superfluous. You never knew when your equipment might fail. How long would it be until Alliance ships turned on their own, as well as the Secess', to steal the dwindling supplies of components, concentrates, all the never-to-be replaced stores for which production lines had all but ceased?

Two of the riderships passed by a massive asteroid with a dense metallic core, a deliberate feint to draw out—there! as if they blinked into existence, there glistened the formation standard to Secess' pilots, a pentacle arrayed along the three axes of space battle. Then another, and another. And where was the base ship that had released them?

Predictable, Pauli thought for the thousandth time. But what was never predictable was the speed with which that formation seemed to materialize, the precision with which the Secess' flew, their cold ferocity, and the deadly teamwork that made each ship of the five react like a finger on the same fatally capable hand. Almost inhuman, it was: never wearing down or fearing, like the pilots she knew. Like herself. Pilots who tired, whose eyes bleared, whose hands shook, and whose breath came hoarse and husky in the fetid cocoons of lifesupport.

Once, just once, before the captain had entered, wardroom rumor whispered of proscribed biotech, of spies vanished, doubtless suicides or painfully dead on Secess' worlds in vain attempts to discover whether the babble about clones and augmentation contained even an atom of truth.

She chilled: even a moment's reflection might prove fatal against Secess' pilots. Whatever else they were, they were geniuses at seizing the opportunity, yes, and one's life with it.

And here they came.

Beyond the five-pointed stars emerged the hull of the Secess' base ship, not burnished like its riders, but scratched and pitted by micrometeorites into a kind of dullness. At the orders of *Leonidas*'s captain, the riders broke formation, changed attitudes, and engaged the

Secess' pilots. Shrewd targeting set violet-tinged spurts of light ravening into hardened metal and fragile systems. Damn! That one had hit a power source. Scratch one ship. Pauli had known the pilot, who had been no fool, just a little old, a little slow. Too slow for the Secess' pilots. They were damned fast, like a schizophrenic divided into five separate, murderous intelligences.

The survivors re-formed and accelerated. A whine underlay the white noise in Pauli's cockpit, and the apparent motion of her companion ships increased. She fired quickly, felt the ship jolt to compensate—and that was the first indication that her ship moved at all. Then *Leonidas* shot forward toward the Secess' so rapidly that she saw it both on grid and in actuality.

Pauli pressed in, one hand thumbing frantically for communications. All around her crackled the chatter of ship-to-ship communications: all chatter from the Alliance side. Never mind jamming: the Secess' were silent, all save the one cool voice per pentacle that had announced the opening of hellmouth for too many of Pauli's friends.

"They're on my tail . . . *cover me-eee*!"

Before a wingman could turn to aid him, needles of violet slashed into the ship and it broke apart, fragments spinning, globing around a central core of fire and instantly freezing vapor. That pilot had been unlucky. Usually the Secess' struck so efficiently that their quarry hadn't even time to see it coming, let alone scream. So, they could be rattled. That, at least, was something. One listed, attitude wobbling; and she fired, taking a ruthless delight in the way that ship veered off, losing control.

"*Daedalus, Amherst . . .*" that was the voice of the *Leonidas*'s captain. "Get out of here. Prepare for Jump."

"Captain, that last jump . . . Engineering reports chip fissures on NavComp. The main boards, not the backups. We can't risk Jump if they melt."

"*Daedalus*, retreat and test then! *Amherst*, prepare for independent Jump. Do you copy?"

"Negative, *Leonidas*, negative," came Captain Borodin's voice in an unusual display of control. Then, more predictably, he roared, "Not goddamned likely, *Leonidas.* We're backing you up!"

Not with all those refugees and civs on board, they couldn't. "This is—"

"Never mind who you are, *Captain*! My commission antedates yours, and I said I'm backing you up!"

"—this is Federal Security Marshal Arnaut, Captain. On my authority, you will retreat and prepare for Jump. Or you will consider yourself removed from command."

In a battle? Pauli could imagine Borodin's snort at the deskflier who would try an empty threat like that. With that snort would come a return to humor, sanity, and craft. Likely, Borodin would bide his moment, then attack. Sure enough, *Amherst* began a tentative retreat. Pauli signalled her own squadron and accelerated toward *Leonidas* as she headed toward a deadly interception with the Secess'.

"Shields on. *Daedalus*, you too; *Amherst*, faster now, get *back*!" Command crackled over the circuits, faltered, then grew loud again as overused commgear achieved a fragile resolution.

"What kind of people are we if we abandon our own?" came Borodin's voice. Pauli felt an incongruous stab of pride. Despite her promotion—for such it was—to the *Leonidas*, Borodin was still the captain under whom she'd first survived fire.

"Smart ones. You have the kids to protect, remember? You really going to let them see battle again, just when they thought they were safe?"

Pauli grimaced. That marshal was crafty, maybe as smart as Borodin. She wondered if the one on *Amherst* was that clever, too.

She got the nearest Secess' in the armscomp sights, heard the satisfactory *beep!* of aligned axes, then opened fire. Clean hit! The other three ships in the format flew wide, then re-formed more raggedly as they, and she, rode out the inevitable buffeting.

She could imagine the chaos on the barracksdecks, and her old friends trying to work with hostile civs to calm them down: Ro, who wore a uniform only because war broke out and she had no choice; Rafe, half a civ himself . . . best not think of Rafe or that last fight when she had finally abandoned their dream of becoming a first-in team, or transferring from the *Amherst* to the more sophisticated *Leonidas*. The kids screaming and crying, wetting themselves, some of them, maybe; the civs struggling to hold to some sort of order as the lights flickered to conserve power, sending it to armscomp and the shields, and the comfort of yellow light faded to uterine crimson, then to twilight.

Her boards showed the haze of screens encircling *Leonidas* and the Secess'. Just one glancing hit, just one, and metal vapor would cloud those shields, make them visible to the naked eye. The screens hazed as *Leonidas*'s lasers slashed out. The running lights dimmed on the big ship. Inside, even the thrum of its lifesupport would pause for the space of a gasp, then resume as power flowed away from armaments and throughout the ship, then gathered for the next surge.

She herself targeted and fired—not mechanically, but with the maniacal precision of a chessmaster forced to choose a move in microseconds. The ship yawed, then resumed attitude. She scanned damage control: assuming nothing else failed, the hit wasn't major. She could press the attack, and she did. Acceleration touched her, pressed webs against her, and apparent motion increased. She fought.

Once again *Leonidas*'s lasers seemed to coil and spring; the Secess' ship returned fire. A pallid haze enveloped both ships, glinting as the white dwarf's savage light struck clouds of frozen vapor into ferocious rainbows. The light intensified about the ships, then widened as power was diverted from other systems into protection.

"Keep *back*!" Pauli whispered. Signalling to the three ships nearest her, she headed toward *Leonidas*, careful to use all available cover to dodge the Secess' one-man craft. On unattainable Earth, she had heard, there were beasts who fought each season over mates. Their weapons were immense racks of horns which they would lower and aim at one another. But once those horns . . . those antlers . . . locked, the beasts were too stubborn, or too stupid, to be willing or able to disengage. Some, she heard, died that way, to be found, seasons later, as racks of bleached bones, their fatal antlers still, inexorably locked.

Once, and once only, she had seen firelock: two ships of roughly equal strength committed, shields and weapons, to destroying one another, as weapons and defense reached a balance in which the captain who diverted power to weapons was instantly consumed as his shields weakened, or the captain who reinforced shields was driven back and driven back until, inevitably, he had to weaken them.

Firelock ended one of two ways: swift, vicious intervention by ridercraft or another ship; or mutual annihilation as systems failed, or overloaded. A brilliant pilot might elude it; but *Leonidas*'s master was no such thing. In the past three years, they had started promoting senior engineers rather than strategists in order to safeguard those ships still in good repair. He might not be pilot enough to avoid firelock, but Pauli was about to stake her life on his being a good enough engineer to hold out until the riderships managed to break it.

They regrouped outside firing range of the two huge ships, now enveloped in light, punishing even as the viewscreens polarized. Half the riders reconfigured as guards against the Secess' single fighters, while the others prepared for the first of a series of quick onslaughts against the base ship: in fast, fire hard and full power—then out again before the ship's heavy armaments could skewer and melt them at a beam. This would either weaken the Secess' ship long enough for *Leonidas* to strike hard, killing or crippling its enemy, or enable *Leonidas* to pull back and retreat.

Ship-to-ship transmission crackled and whined in and out of phase, weakened by passage through the screens.

As the riderships poised for their first strike, words emerged from the static created by screens and Secess' jammers . . . "will begin pumping . . ."

"What?" That cry came from a pilot several hundred kilometers out . . . the emissions of her ship shone more clearly on her status boards than the actual ship itself to the naked eye. Pauli knew that one too: before the war had pulled her from her labs, she had had an interest in physics.

". . . all Jump-capable ships retreat, prepare for Jump on the mark . . . others link with *Amherst* and *Daedalus* . . . prepare for upconversion."

She remembered now just why the man had received his captaincy. It wasn't just that he was an engineer; it was that he was a weapons specialist. And when he got started talking, he was a spellbinder. One off-watch, he had entertained an entire wardroom with his plans for converting the ship's weapons to gamma-ray lasers. The problem wasn't breaking the atomic nuclei to produce gamma rays—more than one planet knew that to its lasting and highly radioactive sorrow. The problem with gamma-ray lasers lay in pumping the material, then raising it to a uniform energy level from which the actual laser would be fired—all without melting the systems . . . even the adamantine components of plated diamond that served shipwide as microprocessors and were all but indestructible . . . or letting the laser beam degrade. Thus far, the captain's engineers had managed to store energy from the ship's power plant in what the techs called an isomeric state. The problem was altering its energy level. Where would he find an outside . . .

An outside source? He had an outside source: the firelock.

"Lee, don't!" Borodin's voice crackled through the fragmented communication, then squealed out. "*Daedalus*, what's your status . . ."

"Jump plotted . . ."

"You don't know this is going to work," Borodin argued.

"We don't know it won't," came Captain Lee's voice. "In any case, I have been ordered to use any and all means to safeguard your passengers."

Arnaut and those other damned marshals! That was a whole ship out there they were talking about hurling into the equivalent of a very small nova. Not only was the ship not expendable, it had a hell of a lot of fine people on it, friends and comrades of Pauli and the other pilots.

Quickly the pilots conferred on ridership frequencies as, all around them, the Secess' fighters struck, attempting to break their formations, weakening their chance of ending the firelock. Disobey orders? Retreat? Turn and fight all comers? Counterpointing their hasty quarrel over the best alternative was the captains' argument: *Leonidas*, stubborn, sure of its strength; *Daedalus*, frantically testing systems and backups; and the *Amherst*. Voices rose and fell, cleared, then phased out as the firelock intensified. Pauli imagined that her short, sweat-damp hair stood on end from the energies that *Leonidas* prepared to harness.

A short bark, and a spate of sounds comprehensible only as orders silenced the captains until Borodin's deep, slightly accented voice took over the comms. "All ships!" he cried in the archaic slang of a planet probably lost to all of them forever. Slang was better than code for emergency messages. Code could be broken. Slang could only be understood—and the Secess' had moved so far from Alliance that they no longer shared many of the same referents. "Mayday! *Sauve qui peut!*" It was the call of uttermost disaster, old even as Earth counted age, a cry for flight so desperate that those unable to keep up must be left behind. And if Borodin sounded it, it could not be disregarded. He was too canny a fighter to cry rout where none existed.

Pauli's ship sensors fluctuated wildly. The radiation detectors emitted a steady beeping which meant, if she were lucky, a clouded badge and a warning, and if she were not . . . she didn't expect to live long enough to have any children, so it made little difference. Firing at the Secess' fighters who pursued gleefully, she and her companions turned and fled toward the two refugee ships. Acceleration pressed her into her couch, which tilted back to enable her to withstand the pressures. Ahead of her and behind, the starlight dopplered as she neared lightspeed. Her breathing deepened, then turned to panting as pressure really took hold. Raising her hand to adjust the angle of the NavComp readout became a supreme effort. If it had not been for the ache in her head from recycled air and the shock to her eyes of explosions too quick for polarization to shade, she might have dreamed that this was a particularly brutal simulator. More pressure, and her vision reddened, her focus narrowing to that one precious readout. She grunted as she forced a stiffly gloved hand up toward NavComp, keying for intercept with *Amherst*.

The overstressed detectors hooted a final time, then were silent. Only the digital readout continued to climb. "X rays," Pauli recalled. Lee had planned to use X rays to trigger the upconversion from which the actual laser would be fired.

As if sensing something new and hideous, the Secess' ship's rate of fire slowed, and its shields intensified . . . "Too late," muttered the pilot turned physicist. "He's engaging it now! Prepare for Jump on *Amherst*'s coordinates!"

The pilot had anticipated her order: well enough. Pauli was no scientist, and the other knew it. She concentrated on breathing and her boards. Around her, the other pilots pressed for maximum speed. One stopped dead, power gone, until a Secess' blasted it to shards and gleaming vapor. Others, unable to maintain the pace, swung wide, hoping to avoid the shockwave to come.

"The drive . . . I'm on overlo—!" Yet another ship veered sharply off, tumbled, then exploded as its drive overloaded.

Behind the fleeing riderships, light rippled about the firelocked craft. In less than a microsecond it peaked, stabbing into an explosion of such speed and brilliance that the ports had no time to polarize. Pauli squeezed her eyes shut and prayed that the ships could make Jump before the shockwave hit them. At least the distress buzzers were out, she thought as the first tremors of the wave buffeted her. Ahead of her loomed the *Amherst*. She forced leaden hands to controls, cutting speed and Gs so fast she almost retched. Half by instinct, she headed for the blessed familiarity of the flight deck's landing bays and the welcoming symmetry of their bright landing grids.

Her ship touched down, and the lights died as the landing bay closed. Her boards ran through their usual spectrum of powering-down, and she sagged against her webbing. How many ships had made it into the safety of flight deck? The others would have to ride out Jump alone. She'd done that once in a ridership, and would probably do it again—if she were lucky enough to survive—but she didn't envy them the experience.

Borodin's voice barked out the command, "On the mark, all ships *NOW*!" Control boards bent and shimmered, gravity faded, and the ships Jumped . . .

Realspace contracted and expanded simultaneously in a frenzy of infrared flickering to violet, then back, rocking and racking the ridership as the shockwave struck, and Pauli yawed back and forth until Jump . . .

. . . Motionless . . . away . . . hell exploding, worse than the heart of that white dwarf star in the binary system . . . a hideous scream, thought, not heard, never to be heard, from the throats of *Leonidas*'s crew, which had created its gamma laser, and died of it—but had obeyed orders to the last, and taken their enemies with them.

Gravity seized and released, and Pauli screamed soundlessly—*like* Daedalus; *like the damned*!—as *Amherst* dipped and plummeted down the bubbles some madmen said underlay space, skimming the treacherous supercurrents of radiation so bright that even quasars seemed dark, a froth of tachyons and fermions, then slid into a trough of soundless, timeless darkness.

Buffeting subsided as the ships Jumped, base ships and riders. Time twinged and trembled in their wake. Then space curved about them, silent and protective, and they left a timeless, trackless hell behind.

CHAPTER
2

Communications had long since been lost—*my God, how long*? Pauli looked for the chrono. It was not in its usual place on her boards, which twisted and shifted even as she stared at them. She put out a hand, and saw it shimmer, deform, then remold again before her eyes. An instant later her eyes seemed to pierce the seals and articulations of her glove, and she saw her bones glowing through the insubstantiality of her flesh. Her body began what felt like a slow churning, simultaneously inside and out.

For the moment, she was deaf and blind; in the next, she was deluged with sensory impressions, crawling along her nerves until she screamed, though she heard no sound. Realspace impinged. Communications resumed, a babble of panic, then squealed out; and Jumpspace folded them into its hideous self once more. It was not a place for humans, had never been. Time stretched out . . . *are we trapped?* To be trapped in Jump: after the first long Jump, when you suffered the distortions of curving space, there in the frothing realm where galaxies were born. Time was suspended there, and matter. And to wake there, eternally, in your flesh, an unholy resurrection, why that was the one fear that, more than combat, brought you shuddering up out of uneasy sleep. You did not really exist in Jump; you entered it and left. If you entered it and could not leave, you could not die—having never really existed there in the first place.

Gravity and weightlessness pressed simultaneously, and realspace beckoned, tantalizingly close. *Come on, come on, this shouldn't happen!* Pauli thought, her consciousness straining toward thought as her eyes, trying to see light in the darkness, created an aurora of scarlets and yellow against her eyelids. *Realspace will exist if I must inv*ent *it!* she declared soundlessly. She considered stars, and planets, seas, and starships: *let them be!* she declared, a mental howl.

Amherst *slid down the wave of no-time and place.* Very well: if the situation called for blasphemy, then let blasphemy exist too. *"Let there be light!"* she screamed.

Absurdly she heard her voice shrill up, then crack. In a "second" more, she would laugh, assuming she could hear or feel it, at her megalomania. Well, if they did not escape Jump, she would have all of a mad eternity to appreciate it.

Realspace tore through the illusions then. The rasp of her own labored breath, the smell of stale air, of chemical cleansers, and of her own sweat came into manifestation once again as communications growled, then exploded into life. The chrono solidified, mute testimony to the fact that they had spent close to two minutes conscious in Jump. Any longer and they might not have been able to pull free. Or be sane thereafter.

"Riderships by the numbers . . . report in, please!"

Faint voices crackled over the ship-to-ship bands as the craft who had ridden out Jump divorced from their base ships called in.

"Do you require assistance to dock?" Borodin asked.

"Negative . . . but I'm going to kiss the deck once I touch down!" one pilot replied, then laughed hysterically. Other voices sounded weepy, exhausted, and nakedly relieved. But there were too few. At least two riderships had not pulled through Jump and . . .

"*Daedalus* . . . do you copy? *Daedalus*, please reply!"

"God, no," Pauli whispered. Instead of cracking the hatch and swinging out, she sagged back. That whole ship, plunged into a maze it could never escape. Lost, its crew; and all the civilians, and the refugees. Tears threatened. "God, help them. They never had much of a life," she whispered. "But at least, now, they were about to have a chance."

"Yeager, are you there? Report!" Borodin's voice cracked sharply, snapping her back into alertness.

"Yeager, aye. Request permission to come to the bridge."

She cracked the hatch, swinging out and down, her boots echoing on the textured metal deck of the landing bay. The lights outside the bay almost blinded her, and she leaned against a bulkhead with several other pilots who emerged almost at the same time. Behind them rose the whine of machinery closing the docking bays, activating the catapults that hurled another shift of pilots into space. Please God, no Secess' lurked in this system as well.

"We shouldn't have left them out there," one woman told Pauli.

"Ought to be an explanation," muttered another man to low growls of assent. Someone owed them some answers: why the secrecy, why the haste, why the *Leonidas*, with its irreplaceable crew and systems, had been condemned as expendable?

"Where are we going, anyhow?"

"I'm headed for the bridge," Pauli announced. "To get some answers!"

Profane agreement growled out. Still in the aftermath of that appalling Jump, Pauli lurched against a bulkhead, steadied, then aimed toward the nearest elevator. The other pilots crowded in.

And nothing moved. Nothing in the elevator, that was. Pauli thumbed for communications. What the hell kind of stupidity was this? After that abortion of a Jump, damage control parties would have to scour the ship, system by system. God knows, the medical staff would need to tend the refugees, or any crewmember whose grasp on reality might have snapped in transit. But the elevator was not moving.

"Backup power doesn't work either," reported the woman nearest controls.

"Down the corridor. Try the next one."

"It's not going to work," Pauli called out at the backs of the pilots who left to take that advice. Only moments ago—but parsecs away—she had called herself paranoid. Now she began to suspect her own skepticism.

"Engineering? Yeager here. Trying to reach the bridge. We don't have elevator power here. Is this a malfunction?"

"Neg . . ." the comm squawked, then went dead.

Interesting. Predictable, too. Why keep the pilots from the bridge? Paranoia threatened to overwhelm her. Pilots were the one group capable of asking questions that someone didn't want answered, or learning the answers on their own. Answers to questions such as where they were headed, and by whose orders, and why *Leonidas* had died. She didn't think that this was Captain Borodin's idea; it wasn't Borodin's style. But then, it wasn't Borodin who had ordered her back to the *Jeffrey Amherst*, either. A marshal had taken command in the battle. But she couldn't expect one of them to tell her anything helpful . . .

The nearest ready room had computer access, she thought, and trotted toward it. Her legs were steadier now. Punching up diagrams of the ship, she nodded to herself. There they were: service hatches, ladders, crawlways . . . she was walking faster and more steadily now, glancing about from side to side as if she herself were a ship expecting attack. It was like arriving in a new system and conducting reconnaissance for Secess'. She spared a brief thought for the pilots who were doing that right now. *Good luck, brothers.* What system were they in, anyhow?

She punched up the codes to access navigation. ACCESS RESTRICTED flashed on and off on the tiny screen. The red light spread out over her hands where they shook on the keyboard. Raising an eyebrow, she used a higher priority, and was unsurprised when that failed too. Muttering to herself, she headed for the hatch she had noted on the ship's plans.

The man standing guard at the accessway surprised her: Becker, the most senior of the Federal Security types who now infested their convoy. Why hadn't he stationed himself on *Leonidas*?

Because, the answer came readily, *since it was pure military, he knew it was expendable; and he doesn't want to die. No more than I do. What else does he know that I could use*?

She must have asked that question aloud.

"What else do I know, Lieutenant? I know that your questions to computer alerted me. I also know that right now the last thing Captain Borodin needs on the bridge is a mob of pilots still wobbling from Jump and a bad case of righteous indignation."

Her own righteous indignation balled her hands into fists. For the first time since she had met the man, he was speaking to her as if he were human, and not an official bound to speak to junior officers as if he were the voice of Regulations itself.

"Don't even try it," said the Fed Sec, and raised one hand slightly. Armed. So there was more to the man than bureaucracy. She might have been intrigued if she hadn't been ready to fight.

"Right now, you only have two choices. Either get yourself back to quarters, or round up your friends and tell them to make themselves useful with the refugees."

"And if I don't?"

"Then I report that you were uncooperative."

Pauli snorted. Uncooperative. The war had blasted every known system to pieces, taken her life apart . . . and this fool expected that the imbecilities he had probably learned in some deskbound leadership course would work. On a combat-blooded, combat-drained pilot.

"They need your help, Yeager. Think of it. You were on Wolf IV. You saw the children we picked up. That was a bad Jump for you, and you knew what you could expect. What about those children? They know *nothing*. And if you're not worried about them, think of your friends"—Becker actually grinned at her, his eyes knowing—"who are in there with them. Unarmed, among children who have probably killed to eat. Children who have lived with terror, and fought through it."

The fury at the base of her skull felt like laserfire as she glared at him. But her rage was deflected by that damnable grin. "You stationed yourself here. You were looking for us," she stated.

"Looking for someone," agreed Becker coolly. "You. I judged you were most likely to think it through. And I was right."

"Becker, you tell the captain . . ." Technically, the civ outranked her, outranked a captain, if he and Arnaut had been throwing around the orders that blew *Leonidas* and put the *Jeffrey Amherst*'s bridge off-limits. The hell with it.

"That you want to see him? As soon as our course is laid in." Becker's smile became less sly, and more confident. He knew he had won. *For now*, Pauli told herself. *I'll get some answers somehow.*

"What is our course?" Pauli asked.

The marshal smiled. "That is another of the things that is classified for now. As soon as possible, however—"

"Have me paged," Pauli ordered, covering her frustration with a show of dignity. Becker would probably page her when that white dwarf in the last system cooled down. "I'll be in emergency quarters."

She turned on her heel and strode away, then whirled. "Becker, are you going to release elevator access, or do I have to suit up, go outside the ship, and climb back in?"

"Such temper," scoffed the marshal. "If you go back to the first elevator you tried, you'll find that power has been restored. You can go anywhere you want. Except the bridge."

Pauli stalked into the elevator and slapped the panels for the main landing bays on the deck below. The door slid shut, and she felt the minor hum of power engaging. The door opened into reddish darkness and pure nightmare.

Someone must have sprayed disinfectant about the bay not long ago, but even that acrid, eye-watering smell could not overpower the stinks of food, of faulty air exchange and improvised reclamation chambers which leaked the vinegar and naphtha stinks of human urine or sickness. She smelled sweat, including her own. In the darkness Pauli grimaced. But the stinks of crowded humanity and failing systems were not what made her scalp and hair, soaked from her helmet, suddenly prickle and go chill. Years in a ship's artificial environment had made her increasingly sensitive to smells. After all, a gas leak or concealed fire might mean the death of the entire ship. What brought her alert and wary now as she stared. into the darkness of that converted docking bay was fear. Not panic, but the type of watchful, practiced fear that could become the murderous attack of a cornered beast.

She had smelled that before. The *Amherst* had made planetfall by one of Wolf IV's cities and sent armed parties out to guard the civ task force who had come to reclaim the children. Lifesupport revealed many bodies in one building that looked like the ruins of a school. In any case, it still had parts of its roof, which made it unique. The power cells had faded, and the wall panels had darkened to the twilight ruddiness of a lair where desperate creatures knew every pathway, and in which they had gone to ground.

Instinctively Pauli's hand dropped to her sidearm, snapped open the catch that secured it. Until her eyes adjusted to the gloom, she was exposed here; and she didn't like it.

A gasp rose from somewhere in that vast space turned into something that was neither relief station nor den.

"I wouldn't," came a quiet, deliberately expressionless voice. She might not be able to see the speaker, but she knew that voice. Raiford Adams. Once, they might have made a good team, the pilot and the xenobiologist. They had been a good team in other ways. But when pilots measured life expectancy in terms of numbers of missions flown, Rafe had tried to talk her into another field.

Persuade her out of flying? Easier to find another man than another field, she had thought at the time.

Behind Rafe's tall silhouette she heard rustles, and whispers. Someone stumbled, cried out, and was quickly hushed.

"Why do you keep it so dark in here?" Deliberately, Pauli went on the offensive. "It's like a damned cave."

"What about lights, David?" Rafe turned and called into the dusk.

"I've got power restored, I think," came a deep man's voice. "I'd have to see your boards, but I'd say that that last Jump almost wrecked lifesupport. Can't say much for your backup systems either."

The lights came on, and Pauli blinked. Rafe turned away. His eyes were suddenly too bright, and he shut them, but not before she had seen.

That had to be relief for her, not for the people who crouched around him. The entire docking bay, usually bare and clean, was heaped with bundles and turned into a maze of makeshift corridors, some made by the sound-deadening plastics and composites that, in more prosperous times, were what ships used to throw up temporary quarters. When those had run out, they had hung foil blankets that rippled with every passing body, or the almost imperceptible air currents in the vast bay. In each one of the spaces partitioned off crouched at least one child: dark children, pallid ones, tall children, and toddlers. There was no way to assign one specific genotype to those children, for they were refugees drawn from several worlds.

Two things stamped them as kin: their thinness, even after weeks on ship's food; and their eyes, frightened, yet speculative. Seeing Pauli, a newcomer in a uniform, they had fallen silent. Now she felt the intensity of their gaze, a gaze focusing, in most cases, on the sidearm strapped to her thigh.

But they are children! she reminded herself.

A tall blonde woman rose from the side of a child who coughed until she bent double. "Lieutenant Yeager? I am

Alicia Pryor, senior medical officer here. I met you before you were transferred to . . . my regrets, Lieutenant, on the loss of your ship."

"Ship?" asked a boy.

"Her ship," Dr. Pryor explained patiently. "It exploded, and her friends were killed."

The intensity of the children's scrutiny faded somewhat. If Pauli were, like themselves, a person who had lost something, perhaps she was not an enemy. Had Pryor deliberately created that impression? It was a foolish speculation, but as Pauli walked farther into the bay, echoing with cries and questions, she could not put it out of her mind.

"What about the other ships?" asked the man who had restored lighting to the bay. Pauli remembered his name. Ben Yehuda. David ben Yehuda. A refugee himself, with two children, older and more robust than many of the others.

She shook her head. "You know about *Leonidas*."

"That was some shockwave. For a moment, I thought it would deform Jump," ben Yehuda said. "The children were terrified."

"It did," said Pauli. "*Daedalus* and three of my riderships failed to come through."

Rafe caught ben Yehuda's arm as he reeled. "Forgive me. I've been at least three watches without sleep. We're short-staffed here—"

"You won't be," said Pauli. "They're keeping the pilots—those who made it through—off the bridge, funnelling them down here to help out."

"I hope they're of some use," snapped a black woman from her position at the food dispensers. "Pilots! What we really need is a maintenance tech."

"I'll get onto it," said ben Yehuda. "Next. In a moment. You say they didn't survive Jump?"

Engineer the man might be, but he was a grounder, Pauli realized. She shook her head. "You don't really live in Jump," she started to explain.

"So you don't die there. Ever?"

"We don't know," she sighed.

"No rest, no peace forever, like the Wandering Jew," said ben Yehuda. He bent his head, muttering. "*Yisgadal v'yizgadash sh'meh rab'bo.*" To Pauli's shock, tears ran down his lined face, and his children—a boy and girl so close in age and appearance that they might be twins— huddled about him. A third child, one of the boys who had stared most intently at Pauli's sidearm, watched, his head cocked. A tiny girl clung to his leg, whispered to him, then released him and started over to the weeping man and his family.

"He hurts!" she hissed at the boy.

For a moment he stood irresolute, as if trying to solve an equation. He glanced over at Pauli again, this time not at her weapon but at her face.

"It's grief," Rafe explained quietly. "Yes, I know. He doesn't cry because he is hungry; and he isn't sick. He cries because other people died (or worse than that)."

"He won't see them again," the boy muttered. His voice seemed rusty and unused. "When they go away, when they get sick, after a while they don't move. Then *they* go away, and you have to leave where they are."

Ben Yehuda turned to the boy. "That's right, Lohr. You remember it, and—"

"I hate it!" cried the boy. "I don't want them to go, I don't want to leave them . . ."

"Hush, there, hush." David ben Yehuda knelt and held out his arms to the boy. The hundred or so children nearest had all fallen silent. What struck Pauli most was the quality of that silence. It was wonder. These children were all familiar with death, with people who had "gone away," leaving their bodies behind in lairs that the children would avoid from then on. They had taught themselves to conceal pain at death, to blank it from their awareness; and now ben Yehuda reminded them.

"We'll have hysterics in a moment," Dr. Pryor murmured. "Can you handle it?"

The black woman muttered something.

"Quiet, Beneatha! Right before Jump, you were the

one who complained that these children are too stoic. Now that they're beginning to feel again, you want to blame it on the military."

"You didn't have to spring it on them," Beneatha accused—who? Pauli? Ben Yehuda himself?

"As long as it happens," ben Yehuda said earnestly. "Lohr," he spoke to the boy, "it's all right. See, Ari is still here. Ayelet is fine," he gestured at his son and daughter, who sat and stroked the hair of the tiny girl who had left Lohr's side. She was crying now, and Lohr watched her, appalled. He started to shake, and a bead of spittle appeared at the corner of his mouth.

"She is crying, Lohr," said Rafe. "It doesn't mean she is going to die. It just means she's sad because someone she cares about is sad. You care about David, don't you? Hasn't he taken care of you and 'Cilla since you were brought in?"

The boy's mouth worked. He gulped and ran his hand over his lips. Ben Yehuda held out a hand, encouraging the boy to cry and be comforted. "Let it out, Lohr," he whispered.

Pauli found herself holding her breath. The boy started forward. *They've got him*! she thought. Relief caught at her throat. Then he bolted for the nearest corner of a rat's maze of hanging blankets, tilted partitions, and heaped-up supplies. A warren formed by hanging blankets. For a moment, sobs trailed after him, but only for a moment. The child 'Cilla ran after him, shaking her head at offers of company.

"How old do you think he is?" asked Dr. Pryor.

"Nine, ten?" What did Pauli know about the age of children?

"He's as old as Ari and Ayelet here. Almost thirteen. Practically feral. You were right to guard your sidearm when you came in, you know. Lohr had his eyes on it. He's not a bad child, you know. He's just never really been a child: that's all. That little girl, the one David calls 'Cilla—we think she's Lohr's sister, though they don't look a thing alike. See how frail she is. There must have been times it would have been easier for Lohr to survive if he had abandoned her. But he never did."

"Sometimes he cries in his sleep about her," said David. "I think he's killed people to protect her. There's anger in him, and fight, all bottled up. But I think I can turn him around. He knows he exists, rough as it's been for him. Some of them aren't sure. We even had to name a few kids who'd forgotten what their parents called them."

Pauli found herself pacing, watching the pile of blankets into which Lohr had burrowed, hoping that he would sob himself out, then emerge. To her astonishment, she wanted to talk with him. There must be something she could say, words drawn from her own experiences on Wolf IV, assurances that all adults—especially adults who wore uniforms—were not evil. But he never emerged.

Beyond her, from the corner of her eye, she caught sight of others of the pilots working with the civilians, squatting down by a sleeping child, carrying piles of equipment, talking in a circle of thin, preternaturally cautious survivors camouflaged by immature bodies. They were of many races and sizes, but a single look of wary, fearful hunger stamped them as kin.

Abruptly the air currents failed again, and the lights went dead. The silence, even of those children most distraught by the invasion of these uniformed adults and their unwelcome news, was uncanny. Occasional rustles and whispers told the adults that the children moved.

Pauli had been this silent herself in survival training, had felt the same buildup of tension as she searched out a new star system for enemies who might, at any moment, reduce her and her ship to frozen vapor. That was her risk: she was an adult who had chosen combat flying. It sickened her that a child would understand those fears.

"No one's hunting us," she announced, making her voice deliberately cheerful. "Why is everyone so quiet?"

"Oh, well done!" whispered Alicia Pryor.

The rustling increased, came closer, like rats padding

in a slum. If someone flashed a light across the room, she had the sensation that all over the room, drawing closer and closer to her, would be pairs of eyes, gleaming like the eyes of wild beasts. She wanted a wall at her back, and preferably someone else to defend her back for her.

"Not again," grumbled ben Yehuda, deliberately jovial. "Ari, get my torch. I never get any rest around here."

Thin, nervous laughter spattered out.

"You think it's funny that I don't get to sleep? I don't. I will give those lights until three to come back on. And then I will be seriously angry at the lights. One . . ." the children's laughter intensified—"two . . . you don't believe this, do you?" Now more of the children laughed. Even their footfalls had more sound now. "Say, I don't think this is working. Two and a half? Lights . . . anywhere?"

"Try two and three-quarters?"

"Well enough, Lohr. Two and three-quarters . . ."

With a hum and a sigh, the lights flashed back on, and the hum of the air conditioners resumed.

The children laughed and cheered. At least they laughed and cheered until they saw the tall, pale man in the dark uniform of the Federal Security marshals standing in their midst.

Becker had crept in like a hunting cat or a wild child himself. How long had he stood there, his pale eyes scanning the entire bay, pausing to evaluate each officer who had been dispatched to assist the refugees?

"Dammit, did he stage that?" asked Pauli in a furious undertone. "Kids have enough problems without his setting up dramatic entrances."

Rafe shrugged. "Becker's not all that bad, for a marshal. The evacuation from Wolf was mostly his doing. He won't say, but I think—" he thinned his lips, his usual signal for ending an unwelcome discussion. "Sometimes he comes in and talks."

"If you want to hear regulations, why not access armscomp? It doesn't pretend to be human."

"Becker knows what he's doing. And you're talking like one of the civs. You're a pilot, not a social worker. At least, that's what you told me when you accepted assignment to *Leonidas*."

Another futile argument with Rafe! Under the sweat and grime, Pauli knew she was flushing. She wanted a bath and a rest, and to get herself away from Rafe before she did or said something irrevocable and idiotic. But Becker stood there, tall and dispassionate, scanning the mob of children and civilians until he caught sight of her in her drab flightsuit.

"Lieutenant Yeager? You're wanted on the bridge."

"Now?"

"Right now. That's a direct order. From me."

All around her the children murmured, their whispers intensifying into a growl. Pauli started forward, and two or three of the girls caught at her hands. She remembered how on Wolf IV they had scratched and screamed at any attempt to separate one of them from a group—and the silence that fell after the child was removed: as if she were gone now and, since it was irrevocable, there was no point in tears.

"No one's going to hurt me. Or you. They're on our side," she called, even as she hurried over to Becker, easing past a knot of refugees who tried to block her way. "I'll be back. I promise I'll be back."

Now what had inspired her to say that? In order to convince the children that not all authority was murderous, now she'd have to return: and this place, these refugees, broke her heart even as their tension, their thinness, and their unnatural quiet made her want to retreat. She would have to burn her flightsuit, she decided, wanting to scratch all over. How long would it take the *Amherst* to get the stink out of this bay?

She started toward the exit, and the children followed her.

"Get back," the marshal gestured sharply. They obeyed, but only just. In the moments, apparently, that Pauli had spent in the bay, quarrelling with their caretakers, the children seemed to have determined that she was an ally. She was small—as short as the black woman she had heard Dr. Pryor call Beneatha, and far shorter than

Rafe or Pryor, let alone the marshal who appeared to have her under custody. She had wanted to comfort Lohr. Though she wore a uniform and a sidearm, she had not smelled like a threat. And now a man in a uniform appeared to threaten her.

The children growled. Even Lohr emerged from wherever he had hidden. Becker raised one eyebrow, then deliberately turned his back and headed for the door, his steps measured, slow, as if he sought to bluff wild animals.

"Well, Lieutenant?" his voice lashed out. A muttering rose.

"Quickly," murmured Rafe.

Pauli forced herself to smile at the children, wave reassuringly, then follow the marshal. Two of the eldest children started to follow. Then Dr. Pryor walked forward. Though her movements seemed as leisurely as the marshal's, she reached his side quickly and gestured the children back. Then, with practiced, unhurried speed, she waved the marshal and Pauli out. The door slid shut, but not before Pauli heard a scream of anger that died away into the wail of a frightened child.

"To the bridge," ordered the marshal. "And move it!" He headed toward the nearest elevator at a pace that made Pauli break into a lope to keep step with him.

"Obviously you're not going back in there," Pauli retorted. "Why did you set that up? Rafe Adams told me you'd been in there before, that you'd acted human in there before. Now, if you go back in, you'd better go guarded."

"I said move! You're needed on the bridge, and so am I," Becker told her. He all but thrust Pauli into the elevator that opened so rapidly after he slapped the wall signal that she suspected he had locked it there to wait for them.

"Bridge. And fast," he ordered. The door slid shut, but not quickly enough for his taste. His long fingers tapped beside controls where Pauli saw herself reflected: nondescript and sturdy, her face grimy, her shoulders sagging under the weight of her flightsuit. The weight! Abruptly it felt like nothing at all. She felt herself begin to rise, her stomach threatening to precede the rest of her.

Free fall! Pauli lurched across the tiny cubicle and slapped the glowing crimson alarm panel. Hooting rang out, then subsided as backups cut in.

"Damned Jump," she muttered. "What this ship needs is planetfall. I'd dump every system on board, then test and reload before I tried to Jump again."

Becker was nodding. "Very good, Lieutenant Yeager. *Very* good. You justify your captain's faith in you."

"My captain died on board *Leonidas*," Pauli reminded him.

"And Captain Borodin?" The whine of the elevator subsided and the door slid aside, pausing halfway. Angrily she slapped the "manual open" and stalked out onto the bridge where too many people stared at boards and glowing screens dominated by red and amber lights. Commander Banez, Borodin's exec, had turned to ask him a question, but she stopped dead when Pauli and the marshal entered. Curious, that: Pauli would have bet that only a laser would have kept Banez from any decision she wanted to make.

Amber and even scarlet lights gleamed, some of them on the primary systems boards. *More malfunctions*, she groaned. Tiny knots of people stood or crouched before their duty stations, one or two calling out instructions to other people who knelt, heads and shoulders hidden, as they sought to repair what needed a shipwide refit. Banez glanced at them, then turned back to the captain, dismay etched into a face that should have been plump and cheerful.

Captain Borodin was slumped into his chair, security webs still loosely fastened about him. He stared into the holographic system display projected by NavComp as if it were a campfire at which he huddled, seeking warmth and refuge from wolves.

"Lieutenant Yeager reporting, sir," Pauli said softly. She had meant to be crisp, angry; she had a right to her anger and sorrow. But then the captain turned. He had not been a young man when she had started this tour of duty, but he had been vital, energetic. Now his hair shone pale in the dimmed lights of the bridge; it had turned gray, and was slick with neglect. Dark circles surrounded his eyes, and his cheeks seemed to sag. He seemed as tired as the ship itself: would he break down too?

He nodded absently. "Damage control?" he asked the comm panel set in his chair . . . "malfunctions ship-wide, sir . . . lifesupport . . . we're on backups now, but they're failing. Possibly twelve hours before we go to stored power . . . we only have the one set of replacements . . ."

"*Bozhe moi!* you won't think of it, much less hint it!" Borodin snapped. "Before *Amherst* turns scavenger, I'll blow it up like *Leonidas*!" Borodin slumped back into his chair. Tactfully Banez turned away. The captain drew a deep breath, then shivered all over, as if emerging from deep waters. Finally, reluctantly, he turned back to the newcomers.

"Captain," said Becker, "call in the riderships."

"Riderships haven't finished preliminary scan," Banez reported. "Shall I activate stealth features?"

Borodin nodded. Instants later, interference twisted the view of space from the bridge and fizzed in the in-ship communications gear. Stealth used immense quantities of power.

"Captain," Becker said in that same expressionless tone, "ask your helm to lay in a trajectory for landing."

Becker glanced sharply at him, and Pauli froze. Like all Jump-capable ships, *Amherst* was built in space. Though such a ship could make planetfall, deceleration and gravity would strain to the limits a freshly refitted vessel approaching a fully equipped landing field, let alone a ship like *Amherst*, whose systems were stressed by faulty components and hard running.

We won't survive reentry, Pauli thought bleakly, and glanced at the captain. All during the rescue operations on Wolf IV, he had been imperturbable, a source of refuge for crew who found themselves unable to deal with the survivors and their own guilt at never having lived on a world slagged by hostile ships or—as happened on Marduk's World—atomics. In this one last Jump, he had aged years. *If we weren't at war*, Pauli thought, *if we didn't need him, he wouldn't be in space now. He'd have some comfortable ground or station berth, and die that much faster of boredom.*

The captain turned toward her. "Lieutenant Yeager. Your recommendation as regards the proposed landing?"

"I'd want to refit before we Jump again."

"Log that into the records," said the captain. "You do realize, Becker, that this ship isn't in optimum shape for a landing, that we're already depleting resources by using stealth gear when we might just have easily used our riderships to conduct a preliminary investigation?"

"On my authority, Captain," said Becker. "Your engineers indicate that the ship can survive planetfall and liftoff. Which do you prefer: landing, or detaching riders to ferry the refugees down to the surface of . . ." he gestured and, though the navigation holos were allegedly keyed onto the helm, the configuration altered until Pauli saw the planet at which he pointed. In its simulation, rapidly scudding clouds covered much of the northern hemisphere where high mountains loomed.

Pauli studied the holo intently, hoping to see the familiar glow of an Alliance outpost, blue against the glow of planets and stars.

"We will be landing shortly," Borodin announced.

He raised his head and met Pauli's eyes. *Assuming the ship can land*, the weariness in his gaze appeared to say.

"Landing, sir?" She could ask at least that much.

"There." He gestured, and the holo changed configuration again, rotating to give Pauli and the captain a better view of the world toward which *Amherst*, however feebly, made its way.

"Instituting preliminary surveys," announced one of the bridge crew.

"You don't have a First Survey report?" demanded Borodin.

"Storms," reported the junior officer . . . "wait, Captain: we're getting interference here . . ." his hands crossed on his boards as he struggled to turn up the information feed. "Too much of a power drain; we can't get much input on account of the stealth."

And if they turned off the stealth features, they were exposed to any Secess' ships in the system.

Pauli raised an eyebrow, asking for permission to inquire. No human settlements, Alliance or Secess'.

"I thought we were headed toward resettlement," she remarked. "One of the refuge worlds like Halcyon or in the Marduk system."

Borodin shook his head. "Helm!" he called. "You're off-shift. Get your relief up here. Pauli, you assist."

"But, Captain . . ." Borodin was sending the senior helmsman below because the man was tired? If he wanted someone fresh on the boards, just how serious was this problem?

"You're worn out. How long do you expect to stand on watch without steering us inside a planet? Move it!"

He grinned at the retreating helmsman. "And watch the elevators too. Apparently they're as dangerous as Secess' these days."

A guilty spatter of laughter lightened the air on the bridge. Even Becker's thin lips relaxed. Then he bent over his boards, double-checking as helm laid in a course that would bring them to preliminary orbit, then enable them to leave it and land.

Pauli took a hand-wave as invitation, and went over to take the helm. Coordinates for approach had already been laid in. She called up survey information on the world they neared. It was surprisingly scant.

"How many orbits before touchdown?" she asked. If this had been her ship, she would have wanted to delay landing as long as possible in order to collect as much data as possible on the planet—for a start, had this godforsaken world a name?—its landmasses, resources, weather patterns . . . inhabitants? She had to assume that it would have no inhabitants. The Alliance never settled citizens on worlds with intelligent cultures. Then, and only then, would she choose a landing site.

"Eos system," computer reported. Somewhere she had read, or perhaps heard from Borodin, that *Eos* meant dawn. "Planet Eos IV . . ."

"Survey called it Cynthia."

Pauli turned toward the captain, who studied the glowing screens as intently as she. "A by-name for the ancient goddess of the hunt on Earth," he explained. "Hunting should be good on that world. It's damp; look at the cloud cover. Air pressure's a little higher than we're used to; gravity is about .8 standard."

"Inert gases?"

"We can breathe the air," Borodin's voice was sharp. "Or we wouldn't have put in for this world."

He gestured. "Recommendations?"

The northernmost continent, though much occluded by heavy clouds, looked green and promising. Even this far away, Pauli saw threadlike veins of blue-green, and stepped up magnification: a river with an alluvial plain. The southern continents seemed sere, and seismographic scans revealed major land instabilities and traces of vulcanism. Cynthia the huntress was a young, turbulent world.

"North continent, sir," she spoke at last. "On that plain, near the mountains."

Settlers would have hydroponics, but such a location guaranteed them fertile land and ample rain, just in case. The planet had two moons (as yet unnamed) and therefore freak tides. An interesting, violent world.

"We're going to set down there now?" she asked Borodin. Despite her best efforts, her eyes slid over to Becker.

"That's right, Lieutenant," said the marshal. "Prepare to initiate landing procedures."

Pauli locked in a course, then bent to the scanners. In the few moments that they remained in orbit, it was a matter of survival to gain as much information on this new world as possible.

That was when stealth systems abruptly ceased.

"We're visible again!"

"Go to backups," ordered Borodin.

Pauli's boards flashed toward amber, then—too many of them—into red. Moving quickly, she began to shift navigation over to backup computers. The ship lurched, went briefly A-grav, as even the incredibly durable processors, coated with diamondlike adamant from an alchemist's dream, fissured and failed.

"Abort survey!" ordered Borodin. They were exposed here, vulnerable to a ship or ship's sensors.

Pauli fought the ship into a braking orbit, and from there into a steep, pitching descent. She could imagine the terror of the children in the docking bay, terror that could turn to fury, could turn on the adults who tried to protect them, if the children could reach them.

Lights flickered and failed. Shadows lanced across the bridge as red distress lights strobed, glancing off the sweat on Borodin's jaw. Air circulation faltered, then started up again.

"Diverting power from weapons to engines, sir," came a voice which trembled slightly.

"Retain backup lifesupport and navigation," ordered Borodin. His taut fist punched lightly on the arm of his chair, then clutched until the bones showed yellow beneath the weathering of his skin. He leaned forward and took over helm control.

"Hull temperature at 4800 . . . 3500 . . . 3000 . . . firing retros . . ." the ship yawed as it turned upright, preparing to land. They lost altitude rapidly, a plunge barely controlled by the helm. Atmosphere thickened about them, threatened to buffet them worse than had *Leonidas*'s death. The shaking intensified as the ship lost speed. Sensors, those not blinded by processor failure or burnt out by the heat of the ship's passage, reported stratospheric gales which gave way, as *Amherst* decelerated yet further and gravity clutched them all in a leaden fist, to less predictable and more treacherous gusts. Briefly Pauli wondered how the civs would manage to cross this planet's seas if the storms were always this severe.

They were falling out of the sky! she thought. Either the Secess' would attack or, the instant they tried to refit and test engines on this godforsaken world, the ship would blow crew and civilians to the fate they had managed, so far, to elude.

Borodin's eyes were very bright. Behind him, Marshal Becker clung to a safety rail.

"Get us down now!" someone whispered.

A sane man or woman might have despaired in those last, nightmarish seconds, but Borodin, by that time, was maddened by some compulsion to beat fate, beat the odds one last time. Still the ship wavered, and he fought for stability, lost it . . . *damn, it was no bad way to die, admiring the man's skill!* but in the next moment, Pauli saw the opportunity his slower fingers were letting slip. She lunged forward toward helm, and gradually the ship came upright, steadied, slowed yet further. Gravity pressed down, and she panted as she fought *Amherst* toward safety. It was madness, worse than combat against a Secess' fivefold formation, but even as her limbs grew heavier and heavier, it seemed as if she were flying, her arms outstretched for balance and for lift, to bear the ship, to ease it down to safety.

Amherst touched ground, not a feather's touch, nor yet the three-point landing of pilot's training; but they were down (albeit somewhat on a slant), and they had a ship that they could walk away from. Pauli glanced down, amazed, then began shutting down systems. Long after she was finished, she let her hands linger on the boards, almost caressing them.

"We're down," Borodin reached up and rubbed his temples with shaking hands. Gray shone between his fingers. Becker leaned over him, speaking rapidly. The captain shook his head, then gestured, one palm up.

"Damages?" Borodin demanded. From all areas of the

ship came reports that might have spelled disaster in deep space: many systems failed, and even backups faltering. They would have to dump all computers, install new processors, then test them. It was a time-consuming, aggravating job, even given planetary facilities: it would be a demon here in the No Man's World of Cynthia. But *Amherst* had been built to survive.

Pauli unstrapped herself. As always after a pitched battle and acceleration, she felt sweaty, stupid with fatigue. She swallowed hard after so many hours in freefall, unwilling to retch as her first act in this new world. Now that *Amherst* was safely down, she realized the enormity of her offense: senior pilot or not, she had taken over ship's controls. She could be court-martialed—*I saved the ship!* reason insisted, but regulations were something else.

She ventured to look at her captain. "Sir?" she began. "I beg the captain's pardon. I acted without thought."

"Thank God you did," whispered Banez. Like the rest of the bridge crew, even Becker, she had gone white to the lips, but now her color flashed back, rose into a flush as she realized she had been overheard.

"I do indeed," Borodin said, and Pauli remembered. Unusual as it was for a citizen of Novaya Moskva to attain command rank, Borodin had not shed his homeworld's religious faith as he rose through the ranks. It had always been oddly, enviably reassuring. Now it seemed only old. Like Borodin himself. Even as damage control reports came in, and the civilian refugees demanded immediate information, escape, or whatever it was that shrilled in Pauli's ears, for that one moment she shivered. Borodin was old. Like the ship. Like the war.

Like she felt at that moment. She allowed herself one more luxury, and lay back for a last instant in her chair as the sweat dried on brow and body.

Borodin rose. Reluctantly Pauli lifted her head. Becker came around to face him.

He raised an eyebrow, clearly waiting for some command or explanation. Captain Borodin drew himself up.

He had not forgotten, and probably would never forgive himself for the moment in which he had proved too worn, too slow. But he still had his dignity.

"My orders," began Borodin, "indicate that here on Cynthia, you are in command. Your orders, sir?"

CHAPTER
3

Cynthia's sky was gray and cool, darkening toward violet at the horizon, with delicate cirrus clouds etched high above. The air was cool, pungent, and moist from the presence of a brownish river, the confluence of several streams frothing down from the foothills of the range that *Amherst* had seen from space. That was the only way Pauli would probably ever see those mountains, she thought.

Wearily she tramped away from the great charred patch in which the *Jeffrey Amherst* rested while the crew—*the active crew,* her thoughts kept cycling back to the new, unbearable pain as if it were a rotten tooth—replaced and tested, sweated and swore, and probably thanked God that they weren't on the short list that Becker had decided to detach from the *Amherst* and assign for duty here on Cynthia with the civs.

Bodyguards. Babysitters. And damned tired of it. It had been three watches since she had slept, then four—and then Becker had read his damned list. She walked farther out, seeing the domes rise in the field beyond the ship. The ground cover, an unlikely combination of grass, thorns, and leaves, crackled underfoot and sprang back up after she moved on.

She snorted. Some of the civs had thrown a fit about the charring *and* the domes. Hadn't wanted to "damage the ground cover," they'd bleated. She kicked at a particularly thick stand of it, which looked like it could take a lot of damaging. Becker, rot his soul, had been diplomatic, reminding the civs that the children would need housing until they adjusted to their new world, or, for that matter, any world that didn't look like the aftermath of a battle. And the children's adaptation, their sanity itself, had to be the settlers' main concern. For many of them, Cynthia was the first planet they might know as a home, or, if the war dragged on, the only one. When they first landed here, Pryor and the gentlest of the civs tending them—and Rafe was among them— had compelled the children out into the open air. They had huddled by the domes as if they were spun from skeletal supports; only gradually had they ventured into the open and began to run.

She supposed Cynthia wasn't a bad planet. Counting New Patuxent, the base where Pauli had longed for reassignment, it was the fifth she had seen. Her fifth, and probably the last, she had realized only after the domes were up, the civs' supplies were offloaded, and she had turned back, with the other officers, to begin the long task of testing and preparing for liftoff.

But Becker had held up a hand, and Borodin—hell, even her own captain—had halted, at the orders, again, of that blasted marshal and his people. Well, she thought at the time, that was one consolation. He'd be staying here. He had pulled out a sealed report—printed orders. In all her years in the service, Pauli had seen such a thing only once: when she was commissioned. Becker had read out the contents—orders which assigned Borodin and the officers who had worked most closely with the refugees on board the *Amherst* to detached duty on Cynthia and the formation of a military government until such time when a duly elected civilian government might replace it—which, in wartime, might be never. She had had a moment's pang—*never see Rafe again*—and then she heard her own name mentioned. She too was grounded. Then Becker stepped back, with the air of a prudent man putting himself out of range, but otherwise refusing to change his mind.

"You're taking me off my ship?" Borodin asked. "My ship's orders were cut for Novaya Moskva by way of New

Pax," he added with the mildness that generally heralded one of his more memorable rages.

"Your ship's orders," said the marshal. "They said nothing about its complement."

"And myself?" Still that mildness, but the anger was gathering, reddening in the darkness of Borodin's eyes. In an instant more, it would reach critical mass—

Becker reached into his tunic's inner pocket and pulled out something. Then there had been a snap, as if the marshal unsealed something. He handed the wafer to the captain.

"A sector governorship?" asked Borodin. "But I thought that you would be remaining here."

"Thumbprint here, Captain. Do you deny my authority to reassign you now? Here are your new orders: to take charge of this part of Project Seedcorn. You had best read it now, and fast: air contact will destroy the message soon."

Borodin lowered his head and read these new orders, then reread them until the message deteriorated. He threw the fragments down, and rubbed his fingers against his thigh as if he sought to wipe them clean. Project Seedcorn, Pauli had thought at the time, numbed by the shock of reassignment, must be quite something if it forestalled Borodin's explosion. When that finally came, it would be a supernova, she thought. Perhaps the heat of his fury would warm her.

"Will you accept posting?" the marshal asked finally.

With the Secessionists busy grabbing planets, and Becker claiming a sector governorship, Borodin either accepted this assignment or boarded *Amherst* a prisoner, to face charges of sedition or mutiny (since Becker had been in command since planetfall) on the first world where the *Amherst* made planetfall. New Pax, probably. They were strict about such things on New Pax.

"I must accept," said Borodin. "But I repeat: you're taking me off my ship. So I think that means you owe me more than 'theirs was not to reason why,' Marshal."

"Captain Borodin, you saw it during landing," said Becker. Pauli gasped at the cruel logic of the statement, and Borodin stepped back a step. "Your reflexes are down; it almost cost us our lives. All right, maybe that was Jump stress, especially that last Jump. And maybe, once you rested up on New Pax, you could scrape past your proficiency tests. This year. But what about next? And what about your first scramble with a Secess' that wasn't on the run? What if you didn't hit weapons or Jump fast enough, or were slow at the helm that time too? We'd be out one very expensive ship and its expensively trained crew. And those are getting to be scarce commodities."

Borodin shook his head, his eyes going from Becker to the clean new domes to the sleek hull of *Amherst* with the desperation of a creature who sees the shimmer of a forcefield between himself and freedom. Then he looked at Pauli and gathered himself up to argue further.

"You think that the war's not going to end soon. Our briefings say otherwise."

Becker snorted. "Why else do you suppose I got authority for Seedcorn? Ordinarily—and if I thought this was an ordinary time, I'd have proposed it myself— I'd intern these people. Maybe they could have been set down on Marduk's World. The whole southern continent's been turned into a hospital to tend the survivors of that first raid . . . and their children. Whatever they'll grow up like."

Standing with the other civilians, one hand resting on the shoulder of a young girl with the eyes of an old woman, Dr. Alicia Pryor winced. Marduk's World had been hit by old-style atomics; the southern continent was the only part of it that had not been struck by blizzards, a winter that might last for years and had already devastated its biosphere. That was no sort of internment camp for these children; and Becker knew it.

"I wouldn't send these children to Marduk's World," he continued. "Even if we win, we're not going to be able to count on having an undamaged gene pool to come home to. Did it ever occur to you, Captain, that—war or no war—we may all be defective in some way or other? Since the Earth blockade, how can we even be sure what's standard human anymore? Do you know what pure human stock is? This world's listed as .8 G. Feels good, doesn't it: after acceleration or zero-grav? But have you ever been on a perfect one G?"

Borodin grimaced.

"Look, man, I'm not retiring you. I need you and your skills—your command skills—here. Turn the bridge over to a younger pilot."

"A younger pilot," repeated Borodin. "What about Yeager? Why does she have to remain here? Dammit, man, she's service to the core. Her family's been service for generations. And she lives for flying."

Becker glanced at Pauli, and shook his head, his lips thin. She had the idea that he saw more than the thin, short-haired woman who watched him out of eyes that burned with lack of sleep and now, soon, lack of a future. "Yeager's got more potential than pilot's training knows how to exploit. Project Seedcorn needs that potential, her reflexes, her flair for math and spatial relationships, her heredity and health, more than we do another pilot. Especially when *Amherst* won't have ships for them all after this last refit. Even if we take all the riders with us." He added that last almost reluctantly.

"You aren't leaving us a single ship?" Borodin did explode that time. It was better than begging.

"I cannot," said Becker. "You know how much *Amherst* needs equipment. And besides, sensors can track a ridership capable of Jump. Be reasonable, man!"

He gestured Borodin away from the civilians. He followed, Pauli following him, appalled into at least temporary obedience.

"Look, Captain, I have to have people I can trust overseeing these settlers. Look at them, will you? Alicia Pryor may be fine as a chief medic, but the rest of them—aren't they as unlikely a crew to represent Alliance government as you'd ever want to meet? You heard that chatter about the domes, didn't you? That xenobotanist—Angelou, or whatever her name is—didn't want to tamper with the ecosystem, did she?

When it gets cold, will she allow the civs to build fires, or weep about the trees?"

Against his will, Borodin had chuckled sardonically. "No. We're going to win this war. And someone—not me, perhaps, but someone—is going to come back and pick up these refugees. They're our future. So we have to leave them with people we can trust. Which is why you're staying here, Captain. You have full military authority, including the authority to decide whether or not they get to hold elections."

"But Yeager?" Borodin protested as if he led a suicide flight.

"Yeager stays. Even though I can't leave you a ship, she stays. She's command track, unlike the other officers here; and I saw her with the kids. They like her, and she's good with them. Even while we were offloading, she made time to talk with them. So I checked personnel files."

Borodin grimaced, his eyes old and bitter. "Those records should have been classified."

Becker shrugged. "Yeager is the most flexible of the pilots you have left. You may need her here; and Seedcorn certainly does. I'm sorry, Captain. I'd like your consent. But I'll have to demand your obedience. I'm shifting command to Banez. She has orders to lift the instant the *Amherst* is operational."

And that, Pauli thought in despair, was that. Becker started to walk away, and 'Cilla, the child with the ancient eyes, danced up to her, then backed off, thin hands covering her mouth. The child was preternaturally sensitive, Pauli thought. A survival mechanism, perhaps? Her too-big eyes filled—*for my pain?* Pauli wondered—and she ran away to hide her face against Rafe Adams' leg.

"Just a moment, Marshal," called Borodin, his voice rigidly controlled.

"Yes?" Becker's voice iced.

"Your . . . cohorts. The other marshals on board *Amherst*. Send them with Banez too."

"I had planned to assign several of them here, to assist you."

"Dammit," roared Borodin, "you've assisted me out of a job, and one of the best pilots I've ever helped train out of a future. I don't need them, man. I don't want them interfering. If they stay here, God knows what sort of sealed, imbecilic orders they will produce to tie my hands with. God may know; I don't want to deal with it."

"Captain," said Becker, his thin face twisting with what Pauli realized was genuine distress, "we can talk about this when you are less—"

"We are talking about it now! Either I am in command, or I am not. If I am not, let me know that now; and I'll resign my commission right now and ask to be repatriated, either at home or here on Cynthia. If I am truly in charge here, then I tell you frankly, I will not have your precious marshals threatening to pull new sealed orders out of their sleeves every time I make a command decision. Now, which is it?"

"You are in command, sir," said Becker. Unwillingly he grinned. "And there will be a few of my colleagues who will thank God that you have taken such a hard line. No marshals: you're on your own. Will that content you?" Abruptly his voice went from ironic to imperious.

"It must," said Captain Borodin.

The marshal nodded and turned away. His footsteps crunched away toward the ship, the ship that was no longer Pauli's or the captain's.

Well, have you the guts to face him? Sarcasm lashed her forward to meet the captain's eyes.

"I tried," he told her. And then, to her horror, "I should say I'm sorry. But you, at least, will have a chance to live."

If she didn't walk away now, she'd break. "I know you tried, sir," she tried to sound confident. "So it's TDY again, isn't it? Just this time, it's not all that temporary."

In the days remaining before Commander, now Captain, Banez took *Amherst* away, they helped unload the supplies that must suffice until the colony became independent. Food concentrates for several years. With luck, they would be growing their own crops before the concentrates ran out. Without luck . . . colonies had starved before, even on the same world as their founding nation. A limited number of hydro canisters and chemical tanks. They'd all have to turn dirt farmer! Pauli shook her head, appalled, and stared venomously at Becker, who had lugged his own share of the burdens. He straightened up, rubbing hands that had blistered very satisfactorily. She hoped they turned infected on him.

Undamaged genes . . . racial survival, my ass! she grumbled silently. Piece by piece, the settlement took shape.

The evening that the *Amherst* departed, Rafe finally walked over to talk with her. Couldn't he see that she had managed to avoid him since planetfall, that she wanted it that way? Probably he could. Perhaps that was why he had brought the captain with him.

"Pauli, can I talk with you?"

"You're talking," she said. Rafe would probably like it here. That was part of what made her so angry at him. Despite his commission, he was a xenobiologist, and xenos were practically civilians themselves. Like the anthro officer Ro Economus, whom Becker had also marooned here. She'd signed up for the service late. But that wasn't all that explained why, at age thirty, she was still an ensign. Even grounded, however, Rafe and Economus could still do the work they'd joined the service for while she . . . Pauli avoided looking at Rafe: tanned, the weathering carefully maintained under ship's UVs, reddish hair, rangy strength. He was lantern-jawed, pleasantly homely. So all right, pilot wisdom decreed that the pilot who got involved with anyone but a pilot was a fool. Rafe had hoped to move into explorations; and that had been Pauli's first choice too. So Pauli had thought things safe enough to plan and to dare have other hopes. And on the strength of them, she'd made plans for a different future, a future so warm and venturesome that even a fighter ship seemed dull in contrast. As the pilots said, a pilot who got involved with anyone else was a fool.

That went double for her.

Adams glanced desperately at Captain Borodin.

"Alone, if you will pardon us, sir?"

"What's to say, Rafe?" Pauli asked, saying it. "All my life, I trained to be a pilot: some kind of pilot, in any case; and now I'm grounded. *You* still get to be an xenobiologist, but what am I? An ex-flier with great genes. Leave me alone, can't you?"

Borodin jerked his chin at Adams, enforcing the suggestion. Reluctantly the lieutenant left.

Pauli headed farther away from the settlement, tramping down the underbrush, wishing it were Becker she stamped underfoot. Damn the man: if his conviction hadn't carried the ring of an obsession, she might have found herself respecting him. He might have interned the refugees, until isolation and hopelessness honed their fear and anger to such an edge that they could be used for shock troops; yet he had not. They were seedcorn, and must be guarded, not expended, so they might be harvested.

The sky looked very clear tonight. She remembered her last flight, the last one she would ever have, she supposed, how she felt as if she were the ship itself, her arms outstretched to balance and protect it against the buffeting of treacherous downdrafts or wind shear. At least she had one last exhilarating flight, she supposed. She hunched down, watching the ship, as the last loads were dumped a safe distance outside and the crew then withdrew, to seal themselves into the ship and prepare for liftoff.

By the time anyone came—*if* anyone came—to retrieve them, she would probably be too old to fly ever again.

Liftoff came promptly at 19:00. They had backed off to a safe distance and paired the refugee children each with an adult who would be sympathetic or firm, as needed.

Smoke rose about the *Amherst* as the charred ground cover smoldered anew. Then, slowly, the ship rose, gained altitude, and then arced up, leaving only a burned-off field and a shriek of sound, like castoffs, behind. Pauli stared at the sky until the *Amherst*'s trail faded into the sunset. She was not the only one.

Gradually the night wind dispersed it, and two of the civs started building a fire. No one suggested breaking out the heatcubes that Becker, guilty at the last moment, had left behind. *Probably they don't want to waste power. Against their ethic, or something*, Pauli thought mordantly. Still they had to have light.

She thought back to some of the psych briefings she had endured since her assignment had become generally known. The children, 'Cilla especially, feared the dark. 'Cilla . . . they had found her in the wreckage of Wolf IV's scout base Gamma along with her brother Lohr and a boy named Washington. 'Cilla and Washington still winced at sudden noises. Lohr, though, around twelve years old, and with a dark, clever face, was moody. Pauli remembered that one. Whenever he was around, she had a hand on her sidearm, and had a pilot's wariness—around a child, for God's sake!

For now, however, Lohr was no problem. He had stared all that day at Captain Borodin until the captain, kind by nature and necessity, had beckoned him over. Lohr gestured excitedly, miming what Pauli realized were air currents. Now they were deep in talk.

"One thing you learn as a medical officer," murmured Alicia Pryor at Pauli's back, "is never to say, 'I cannot believe it.' I had thought Lohr might never acquire totally normal speech. And look at him with the captain, jabbering away. What are they talking about?"

"Gliders," Pauli muttered. Gliders might be all the flight she had left.

"We've got two pilots now, seeing as how Lieutenant Yeager's completed her training." Lohr glanced her way, with a stare like a young animal, hoping—she realized with some surprise—to play; and she smiled back. "But no ships. Since we're human, and humans are a building sort of animal, I will bet that we are going to make something to take the place of ships."

Abruptly Borodin seemed to be adapting to his new position and surroundings. "Now, I think we could build gliders like the ones I flew at home before I entered the service. Once they're built, all we have to do is find a high place, like those mountains, wait for an updraft, and step right off into it."

Lohr laughed.

"Would you like to try?"

The boy followed Captain Borodin's hands as they described the flight of his hypothetical hang glider. The boy's eyes glowed and he nodded enthusiastically. *He's quick and eager. He might have made a good pilot*, Pauli thought sadly. *But now? Mud farmer, grass-grower, hydroponicist at the very best he can hope for* . . . Well, wasn't that a fine surprise? At least this time, Pauli was sorry for someone other than her own wretched self.

'Cilla edged up next to her again. *I think I've been adopted*, Pauli thought. This time the girl thrust a scrap of fax into her hands. Sketched crudely onto it was a glider. *A talented child, perhaps. Were there paints among the supplies Becker left us? I'll have to check.* So many talents. It was like mining: how could you find the gifts beneath the damaged exterior of the child?

"Our resources are limited, Captain," Dr. Pryor told Borodin calmly as several of the civilians began to nod. "We should not waste them on adventures or toys, even camouflaged as ways of enabling us to investigate our new home. Besides, the gliders you describe are risky."

"Risky to the badly trained, or to the careless, Doctor," retorted Borodin with more spirit than he had shown since *Amherst* landed. "None of my students are ever careless."

The blonde, austere physician glanced skeptically about the circle of civilians, then met Borodin's eyes. He wasn't going to be able to charm this one, Pauli thought. She was canny and underneath the age, the tiredness, and the concern for the children, there was a sophistication and intelligence that would make the medical officer a canny ally or a bad antagonist.

Rafe tried to catch Pauli's eye and grin over Borodin's rather heavy-handed attempt to conciliate the medical officer. His sense of the ridiculous was catching; in fact, years ago, it had helped catch Pauli too. But tonight, she didn't feel like laughing with him. Tonight—she remembered the *Amherst*'s trail arcing up into the darkening sky, then dissipating with the night wind. She had stared at it until it was gone. There would be no more ships: she was sure of that.

Good genes, she thought. *As if I were just a set of chromosomes to be put in freeze. Breeding stock.*

They might be stuck out in the No Man's Worlds, but if Rafe tried to presume on that, he would be very sorry.

After a moment, Rafe looked away. Then he rose to throw wood, carried down by the river and cast up on its banks, onto the fire. Sparks cascaded upward in a preposterously magical, comforting torrent. It was almost as bright as noon. Even Ayelet, the more sullen of David ben Yehuda's twins, smiled. Her father looked up from the tiny engine he was stripping and smiled too.

It might work. Hope kindled on Borodin's face. All over the camp, children turned to the adults. Those children's futures depended on the adults' ability to bring them back into human emotions, a human way of life. It wasn't just caretaking, though; the adults wanted so much to love them. 'Cilla backed away from the fire, and Lohr caught her arm, brought his face up next to her thin one, and whispered urgently.

Instants later, the little girl laughed and ran off to speak with other children. Was Pauli imagining it, or had Lohr warned her not to fear the fire?

Lohr looked after his tiny sister and smiled, the unfeigned, free grin of a tired child. Then, abruptly, he stiffened and pointed at the night sky.

"There!" he cried, and his voice turned into panic and rage.

Enemy ships, thought Pauli. *Not already; and me,*

unarmed. She had no ship with which to pursue them, even though such pursuit might spell death for the rest of the colony.

Longing for the armaments of the *Amherst* and a good armscomputer here on Cynthia, Pauli leapt up. Instinctively her hand dropped for the sidearm that should have hung at her belt. She swore horribly. She'd laid it aside in deference to civ opinion that the sight of weapons might interfere with the children's readjustment.

Such as it was.

Pauli glanced up at the sky, hoping to see the same illusions that the children saw, then dispel it with a stunning display of logic.

But it was not enemy ships that she saw.

'Cilla gasped, a sound more of wonder and welcome than of terror.

Rafe rose to his feet, his face stunned. Apparently, then, the survey that chose Cynthia as a good home for Becker's refugees had not studied the world long or closely enough to discover if it had any inhabitants.

High above the camp, hovering in the thermals that made the flames of the settlement's first fire dance, as if they had been lured away from the mountains by the flame's flicker, fluttered a splendor of immense wings.

CHAPTER 4

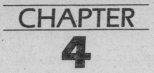

'Cilla struggled free of the adult who tried to embrace her and protect her from the sight by hiding her face against his shoulder, but she remained motionless.

Rafe rose to his feet, his mouth almost slack, his eyes glowing. *So he hadn't guessed either*, Pauli thought. He tracked them as they swooped across the night sky. *Huge*, she judged them. But as they flew nearer, she saw that most of their apparent size lay in the vast wing-spread that had so dazzled her when she first saw them. Firelight, reflected by some bioluminescence in their pigmentation, made them glitter with all the colors of deep space. Indigo galaxies shone on their front wings, and on their scalloped, elongated rear wings flickered whorls of silver and violet nebulae.

They were fliers by right of birth, unlike Pauli, who had craved the power of flight all her life, and had just been grounded by someone else's whim. Fliers, and therefore kin to her; winged and beautiful, and therefore wholly wonderful. Grief, jealousy, and a sudden fierce love for the winged creatures warred within her. She looked over to see Ro nod at Rafe and bring out the comm equipment and a compterminal. That was precisely the sort of first-in work that she and Rafe had planned to spend their lives at. But they had quarrelled, had drifted asunder, and now she had neither the right to work with him nor to touch the tears that glistened on his face. Pauli sighed, then rose and walked toward the tangle of equipment.

"Look at the antennae on those creatures!" Rafe whispered. "Set the receptors for high frequencies."

Pauli leaned forward, faster than Ro, to make the adjustments. Her eyes strayed to Rafe's face, rapt, confident of his skill.

"The antennae are quivering," Rafe observed. "That has to be communications. I wonder what they're saying about us." He welcomed intelligent aliens to study, desired them the way she desired a ship of her own and free space to fly it in.

"You wouldn't think anything that big could get off the ground," muttered Ari ben Yehuda.

"Air pressure's heavier here," said Rafe. "And their bodies are probably a whole lot lighter than ours, even in .8 gravity. Chitin, not bone, for support material, maybe a more efficient circulatory system . . . I can think of many adaptations that would make a creature—a person," he corrected himself with a smile "—flight-worthy."

"I read that in order for there to be intelligence, the brain has to weigh a certain amount," said ben Yehuda. Skilled with all forms of tools, a great reader, he was out of his depths here, and knew it.

"Intelligence as *we* know about it." To Pauli's astonishment, Lohr spoke up. Concealing his surprise, Captain Borodin ruffled the boy's hair approvingly. Dr. Pryor smiled at him the way Rafe smiled at the Cynthians.

"Do you know why you're right?" Borodin asked the boy.

Lohr flushed at so much adult approval and shook his head. He started whispering at 'Cilla, who was scribbling again. Her shoulders were hunched, but in concentration rather than fear.

"I'll tell him," Rafe offered. "Relatively speaking, in our own brains, the synapses—the links by which impulses are transferred—are distant from one another. Move them closer together, pack them in the way you've been packed into the docking bay, make the other modifications that I suggested, and presto!" The children laughed delightedly at his imitation of a magician. Even the aliens' wings swayed in the breeze, sending sparkles of color glittering above their blue and crimson surfaces.

"That's how you might get one large, light, and presumably intelligent creature. Such as the ones we have here."

One large, light, and winged creature. Since gravity was .8 of Earth-normal here, such a being would have less need of long runway space or a high takeoff speed. Probably, given the updrafts in the mountains and the wind currents that made passage across the seas perilous on this world (if they had a ship to attempt it), such creatures could fall languidly into flight and soar for hours.

They had to come from the mountains. Desire slashed through Pauli to take one of the gliders that Captain Borodin planned to build and fly into the mountains to see the Cynthians dancing in the gusts and downdrafts of the high passes.

"Perhaps we should move clear of the fire," she suggested. "If you recall, on Earth, there were creatures that used to dive straight into flame. Wishful thinking aside, we don't know for certain that these beings are really intelligent."

"You think there might be a similar tropism?" Rafe looked up from his adjustments to the communicators' frequency. "They haven't dived at the flames yet. In fact, I'd say that they had been rather careful to stay out of range, which makes me think that they've at least got a well-developed survival instinct. But your point's good, Pauli. Maybe we should move away from the fire, away from the camp itself. They didn't come out during the day, or when the ship was still here. Perhaps they're shy and nocturnal."

He looked around eagerly, almost unable to wait to lure the creatures into landing.

"Lohr, please get me the spray canisters we stacked in the supply dome," he said.

The boy ran off. When he reemerged with the canisters, Rafe examined them, then nodded. He sprayed the first one. Sweet. The second was more pungent, underlaid with a sort of green fragrance, doubly welcome after weeks of a ship's recycled air. With a mutter of satisfaction, Rafe tucked the canisters under his arms and moved out of the fire-lit circle.

There was a story, Pauli remembered, an ancient one from the days before spaceflight, about humans who conversed with alien sailors by means of scents and powders. Was that what Rafe was going to try? Let orange stand for pi, or vinegar represent Avogadro's number, or the square of the hypotenuse, or something? Assuming, of course, that these creatures would even have mathematics.

Attracted by the scents, the Cynthians circled in. Pauli tested the speed with which her sidearm would pull free of its holster, then helped Ro to carry the comms out where Rafe waited in the darkness. Then she gestured the anthropologist back. In a settlement like this, Ro Economus was far less expendable than a grounded pilot.

"I wonder how long it'll take the microcomp to break their language patterns," she muttered.

"Now who's overly optimistic?" asked Rafe. "We'll be lucky to convince them to meet with us again and try to communicate."

"Get the tapers. We'll record all of this," Pauli told Lohr. Then she went back to watching the Cynthians, circling lazily in the sky. They seemed to come in two sizes, one about a third larger than the other; and both types were descending. "Move it fast!" she hissed at the boy and wished, when he scurried off, that she had at least been gentler.

"They're going to stay," Rafe murmured. "Maybe those smells intrigue them. Or maybe we do."

Lohr and 'Cilla ran to Pauli with the recording equipment. The firelight cast gigantic rippling shadows of their running figures on the ground cover and dancing high on the curved walls of the domes.

Sudden static snarled out of the computer's voder. Two of the larger Cynthians detached themselves from the main formation and dived near the children. Their antennae quivered so fast that Pauli could barely see them. Iridescent heads lowered. Between the violet compound eyes, horns stiffened and grew bright with drops of some viscous fluid.

"Move very slowly," Pauli told the children, thanking God that her voice stayed low and calm. "Get back . . . right now . . ."

In an instant more, she'd have range enough to draw . . .

"*No!*" Rafe shouted, and leapt forward. "We're friends!" The lights on the comm danced a frantic pattern, while sounds squealed up painfully until they were too high-pitched for human ears.

Pauli rested her hands on the children's shoulders and walked them back to the fire where Dr. Pryor received them protectively.

"Pauli, get back here. They're going to land!" Rafe cried. No thought of danger, of where she might be needed, but "get back here!" he ordered, and she still dropped everything to be near him.

This time Pauli drew her weapon, ignoring various civilian scowls, before she left the fire. Borodin, she was glad to see, also drew. The significance of those horns, and their gleaming tips, hadn't escaped him. That had to be some natural defense.

"Look at that!" murmured the botanist, who had put up such a fight at any military personnel being allowed— allowed!—to remain on Cynthia. "Why must they automatically assume that these . . . flying things are hostile?"

Pauli wanted to snarl at her. But it was more important to get out there in the dark and help Rafe. He was hooking the commgear to the ports of the readout display. From time to time, squeals and screeches and flutters of dazzling wings showed that he was making some progress.

Finally he stood, weariness apparent in his stooped shoulders. The sky was beginning to pale; and the fire had burned down. The Cynthians took off and circled about the camp once before they headed back toward the mountains.

"We can't just let them go!" Ro whispered, her voice hoarse.

"We won't," Rafe said. "They'll be back. They're just as curious as we are." He rubbed an aching spot on his back, stretched, then shook himself. "I managed to intrigue them . . . I swear I did. That should give us the time we need to learn to talk with them."

He turned to walk back toward his own quarters, and never once spared Pauli a glance.

Why not talk with these creatures? she thought with a return of that morning's bitterness. *After all, what else do we have to do?*

It took weeks even to work out a simple code, long frustrating evenings in which no one could tell whether the Cynthians would even appear or not, or whether the settlers were too weary to do more than stare at the winged creatures and tap out a few desultory experiments on the computers. The planet was hospitable, after a fashion: after its own fashion, which was to demand work of those who hoped to live there.

A day of storms, of struggle even to move from dome to dome, and the Cynthians could be counted on not to appear. On such days, clouds would hide the mountains that served, effectively, to isolate them on a broad, fertile plain. Many times, Pauli wished to explore, to take the flier she no longer had, or even the gliders that Borodin had spoken of, and soar over the plain, up into the foothills—but usually, when evening came, she was content simply to sit with the others.

After stormy days, or on windy evenings, the Cynthians would not appear. But on the clear nights, or those with only a few freshening winds, that the Cynthians did appear, no one could ever tell what might startle them, hurling them aloft and back to their mountains. Perhaps it would be the smell of meat cooking, or a too-rapid movement by one of the settlers.

Anything could jeopardize the fragile accord Rafe was building between himself and the winged natives of the refuge world.

But gradually he reported progress. Gradually he moved out farther and farther from the camp to where the Cynthians would be willing to land. Their visits increased in frequency. Rafe had been right, Pauli thought. He had succeeded in intriguing the Cynthians. After a time, not even a storm that might have shredded their wings could keep them away from the fires, from Rafe, and from the signals that he, and they, tried to send to one another.

"Their semiotic usage—their system of signs—is vastly different from ours," he reported to Borodin after one particularly successful visit. "No specific nouns and verbs; just concepts that can be adapted to either. Most of them have to do with flight . . . you wouldn't expect winged creatures to have a sign for swimming; and sure enough, there isn't one. This doesn't surprise me.

"They've got a sign for fire. It's semantically allied— do you see?—with the sign for destruction. Your analogy of Earth moths, Pauli . . ."

So that first evening, it had been the fire that frightened the Cynthians. *Odd*, Pauli thought. *At first, I thought they feared the children*. But how could anyone fear children, especially those as badly traumatized as the ones here had been? Strange: she had always assumed that one good way of establishing contacts with aliens was through the young of each species.

"There's something that's been puzzling me," Rafe spoke up the next evening, after the Cynthians braved rain and wind to appear at the tiny camp. "I want to get a sample of that fluid on their horns."

"Rafe, if they turn on you, we haven't got an antidote for that," Pryor warned him.

"I think they know they can trust me," he replied.

"You'll cover him," Borodin mouthed at Pauli, who moved in.

"You'd better let me take the sample," she told Rafe.

He was too valuable to risk, and she—she knew her reflexes were faster than most. After all, she was—had been!—a pilot.

Taking a slide, she dabbed with it at the horn of the nearest Cynthian, then leapt back before it could do more than rear up in surprise. She smelled the alien: dusty, like old leaves in the autumn on the homeworld she remembered now only in the sort of dreams from which one woke crying. Perhaps, if she were lucky, she could remember it thus, not as a nightmare vision of a world charred until it no longer had autumns or any other season, or a world irradiated into a trackless, endless winter.

Some of the dust from the Cynthian's scales seemed to cling to the slide along with the fluid she had dabbed from the protective horn along its mandible. Even as she watched, frowning with an absurd sense of guilt, of having trespassed upon another creature, the horn went flaccid, the fluid it had secreted evaporating.

When she gave Rafe the slide for analysis, he stopped glaring at her long enough to process it. "Strong neural toxin," he announced. "Must be their major weapon. Their mandibles are imperfect; it's a wonder that they can eat at all. I'd say that their backup defenses are the barbs on their wings and those forearms. My guess is that they'd use them to grasp an enemy long enough to bring it close, then shred its wings or brush it with their poison."

A Cynthian battle . . . horns glistening, winged Cynthians darting, dodging, reaching out with those hooks and claws . . . what a beautiful, lethal sight such a battle must be.

Pauli hoped she never saw one.

CHAPTER

5

Rafe Adams stared at his printouts. Human/Cynthian equivalences . . . this world's Rosetta Stone. Behind him murmured voices. Sparks from the nightly fire crackled. That fire had turned into a ritual that comforted the entire settlement and drew it closer together. Pauli too—they were working together now, almost as they had planned. Only she was still reserved around him— except when she should be, he thought.

Damn the woman! Who had told her to leap at one of the Cynthians like that, armed only with a slide, deter- mined to protect him from the consequences of his own research? Was she so unhappy here that she courted death? God, he wished she would court him instead, then grimaced at the absurdity of the image. She had to be crazy to think he liked being stranded here either, or to imagine his delight at her presence here with him caused him anything but guilt. Perhaps she would come around.

Pauli . . . alive! he thought, guilty in his relief. Once he had watched ships die; now he watched her. All too often, since planetfall, her face had been leaden, lifeless; the moment's risk, the moment's protectiveness, made her face lose the masklike resignation that had hurt him, even as he sought to break through it.

After all, things could have been much worse. The settlement was beginning to pull itself together, to cope with Cynthia's turbulent climate and to develop some type of local economy.

And, as important, the children at the tiny settle- ment's heart were beginning to live again. Today Ayelet had been a brat, the real variety, even down to the selfishness and sullenness of a child never balked of a toy or a sweet. So, on Borodin's orders, Ayelet had been sent into a dome to go to bed early. Rafe was delighted: Ayelet had acted like a child. Well enough—she had a father and brother alive.

But 'Cilla—frail, tiny 'Cilla—had snapped at her brother Lohr for spilling her paints. They were important to her; she had turned out to have real talent, and was quickly becoming the group's artist. Lohr, however, had snapped back loudly, instead of with the watchful quiet that made Pauli go cold around him and check the position of her sidearm. Dr. Pryor could scarcely conceal her exultation. After all, it was remarkable that children who had been brutalized as badly as these could make a fresh start. Autism was far more likely.

Each day the refugee children, especially the ones whom the larger children called "the littlests," were laughing more, losing the preternatural control and jumpiness that still made some people nervous when they had to be around them.

With a great show of studying his screen (and a more subtle scrutiny of the children, as well as the winged Cynthians), Rafe decided that much of the children's adjustment was due to Pauli and the captain. Probably because they knew no other way of acting, they treated the children like cadets. Perform well, and they handed out rewards, chief among them work with the gliders. Shirk, and there were punishments, like early bedtimes, no gliders, and no sight of the Cynthians, who fascinated the children, unlike human strangers, who made them hide, growl, or reach for the nearest rocks.

But what child would not have been fascinated by the Cynthians? Rafe thought of the younger brothers he had. *Had* was the operative word; his family had lived on a station when the Secessionists struck it. And he had better not think of that again now. Or ever, unless he wanted to submit to Dr. Pryor's attempts at therapy.

Ben Yehuda sauntered over toward him and grinned,

undisturbed at Ayelet's punishment. Rafe tossed more wood on the fire and coiled himself down beside a pile of logs to wait. Pauli stationed herself at the comm. If habit were any indication, soon the Cynthians would begin to arrive.

Two in particular turned up almost every evening. Some odd whimsy of Pauli's had made her dub them Uriel and Ariel; he wouldn't have assumed that she even knew those names—and he would have wagered on her not knowing what they meant.

"I'm a pilot," she had always told him, half-boastful, half-apologetic, whenever he had tried to draw her away from talk of them or of the day-to-day into visions of art and peace. "Specialized. How would I know anything about that?"

And then she would smile at him, and he would lose his train of thought. She had dissembled, he knew. Pauli was better educated than her boasts.

So, she had named the Cynthians, and the names had stuck. Uriel and Ariel were among the largest of the Cynthians and, assuming that the pallor of their fluorescent wings indicated age, they were probably among the eldest. Rafe chuckled, thinking of Uriel and Ariel as having to keep order among the younger, more brilliant Cynthians—*you raced one another despite wind shear, so no visit to those wingless freaks by the river tonight!* (The possibilities for Cynthians'-eye humor made him suppress laughter.) They might have many of the same problems as Captain Borodin.

But now as Rafe looked up, he saw a gleam of wings descending from the foothills.

"They're coming," he murmured.

"Good. Can you ask them if there's a cold season and, if there is, how they manage to survive?"

"I can try," said Rafe. The Cynthians circled and landed, dipping wings in a gesture Rafe had concluded was a form of compliment to the humans. Rafe tried to imitate the gesture with his arms and shoulders, but, as always, failed gracelessly. After an exchange of ritual phrases, Rafe repeated the captain's question to the

Cynthians. The sound of his words went into the common-coder and appeared on the readout as symbols: *cold/visualization of a Cynthian/interrogative.*

Antennae quivered. The screen blanked, then lit with the symbols of the Cynthians' reply: *mountains/hollowed-out caverns/Cynthians, wings folded, within.*

"Nice work," hissed Borodin.

At least human eyes perceived some of the same wavelengths as Cynthians! Rafe thought. Otherwise communication would have been impossibly hard, instead of just arduous. Studying the signs on his screen, Rafe concluded that the Cynthians were not just primarily nocturnal. They hibernated too.

But wait. Now new symbols were forming, replacing the previous analogy. *Cold.* The screen split into two displays, preparing for the analogical constructs that seemed to be such a major characteristic of Cynthian thought or "speech." *Cynthians/mountains; humans/domes.* Assuming the unattractive stick figures were humankind, that was plain enough. Cynthians lived in the mountains; humans lived on the alluvial plain.

The screens lit again. *Humans/mountains.*

"They're asking us to move," Rafe said.

"We can't!" Beneatha, the xenobotanist, argued. "For one thing, how do you expect us to pack up the hydro tank into those hills?"

Rafe sighed, as he usually did whenever Beneatha opened her mouth, wishing, as always, that Beneatha were less hostile toward the military members of the settlement. He'd have liked to study the Cynthian diet, for example, and he had asked for Beneatha's help. But the one time he had approached her, she had barely been civil. Even to him, whom Pauli had accused of being three-quarters civilian himself. Perhaps if he had not been—if Pauli's preoccupations with flying, with the traditions of the service, had meant half as much to him as she did herself . . . Rafe shook his head. There was no time now to waste in regrets.

He glanced over at the woman who was the source of

most of such regrets for him. She had hoped, he knew, to command a ship like the *Amherst* herself. Once they had made plans together for such a ship. That and service in exploration might have meant a life together of discovering and surveying planets such as this one. But now, with the Secessionists grabbing and fortifying undefended planets, Pauli could only hope for advanced pilot training which would qualify her for the type of combat duty that was more suicide than combat.

Oddly enough, she resented being deprived of that. But at least she was alive. Rafe was glad of that. There had to be something wrong with a system that condemned its bravest, brightest young people to early deaths, something even more wrong when those people themselves acceded to their death sentences—and you didn't have to be three-quarters civilian to think that.

Rafe became aware that he had been silent too long. People were staring at him. So, for that matter, were the Cynthians. One of the smaller, more garish creatures mantled its wings, then settled back as Uriel half turned toward it.

He brought himself back to the present. "I'll tell the Cynthians we can't join them in their mountain caves for the winter."

He selected his symbols carefully. *Domes/plants in rows. River/humans.* That ought to be clear enough, even if you left out Beneatha's protests about the hydroponics. The humans had to stay near the river in order to find food, water, and shelter.

Ariel's antennae quivered and stiffened. The poison horns on its head extruded themselves, gleamed wetly, then withdrew quickly. Wings flapped and scattered spangles of violet and silver across the night sky as it rose and vanished in the direction of the foothills. Why had Ariel fled the human camp?

"That wasn't a retreat, that was a withdrawal," Pauli commented. "What did you tell it?"

"That we had to stay where our home was."

Uriel, ink-blue body with pale-green and silver mottlings, wrapped its upper wings firmly about its body, indications of fear and distress. The screen filled with the elder's message: *humans: caves . . . humans: caves . . . humans: caves . . .*

"Insistent, isn't it? And we have months until winter, too?"

Before Rafe could respond to either, Uriel also lifted away from the camp, followed, more reluctantly (or so it seemed), by the other smaller Cynthians. Powder from their wings sprinkled down upon the watching humans.

Why would they want the humans to move up to their eyries? You'd think that the Cynthians would be territorial . . . unless winged creatures were not as turf-conscious as landbound ones. If that were so, it would be the first case of nonterritoriality that Rafe had ever studied.

I'd like to get into those hills, he thought.

A hand fell on his shoulder. Borodin's hand.

"If you're thinking what I think you are, Lieutenant, forget it till we learn more about this planet. I'm not about to risk you."

"I'm getting a little tired of being too valuable to risk," Rafe pointed out. "How about ground recon? That's usually in my job description. Since you don't want me heading for the mountains, why not let me take a team into the river plain?"

Borodin chewed his lip, unable to see a reason to refuse. "Fine. When would you want to leave?"

"I doubt that after tonight's little talk that the Cynthians will be back tomorrow. I could leave at dawn."

Borodin nodded. Rafe's gaze slid involuntarily over to Pauli. *Come with me? Please?* But she was staring after the Cynthians, then looking down at the gleaming dust on the hand she had raised to her lips as the younger ones had risen, a concerted splendor of wings.

Rafe sighed, knowing that nothing he could offer would ever replace her dream of flight.

Then he shrugged, and went to choose those civilians

and children who would accompany him. Dawn came early on Cynthia.

Carefully Pauli stored her glider and started toward the dome they had designated as the settlement's dining hall. Great flying weather, she thought in satisfaction. Even the experimental, short glider flights she had tried in order to test them had given her a dizzying sense of freedom. She loved the way that the wind rushed against her eyes and forced tears into them, turning the patchwork land below a green-blue. Risky, the civs clucked. Sure: but a one-man ship was riskier, and that was the ship she had wanted.

Were any of her friends at New Pax or on board *Amherst* still alive? Involuntarily she glanced toward the plain in the direction that Rafe and his scout team had taken. If the wind had been right, she might have flown after them.

Maybe the war would end soon, and that Becker would return with the *Amherst*, and new orders for them all. Or maybe, a more cynical voice whispered to the darkness behind her eyes, maybe the war would only end when no one was left with the strength to fight it, or even to endure it any longer.

Well, for her, the war was definitely over.

"I expected Lohr to join us today in testing the gliders," Captain Borodin commented as he entered and hung away his own glider. "He's been panting to test out his wings."

"Lieutenant Adams convinced Dr. Pryor that his recon was a field trip, and thus took priority over joy riding," Pauli said. Her voice was harsh. "Frankly, what I think was that 'Cilla wanted to see the plain, so Lohr went along to watch out for her. You know, lately she's shown a tendency to break away from the crowd and run on ahead. Besides, Ayelet was going with Rafe, and Lohr likes her."

"That'll be useful to know in a couple of years when the children all start pairing off," Borodin said. Then, after too long a meaningful pause, "Adams is doing fine work, don't you think?"

Speaking of pairing off, are you, Captain? If the captain wanted to praise Rafe, let him put a commendation into the computer log.

As they came out of the dome, someone ran into Pauli, sobbing hysterically.

Ayelet! Several of the civs ran to soothe her. Was Rafe's expedition aborted so soon? Where was the rest of the party? Where was Rafe himself?

Pauli forced herself to meet Borodin's eyes. What if Rafe was dead?

"There he is!" The captain pointed at a tiny figure that seemed to stagger as it hurried toward them.

She hurried to the arms locker, then headed out to meet him. Rafe was carrying 'Cilla, and weaving as he ran. The little girl's face was gray and slack. Spittle glistened in the corners of her half-opened mouth, and she shivered convulsively.

"Dr. Pryor! We've got casualties!" Borodin was shouting. Pauli glanced behind her. The captain was helping the children, now staggering in one by one, to sit with their heads between their knees. One or two retched from the long run and the terror. Lohr bent forward in the long grass and tried to be sick from exhaustion. But he was too controlled. Borodin patted his shoulders.

"Don't let the kids come any closer to 'Cilla," Rafe gasped at Pauli.

She bent forward to examine the child herself. 'Cilla's right boot was gone, except for a few shreds of curling leather that clung to her shin. Four deep punctures showed blue on her ankle. The entire foot looked as if acid had spilled on it.

"What did this?" Pauli demanded.

Rafe shook his head. "Another lifeform that survey didn't turn up. Damn them! Damn them all!"

CHAPTER 6

Pauli thinned her lips as she bent over the unconscious child . . . *that time during basic training in lab . . . Leslie was trying to concoct archaic liquid fuels . . . washed out of flight training on disability pension . . . no funds or time for regrowth . . . and besides, you needed two good hands to fly . . .*

Had 'Cilla survived the slagging of Wolf IV only to endure this? What would her injury mean to the rest of the children, who must know now that the adults could not protect them against enemies even on this refuge world? Would they be able to survive at all?

For the colony to survive, they might have to call on the gutter-bred survival abilities of the children whose memories and lives they had hoped to ease.

Alicia Pryor seemed to materialize, yet she did not look as breathless as Pauli felt. She knelt beside 'Cilla.

"Will she lose the foot?" Pauli asked.

"Depends," said the medical officer. "She's deep in shock. Unless she wakes, I won't risk sedation or pain-killer. No, Rafe—don't touch her! Whatever acid she stumbled into, if I don't neutralize it fast, it's going to dissolve her foot!"

"Not acid . . . a bite . . . I saw . . ."

"First I work on 'Cilla. Meanwhile, you bury everything—starting with the clothes you're wearing—that may have come in contact with this acid. Then you can tell me what you think you saw."

Rafe tried to protest.

"All right, then: what you know you saw. I can use all

the help I can get. For example, from the way the flesh is torn here, it looks like some sort of lizard; but, given a bite of this size and a child no bigger than 'Cilla, if that were venom, probably a nerve poison, she'd have died before she hit ground."

Pauli shuddered. The dash and detachment about death with which pilots tried to armor themselves were nothing, she thought, compared with Pryor's particularly chilling brand of scientific objectivity. Yet, at the thought of her death or, right now, of 'Cilla's, Rafe had cracked.

Now he groaned. "Not a lizard. Horrible things, like grubs or maggots, and a meter long . . . God, I have to . . ." he gagged, then swallowed convulsively, restraining himself.

Another world . . . another life . . . but Rafe had been similarly red-eyed. Beads of sweat had stood out on gray skin, matted the springing hair. *"I won't wait to know if your ship blew, or if you'll be flying back, Pauli,"* he'd sworn the night after a pilot from his home station had been blasted by Secess', working in that precise, hellish unanimity of theirs. *"You choose, Pauli. Flying or . . . our future."*

Unless she and all of the other pilots like her flew, what future could anyone have? It had not been a fair demand; Rafe had been too afraid, too anguished, for fairness, which was, Pauli sometimes thought, a peacetime luxury, in any case.

To spare them both, she had chosen flight. Had she chosen wrong? He retched dryly; that would change in a moment.

"Not here, you can't," Pryor's hand, pushing him away, was gentle. "'Cilla's foot's already septic enough. Get him out of here, Pauli . . . Pauli? Move it, Lieutenant! I haven't time for you now."

Pauli drew her gloves on and led Rafe to the riverbank. He gazed about, studying the ground with frantic care. Then he collapsed the way Lohr had and vomited at the water's edge.

"Steady now," Pauli murmured. "Whatever else happened, you got the kids back alive. And you've given 'Cilla a chance. She's tougher than she looks, you know. Lie back and rest."

Careful not to brush against Rafe's outer clothes, Pauli removed them. Already the acid from 'Cilla's foot had begun to eat through the tough synthetic of his trousers, and had made inroads into the leather of his jacket.

Digging a hole in the soft, easily turned mud of the riverbank, she buried first the contaminated garments, then her own gloves. Covering the spot, she marked it with a large, flat stone. Rafe shivered convulsively, and she stripped off her own jacket and wrapped it about him, then moved to put herself between him and the wind.

"Let me get you a blanket," she offered. But he grasped her wrist hard.

"Don't go, Pauli. You stay and listen. Someone's got to listen to me, Pauli, listen now, so I won't forget, and so I'll know I'm not crazy."

"You should tell the captain . . ."

"The captain's got all he can handle now. Damn it! Girl, just this once, don't play things by the book . . . *please*." Rafe clasped her hands between his. His fingers were clammy and they trembled.

A second chance, Pauli thought, and chafed his hands.

"All right, Rafe. Let's hear it."

"We headed south toward the flats. At noon we stopped to rest. About that time, we saw rock formations in the distance."

"I didn't pick them up," she muttered.

"Scan registered them as about five meters high; you wouldn't have. Curious thing about them too. They were all oriented along this world's magnetic field. Exploration never mentioned them in the preliminary reports on Cynthia."

"Were they artifacts?" Pauli asked. "A technologically advanced lifeform here—and hostile?"

"I don't know, I don't know." Still clutching at hers, his hands rose to hide his face. Pauli stroked his hair back from his forehead.

"'Cilla was sure Ro would want pictures, samples of the rocks. She got very excited about the possibility that they might even have inscriptions on them. So we headed that way."

Rafe shook his head. "She had been frisky all morning. Twice already, I had had to order her not to run ahead of the group. So of course she got away again to be the first to take a close look at the rocks. I shouted at her to wait up, then headed out after her. She kicked one of the rocks, and it cracked. Up till then, if it hadn't been for the scanners, I'd have sworn that it was rock, solid."

"'It's not real rock,' she yelled." Rafe squeezed his eyes shut, as if trying to blot out memory along with vision. Pauli leaned forward and brushed her lips against his forehead.

"That was about the time she started to scream. I ordered Lohr and Ayelet back, then grabbed my weapon and motioned the civs to fan out. My God, there must've been sixty . . ."

"Sixty what?" Pauli finally succeeded in pushing him down to lie on his back. In the next instant, however, he had risen again.

"I don't know what you'd call them. Grubs. Maggots. Segmented, with thick black hairs on each segment, and splotchy patterns. Each one of the things must have been a meter long, most of it mandibles. Did you see the marks on 'Cilla's foot? One of the things grabbed her. I don't know which it was, the bite or the acid, that hurt her so badly."

Rafe sobbed once. "She was brave, so brave. I knew she wanted me to get her free, but some more of the grubs started coming at us. I burnt a circle around 'Cilla and me, then blasted the one that was gnawing on her. And she trusted me to do it! God help me, I don't think I did it quickly enough. Once I got her free, I picked her up and jumped the fire. After I got clear, we laid down a barrage and sent all those things, and the rocks, up in flame."

He rolled closer to Pauli and buried his head against her shoulder. Before she realized what she was doing, her arms went around him. There was an astounding ache in her throat, a tightening in her chest. *If they had gotten Rafe too . . . !* "You got 'Cilla out, and you warned us, Rafe. You did your job and did it well. That's all that's important right now," she told him, and knew that wasn't the truth. He felt right in her arms, as right as the glider had felt that morning.

Rafe's hands clasped her shoulders tightly, kneading them. "Pauli, what if that wasn't the only infestation?"

"Then we'll wipe them all out," she told him. She was only a pilot, a grounded pilot. All she had ever known was how to fight and how to fly and how never to give up until she died.

But now she knew other things, things like protectiveness and love. They burned in her empty belly like the acid that had crippled 'Cilla's foot.

Flying and combat had been easier by far.

Still, there was no need, though, for Rafe to suffer right now.

She tried not to tense. "You've done all you can for now," she soothed him, and pressed his head against her breast. "Rest now. Try not to worry about the eaters."

"But they remind me . . . what . . ."

"I said, 'Never mind!' We'll manage. Hell, Rafe, any race that can move itself from caves into starships ought to be able to keep some grubs in check. Let it go for now."

A race that fought planet-breaking wars, against grubs that spat acid and attacked children . . . and seemed to be on an interception course with their fragile settlement. They were stranded here; with no fliers to move them, and mountains and a river to cross, they had no choice but to hold their ground.

The civs are going to love this! Pauli made herself sit motionless, and finally Rafe dozed, his head in her lap, her arms wrapped about him protectively under her jacket. He was warmer now, and the feel of his skin distracted her momentarily. But the afternoon wore on, a faint mist rose from the river and began to thicken about them. Painfully she worked one hand free of Rafe and fumbled her sidearm free of its holster, then balanced it on her knee, carefully so it might not touch the man who had found his way back to her.

What would become of him now? What would become of all of them? When she cared—or claimed to care—only for flying, her life had been simpler. But she had been lying, and now her punishment was upon her: to wait here while the mist wreathed about her, hiding possible enemies. For the moment, however, she could not fight. Having no other choice while Rafe slept, Pauli sat and contemplated a bleak future until Borodin came to collect them.

The river mists had blown away, and both moons shone, blurred by the shadows of a few clouds. Captain Borodin stood by the fire, his hand on his sidearm, waiting, as Rafe knelt by the computer, painstakingly working out the questions they had to have answers for. Several hundred of them, in fact. And, in return, he had to be prepared for whatever questions the Cynthians would ask of them.

Behind them, between the fire and the safety of the domes, waited most of the settlers and those children too restive or too stubborn to let themselves be convinced to rest and let their elders handle things. Their eyes gleamed too brightly, with that preternatural alertness that had made Rafe shudder the first time he met them. Only the knowledge that 'Cilla would not lose her foot had prevented general hysteria. If they were not to revert to protective savagery, they especially needed answers.

The night wore on. Though several of their elders yawned and shook themselves reluctantly awake, the children waited, crouching by the fire, occasionally glancing at one another or whispering things that they refused to tell their guardians. Finally, moonlight picked out the familiar whorls and stars of the Cynthians' wings. Uriel and Ariel hovered above the settlement for a long time before they descended a safe distance from the dying fire.

"They sense something," Rafe muttered to Pauli, then

bent to call up one of the new symbols he had created: small, segmented, and long-fanged.

Two of the younger Cynthians mantled, then subsided. One actually displayed the poisoned horns that were their chief weapon. Antennae quivered; simultaneously the agitated Cynthians withdrew, and Rafe's instruments registered transmissions so rapid that they could not decipher them. He flung out his hands reassuringly, gesturing at Borodin to lay aside his weapons. Gradually the rate of transmission slowed, and the blur on his screens coalesced and gradually resolved into identifiable symbols.

Rafe turned to the captain. "There's a lot of static about this concept. If these creatures were human, I'd say that it's got strong emotional connotations for them. It makes translation difficult. The closest equivalent I can get is 'those who eat' . . . eaters. I don't think, sir, that I can finetune the resolution any further."

"Ought to blast them all," grumbled David ben Yehuda. He had an arm about his daughter; her twin sat on her other side. Both the father and the son kept flamethrowers close at hand. It had taken a direct order—"You're ordering me? I'm not under your command!"—to keep ben Yehuda and his cub from starting out that very night to hunt down creatures such as Rafe's party had blundered into.

"Rafe, ask what the Cynthians know about these eaters."

Pauli shook her head at the captain. "They think in analogies, sir. You've got to break your questions down into that form. It may take some time."

Enemies, Rafe thought. Symbols formed under his fingers: *Cynthians/mountain caves; eaters/rocks on the plain.* That was the basic situation. Now for possible conflict: *a broken-winged Cynthian/on the plain; eaters/ devouring Cynthians along with plant life.*

Immediately the screen blurred and filled again with symbols. *Cynthians/caves; humans/caves; eaters/plains.*

"It's the same story, sir," Rafe spread out his hands and shrugged. "The Cynthians flee the eaters. Since they like us, they want us to run too, and suggest evacuating into their caves. I don't think they're equipped to put up much resistance; may be why they run. They're pretty awkward on the ground."

"But we could fight them!" Pauli cried.

Borodin watched the pilot carefully. Her commission date had preceded Rafe Adams'; despite her age, she was seasoned and wary. Why had she suggested a fight? That answer came more quickly than replies from the Cynthians: a fight would be one way to remove the strain from Adams. She stood very close to him. That, at least, was something to be grateful for.

A flicker of color drew the captain's attention. Ariel's wings were drooping, their luminous colors subdued. Borodin felt a moment's sympathy for the Cynthian: older, and presumably stuck with responsibility for the smaller Cynthians such as the ones it had evidently ordered back to the safe hills.

"What would you suggest, Lieutenant? Besides ben Yehuda's dubious expedient of blasting the lot of them."

As if Uriel could interpret the emotional tensions among the humans, it fluttered its antennae, swept palpae back and forth, and beat its wings two or three times as Pauli considered her words.

"I say we push the eaters hard. Given our own limited food supply, we can't retreat to the Cynthians' caves and expect to be a drain on their resources. Whatever their resources are," she added. "So I'd suggest that first, we guard the camp by burning a clear zone on the land side. If there's nothing to eat in it, the grubs won't try to cross. But we'll be planting, and our crops will tempt the things. That means we'll have to set up watches. And every time we see eaters, we burn them out. And"— Pauli collected herself and drew a deep breath as she came to the most controversial part of her defense strategy—"I further suggest that we develop a pesticide that will stop the eaters permanently. Sir." His title came tacked on as an afterthought, and the woman tensed, anticipating his reaction.

Pauli, I think you just went too far, Borodin commented silently. *Not that I disagree, but I think you're going to have to take the consequences of those words.* The civilians were muttering again. *Bozhe moi*, the civilians were always muttering. Sardonically Borodin quoted a proverb from Novaya Moskva, his homeworld: you couldn't make omelets without breaking eggs. His people, even from the time before spaceflight, understood that. Their continued survival could be attributed to a genius for enduring times when large numbers of eggs were broken: accepting the horrors, and the consequences, then hunkering down till the trouble retreated. As it always did. These civilians might be more humane; they were far less patient. It was a weakness.

He sighed. After a lifetime in space, he found planetbound life painful; dampness made his back ache; the civs' tendency to fight him made his head ache. And the injury done the child who was his to protect? They were sentimental on Novaya Moskva; and his heart ached for her.

"I don't want to hear any talk of poisoning alien life," Beneatha Angelou stated.

You can't antagonize the xenobotanist, Pauli girl: we need her too much, Borodin warned his underofficer silently.

"Would you rather have an eater latch onto *your* foot?" cried Ari. His father motioned to his son to hush.

A moment later, everyone still gathered near the fire and the bristling Cynthians had leapt up and seemed to try to make an angry speech at once. Several of the children screamed, high and piercing, drawing Ariel's attention. Two others had curled up almost in fetal positions.

"Look what you've done!" Borodin snapped. "Someone take those kids inside." He waited until they were removed. "I hope we didn't do them any damage tonight. Now look, I didn't want to have to say this. I suspect you've all wondered why Marshal Becker assigned me here. It wasn't just because my age and reaction time made me a bad combat risk. If it comes to that, I'm still more than a match for you. That's not the issue. This is. I don't know if all you people realize that Becker and the Alliance are counting on us to be waiting for pickup after the war . . ."

"Assuming they live through it . . ."

Borodin let that muttered comment pass. *That's close to sedition. If I notice things like that, I'll have to declare martial law. Then I can say good-bye to any hope of rapport with these people.* Banking on any goodwill that they might have—for Rafe or his other officers, if not for him—he pressed on quickly.

"A couple of years from now, if we're not picked up, I don't even want to hear whispers that maybe we lost. It doesn't have to mean that. Think of what else it could mean," Borodin lowered his voice. "It could mean, for example, that there's nobody in shape to pick us up. No one with spaceflight—or even no one alive." *Darkness and cold, ice and snow covering the steppes, hiding the bodies until the spring that would come as it had come every year for the few who survived.*

"So we're going to have to get used to thinking of ourselves as the human race. For all we know, we may be what's left of it. I say we keep it going; it's worth keeping going. None of you look to me like potential suicides. So I think you'd better consider Pauli's plans for defending this place, unless you have things to add."

The xenobotanist rose, hostility making her thin body taut.

"I'm coming to that. Now, Beneatha Angelou has raised a serious moral and ecological issue: destroying alien life. Rafe, would you say that killing an eater is destroying intelligent beings?"

"God, no!" Rafe shuddered. "I'd call it pest control. Or getting an animal before it gets you."

"Please ask the Cynthians how long these incursions last."

Symbols formed on the screen which blanked, then lit with the answer. "Every two seasons, sir." That answer came with commendable speed. More symbols came, and Rafe shook his head, unable to understand the jumble of light and pattern. He swayed, then caught himself.

"Then, as far as I'm concerned, that settles it," said Borodin. "If they come every other year, you'd be spending half your lives as refugees, or in constant fear of going out one morning and coming back like 'Cilla. Or not coming back at all from a very unpleasant death. Which option do you choose?"

"Your lieutenants were quick enough to adjust the comms to 'speak' to the Cynthians," Beneatha lowered her head, as if planning to attack. "Why can't they adjust it to transmit offworld so we can leave here? Or"—she raised a hand for attention—"you listen to me now! I've listened to you. All right, I understand that we're supposed to be safe here. Can't we move?"

"We haven't even got a flier," ben Yehuda replied. "You tell me how I can build transports, and I'll start tonight."

"You don't really want to risk the Secess' interpreting the message and finding out our coordinates, do you?" Borodin asked. Was the xenobotanist being difficult on purpose, or were her objections based on arcane civ principles, or just wishful thinking? "Never mind my orders," he went on, making his voice warm and persuasive. "I think we have an obligation to protect ourselves and the children. It hasn't been much of a life for them so far; one reason we brought them here was to give them a chance at a better one.

"I hate to say it. But if we can't contain this . . . infestation, well, I don't like it either, but the eaters won't be the first extinct species our race has racked up, starting on Earth and moving out into the stars."

"Perhaps," suggested Dr. Pryor, "your officers might ask the Cynthians if they have any ideas for helping out." Borodin inclined his head to her with the courtesy he hadn't used since his last home leave. She was a civilian, and an aristocratic-looking one at that, but he liked her calm resourcefulness. The instant she spoke, the noise level sank noticeably.

"Try it," he told Rafe.

But as the underofficer transmitted the question: *Cynthians/eaters . . . Cynthians/interrogative?* the winged creatures mantled. So much for that good idea. Rafe tried again, but the aliens grew increasingly agitated.

"Sir, he's ready to pass out," Pauli hissed at him.

"Then I'll try," Borodin said. He might have been born patient and learned tact in space, but standing back and letting other people conduct the negotiations went hard with him. He took over the comm from Rafe, who sat with his head buried in his hands, and tried to assure the Cynthians that they didn't have to fear.

But he was clumsy with the symbols, unfamiliar with the analogical reasoning Rafe used to communicate with them; and the winged creatures grew more and more agitated. Finally they went into full threat display, their horns out and gleaming with clear venom. Their antennae quivered too quickly for human eyes to follow or the equipment to receive.

"They're terrified of the eaters," Pauli whispered. "Or of what we're asking."

As the communications gear crackled and squealed, the Cynthians mantled again, their wings hurling them into the air with a scatter of metallic-colored dust. Their wings flashed so brilliantly in the moon and firelight that for a moment, no one realized that the comm lights had blinked out. Even the screen blanked, except for the small green point that floated languidly from left to right on the now-dark panel. As if waiting for that, the fire crashed in on itself, burnt logs crumbling into ash and glowing embers, then subsiding into darkness.

"That must have been some speech," Pauli whistled. As usual, she was the first to recover her composure.

Borodin nodded. "Tomorrow, on my orders and my responsibility, we will organize our defenses. I think we can conclude that the Cynthians can't be expected to help us on this. So we will burn off that strip, set up our watches, and see what we can manufacture in the way of pesticides to be used only as a last resort. Is that clear?" He glared over at ben Yehuda.

"I don't *like* killing things," the engineer said. "Why look at me?" He glanced down at his and his son's flamethrowers, then grinned wryly.

"One last thing: every morning some of us will sortie to make certain our local environment is clear. Understood?"

In what seemed like another life, she and Rafe had dreamed of such missions; in their dream, though, they had found only friendly, beautiful life . . . like the Cynthians who, unaccountably, had fled. Well, this was as close to that dream as they were going to get.

Why did it feel unfamiliar, as if she prepared not for a sortie, but to solve a puzzle for which, somehow, she had lost the critical pieces?

CHAPTER
7

"Dr. Pryor told me that 'Cilla's fever is down." At least Pauli could begin her report cheerfully.

Borodin nodded, then promptly won an argument by ignoring the possibility that it might exist. "I'm going to be the only one taking a glider with me, Pauli. You may be lighter and quicker than I, but I've got more flight experience."

"Are we going to need that glider, sir?" Rafe asked. "What do you plan to launch from?"

"Those, if I have to," he pointed at some distant rock spurs. "It's an emergency measure. I'll use it only if we have to get a message through and something blocks our communications. We'll have a backup. Me."

Pauli grumbled, then subsided. Pilots relied on instinct, trained over as many years as they stayed alive and flying. Borodin, as he said, had the experience. If he thought he might need to fly out of a situation they could handle until he brought in backups, she had better let it stand. She smiled encouragingly at Ari ben Yehuda, whose flamethrower made him bend almost double until his father adjusted its harness. Then she turned to give her own final instructions.

"Strip the settlement's perimeters. Start digging a trench and fill it with brush, dried ground scrub, or anything else that's flammable. If the eaters come, pour oil into the trench and shoot. If we see smoke, we'll approach from the river."

Beneatha looked stubborn.

"*Do it*," Borodin said. "I can't risk leaving Pauli or Rafe behind to see that orders are carried out."

"That marshal prepared you for everything, didn't he, Captain," the xenobotanist gibed. "Weapons, which none of us have access to. Martial law. Secret orders. But they didn't prepare you for the eaters. So naturally, now, you have to kill them."

"You'd prefer that they'd killed 'Cilla instead?" another scientist snapped, much to Pauli's relief. Things were getting too polarized: military on one side, civs on the other. "I'll round up the older kids. They can help."

By afternoon they had passed beyond the sections of the plains explored on previous scouting trips. Here rock spires jutted out, and ben Yehuda turned scanners on them. "I don't know how you guessed, Captain, but they'll block transmissions from here."

Pauli grinned. No fog from the river spread out this far, and the spatter of rain that usually came from the mountains at around noon had long since dried, leaving only a smell of green and of freshness. The sun shone, and the winds were lively. *I could like this world*, she assured herself.

"The rocks look like jaws," Rafe told her.

The muscles along his eyelids and jawline twitched. In the warm sunlight, his face seemed as remarkable to Pauli as his body had felt the night before. He had clung to her as if her touch, her heartbeat, were all that protected him from the eaters, or from his dreams of them.

"Can't you think of anything better to talk about?" she asked, grinning reminiscently and not minding ben Yehuda's knowing, gleeful "oh *ho*!"

Rafe turned to her and smiled. The strain in his face lightened, and seeing it, Pauli was even happier.

Carrying communication gear, Borodin headed for the peaks.

"Heads up, sir!" Pauli shouted. Overhead, brilliant motes glinted and danced above the rock teeth. "I thought you said that the Cynthians were nocturnal, Rafe."

"I said 'probably nocturnal.'" He drank from his trail flask and wiped his mouth on his sleeve, then smeared his hands down his trouser legs before answering. "Apparently they can come out during the day if they have to." He paused, watching them. "They're watching us. Wonder why they don't land? They've always been friendly." He grimaced as if he too tried to remember something—as if he too groped for a missing piece in a puzzle that he only half understood.

"They've been watching us all morning," ben Yehuda lowered his field lenses, rubbed his back to ease it, then swung his flamethrower back over his shoulder. "First few times I saw it, I thought my eyes were playing tricks. And you two were . . . let's call it, preoccupied."

Rafe turned on him, and he held up a hand. "With your work, of course. What did you think I meant?"

"Captain was really right about the idea of a backup after all. Never mind the rocks. Even if we could transmit past them, those Cynthians can generate enough interference to make any transmissions impossible."

She activated her own lenses. They whirled almost sickeningly, seeking rapid resolution and polarizing against the sunlight. Distance grids and markers snapped into place.

"More rock spurs at four hundred meters," she said. "Rafe, do they look anything like the formations you saw before?"

"There's the captain," ben Yehuda pointed.

Borodin had clambered three-quarters of the way up the nearest peak. He shook off his pack, then flung his arms wide and shook his head to indicate that the comms were not working.

"Comms are out," ben Yehuda interpreted, but neither Pauli nor Rafe paid attention to him.

"The rocks . . . not quite like the others. It looks like the eaters have already broken free," muttered Rafe. His lenses fell from his hand and slapped against his chest. Then he looked up. Swooping at them with a breathtaking, precipitous urgency that delighted Pauli even as she started to back away were five Cynthians. Two of them were the larger, more somber elders.

She gazed at them, unable to dismiss a sudden, horrible idea. "Did the eaters break free of those formations?" she asked slowly. "Or were they hatched?"

Adrenaline made her dizzy and sick in a way that she had not been for years.

Rafe turned around to stare at her, his lips going white.

"Hatched," he repeated. "Hatched. Call myself a xenobiologist, damn it. I didn't want to think of that, either. Enough happened right away that I didn't have to. Hatched. You do understand what you've just implied, don't you?"

In her dreams, she had tried to solve a puzzle, had lacked the essential piece. Now it came to hand, and it cut shrewdly. Dammit, how could she have known? She was a pilot, only a pilot; her talents were for math and flying; *yes, and killing enemies*.

"The Cynthians aren't watching us," Pauli said. "They're guarding them. The eaters . . . that's who they're protecting." She wanted to bend over and vomit. No, the eaters weren't sapient . . . not at this stage of their life cycle. They were merely hatchlings, voracious, driven by their instincts for survival to devour everything within range until the weather cooled and they encapsulated themselves once more, to emerge as . . .

No wonder the Cynthians fled questions about the eaters. No wonder they refused to help find a solution that would block the eaters' movement from pasture to pasture. They might urge their newfound, oddly shaped friends to move, but in the end, if the newcomers did not move, they would be abandoned. Even if it meant their lives—for what were the newcomers, against the life of their own species?

Fire lanced down to char the nearby brush.

"Get moving!" Distance thinned Borodin's voice. He

had one arm already in the glider's harness but he waved his free arm frantically, then fired again into the bushes. "Eaters!"

There they were, heaving away from the crumbling structures across the plain, between the rock teeth. The ground was mottled and roiling with them. Pauli started to tremble. She imagined that she could already hear the gnawing of the eaters' huge mandibles and the hiss of acid. This was nothing like the fast, savage cleanliness of ship against ship in the silence of space. Rafe stood at her shoulder. He was no fighter, not really. If he had survived this, she could too.

"Get them all!" shouted the captain. "I'll fly the news back."

She wanted to scream at him to wait, to warn him that the eaters and the Cynthians were different stages of the same race, but he was poised now, waiting for an updraft, he had found it . . . Pauli drew her weapon and waited for the eaters to come within easy firing range. No use wasting the charge. Her hand shook. How strange that she hadn't expected revulsion to slow her down. It wouldn't have done so in space. She was damned if she would allow this to happen to her.

"Do as much damage as you can, then retreat," she heard Rafe instruct the ben Yehudas and the other civilians on the flamethrower crews. "If you're cut off, head either for the rocks or the river. I don't think they'll follow you there."

She was *not* going to freeze. She waved at Borodin, the signal of a mechanic to a pilot before the catapult engages. He grinned and signalled back, then stepped off the bluff, and into smooth flight.

And, circling high above, the Cynthians folded their great, luminous wings, and plummeted down to block him. Their arc held a deadly beauty.

"Don't engage them!" Pauli shrieked. "Get back, Captain!"

The puzzle . . . the puzzle . . . no time to think of it. Of course, they'd try to stop him. The eaters were revolting, but they were the Cynthians' offspring. *And were they any less the same species for looking so different? Look at the children that the settlers protected. When they were rescued, they had all but degenerated into scratching, biting animals.*

"What's wrong?" Rafe cried. He was methodically burning off the first eaters to crawl within firing range.

He wasn't a pilot. He couldn't read the conformation of the Cynthians' flight pattern the way Pauli could. A concerted dive like that meant deterrence. And if it failed to deter, it could be turned into an attack.

Borodin, seeing the menace in those diving creatures, banked in a wide circle out over the plain where the eaters swarmed. Fiercely Pauli willed his glider to maintain altitude. It swayed in the crosswinds, and she felt the vibrations run up and down her arms as if she, not Borodin, were the one flying it.

"For God's sake, keep on firing!" Rafe shouted. The eaters were ominously close. They were hideous things, but except for those jaws and the acid, they were easy to kill. Just like the beautiful, sensitive creatures that circled overhead, trying to protect their ghastly offspring long enough to let them fatten themselves on the moist lowland grasses and enter dormancy—and then emerge as winged Cynthians.

Borodin veered and banked again, his wings slanting against the clouds and picking up the sunlight. Now he seemed to head back to the settlement along the route he had first chosen. The Cynthians dived at him again. This time they came even closer. They slashed at the glider's wings with their prehensile, gripping foreclaws. Again the captain banked. He lost altitude almost disastrously. Only a fortunate gust swept him aloft again.

Now, ben Yehuda and his son marched past Pauli. The muzzles of their flamethrowers wheezed and whistled blue fire. Three Cynthians dived at them. Ari yelped and bolted, then returned to retrieve his weapon.

One of the larger Cynthians saw Borodin making his escape. It launched itself at the captain and dragged its foreclaws on the metal fabric of the glider. Sparks ripped from the cloth. Then the Cynthian somersaulted backward, righted itself, and attacked again.

Borodin was only human, Pauli thought. He couldn't fight and fly a glider simultaneously. But compared with a Cynthian, what was a human pilot but the crudest interloper in the skies? The captain's attitude steadied; he gained altitude, then counterattacked by diving on the Cynthians.

Madness, Pauli thought. *Madness. But what's his option?*

She raised her gun, steadied it in both hands for a long shot. She had found the missing piece of her puzzle now. Judging from his expression, so had Rafe. And it had turned out to be sharp-edged and deadly.

"No!" One of the civilians hurled himself against her arm. Her gun jerked aside, and the energy bolt went wildly astray, sizzling across ground cover, narrowly missing another of their party. "That's an intelligent being!"

"So is the captain!" Pauli shouted. "And he's ours, like the woman you almost made me burn down. What do you call *these* things? We have to kill eaters. Does it really matter at what stage of their life cycle we kill them?"

She flamed down three eaters, then backed away to watch the captain. She gestured to the others to fan out and increase firing, but that one man still shadowed her. She'd been lucky when he'd deflected her aim the last time. If he did it again, someone might get killed. Like a civilian. Or Borodin, whom a bad shot could bring down.

The Cynthian he had dived at evaded him, then lifted, to swoop at him from the side. Borodin dodged it, so intent now on this one adversary that he didn't notice how the others had climbed high overhead. In a ship-based scramble, his boards would have warned him. But in the air, in a glider, he had only his naked, insufficient senses.

"Watch it," Pauli whispered, knowing that her voice couldn't reach him.

One of the Cynthians launched itself into a power dive. At the last possible instant before swooping below the captain, it jerked its head sideways and brushed the captain's hand and arm with its poison horns. Sunlight glistened off the clear venom as it spattered onto his face as well.

Borodin screamed in surprise and agony. With his hand and face burnt, his arm paralyzed, he couldn't keep the glider level. Like the Cynthian earlier, he went into a somersault, head over flailing arms and legs, tumbling out of the sky with the now-useless glider, slamming against a rock spur. The struts of the glider twanged and snapped, and the metallic cloth tore. Then the broken man and the broken craft fell to the plain where the eaters swarmed.

"I hope he died before he hit ground," Pauli whispered. Sunlight, shining like the spurt of venom that had killed her captain, threatened to flood her eyes.

"Oh, God. I didn't mean it," muttered the man who had spoiled her aim. She turned her back on him. She didn't want to hear his voice or see his face. If she noticed him at all, she might kill him, and she needed him alive to kill eaters.

She began to shoot again, and eaters crisped under her harsh, steady fire. The stink of their execution became intolerable. Rafe and ben Yehuda were retreating, gesturing for the others to pull back too, but Pauli kept on shooting, kept on walking forward.

She wanted to reach the center of that plain. There had to be something left of Borodin for her to recover—his service disks, a belt buckle, even a broken strut from the glider. Pauli would kill all the eaters, then go after it.

People were running past her, coughing and retching from the stink. "Get back, Pauli!" Rafe screamed. He ran over to her, had her by the arm, was forcing her away from the dead place. "You can't do anything for him now, and we have to get back."

She let herself be led to safety. Overhead, the Cynthians flew back to the refuge of their mountain caves, high in the hills which their hungry, mindless children could not scale.

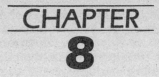

CHAPTER
8

Pauli stared up at the night sky and shivered. "Can we build up the fire?" she muttered in a plaintive voice she barely recognized as her own. "Eaters are afraid of fire."

Now, she was afraid, not only of eaters, but of the beautiful creatures who might come swooping out of the starlit sky, bearing stars on their wings, and death on their horns; creatures who had resolved their dilemma of whether to protect their own kind or their friends in a way Pauli now would have to emulate. If she would be allowed to. Right now, the civs' priority seemed to be debate. She couldn't afford the luxury; she had to defend.

The only defense that she saw terrified her. Easier to die.

She started to lever herself up, to sit nearer the fire. "It's warm enough, Pauli," Alicia Pryor told her firmly.

Rafe reached out and gripped Pauli's shoulder, returning the comfort she had lent him just the day before. Somehow it felt like years. At least, that much was right again. Before the physician could intervene with her drugs or her counsel, he bent and tucked the foil blanket firmly about her. He heard her whimper, buried in the hands she clutched about her mouth, and hugged her reassuringly. She turned her face against his chest.

Then the full reality of the situation hit him. With the captain zeroed out, command fell to Pauli. Sure, she was younger than he (though not by all that much), but commission dates and specialties were what counted in chain of command: her commission preceded his, and she had elected command track, as opposed to his own research specialization. He had promised her all during the hike back to camp that he would do anything, anything at all, to help her, but not this. He was devoutly grateful that their positions were not reversed.

At least we're together again, he thought. Otherwise, Pauli might easily have retreated from him into her new rank. But now what? Would she try to convince the Cynthians to set boundaries to offspring—you could hardly call eaters "children"—they feared and couldn't control? But even if they could control the eaters' feeding frenzy as they moved from pasture to pasture, would they? They were fliers, and fliers recognized no boundaries.

"What worries me now," said Pryor, "is the next wave of eaters. We can retreat into the perimeter defenses, but inevitably we're faced with problems of food, sanitation . . ."

"They didn't know they would kill him, Rafe," Pauli whispered. "They were only trying to warn him off. They treated him like one of their own. They didn't, couldn't, know how limited his maneuverability was, or that he'd try to fight them. And they had to protect their young."

"As we must?"

"What else can you expect, man?" asked ben Yehuda. His big, capable hands twisted, then dropped down on his knees. "Do we just sit here, depleting our resources, every year a little more gone, a little less hope? You call that living? What sort of life would that make for the children? Look: my kids have seen enough. I can't tell them no, you can't go out, you can't walk about freely because there are things crawling around there that will eat you up, like a bad fairy tale."

"That's not the issue!" shouted Beneatha. "This isn't our world; it's the Cynthians'. And if they and the eaters are truly part of the same race . . ."

"Why doesn't she just come out and say it?" Pauli murmured. "The word is *genocide*."

Someone heard her and repeated the word. Like a curse, it hissed from mouth to mouth. Genocide: forbidden by treaty and moral imperative since before the first ships had left Earth.

"That's what you call it when you eliminate an intelligent race," Rafe said. "We might as well call it by its rightful name. The only problem is that in our situation, any other option may be suicide. Very possibly, if you'll remember Captain Borodin's speech, racial suicide. All right! My friends, you may be willing to accept death for yourselves, but will you let your children die too? And seeing the death that the eaters deal out, will you help them to an easy death?"

"What about *you*?" Beneatha asked ben Yehuda brutally. Black face and weathered one locked eyes, and neither bothered to look away.

"You would have to remind me," he murmured, and shook his head in sorrow. "Genocide. Can you really call it that? After all, for all we know, these creatures might live on every continent. Maybe, we could just . . ."

"Just wipe out the locals?" Beneatha asked sarcastically.

It was strategy, just strategy, Pauli told herself. But she had never been able to look past the abstraction of the armscomp grids to the actual ship that she targeted. She realized now that that had been a mercy. Now, she could not look away either, nor permit anyone else to do so. "Dave," she broke in, "think it through. You're right. For now . . . for this season and maybe for the next few, all we need to do is secure this area. But we don't know if these creatures . . ."

"They're *Cynthians*," Beneatha put in. "Cynthians. And they're sapient."

Fighting a rush of bile to her mouth, Pauli raised her voice over Beneatha's . . . "if these creatures breed with other, other, let's call them flocks. If they do, anything, any biological measures we might take against them are likely to be spread."

And then there would not be the slightest relief, the slightest mitigation of what she knew she must do if she was to protect the littlests—her children!—from suffering like 'Cilla.

Alicia Pryor grimaced and looked away.

Pauli could not command them in this, though obedience might, in this case, be a blessing, be, perhaps, even a form of absolution.

For people other than these civs and survivors, she realized. Not for these people. She would have to persuade; and that would mean that they would share in the deed.

She blinked hard. In a much lower, huskier voice, she continued, "Does it matter if we kill them all? The intent in this case, it's as bad as the deed. Look at 'Cilla's foot, people. Look at it, and then tell me this: if you could press a button and wipe out what caused it, if you could prevent any more of the littlests from suffering, wouldn't you press that button?" Her eyes found Dave's, held them ruthlessly. "Well, wouldn't you?"

He covered his eyes. "God knows. Perhaps . . ."

Ayelet looked up at her father and interrupted. "You used to tell me the stories from before the Earth blockade. I remember: you'd say, 'Ayelet, you're too young to ask; so you must be told. You must remember. So you told me. About the camps. A thing called the final solution. Do you know, when we escaped Gamma, I thought that must have been something like what we escaped. And then there were other stories too. Do you remember the one you told me about a place called Masada? All its defenders killed themselves. Very heroic, you said . . . but very dead. Weren't you the one who told us, when Ari and I wanted to lie down and sleep more than anything else, 'Masada must not fall again.'"

"I don't want to die," her brother Ari added. "Not if we can think or fight our way out of it."

Pauli looked about for someone to take the lead, someone able to exploit the change in mood wrought by the twins' confession. Rafe? She turned to him, but he shook his head and gave her a tiny, encouraging shove. They were watching her; she had to be the leader now. *God, I don't want this. Especially, not now.*

You chose it, she reminded herself. She sighed, then rose and stood before the fire.

"I haven't got Captain Borodin's experience, and you know it," she began. "But I guess I've inherited his responsibilities. I'll do the best I can. With your help—if you'll give it to me—I'll try to do what he'd have wanted, I think: build us and the children a safe place to live. A home, please God, not a fortress." She aimed those last words straight at Rafe. *Don't leave me. I can't manage this alone.* He smiled at her, and her voice grew stronger.

"The problem's been stated and chewed over. We can retreat and employ strategies to buy time. You all know what they are. But if we don't turn self-sufficient, the minute our reserves are gone, they're gone, and we starve. I don't think we can count on the Cynthians for help. So living off our own fat will just drag out our defeat: you all know we've got to farm here if we're to have enough food for the coming years.

"But then, we've also got to consider the prospect that we're here permanently. I suppose the moral thing would be to suicide straight off, and not inflict ourselves upon the Cynthians. Ayelet and Ari, though, have just given their reactions to that." Pauli squared her shoulders. Her new authority felt like a lead cape settling down on her for life—*and ever afterward. How will I be remembered? As a genocide?*

"You all know I didn't want to be stranded here. By the time"—she laughed a little hoarsely—"the captain got finished explaining that, I think the whole camp knew it. But now that I'm here, I'm damned if I want to die. I don't think I'm alone in that thought, either. But even if I am . . . even if some of you are . . . there are still the children to consider. They're not voting members of this group yet. But as you know, they haven't had much of a life so far. That was the point in coming here, wasn't it? To give them, and perhaps the rest of humanity, a chance at a future."

But at the price of eliminating the Cynthians? What sort of future could they have, with the memory of that weighing down their lives?

"I think all of us ought to reconsider," Dr. Pryor spoke up. Her voice, usually soft and thoughtful, rang out with a surprising resonance. "Lieutenant . . . no, *Captain* Yeager . . ."

Pauli shuddered and shook her head, repudiating the title she once had longed for.

"She's the one who had the guts to bring up the word we all were talking around so carefully. As if that would make the reality go away. *Genocide*. It's an ugly concept. But keep this in mind: before we knew what the eaters were, we were all set to wipe them out. It wasn't genocide then; it was pest control. You might also keep in mind the fact that we've seen that the Cynthians too are revolted by the eaters. But still, they protected them. Can we do less for our own children?"

"We've got another problem," Rafe said. "I hate to bring it up. Hell, I even hate to think about it. It isn't just the eaters that we have to deal with. Even if we do eradicate this one colony, it's only one generation of eaters. The full-grown Cynthians will simply build more hibernacula and breed more."

"I don't want to kill Cynthians," Pauli said softly. She scrubbed at her eyes. Spots flamed, bright as the whorls and stars on a Cynthian's wings. If they made the world safe for the children, there would be no more Cynthians to exult in the cross-currents or the high passes. For their attempt would have to be as global as they could manage it. The survey of this world had been flawed; and now they must suffer for it. Who could tell them whether or not the Cynthians could survive a flight over this world's turbulent seas—or even if the same winged creatures lived on the other continents?

And did it matter? Whether or not they succeeded in killing all the Cynthians, they were genocides. It wasn't efficiency that mattered. It was intent.

No more Cynthians. She had always loved their beauty, found in it some consolation for not being able to fly herself. For she would probably never fly now, not even the gliders. She was the leader; she could not be risked.

"Can't you all think of anything else?" Beneatha's voice was husky, stripped of its usual belligerence as she sat with her arm about Lohr. The boy was still groggy from the sedative Pryor had to force down him when he refused to believe that the captain wouldn't suddenly fly back home. Three of the other children had found him sneaking out of camp to go look for the man who had become a father-presence for him.

"There is something else to think about," Pauli said. "Marshal Becker told us that we were planted here as part of a project, a sort of genetic . . . seedcorn, he called it, to be preserved in case the rest of humanity became gene-damaged or sterile in the war."

"What sort of legacy would we give the rest of humanity with our genes?" asked another one of the scientists, who frequently allied with Beneatha.

Pauli sighed. "The ability to ask questions like that," she said. "Yes, I know that's glib. They may need us. They don't need to know what we've done for them, do they?"

She stared around the circle of faces: some pale, some dark, bearing the racial and ethnic traces of many worlds, but all with the stamp of their ultimate home upon them. They were silent as they stared at her, then one another.

"Since command has defaulted to me, I will take the responsibility," she said. "Rafe, is there some way to make sure that this generation of Cynthians is the last? I do not want to kill the adults, but they must not reproduce themselves."

"Interfere with their breeding capability?" Rafe gnawed at his lower lip. "There's got to be a way. Say that we gave them something they liked. No," he was muttering to himself now, intrigued by the logistics of the problem, "they'd detect the taste of an additive in a sweet syrup . . ."

Pauli glanced out over the listening settlers, relieved past speech that Rafe, with his skills and his ease with people, was on her side. *Accomplice.* She would try not to think of him in such terms.

* * *

He shut his eyes, dizzied by his attempt to reach a quick solution. A nagging ache at the back of his skull warned him that he was on the track of something. But he was worn out. They all were, Pauli especially. *Call this meeting off!* he willed his lover silently. They all needed sleep, and she would be in need of comfort.

He gestured away Ayelet, who approached with more fuel for the fire. Let it burn down. Smoke coiled from its embers, sweet-smelling, overwhelming the scent of the river, the plants, and his remembrance of the stink of charred eaters. He'd never truly be free of that smell.

Smells . . . the Cynthians were incredibly sensitive to smells. And mating season was near, when they would breed a new generation of eaters, attracted to one another by . . . madness . . . brought on by pheromones.

"I've got an idea," he said quickly. "It's near mating season. And we know that smell is a powerful stimulus during mating—any species' mating—but especially to creatures like the Cynthians. Smell, and color. Like the colors on their wings. What if we gave them something that enhanced those colors, made them shine like the morning star, while eliminating their capacity to breed, or, at the very least, to produce viable offspring."

Radiation might be one way to accomplish that, he thought.

"No atomics," said Dr. Pryor.

"I was on Marduk during the initial relief efforts," a medical technician whispered. "Had to be transferred off. So I came here. I don't think I could bear that."

Atomic poisons were too treacherous, Rafe thought. They could so easily contaminate their users and their land. But even as he dismissed the idea of using radioactives, he realized that the merest hint that they might be used would make any other suggestion more acceptable. That would spread, all right; spread and contaminate the world that they needed so desperately that they would steal it from creatures native to it.

That might be one escape. They would die along with the Cynthians they slaughtered, die rather than live with the knowledge of what they had made themselves become.

Except that the littlests would die too, and they had not consented, to the deed or to their death, any more than they had consented to the war that slagged their worlds. Pauli was afraid that she and the other adults of Cynthia colony were sentenced to life.

"All right," he said. "All right! You don't need to remind me. No radioactives. Besides, I don't think we could develop or apply them with an acceptable degree of safety for us and the children. So what's left? Organics. Our trap will have to be chemically based."

Rafe would need time, Pauli thought, and ended the meeting quickly. Both of them would be too worn out for anything but sleep. Still, there was comfort in huddling together until they slept: more comfort, if the truth be known, in huddling than in sleeping. For that night, Pauli dreamed of the story of the ancient aristocrat who sold contaminated blankets to natives, and of an island where natives died off within a generation after they had been discovered by "civilization . . ."

"All I ever wanted was to fly," Pauli whispered once her tears had waked Rafe, and he had shaken her from her nightmares. "How will they remember me, Rafe?"

"Was flying all you ever really wanted?" He drew her closer, coaxing her to rest in his arms. He could foresee that in the years to come, this would be one of his most important roles: to calm her and comfort her as she struggled with a burden she didn't want. Seeing as he didn't want it either, but hadn't been in line to have it dumped on his back, this seemed like the least he could do. The very least. He tightened his arms about her.

Pauli rubbed her cheek against his shoulder. "Not quite all that I wanted," she murmured sleepily.

"Pauli . . . Pauli . . . Captain?"

The title brought Pauli wide awake. For one moment, as she leapt from a tangle of blankets, she had the mad hope that Borodin was back. Why else would anyone be calling for the captain? Then she remembered, and sank back with a groan. Behind her, Rafe had scrambled up and was dressing hastily.

"Don't call me that," Pauli told the woman who had waked her. "Am I late for today's meeting, Dr. Pryor?"

"When are you going to learn to call me Alicia?" asked the physician. "The meeting can't begin until you get there. You have time to eat yet."

"Food?" Pauli said with disastrous candor. "I'd be sick."

Pryor eyed her speculatively. "It's too easy to tell that," she remarked, then grinned. "Seriously, I wanted to tell you that you haven't got a thing to worry about. Just leave it to me."

Heartened by the physician's words, Pauli found she had an appetite, and ate hastily. Dressing in full uniform for some reassurance, and accompanied by Rafe for even more, she walked outside to call the meeting to order.

Pryor nodded almost imperceptibly at her, rose immediately, and asked to be recognized.

"David," she turned to ben Yehuda, "last night you recoiled at the thought of killing the Cynthians even in their eater stage because you thought it was genocide. Now, let me ask you a related question. If you knew for certain—for absolutely certain—that we were the very last . . . dregs of the human race, would you still feel that way?"

"Ayelet changed my mind for me. We have to stay alive."

"I think," Pryor said, "that this is the question that Pauli's wanted us to ask ourselves all along. But she's been too tired, to say the least, to force the issue. Certainly, we liked the Cynthians. And they've liked what they've seen of us. But when they had the choice, they chose for their own children. And they'll go on fighting to protect them, no matter how horrible we think they are. That's the issue: nothing else is relevant."

"I can't give you orders on this issue," Pauli said. "In any case, I wouldn't try. Let's put it to a vote." Perhaps

Borodin wouldn't have done that. There was room for only one captain on board a ship. But this wasn't a ship, she wasn't a captain, and she certainly wasn't about to try to fill Serge Borodin's boots. Yet, it wouldn't be shirking her responsibilities to make certain that they shouldered their own.

Rafe set to work. The communicators and the microcomp had preserved not only the Cynthians' sign activity, and their curious, analogical language, but also their pattern of antenna activity and the frequencies on which they communicated. From them, Rafe discovered just what chemicals caused Cynthians to enter mating readiness and to respond to one another. The pheromones were multicomponent—long-chain, unsaturated acetates, alcohols, aldehydes, with a few hydrocarbons tacked on. Sweet. Rafe tested them first in solution, then sprayed them into the air to test them that way, since exposure to the air might dilute them, or make them act differently.

After several weeks of tests, his sinuses ached whenever he even thought of a Cynthian. He could barely breathe while doing his tests. Ironic, he thought, wheezing, that these smells that signal *here is life!* to the Cynthians almost asphyxiate me, and will—if all proceeds well (and I must think of it in that way)—bring about the death of the entire species.

On some worlds, people baited the creatures they wanted dead by poisoning foliage. The Cynthians were herbivores, so this seemed quite logical to Rafe. Too logical to work, he sighed, wincing, as Beneatha hurtled onto her feet.

"Not here you don't!" she insisted. "You don't know what the effects of your poisons will be on the entire ecosystem, let alone on us. Long-term, as well as short-term, since you all seem so interested in preserving our . . ." Thank God, Rafe thought, closing his eyes, that she managed to stop herself before she spat out the words *racial purity*. He saw Pauli's eyelids tic, and knew that she had anticipated Beneatha's words.

"As I was saying," the xenobotanist continued, "I haven't the resources, much less the training, to heal anything you ruin. Since we're going to be here quite a while, I think it's important to consider the effects of anything we do on what's now our home." She spoke, and looked, as if she hated the idea.

"Rafe, I've got to agree with Beneatha," Pauli said.

"Then what's left?" Rafe asked. "We'll have to apply the pesticide directly. Anyone have any suggestions as to how?"

"Make up some scent that the Cynthians would like," Lohr's voice (which had started to crack) came from the blanket on which he sat with his sister, her foot still immobilized, as she covered sheet after sheet of reusable plastic with gleaming swirls of paint. "Then make them trade for it."

Rafe wanted to slap the boy. The idea of profiting from the death of a species was indecent. *How long, though, has the boy even known what decency was? What does he know: all right, he protected his sister. Then the Cynthians hurt her; so now, naturally, he thinks of ways to stop them.* And he had a point. After the Cynthians had killed their captain, they had avoided the settlement. It wasn't likely that they would accept an offer of a gift from the people they had injured: aliens they might be, but they were intelligent—*which is why we're in this situation*, Rafe grimaced to himself.

"What would you suggest?" he asked the boy. "You wouldn't accept food from enemies, would you?"

The boy laughed bitterly. "I might," he said. "But giving it to me would be the last thing they'd ever do. I can see what you mean, though. Why does it have to be food?" He glanced around as if for inspiration, and his eyes fell on 'Cilla's artwork. "Why not paint? They like colors, don't they?"

In the end, Rafe could come up with no better ideas

for dispensing the toxic pheromones; and he had little time for trial and error. If he had been wrong, if the toxins didn't turn this mating season into sterility and death, the next generation of Cynthians could probably destroy the tiny human settlement.

For the last time before she started up the rock chimney, Pauli wiped her hands on her legs. She only hoped Rafe was right when he claimed that this was the way to the Cynthians' hibernacula. It was ironic that those were the very caves into which they had attempted to persuade the humans to evacuate.

Well, this was as good an approach to them as any; and, since it was protected by a rock passage too narrow for the Cynthians to enter, it was safer than most. That is, if Rafe was right. If he was wrong, then one of the smaller aliens, the nymphae as he called them, might well swoop down into the chimney to touch them with poison horns and send them toppling and screaming to the sharp rocks at the bottom of the shaft.

In that case, there would be no eaters to finish them off, as there had been for Borodin. (*Dear God*, Pauli made the familiar prayer, *grant he died quickly!*) They could lie there broken for hours.

Pauli had refused to allow Rafe to climb up into the mountains alone. Someone had to cover his back as he stole into the Cynthians' caves. She was small enough and fast enough to do it. More than that, if she had to, she could fly back to the settlement on the glider she carried into the hills . . . *if the Cynthians allow you*, whispered the nagging, worrying voice that had interrupted her thoughts ever since she inherited responsibility for the entire settlement.

This was one betrayal that she would not delegate.

"Look," whispered Rafe. "There they are."

High in the air, the Cynthians were dancing, a mating dance of such beauty that Pauli wondered for one traitorous instant if this trip really was as necessary as they thought. Surely, if they moved, or built barricades —*we haven't the time or resources*, she told herself sternly. *The decision has been made.* But she knew she would regret it lifelong.

Deliberately she blotted out the sight of the Cynthians, darting and swooping on the air currents, their wings hotly aglow, with her last sight of Borodin, falling and smashing against rock *just like what I'm climbing now*. To the end of her life, she thought, she would hear that last scream of his, and the sound he'd made as his bones shattered against the rock.

"I'm going in now," Rafe mouthed. "Cover me." Not three meters away, the rock hollowed out. Rafe disappeared in the cave. Pauli drew her sidearm and prepared to wait. If Rafe couldn't find the clue he needed, she would have to give another order she feared and hated: the synthesis and use of pesticides so powerful that they might poison their own thriving crops if anything went wrong. It would be terrible if they were destroyed by their own weapon, wouldn't it? Or would it be a weird sort of justice? It wasn't a question she cared to debate, even within herself; and certainly not now.

To prevent destroying their own fields, such pesticides would have to be applied directly to the Cynthians. In other words, direct confrontation—war against beings who secreted their own poison.

Now the Cynthians were diving, turning in incredible loops before they paired off. Pauli felt not just like a voyeur but a voyeur who stalked her prey and readied the weapon that would destroy it. Then she shook her head. The lives they fought to safeguard wouldn't be worth living if they used them only to wallow in their own (admittedly monumental) guilt. And such guilt was not fair to the children. Even Ayelet and Ari, who had spoken of Masada, and Lohr, who suggested creating toxic pigments, were innocent of the settlers' decision. If anything decent could be salvaged from it, the children must be brought up as free of their elders' guilt as could be contrived.

Rafe emerged, and Pauli could breathe freely for the first time in hours. She sagged against the rock, then wrinkled her nose at how he smelled. "You smell like

Cynthians, only more so." She wanted to sneeze. The fragments of powdery scales that clung to him and glittered as he rubbed streaming eyes had an odor that was musty, yet aromatic.

"You knew, didn't you, that Cynthians' scales and wings shed. What you didn't count on was the fact that they're excited now, which is why this stuff smells so high. I can do my bioassay now. And if I can't get my synthetics to test out, I'll simply grind up this stuff and return for more."

He'd have to make this climb again, Pauli thought. They had been lucky once. She would be reluctant to have him try again.

"Come on, Pauli. It's getting on toward dusk; and we need light for the climb back down."

Lohr had been right all along, Pauli thought, some weeks later. The Cynthians had to be tricked into acquiring the toxic paints. After Borodin's death, they definitely would have suspected a gift. But seeing 'Cilla (whose foot was healing about as well as anyone dared expect) painting by the firelight, the Cynthians had pricked up and vibrated their antennae at the paints she used—brilliant, full of metallic flecks, utterly enticing to them both in color and in scent. And when they learned (glitter/humans; fruit/Cynthians; glitter/Cynthians) that gifts of fruit or leaves or glittering rocks would enable them to own that paint, they were taken in.

Now even old Ariel and Uriel gleamed with new potency. They cavorted in the air above the settlement with the abandonment of nymphae in their first mating season. When they flew back to their caves at dawn, the sunlight striking rejuvenated wings, they were dazzling. Even 'Cilla clapped her hands in delight. Now she was making plans for a mural. Somehow, Pauli thought, she would have to deflect that particular hope. She had already warned Lohr not to tell 'Cilla of the relationship between Cynthians and eaters. Let her simply think she had run into a wild animal: it was kinder thus.

As summer progressed, fewer and fewer eaters crossed

the charred lines which now marked out human territory on Cynthia. Search parties accounted for some of the eaters. The watches set over the fields accounted for the rest. Then scouts began to report the appearance of structures that resembled those of a year before.

The Cynthians were building them and preparing to lay their eggs. They had been spotted dancing on the thermal currents: more Cynthians than could be accounted for in the one, local, now-dwindling swarm, and more of them glittering with the lovely, lethal paint that had proved such an inducement to prospective mates.

"Come next year," said Pauli, "they'll crack. And we'll have more eaters than we will know how to kill. And the ones that survive will hibernate, to emerge as nymphae and breed even more eaters. So tomorrow, I want fire parties out to attend to those hatcheries. But," she warned her scouts, "*no more Borodins*. You go armed, and one of you has always got to be watching the sky for Cynthians. If you're attacked"—she drew a deep breath and suppressed her revulsion—"aim to kill."

Subsequent scout parties found little need to protect themselves from angry Cynthians. Certainly they trailed the humans, but their flight patterns were labored, as if they were too weak for much resistance. They could be dodged or run from; and this, with a dreadful pity, such scouts did.

Still, every night, a flock of Cynthians would hover around the central fire. Their wings were brittle now, their body scales dulled and falling off in patches. But wings and bodies were stippled by the lovely, deadly paint. Even now they were using it to adorn themselves, hoping that the pungent scents would stimulate them to mate, to produce more young to replace those slaughtered by the humans.

And many of the Cynthians who flew down to the settlement to trade for the pigments never made it back into the mountains. Their wings tore or snapped, and their desiccated bodies fell where the humans could find them. Beneatha and ben Yehuda, their differences laid aside, appointed themselves a sort of dawn patrol; each day they buried such bodies before the children could stumble onto them.

"They smell like dust," Beneatha reported, mourning, "or like dead leaves, rotting after a wet autumn. I can't forget it."

"I can't forget either," said Pauli. "None of it." She turned toward Rafe. "I hope the Cynthians never guess why they're dying."

"That's wishful thinking, love," he answered. "They're bound to, if they haven't already. But the effects of the toxins are cumulative and irreversible. Even if they stopped using the paint tonight, the damage it's done has gone too far to be healed." Though his voice was gentle, Pauli shuddered at the inflexibility of his words.

She remembered the inexorability of that sentence each evening at the fire. The winged creatures still appeared, their wings feeble now, bringing more and more "trade goods" for the glistening paint they seemed to think might restore their strength. That was the only reason Pauli could come up with for their craving for the paint. Each night, Pauli marked that the fruits and shining stones were harder and harder for them to carry. Their dusty, morbid smell filled the air and clung to the garments of the humans forced to approach them with the paints.

The weather was turning much cooler. Since the cold snap started, Ariel had not appeared. But the evening they expected frost for the first time Ariel showed up, leading a band of nymphae. When it saw the paintpots, however, it swooped down and overturned them with deft flicks of its winghooks. Then it stood, wings outstretched, before the avid nymphae as if trying to protect them from the dirtied pools of sweet-smelling, lethal pigments.

Several nymphae dodged their elder to dip wingtips into the poison. Ariel went into threat-display and even everted its poisoned horns. But the nymphae ignored it.

Ariel mantled, then, antennae quivering in agitation. With a convulsive sweep of his great wings, the elder flew above the fire. Brightness fell from its scales into the fire. But it avoided colliding with the nymphae, reluctant, even at the last, to harm them. Higher and higher Ariel climbed above the fire. Then it banked, folded its wings, and dived into the fire's heart.

'Cilla screamed and burst into tears. In all the painful months of her convalescence, not even during skin grafts, she had never wept so bitterly. Pauli hugged the girl and motioned for people to lead away the rest of the children.

The fire smelled of charred eaters, of the field where Borodin died. It made her ill and, ordinarily, these days, Pauli was only ill in the mornings. Which was another reason to have taken the action she had. *Try not to hate me*, she wished the child she bore.

Uriel appeared and flew down toward them. It too looked tired and worn. But the only signal on the comm screen was a simple interrogative.

Why have you done this to us?

Rafe drew a deep, quivering breath.

"It deserves to know," Pauli said. "Tell it!" She raised her face above 'Cilla's bright hair, condemning herself to watch her victim.

Rafe keyed the screen to transmit one symbol: a human child. Pauli remembered how the Cynthians had panicked at their first sight of a child. Seeing how revolting their own were, that had been a completely natural reaction. *Could we have guessed?* Pauli asked. She knew she would be asking such questions for the rest of her life.

"Look at that," said Dr. Pryor.

The screen blanked, filled with the symbol for eaters, repeated again and again, then blanked again.

"I think that Uriel has put it all together," Rafe observed.

Was there a symbol for *sorry*? Even if there was, what good was it? What possible apology could be made for ending a race?

Uriel raised its head, and Pauli thought that it looked straight at her with those dulled, faceted eyes. Its wings quivered, and it strained upward, turning in its last moments toward its mountains. Then, in a little eddy of luminous dust, scattering from its crumpled wings, it toppled.

The skies were quite clear thereafter. Pauli supposed that after a few years she might even get used to not seeing Cynthians aloft at twilight. She still gazed into the skies, the way she had when all she had wanted was to be a pilot and to fly free. She had to: the children had begun to adopt her mannerism—developed after the last Cynthian fell from the skies—of looking shamefacedly away from the heavens she felt as if she had profaned.

Somewhere in this world might be updrafts on which other Cynthians danced. Somewhere there might be relief from the consequence of Pauli's actions—if not of her intentions. Pauli hoped never to see them, never to have to gaze again at a screen where a simple interrogative glowed. It was burned into her mind now. If she was faced again with the test, she feared that she might kill just to prevent herself from seeing it.

I didn't have the Cynthians destroyed so the children would grow up to be penitent, guilt-ridden cowards. I may be a genocide; very well, so I am. Maybe I can't bring those children up innocent. But they were victims, and they must not suffer for my crimes too.

Whatever guilt she and the other adults felt was their private, fitting punishment. Now *they* were the Cynthians. And the creatures they replaced had left them a standard of conduct that would be hard to equal. Cynthians fought to live and to protect their young.

That being the case, Pauli had better gifts for the children than her guilt. Gradually she forced herself to speak again of flying, to enjoy the sight of gliders swooping aloft, to dream of other larger craft that one day they might try to build. After all, she reminded them, the stars were a part of their heritage. That wouldn't change, she vowed, whether the ships came for them in the next hour, the next year . . . or never.

If my child is a boy, I'll name him Serge, Pauli thought. *Rafe would like that too. If she's a girl, then 'Cilla will have a namesake and someone to look after.*

After all, Pauli was a Cynthian now, and would soon bear a child. And all Cynthians must grow up with a heritage of flight without shame. No one knew better than she that Cynthians protected their own.

PART II
Survivor Guilt

And I alone escaped to tell you.
—Book of Job

CHAPTER

Alien greens flourished in the fields still marked out by the scars of trenches where the harsh, resilient native ground scrub had begun to grow back, healing the places where the land had been burnt clean. Beyond the fields half the adults and all the children of Cynthia colony ran and played. Slowly they were forgetting the seemingly endless war between Alliance and Secess', the slagged worlds and the hunger. From here, Pauli Yeager didn't think they sounded any different from children who never wet their beds, or woke screaming from nightmares or from memories.

"Consequently I rejoice," she thought wryly, *"having to construct something upon which to rejoice."*

There were grounds for rejoicing. So far, no Secessionist ships had ventured this far into the No Man's Worlds to discover their refuge. Wide-spectrum immunities protected them from any disease their new home might have had in store; and there had been no predators they couldn't defend themselves against.

She winced, then, laboriously bent down to examine a fretwork of humming rods. It generated a faint violet light which shone around the fields and a generous space beyond, and extended all the way down to the river.

"You can touch them," the techs had briefed her and the rest of the settlement. "A human's electrostatic field won't trigger the charge. It isn't strong enough. But . . ."

The stobors' fields would. As always, Pauli winced at the name. But she supposed it probably had been inevitable. She rubbed the small of her back. Sturdy and weathered after these seasons downworld, she had been slowed only in the last month by the pregnancy that made bending down a penance and prohibited her from joining the scout parties that once again were travelling across the plains and into the foothills and the mountains beyond. *I'm doubly grounded now*, she thought, but contentment had eased some of the old hurt. Something else to rejoice for: Pryor had assured her that if she hadn't aborted spontaneously in her first trimester of pregnancy, the child would probably be undamaged by any radiation she had absorbed.

These days, her back ached constantly. So did her feet despite Dr. Pryor's constant attempts to keep her off them. But she had to inspect the fields that were replacing their hydro tanks, and the defenses that protected the fields against stobor.

She sighed. The stobor had first turned up that spring, another one of the little surprises that survey had failed to warn them of before they'd been landed here. Her husband called them one part lemming, one part platypus, and the rest God-knows-what. Including electric eels, because stobor seemed to come equipped with their own electrostatic fields. Touching one stobor earned you a nasty shock. Stumbling into two or three paralyzed you. After they'd almost lost one man who'd done just that, and who was saved only by David ben Yehuda's rough CPR (which cost his victim a couple of broken ribs), Pauli had ordered everyone in the camp to learn the emergency procedures, down to every child strong enough to manage them.

Contact with more than three would probably stop your heart permanently, not that anyone had felt like experimenting. And of course, the damned things had to travel in packs, herbivores drawn irresistibly to the crops vital to the settlement's survival.

Well, what else could they expect? Ordinarily, the ground would have been scoured by the eaters; and the stobor would have sought elsewhere for forage. But with the eaters gone, and fields sprouting more appetizing crops than the ground scrub, the stobor turned up right on cue. At least they'd figured out how to turn the stobor's natural defenses against them without having to wipe out the entire species. And that definitely was something to rejoice about, even if it *was* impossible to consider the stobor sapient beings.

Brushing grainstalks aside, several of the refugee children accompanied Rafe into the fields. He grinned at them, then had a lazy smile just for her and the baby-to-be before he walked over to the nearest cluster of civilians who, even now, Pauli tended to regard as a foreign species. *He's half a civ himself*, Pauli thought, but she tempered the words with a smile. When she had been a pilot (with a life expectancy you could measure in months) she had kept him at a distance. But now, if she had one reason to go on living, it was Rafe's faith in her.

'Cilla, who had become devoted to Pauli, God only knew why, limped over and took her hand. "How's the baby?" she asked.

Pauli laid 'Cilla's hand on her stomach so she could feel the tiny, emphatic kicks.

The child laughed delightedly. Pauli expected her to limp away, but instead 'Cilla stayed by her side, clutching her hand. The limp, Pryor had assured them, would not get much better; but at least they hadn't had to amputate the foot bitten and seared by the eaters.

Suddenly the hard little hand jerked. "Shooting star!" 'Cilla cried.

A streak of cold fire blazed down the night sky and struck the horizon soundlessly.

"You have to make a wish," the child commanded eagerly.

Pauli gestured at two former crewmembers. *Take all the children inside*, she ordered, her lips moving soundlessly.

I'll make a wish, all right, she thought. *I'll hope it is just a meteorite.*

"Impact coordinates recorded." Another crewmember passed her his macrobinoculars. Pauli activated them, then hissed in aggravation. The haze from the shields, the domes' yellow nightlights, even the spray of light from the beamers carried by some of the settlers, blocked her vision.

"Recon team?" Rafe asked.

Quickly Pauli ran over the list of people she called her reliables. There was no way that medic Pryor would let her lead a team, not with her pregnancy this far advanced. Pryor herself was both too old and too valuable to be allowed to lead a team, even if she had wanted to. Rafe? No way around it; he was the logical choice, and she wanted bearish, quick-minded David ben Yehuda along to back him.

"You'll lead, Rafe," she said. "Take care."

Quickly they passed the word for the team to assemble.

"You'll maintain silence on the communicators, just in case . . ."

"The hills will block communications. I'll need a messenger," Rafe cut in before Pauli could voice her concerns in front of casual passersby. It was always that way with them now: often they found themselves finishing one another's thoughts, anticipating one another's wishes. It meant that Cynthia colony had, in effect, two commanders.

"So I'll want a messenger," Rafe continued. "Sorry about that."

Pauli shut her eyes. Of the few settlers who had had time to master the fliers (little more than old-fashioned gliders), the most skillful was Lohr, age twelve; and they both knew it. He was quick, smart, but if he had a chance to attack a Secess' pilot, the survivor of an emergency landing, could she trust him?

"Look who's coming," Rafe pointed. "So help me, that boy *smells* trouble."

Lohr skidded to a stop beside them. "If you're sending out a team, you need a messenger. I'm the best with the fliers . . ." his eager babble of speech ran down under Pauli's and Rafe's somber expressions.

Pauli looked him over. "And if I said that Rafe and David were just going out to check on stobor?"

"Lieutenant," Lohr burst out indignantly, "not even the littlests believe stobor come down from the hills. They're amphibians!" He brought out the word with pride. "You're sending a team out to check on that meteorite. *If* it's a meteorite and not a—"

"One more word out of you, Lohr, and you're confined to quarters," Pauli interrupted, thanking God that none of the "littlests" were around to be terrified by Lohr's accuracy. "And if I find you've been babbling to 'Cilla or any of the other littlests . . . no, I guess you won't frighten them. Get your gear, then, and tell Ari ben Yehuda that he's going along to keep an eye on you."

Rafe laid an arm across Pauli's shoulders. She wrapped hers about his waist, and they walked toward the dome where the team was assembling. Briefing was quick; farewells quicker yet.

"You come back," Pauli whispered fiercely, her face buried against Rafe's shoulder. "Don't take any risks. You just come back!"

No one knew better than an Alliance pilot just how deadly the Secess' were. Compared to them, the native predators—or even the winged Cynthians they had had to eradicate—were games for the littlests.

By dawn, Rafe and his people were well up into the foothills, but the site where the meteorite hit—he gave it the name he hoped it would keep—lay far beyond, in the mountains themselves, past the high caves which he'd visited once as a thief. Rafe swore and reached for his macrobinoculars. Beside him, Lohr crouched, his pupils contracting to pinpoints. His lips were skinned back, and he all but growled.

"See anything up there?"

"A few sparks," Rafe grunted. "Could be anything."

Lohr hunted through his pack and pulled out struts of metal and a gleaming length of mesh into which the struts slipped until long, flexible wings took shape.

"You won't get any help from thermals this close to dawn," Rafe warned Lohr. "So it's a good thing you're light. Look: I hate to use you like this, but the sooner we all know whether or not there might be Secess' around, the better I'll like it. You won't be afraid?"

"Can I have a blaster?" Cunning aged Lohr's face so that he looked far older than his age. He held out his hand as if he expected Rafe to hand over his sidearm. Stunner, explosive bolts, or laser—they were all blasters to Lohr; and he had wanted one for as long as Rafe knew him.

"Lohr, you know what Pauli told you about weapons," Rafe sighed. "First, you're better off flying light. Second, if you've only got a knife, you'll probably have the sense to run from a fight you can't win. No matter how much you want revenge."

Lohr sized him up, and Rafe held his breath. Finally the boy shrugged, resigning himself—but only for the moment—to reality, such as Rafe's superior height and weight, and the fact that the others on the team would certainly back him.

He strapped the wings to his back and shook himself to settle them.

"One thing more." Though Rafe kept his voice down, it seemed to boom against the overhanging rocks. "Tell Pauli I recommend evacuation."

The settlers universally hated the caves into which they'd practiced evacuating most of the colony—everyone but the ones like Pauli, whose pregnancy made climbing impossible right now, or those people disabled by age or injury . . . plus those few ablebodied who had to remain behind as decoys. The caves smelled of Cynthians. Living in them was like murdering a man, then sleeping in his bed. Rafe hated it too. Of the two options, searching for a downed Secess' ship, or evacuating into the caves, he knew he had the easier task.

Lohr grimaced, then raised his head, testing the air like a wild animal.

Rafe flashed "thumbs up" at the boy, and heard a shaky laugh before Lohr stepped off the rock, dropped for a hideous moment, and then soared. The last of the moonlight gleamed on his wings.

"Damn! I hate sending out a kid while I'm stuck here,"

he groused at ben Yehuda and his son. "Now we just sit here until he gets back. Dave, am I right that scanners could pick us up if we move?"

"There should be enough rock between us and that object to protect us. But assuming it's a ship, not a meteorite, even a quick flyby might have picked us out."

"What if it's not a ship, but just an escape pod?" Rafe asked. Pods were fitted with automatic distress signals and programmed to land as softly as possible. In that case, too, they'd be facing a live enemy.

David tinkered with the comms. "I'm not picking up anything . . . not yet. Too much static."

"You know Lohr's going to want to check out that landing, don't you? What are you going to do about him?" asked ben Yehuda's son.

"First, I'm going to pray real hard that it's a meteorite. But if it's not, *you're* going to sit on Lohr so he doesn't get himself killed."

What if it is a downed pilot, and not one of ours? Rafe worried. Pauli had passed on pilot rumors: that the characteristic Secess' five-ship formations flew so fast and close that the pilots had to be hard-wired into their ships, and that the whole damnable cyborg was configured to a mammoth computer run by some sort of sadist. Highly colorful rumors, he had remarked at the time.

Secess' raiders blew the power core on my own home station, Rafe thought, as he did too often for his own comfort. *At least my folks died fast . . . I hope they did.* Rafe shuddered as he always did when he thought of fading lifesupport, of the air growing foul and thin and cold before the lights went dead. He'd had nights where he'd waked gasping and shaking, dreaming of being trapped in such a place. The cold sweat of panic began to trickle and itch down his spine at the thought of meeting the sort of man who'd taken out his family's home.

"You've got our coordinates for the landing site?" Pauli asked Lohr again. The winds teased up a gust of cinnamon from the fields, their greens highlighted by the eerie shimmer of the electric shields.

She glanced enviously at Lohr's wings, then examined the boy more closely. There were deep circles beneath his eyes. Perhaps, after all, someone else should report back to the recon team.

Alicia Pryor strode up. "The first group to evacuate will leave for the caves in about ten minutes, right?"

Pauli nodded. "I'll be there to see them off."

"Afterward, we've planned for them to be followed by five-person units about every half hour."

"What about you?" Pauli asked. She had wanted their most experienced medic to join the evacuees. Even though practice had turned evacuation into a routine, she hated the thought of subjecting the children to it.

"Well, what about *you*?" Pryor retorted. "Lohr, get moving before Yeager here tries to pull rank on you, and I have to declare her medically unfit."

"Head up," Pauli whispered as Lohr headed for the cliffs, passing the first group of fugitives with ease despite how tired he must be.

"The rest of you, back to camp. Let's make the place look lived in. Come on," she called, turning on her heel. "On the double."

Their defenses now seemed very feeble, their communications link even more so. "I ought to be there—" she told Pryor.

"Forget it! If I thought you wouldn't miscarry, I'd get you up into those caves so fast—"

"They can manage without me." Pauli spoke without bitterness. "Someone else would lead."

"Like Rafe? Or me? No, thank you very much. Look, I wish you'd get it through your head that while you've got opponents here, you don't have enemies. Think it through, Pauli. These are civilians! They're not used to orders, let alone to someone making those orders stick."

Pauli whirled to face the other woman.

"Even after . . ."

"Even after what we've all been through here. You didn't make the decision to wipe out the Cynthians on your own, despite the fact that you're trying to take responsibility for it. But now that the place looks safe, they want to sit down and try to argue things out again. Except for the littlest ones."

"Do you think," Pauli brought up a familiar, poignant topic as they trudged back toward the domes, "that they will ever trust again?"

"They trust *you*," Pryor said firmly. "Which is one reason why I'm staying down here. To look after you."

"What's the real reason?"

To Pauli's astonishment, Alicia Pryor's pale skin flushed, and the older woman stared off toward the distant hills.

"I'm sick of talk all the time. And besides, by staying here, I free up a spot for someone younger. How old do you think I am, Pauli?"

The shorter woman shrugged. "Forty-five, perhaps?" If she shielded her eyes, she could just see Lohr poised high overhead, waiting for the right current . . . there! Sunlight danced on unfurled metallic wings as Lohr banked in salute before veering back up into the hills.

"Add twenty years," Pryor chuckled dryly. "Balliol II had plenty of anti-agathics for senior faculty at Santayana."

"You're trying to distract me, right? Otherwise, if you haven't spilled your guts before this, why do it now?"

"Precisely," the medic agreed. "As I said, I got sick of being safe, and of talk, talk, talk. Probably because I listened too hard to one person. Pauli, have you ever heard of Halgerd of Freki?"

Pauli allowed Dr. Pryor to steer her back to her quarters (so heartlessly bare without Rafe's gear) and ease her down onto a mat.

"Halgerd of Freki? Sure." At one time or another, most educated people for six systems around had heard of Halgerd of Freki, laureate in genetics, who'd curtailed a brilliant research career when the war broke out, resigned his professorship on the safe haven of Balliol II, to return to his homeworld. His *Secessionist* homeworld.

"I wonder what sort of uses the Secess' would put a brain like his to," Pauli mused.

"It's likelier that he's using them. Or that he's dead."

Pryor's voice was muffled as she bent to activate the self-heat tabs on two food packs. "Halgerd's no martyr. He left Balliol for Freki only after his research group was ordered to disband." She paused. "Freki's one of the throwback worlds. Did you know, it even used to be a military oligarchy?"

"Group Two headed out, Pauli." That was Beneatha, shoulders hunched under the weight of a pack.

"Get Three ready to move."

"Right."

"Was your Professor Halgerd one of the oligarchs?" Pauli raised eyebrows as if delicately gauging Alicia Pryor's sympathy for her old colleague. A geneticist with military interests. God.

"Something like that. He never got over his aristocratic background. Yes, you can smile; but I'm allowed to say that. I'm also allowed to feel guilty for collaborating with him for as long as I did. There were a number of us, dazzled by him at first. Later—let's say he left before we could dump his computer. We never got around to it, but I wanted to. Some of his work on cloning—I thought it ought to be suppressed for the duration of the war."

"I thought Santayana never suppressed research."

"That's right, we don't." Involuntarily, and with a sort of bleak pride, the "we" slipped out. For an instant, the Alicia Pryor of the settlement disappeared, and a younger, more arrogant woman sat opposite Pauli, sharing emergency rations with the fastidious manners more appropriate to a banquet. "But it didn't mean I didn't want to. That was another reason I resigned. I not only had lost my objectivity, I didn't believe it was worth the having in the first place. So now the Secessionists have all Halgerd's experiments. And him along with them. Part of that work is mine, Pauli. That means that part of the blame's mine too."

"If you're looking for absolution, I frankly don't envy the people hiding out in the caves. And God knows, you've come to the wrong person."

"That isn't it. For once, I don't want to be exempt because of my age, or my profession, or status, or some damned liability." Pryor's lips thinned. "God, I sound like Halgerd did before he left. It got to be you couldn't be in the same room with him without hearing a lecture on the evils of noninterference. In the end, he convinced me. But not," her voice was soft, sad, "as he hoped."

Pauli shook her head and smiled in a way she hoped was sympathetic. It was hard to imagine the medic as a privileged, sheltered member of Santayana University's dazzling faculty—or was it? But she had heard of the throwbacks. There were a few other such worlds like Freki, mostly settled by one racial or ethnic group, Freki and Tokugawa on the Secess' side, and on their own, Abendstern and Ararat (come to think of it, Dave ben Yehuda had ties there). Usually driven by a dream of former glory to reanimate old languages and older customs, settlers of the throwbacks were generally too tough to be dismissed as eccentrics.

Freki prized aristocrats and warriors—and Halgerd had been both. He'd been Pryor's colleague . . . what else? Pauli didn't even have to guess. The medic was pale and still patrician-looking; years ago, she must have been stunning.

Behind them, the last of the evacuees left the settlement, without Pauli. Pryor had achieved her goal of distracting the younger woman; but now she herself was lost in thought and a years-old sorrow.

Pauli patted Alicia Pryor's shoulder. "As the chaplain used to tell us, I haven't heard a word you've said."

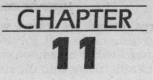

CHAPTER
11

A shadow across the noon sky drew Rafe's attention, and he froze against the rock, all but his gun hand.

Lohr dropped down onto a bight around fifteen meters above Rafe, his wings furling about his feet before he slipped off the flying harness. He scrambled down the slope, showering the recon team with pebbles and dust, and finished his descent with a dangerous skid that might have skinned the hide off him if Rafe hadn't caught him.

The boy was all legs, ribs, and eyes, Rafe thought. His skin was clammy and his breathing too rapid. "Now, rest," he ordered, trying to force Lohr down with one hand even as, with the other, he holstered his sidearm, and snapped the protective flap shut.

Ben Yehuda began to rifle Lohr's pack. "These coords should save us about six, seven hours," he grinned with satisfaction.

"You don't have to stop for me!" Lohr pushed against Rafe's chest, trying to stand on his own. "I can travel. Just let me catch my breath."

"You can travel? Really? Just you try it." Expertly Rafe tripped the boy and eased him down onto the pad Ari ben Yehuda unrolled.

The boy's eyes glared with anger quickly suppressed as the comfort of the sleeping pad and the smell of food got to him. He submitted to being fed, and ate ravenously. But the instant he finished, he began to protest again.

"All right, then," said Rafe. "Let me see you walk."

He managed to struggle to his feet. Turning pale, he got

about four steps before his knees wobbled and he collapsed.

"Convinced now?" Rafe asked, with a smile.

"You go on ahead," Lohr muttered. "I'll sleep, then catch up. I'll fly there . . . you can trust me not to do . . . 'nythin' stupid—"

Beneath the blanket, the boy's wiry body twitched with exhaustion.

"We'll give him two or three hours to rest, then wake him and see if he's fit," Rafe decided. A more carefully reared boy would still be a wreck at the end of that time; but a more protected child couldn't have completed the two flights Lohr had just made, or, probably, coped with the need for them.

The others settled down to wait, or sleep, or watch the monitors. No one spoke of meteorites anymore.

"Over this way," ben Yehuda gestured, never raising his eyes from a small tracker. Pebbles scraped and slipped beneath his feet until finally, inevitably, he tripped.

"Man, are you trying to break your neck?" Rafe hissed. "Or announce 'company coming' to that Secess'?" His neck heated with ridiculous anger, and he jerked David back onto his feet.

"Get down!" Ari whispered, and both men dropped.

Up ahead, in charred and gouged-out scree, lay the emergency pod.

"Good thing there wasn't much brush about, or we'd have had a fire too."

"I'd rather have a brushfire any day than a firefight," Rafe said.

One of the pod's landing struts had buckled. The pod lay canted over, dented, and scarred where it had scraped along the hillside.

"Pod that small—it's got to come from a fighter ship."

"Is its beacon working?" Rafe asked.

Ben Yehuda made fractional adjustments to his instruments. "The pod didn't land stable," he thought aloud, "but those things are built to last. See that dish . . . some beacons still have external components . . . and I'm afraid this one's function—"

Light raved out from Rafe's blaster; ozone abraded their eyes and throats. "Not now it isn't," he said.

"Talk about announcing 'company coming,'" ben Yehuda observed. He had drawn his own weapon.

"The hatch . . . it's heard us," Lohr whispered, his voice cracking up an octave.

The hatch grated aside, then stopped halfway.

"That spar's blocking it," Rafe said. "Good. We can pick our moment to let him out." But what were they waiting for? They might as well get it over with. He sighed, aimed, and vaporized the spar. The hatch cracked open somewhat farther, but not widely enough to free the survivor.

He had a macabre fantasy of prying out whatever occupant was in there . . . in whatever shape the crash had left him. Or she; but Rafe preferred to think of the Secess' as male, not as a pilot like Pauli. As an enemy male. A war criminal. Maybe they should just seal up the pod and let the man die.

"Now what?" asked Lohr.

"Might be safer if we waited, let him wear himself down—"

The grating intensified, then was replaced first by pounding, then a long, long silence.

I don't want to have to go in there after him: that's certain to be a trick. Why'd I get stuck with leading this team anyhow?

"Ki-YAI!"

The roar made them all shout. Blaster fire lanced out wildly as the metal hatch buckled.

One bolt caught a dead tree leaning at an angle above the craft that had toppled it. Now it showered sparks and blazing twigs onto the man who half jumped, half tumbled from the pod. He started to fall, the practiced, graceful roll of someone long drilled in combat techniques, and brought up short with a gasp.

Blood-colored light and caked blood stained pale hair

and paler skin. The Secess' was tall, Rafe thought, probably a head taller than he. With muscles in proportion. Damn. He raised his blaster.

"Get him!" Lohr shouted.

The boy's shout brought the man's head up.

One hand on the rock he'd fallen against, the Secess' pilot levered himself up. His eyes were wild and they didn't track. Concussion, maybe. He stared up into the night, squinting against the violent light of the blaster fire and the paler light of the two moons.

"Now, while he's off-balance," Rafe hissed. "Move in. Lohr, you and Ari stay back."

Rafe stepped out into the circle of fierce light, prepared for anything but the look of incredulous, almost agonized joy on his enemy's face.

"Braethra!" he shouted, or something that sounded like it, and started forward exuberantly, his arms outstretched. Then he stumbled, toppling to his knees.

Rafe forced himself into the firelight. God, the man was fast. Even injured, he was faster than Rafe wanted to tangle with. He raised his blaster, bringing it into the other man's line of sight.

"Braethra?" The word was an accented whisper, pained and disappointed now. Abruptly he gasped, his hands clutching his temples. "Wyn, Fee, Hal. Kane! Ash?"

As ben Yehuda came up behind him, the pilot tried to whirl, to face two ways simultaneously. He screamed once in loss, confusion, and rejection before he collapsed again, his face in the dust. In that instant, they leapt forward and snapped binders on him. Then they rolled him over.

"Let's get some light on the subject," Rafe ordered. The face, even with the blood, the bruises, and a terrible emptiness about it . . . but that face was familiar. Add years to the severely-boned features, thin the hair somewhat, and he'd seen it in texts and recorded lectures.

"Halgerd of Freki," he nodded. "Maybe forty years age difference . . . but this man could be his twin brother . . ."

"He's not breathing." Lohr's voice was shaky. Rafe scanned, and shook the man, then tilted back his head.

"Ari, help me with CPR." He gestured with his chin at Lohr. Like the rest of them, Lohr knew how to restart a man's heart. Pauli had seen to that once they realized what stobors' electrostatic fields could do to you. But *this* one . . . they needed information too badly to trust this man to Lohr's shaky sense of justice. Rafe started breathing for the downed pilot, paused, then breathed again. Ari's hands worked on the man's chest. His young face was earnest with concentration.

Rafe nodded at David ben Yehuda, who started cautiously toward the pod. "I've got some time before you need me. Lohr, help me clear this debris away. I want to get in there, see if there's any information—" Or a functioning transmitter, Rafe thought, though Dave kept quiet on that subject.

As their enemy's chest began to rise and fall shallowly, Rafe sat back on his heels, breathing hard. Red and orange lights, like the swirls on wings, danced before his eyes.

"That ought to do it," he muttered, and threw a blanket over the Secess'. They'd have to move him . . .

"Get him!" As the man spasmed in violent convulsions, Rafe launched himself forward. The Secess' back arched, and his heels drummed on the rocky ground. Then he went alarmingly, bonelessly limp. Rafe was ready with an injection.

"Damn," he said. "I wish Pryor—" then his jaw set as the pilot started struggling again. One hand tore free of the binders and cracked against a rock. Though the man cried out in pain, he scraped his wrist hard against stone until blood spurted from a severed artery.

Binding him again while keeping him from bleeding to death was a messy five minutes' work. Afterward, Rafe sat back on his heels, hoping for a chance to rest. Why had the man deliberately slashed his wrist?

"Not again, dammit!" Rafe grunted as the man stopped breathing. He dived forward, tearing open the man's stained flightsuit and slapping an injection patch over his heart. How much adrenaline could it take before it gave out permanently? The pilot jolted and gasped, his eyes and lips snapping open briefly.

"What's that?"

Rafe bent over him, trying to get him to repeat his words.

Rapid footsteps brought him around on his knees, hand grabbing for his weapon.

"Steady, steady, it's not an attack," said ben Yehuda. "At least not yet."

"That bad?" asked Ari.

"I dismantled a working transmitter. Then Lohr here, nosing around as usual, found this—" Lohr displayed what looked like any other of the miscellaneous batches of hardware that David generally lugged around. "Single burst distress beacon. Omnidirectional . . . and fused upon transmission."

"How's he doing?"

"He's alive, for now. Essentially he's just 'died' four times, but I caught him. His heart's incredibly strong, or I couldn't have pulled him back. But we've got to get him to Pryor soon." *For more reasons than one.* Ari saw the man shiver, and threw another blanket over him.

"Need . . . to die. Let me—"

"So he knows our language." *That means we don't dare talk more than we absolutely have to.* "You'll be cared for," Rafe told him.

"Where?" Awareness kindled in the man's pale eyes. He glanced around, shook his head, and winced. An incongruous expression of panic and bereavement shadowed his bruised face still further. "*Braethra.* Where are they?"

"Looks like you're the only survivor. What's your name?" His voice went tense on the last words.

"You couldn't kill me quickly, then have done, could you?"

"What the hell does he think we are?" Ari snapped. "Butchers like on Wolf IV or Marduk?" The pilot's head jerked at the names of the blighted worlds. Let the civs suspect he'd been at either, and Pauli'd have a lynch mob to deal with along with a war criminal.

"Quiet, cub," his father ordered.

"We don't do that, mister," Rafe snapped. "Our commanding officer's got some questions to ask you, so we're taking you in. Meanwhile, you can start by telling us your name."

The Secessionist officer closed his eyes.

Ari laid a finger on his unbandaged wrist. He's wearing some sort of insignia. Here, I got it." He placed a thin metal band on Rafe's palm. "Like a wrist ID. Numbers, some funny-looking symbol, and 'Thorn'? Is that your name? What's the rest of it?"

The man turned his face away and refused to speak.

Hours later, he still kept silent, clamping his lips against water, ignoring his surroundings. Trying to die again, Rafe thought. What would make him want to die, and make him try so many times? He'd had a set of bad shocks, but there was no organic reason for him to die, not as far as Rafe could see. Rafe's medic friends called such conditions fascinomas—they were more figments of the imagination than clinical states; and he'd heard of one such . . . if only he could remember its name! Maybe the man could travel; or maybe he'd die on the trip back. One thing, though, was certain.

"Dave, I want you to rig up some sort of recorder," he ordered. "If he so much as burps in his sleep, I want to hear it."

If the pilot had survived a battle, that meant that Secess' and Alliance still fought it out, that there were still survivors, still people capable of striding from star system to star system. Unfortunately, though, the transmitter Lohr had found meant that some of those survivors might come after this man, and find them too. Given what briefings had told Rafe about the Secess', he thought it was unlikely; but then, he'd never much trusted briefings. Why had there been a battle around here anyhow? Somehow, they'd have to get a coherent story out of this Thorn character.

Warmth against his side warned him that Lohr had crept closer. "Look at me," Rafe warned him.

The boy's eyes were hot, and his face sullen with a hard vindictiveness.

"Stop worrying that I'm going to turn . . . what's that word you all use when you think I'm not listening . . . feral? and kill the—" Lohr chose an epithet right out of the portside stews. "We need this bastard. But if he won't talk once we get him back home, I've got an idea. You just call me. Me and some of the littlests—we'll make him talk, all right."

CHAPTER
12

Pauli rubbed the small of her back, then laced fingers over a belly she'd have sworn couldn't grow any bigger a month ago. *Kicking again, are you? You'd just better be a fighter*, she told the presence she was increasingly eager to see.

Lohr set a half-empty cup down on the table, and it jiggled from the tremor in his hands.

"What about Rafe and the others?" Pauli asked.

"They're on their way here," he mumbled, rubbing his eyes. "They sent me on ahead." For an instant, his eyes shone with a rage the whole colony had tried to ease. Then he grinned. "They didn't trust me, and I suppose"—he stretched and yawned—"they were right."

"Any idea when they'll get in? Can you remember anything else about the Secess' pilot?" Pauli asked, as she'd asked every couple of minutes.

"No, I can't!" The boy's voice broke. When Pauli held out a hand, he buried his face in it, and curled up at her side.

"I've done all I can!" he whispered, and hid from the light, as he must have hidden many times before. *Have I made him remember darkness and how he'd failed at tasks no child should ever face?* Guilt entwined with her baby's kicking, and Pauli winced.

"Let me, Pauli," Pryor said. "Lohr, think back. Just a little more, and you can sleep. Think back. Think back now, to when this Thorn came out of the pod. Describe it for us."

"What were those names he used?" Pauli interrupted,

and Pryor pursed her lips.

"Strange ones. Wyn, Fee, Hal, Kane, Ash . . . something like that. His wrist-ID said Thorn, too. And 'gerd-something. Rafe said he looked like 'gerd of some-place I didn't hear right. Only younger. I would have listened better, but they kept me too busy. Can I sleep now?"

"Get yourself some sleep now. And get *bathed*. Lohr, you've done a good job, a man's job, and we're all proud of you."

The boy stumbled from the dome. Painfully, Pauli rose and activated the comm. It hummed and crackled, hooting as she narrowed the frequency, boosted the gain to transmit into the mountains, and then, finally, hit the keys for cipher and direction scrambler.

"Yeager here. Report, please."

More humming, during which the medical officer settled in at Pauli's side.

"How are you doing?"

"Sick and tired of waiting," Pauli snapped. She didn't know if she referred to her pregnancy or lag time while the evacuees decoded her transmission, or for Rafe to get back with his prisoner. She was as tired as Lohr of all of them.

"We copy you." *Finally!* "Go ahead."

"Stay where you are for now."

A jumble of voices made Pauli grimace. "I know you hate it. But you're staying there."

More protests.

"I told you: stay. This isn't a debating society. Yeager, out."

Sighing, she shut down communications, walked over to another panel, untaped a stud, and examined it.

Scanners could pick up the screens set to repel stobor. But if she deactivated the shields, they'd have stobor in the fields devouring an entire spring's labor. She sighed again, and decided to hold off. More hurry up and wait, she thought with a grimace. The civs would already be mad enough at her order to stay in hiding up at the caves without her throwing away precious crops for a dubious gain in security. And, God, she didn't even want to think of how they'd react to the presence of an enemy fighter in their midst. She'd best postpone that little announcement for as long as possible.

A bump, a muffled exclamation, and a clatter of rolling plastic made Pauli whirl around to see Pryor mopping at spilled soup, her motions surprisingly awkward.

"Want to tell me, Alicia?" For once, Pauli's voice obeyed her and came out gentle and persuasive.

The other woman looked up. Beneath chagrin at her clumsiness, Pauli read grief and an appalled conviction.

I've got to help her get it out, Pauli thought. Still in that new, gentle voice, she went on, "Did Lohr give you any fresh ideas?"

"You learn fast," Pryor scowled at her. "Yes, he did." She rose from her knees, wadded up the sopping cloth, and threw it at a box. Nothing was discarded anymore. "Remember what we discussed a few days ago—and whom?"

Pauli managed to stop before she blurted out the word she suspected would break the other woman, the name of her old lover.

"You know, it was possible applications of Halgerd's research on cloning that we objected to at Santayana. You've read studies on twins . . . no, *you* probably wouldn't have had to. Well, the basic research on that's very old: started back on Earth. They tracked twins separated at birth. They tended to live very, very similar lives. Some people—and these were the crackpots—even hypothesized that twins could sense things about one another. I don't have to tell you that no one took this seriously. Even prespace, they had some research standards.

"But imagine if you didn't have a twin, but a live, functioning clone. Whom you knew. Whom you worked with. Loved, probably. It would be very efficient, a team made up of clones. Practically telepathic. For all intents and purposes, they'd be the same person. You could train them—tapes, drugs, conditioning. Hell, for all we know, maybe they actually would read one another's minds. And if they couldn't, cybernetic or biotic implants would be easy enough to develop. That's what Halgerd thought.

"He'd worked out the theory—organic fiber cybernetic implants. He'd even suggested deriving the organic fibers from the individual's own cells to avoid rejection by the body. Essentially, Halgerd planned to turn people into human multiplex communications systems. He thought it would be easiest with clones. Of course, on basic humanitarian grounds, we couldn't let him test it."

Pauli blinked at the physician. Granted, she had heard crazy rumors, pilots' talk about the Secess', but no one would really do that to a pilot, or anyone else—

"Think about it. It's hard enough to watch someone die. I ought to know. So should you. It's harder knowing —feeling, as some people would say—when a family member dies . . . especially a twin.

"Just think, though, if you lost a clone. Long before the Earth blockade, some people hypothesized that in a functional clone group, injury to one of the team would probably be felt by the rest. But what if that group were physically linked by the implants? They actually would feel it if one of the other clones died. What's worse, the death agony could be magnified by the perceptions of each clone who experienced it.

"You can see why some people thought that given such a group, the death of one clone could easily kill the others. Even without organic MUX implants. They called it Kroeber's Trauma. Halgerd, of course, called it damned nonsense."

"But you don't think of Kroeber's Trauma as damned nonsense, do you?"

"No." Alicia Pryor sank into a chair. Her long, worn fingers rubbed her temples, and for a moment, her face betrayed her true age. "I think that in his own exhausted, inarticulate way, Lohr has described a case of Kroeber's Trauma."

"What makes you so sure?"

Pryor rubbed her temples again. "Once, when it looked like we might . . . never mind that. In any case,

Halgerd took me to Freki once. Those names Lohr quoted aren't really names, Pauli. They're runes, the ancient symbols that the oligarchs revived, runes with names like Wyn, Feoh, Hagl, and Kaon. The man they're bringing in isn't really *named* Thorn. He's a clone. They've tagged him Thorn the way we tag lab animals A, B, C, or D."

"And this Thorn only 'died' four times," Pauli mused. "Assuming the standard five pilots in a squad, and another on board their home ship—"

One of the Halgerd-clones was probably alive, then. And with Pauli's usual luck, he'd be looking for his brother.

If only Rafe and the others would hurry bringing in this Thorn . . . this clone of one of the most brilliant offspring of a fighting world. God help them all. Freki had cloned its best and brightest; she saw no reason why other worlds like Tokugawa wouldn't follow suit. And no reason why they should stop at a clone of six, or restrain themselves from modifying the clones for speed and strength.

That thought bred worse horrors. Since it was now possible to create a fleet of aces, disposable and replaceable pilots, against whom ordinary pilots (let alone the young ones that the Alliance had to release for assignment these days) had no chance, Alliance would have to follow suit.

How hard would it be to duplicate Halgerd's research? Granted, Pryor had fled Santayana rather than participate in it, but in wartime, how many scientists would share—would be permitted to share—her scruples? Pauli used to think she was an ethical being. But that was before Federal Security had grounded her with the refugees here, before the need to protect what might be the last of humankind had forced her . . .

Her child-to-be kicked. She laid a hand on her belly to comfort the child who might never have time now to be born.

* * *

"They're coming in!" Lohr overflew the base camp, shouting the news, then touched down. "They're all safe, and they're carrying him in!" he yelled and overbalanced, his wings scrabbling in the dirt, his legs imitating an overturned stobor.

"Nice landing," Pauli commented as he gathered up his wings, strut by strut. "How far away?"

"Not far . . . half a klick or so."

"Good," Pauli said. "Tell Dr. Pryor to meet me here. Did you check on how they're doing with the hydro tanks up at the caves?"

Lohr looked chagrined, then sullen. "Go do it. You're the only one we've got who can fly that far now—" *and you're damned right, I don't want you around when they bring him in.*

Idly Pauli burnished the pilot's wings she had decided to wear for the first time in months. The sun felt good on her shoulders, and she was glad simply to sit and to plan. A Secess' pilot . . . her opposite number . . . *but an improved model . . .*

"There," Pauli pointed.

"I'll take your word for it," Pryor said.

Pauli rose as they came nearer. The prisoner was a tall, fair-haired man, paler than most spacers who lay under UV lamps for prescribed intervals. He lay covered, restraints making odd bumps at wrists, ankles, waist, and chest.

Pryor shook her head and murmured something deep in her throat, before she knelt beside the Secess'. Her hand smoothed back the unconscious man's limp hair, and she watched its motion as if it went on separate from the rest of her, as if the caress belonged to someone else. Then she shrugged and raised an ironic eyebrow. "Despite the bruising, he's as much like Halgerd as a twin," she said sadly. "Only forty years younger. He's concussed from the rough landing. Maybe the implant is broken. In that case, it'll probably be dissolved by now, but I'll scan for it anyway. Bring him inside." Pryor led the way to her improvised clinic, talking to herself of "full-body scan, genetic assay, comparison analysis . . . I probably don't want to add any other drugs to what you've given him. Dosage is well beyond normal tolerance—"

But then, Pauli thought, *we're sure we're not dealing with a normal human being.*

When doubt was no longer possible, and before anyone could protest, Pryor unfastened the last of the prisoner's restraints.

She started to say something, then shook her head. "Wrong name." Her voice was husky. "Thorn?"

His eyes opened slowly. "*Hwert emk? Thykkjask thik kenna?*"

"Still groggy," Pryor said. "That's Frekan he's speaking. I'll have to bring him back into the real world."

"You're here," she murmured. "I'll explain. And no, you don't know me." She looked down at his blank face and translated. "*Mik eigi manthu.* You haven't known me for years. Can you talk?" she asked, and helped him to sit up.

How carefully she kept her back turned on Rafe and Pauli.

Pauli studied the man now propped against the wall. They'd dressed him in one of the settlement's all-purpose gray work suits. He was tall, and the way he had unconsciously arranged himself when Dr. Pryor sat him up gave the drab garment a look of elegance. Pale features and fair hair made it look surprisingly formal.

Her eyes flashed from their prisoner to Dr. Pryor. She looked more like *him* than like them, and she had known the original Halgerd. She shuddered, and forced herself not to rub her flight insignia as if they were a talisman.

"Our C.O., Pauli Yeager," Pryor announced neutrally. Pauli had expected that the prisoner would speak a language other than the obscure Frekan dialect to which he had reverted when he was injured.

Thorn Halgerd started to rise, then froze in his place, staring appalled at Pauli's obvious pregnancy. "What kind of people are you?" he demanded, leaning forward, his voice chill. "You use people capable of giving life as pilots?"

Pryor handed Pauli a printout of the tests she had run. *Sterile.*

"I'll ask the questions around here, mister."

He turned to Pryor. "How can you waste . . . and she's weathered too. Don't you have tanks?"

"Which tanks do you mean?" Pryor asked.

"Stass tanks," he said impatiently. "Everyone knows that the distractions of ship's routine between engagements only lower a piloting group's effectiveness." He looked Pauli over again, then nodded. "Maybe there's some twisted logic to it, though. Breeding's cheaper than cloning, though then the child has to be allowed to mature normally—"

Pauli shot Pryor a horrified look.

"So they keep you in stass between missions," Pauli said. She felt the beginnings of nausea curdle in her stomach. Genetically modified, sterile pilots, cloned, carefully kept from any stimuli except those their commanders chose for them. No wonder they fought so hard. It was the only time they were alive. Given what this Thorn betrayed, fighting was the only reason they lived at all.

"We don't do things like that here," she declared. "Our pilots are humans, not killing machines. I was *born* and grew up normally. As will my child. Now, I believe we've humored you long enough—"

"I have no answers for you. And I won't speak to . . . you people aren't even human!" Revulsion as keen as Pauli's thickened his voice, and he turned away.

"The original was even haughtier," Rafe murmured in Pauli's ear.

"Alicia, if he's that used to stass, he can probably take more medication. Put him out."

Pryor hesitated, clearly thinking of the four pseudo-deaths Rafe had already averted.

"Need I remind you, Doctor, this isn't the original Halgerd. He's an enemy pilot who's probably responsible for more deaths than you'd want to count." When Pryor still didn't move, Pauli brought out her last weapon. "You said you left Santayana because you'd lost your objectivity. Just how badly compromised *is* it now?"

Pryor glared, then readied an injection feed, slapping the patch on Halgerd's neck before he could protest.

As he sagged down again, she checked vital signs. "I don't like using neoscopalamine after what he's been through. He's fighting it too. Should have expected that." She sighed and increased the dosage. "His eyes will be sensitive. Dim the lights in here."

Rafe brought out her kit.

"Ready to record," she announced.

Pryor took out a tiny light mounted on a stylus and peeled back one eyelid. "Let me start the questions, will you? I know what to ask."

She flashed the light across Thorn Halgerd's face. "Wake up, pilot. Wake up!"

The light eyes opened, filling with eagerness.

"Name!"

"Thorn, of Halgerd series 6AA-prime. Decanted . . ."

Only twenty years real age. He'd been accelerated to full growth. And how much of that twenty years had he spent in the tanks?

"Orders?" he asked. Even under the powerful drugs, his body quivered, eager for action.

"First you report, pilot. Think back to your last wakeshots . . ."

Rafe closed in with the recorder.

Air struck his face. The light about him, tempered to reddish twilight, was beautiful to his eyes. Someone was rumpling his hair . . . Aesc, his group's Number One. Aesc was ship-liaison the way he and his brothers were pilots, so he was always the first one out of the tanks. Around him were mumblings as his brothers stirred and stretched. The linkage among them pulsed with comfort and welcome.

As usual, he sat up too quickly, but Aesc was ready with the strong shoulder and warm grin that made him Thorn's favorite.

"A fight?" he asked.

Aesc looked troubled. Beneath the hunger any time in the tanks invariably left him with, Thorn felt Aesc's worries and, worse yet, felt his anxieties spread and resonate through the link. As communications core of the Halgerd group, Aesc was most skilled at sending or filtering communications from the outside to his brothers. His implant was equipped with an override, and he had the deep conditioning for stability, to keep the brothers strong until the Republic needed their lives. "You were created from our best and our strongest to protect the life of the Republic," their tapes said. "You have no other, and no better, immortality."

The ones who Ordered told them it didn't matter where they served; they'd be indoctrinated and briefed while under stass. But no system was the same. Good pilots learned to study each one during waketime . . . from the asteroids of the Wolf System, which they had used first as a shield against the defenses of the fifth world, then as a bombardment . . . to the treacherous variable binary in the last system they'd fought in, where they'd lost two groups to a spectacular stellar flare. Those groups had cut it too close, the brothers had agreed. The Republic had no use for bad timing.

"We've Jumped," Aesc said.

No battle? That was strange. Curious, Thorn swung his legs off his pallet and turned to help the others. Hagl was always slower to wake; Feoh was usually shaky, hungrier than the others due to slightly higher adrenaline production. Which made sense, of course: he flew point. Wyn, a double for Feoh; Kaon, about the same as Thorn himself, and the one who looked most like him.

In training, they had been shown holos of their genefather Halgerd, who had created the groups, and they had been told that since they were specially honored in being made from his line, much would be expected of them. Thorn had always longed to meet Halgerd, who used their enemies to gain knowledge, and then came back to the Republic to share it. He had studied what he could find, which wasn't much; it wasn't needful for pilots to know much beyond their ships, flight, armscomp, and their duty to the Republic. If he'd strayed into unauthorized data, he might have been reported—and that would have harmed his brothers too. Most of what pilots needed to know, they learned in the tanks, loaded into memory through their links. But pride in Halgerd was a thought he'd had all on his own.

They were all awake now, assisted by the medical officers to a table and fed their restoratives. In the room beyond, Thorn smelled food, and grinned at the others, a grin reflected on each nearly identical face. The cascade of sensory impressions had to be what born-humans described as intoxicating. As the restorative heated his belly, the awareness that linked the brothers in combat and always let them touch woke fully, and they were one, basking in one another's mere existence. It was good that they had all survived that long. Granted, they were weapons in the Republic's hand, to be expended for the sake of those who birthed them, but . . .

"Sacred Band," whispered ben Yehuda, who had let himself in during the prisoner's drug-induced report. In response to the others' questioning looks, he added, "A . . . rather specialized Theban unit on Earth about 3M back. It was composed of paired men who had sworn to die before they abandoned one another."

"Men!" Rafe grimaced.

Sterile, fixated on one another, on themselves, given the fact that they were all clones of the same person, such a group had no use on a world where increased population and genetic diversity were required. But as human weapons . . . Pauli shuddered and tried to find a more comfortable position. A cramp twisted in her entrails. Just her luck if she'd started labor.

Suddenly she shivered again. The pilot had mentioned Wolf IV. God, had he been mixed up in the raid on Lohr's homeworld? She looked up just in time to see the door slide quietly shut. Lohr was expert in his comings and goings, he'd had to be. She wanted to check on him now, and if he had eavesdropped (which was likely), to comfort and control him—but Thorn had started to mumble again, and she dared not leave here, with his tale unheard. She started to rise, but the cramp stitching itself across her belly again warned her against movement.

Rafe glanced at her sharply, and she squeezed his hand.

"Go on," she told Pryor.

CHAPTER

13

"On your feet," snapped one of the medics as the first officer walked in. Thorn tried not to stare at him; he was regular crew: born, not decanted, unique, not one of a group. Surely the first officer understood that Halgerd group were pilots, not to be distracted from their tasks. But here they were, wakened from the protection of stasis in mid-Jump, brought to face a true-human who bore marks of fatigue and stress that pilots never carried. Pilots died in space, or rested secure in their stasis tanks.

As the first officer finished speaking, Thorn's brothers exchanged glances. They had Orders now, and Orders were never to be protested. Strangeness resonated in the link: so very strange that so many true-humans had been killed. Had the other pilot groups failed them? Then it was justice that the surviving groups must serve watches, must leave their protection and work side by side with true-humans. They all looked to Aesc, who was as used to such contact as any groupmate ever got. Aesc would help them adapt.

"They briefed me before reviving the rest of you, brothers," Aesc said. "This is an honor they're giving us. We are Halgerd, therefore judged most capable to serve." Pride flashed briefly through the link, followed by apprehension.

Feoh started to look shaky all over again. "It's all right," Aesc comforted him, hands kneading his shoulders. "Medcrew has tranquilizers for you until the stimuli no longer overpower you. You'll get used to them. We are Halgerd. We can adapt."

"Is that all?" Feoh asked. "The only reason?" His eyes slid wistfully to the sliding door that hid the safe, comforting tanks from them.

"What's that to you?" Aesc snapped, unusually harsh on Feoh, whose perceptions were generally as sharp as his nerves. "We have our orders."

"Not all," Thorn Halgerd mumbled. "Not . . . not all . . ."

"You have your Orders, your duty shifts, your medications for whenever the stress gets too bad. What else do you need, Thorn? What else can you want?" Alicia Pryor asked, and stepped up dosage.

Boring, that's what it was. Boring had always been just a true-human denotation, but now Thorn had a referent for it. Like spending tank-time wide awake, with sights and sounds and smells added. There were duty-shifts, but there were also long periods of time that the true-humans described as "hurry up and wait."

Thorn had sat waiting until, "Come on," a true-human from CompCentral told him. "Medical's decided that you have to do something constructive with your off-shifts, and they've asked us to see to it."

She took him by the arm—it felt strange to be touched by someone not med staff or a groupmate, let alone by a true-woman—and led him to the ship's libraries, showing him access codes for a wealth of tapes he had never dreamed existed. Glancing about almost guiltily, he noted Feoh and Hagl in nearby carrels, concentrating on tapes Thorn suspected had nothing to do with weapons or shiphandling. He sighed with satisfaction and punched up the first menu.

These tapes! As their library time increased, their dependency on the diazepam-analogs and other antistressors declined . . . which, Thorn concluded with a shrewdness new to him, was probably what medical had kept in mind. At first, he had duly kept to Republic history. But gradually his fascination with the group's genefather Halgerd, creator of all the fighting groups, overcame his guilt and so obsessed him that he had scanned all the available biographies on the databanks.

Once he exhausted them, he discovered Freki, Halgerd's home, with joy, got quietly, tearfully drunk on its proud, plangent songs of victory, even in death, and shivered at its history. The deep inlets, the echoing mountains and twilights that Halgerd longed for in his years of exile among the enemies lured him too until, inevitably, the moment came when he started to think of Freki as his homeworld as well. The way Thorn might choose a weapon (but with a strange new tenderness) he chose the steading he pretended was his home, his favorite animals, and the foods he liked best. He cherished this fantasy in secret, guarding it even from his brothers in the link, because he suspected that now he'd crossed the line from acceptable interest into delusion.

"I thought maybe I should report myself, but . . . I couldn't bear to not-be. That never occurred to me before. And what about my brothers? For the first time, I had words to understand what they meant to me. If the medics euthanized me, what would become of them?" he asked.

Pryor touched his forehead and sent him deeper. Her fingers lingered against his hair.

Then his next delusion took root. To *be* Halgerd, who had been a giant among true-humans. Just to know what he did would be the study of a full lifetime, with no rest in the sleep of the tanks. Thorn began to study feverishly, desperately. And those too were words for which he used to have no referents.

When, in the privacy of pilots' quarters, Aesc asked him what he had learned, he answered with evasions, then winced as unease, and a surprising, complicit guilt quivered in the linkage. Covertly he studied his brothers. How had he ever thought they looked alike? Ship's day by day, they all were diverging from their original unity, Aesc spending more time on the bridge, the others in medical, engineering, even science. Reading. Talking with true-humans, spending less time with one another.

And more than talking. He had roused from concentration so intense on a Frekan poem that he might almost have been in a tank, to overhear two true-female crewmembers.

"What difference does it make? They're not fertile; it's not as if we have to requisition anything."

"How can you talk about them as things one moment, then plan what you're planning the next?"

"How? Boredom, that's how. This eternal waiting for orders, or for the captain and first to decide how they're going to carry out whatever orders we get." The woman was pretty, Thorn decided, slightly bemused at that awareness. And she tugged at Feoh's hand until he left his carrel and followed her out of CompCenter. The link heated with Feoh's emotions, then his act. Half the ship away, Thorn trembled.

Feoh wasn't in quarters until late that ship's night. When he returned, he was smug, full of hints and of talk about factions among the true-humans, in the Republic itself, talk which sparked a response from Wyn.

Hagl—sturdy, stolid Hagl (where had Thorn learned those words?)—banged his fist on the nearest table. "We're not supposed to question. We're pilots, weapons in the Republic's hands . . . not politicians. What's the matter with you?"

"Nothing, brother mine," Kaon murmured at his ear. "They've just gotten a little too close . . . let's call it that . . . to the true-humans and to some of the women at that. Or didn't you have the brains to know what you were feeling in the link?"

He and Aesc had to separate Hagl and Feoh. They all winced at the bruises.

"You know what's the matter?" Aesc asked him later. He looked as anxious as the first officer that time he'd come into Medical Center with the orders that had destroyed their peace and—abruptly Thorn understood another strange word—their innocence.

Thorn shrugged. "Too many stimuli. What can you expect? They take us out of the tanks, and—"

"We're not meant for this!" Aesc interrupted. "We're all changing. Pretty soon, none of us will be fit to fly . . . and what then, Thorn, what then? They terminate pilots who can't fly!"

He started to tremble, then to cry. Maintaining override on the group's linkages was draining him, Thorn thought. He looked years older than the rest of them. Wondering at his own calm, Thorn dialed for tranquilizers. He ought to have felt Aesc's hysteria. What he felt instead was relief.

"I want him to rest before we go on," Pryor said. "You too. You look like you'd be better for—" Her eyes narrowed as Pauli winced at another cramp and her own rotten timing.

"How long since contractions started?" the physician demanded.

"Maybe an hour or so. Get on with this, Alicia! There's one of this Thorn's group alive up there, and that distress beacon has sent a message off to him."

Pryor hesitated, and Pauli searched for arguments to convince her to proceed with the interrogation.

"I'll cross my legs or something. I promise I won't have the baby while you're interrogating him. Just hurry up, Doctor, before this Aesc-character finds us!"

"His heart's weakening—"

"He's a killer, Alicia. But so am I. As you know. Get on with it."

Pryor touched the hypo, increasing the flow of neoscopalamine.

"So you lived with the true-humans, and you didn't like what you felt, is that it?"

Thorn mumbled sleepy agreement. "Finally, though, we got orders. Aesc was so happy."

The old eagerness for battle fired his blood, yet Thorn felt strange. The part of him he'd made into Halgerd's image had a word for that. *Feigr*. He kept it to himself:

fatalism was encouraged; but superstition would probably get him euthanized. That is, if the true-humans maintained proper discipline anymore. Anything could happen, had already happened. True-people had been arrested . . . "They fight among themselves," Aesc had lamented after one of his forays into bridge territory.

But they had arrived in a new system where hostile ships awaited, so they headed down for the launching bay. Before he and his brothers climbed into their ships, they bowed to the six brothers of Tojo-group, then exchanged somber, respectful nods with another group of high-cheekboned, dark-haired men he had never seen before.

Real flying again, thank God, he thought; and knew the relief and the prayer for Halgerd's mindset, not his. At last. The linkage of pilot and pilot awoke strong and clean in Thorn's mind and kindled in the others', bringing a warm, welcome sense of rightness, remembrances of excitement, of victory, and, afterward, desires assuaged.

Then they sighted the other group. Curious: no warning of another Republic ship in the area had filtered down to them; and the strangers made no courteous suggestion that their groups combine forces against an enemy—where were the familiar patterns of the enemy ships?

The stranger-group opened fire, blowing Wyn and Feoh out of space before Thorn's blast shields fully polarized. Half-blinded, he fled behind a satellite with his surviving brothers. None of them felt the two deaths yet, and the knowledge of pain deferred only made him stronger for now.

"Aesc!" he shouted into his comm.

"We're trying for a visual," Aesc spoke fast, sounding half-frantic. "They know the ship . . . they say . . . I've no referent for these words . . . *civil war* . . . we've broken their codes and got them on screen."

The tiny screen which held Aesc's face blanked, then *NO*, he thought aghast, in the instant Aesc shouted, "My God, it's *US!*"

Another Halgerd-group? Thorn flamed with anger and his brother's unfamiliar terror. Aesc might have no referent for *civil war* but Halgerd's old poems did:

> Bræðr munu berjask ok at bönum verðask,
> munu systryngar sifjum spilla;
> hart er í heimi, hórdómr mikill,
> skeggöld, skálmöd skildir to klofnir,
> vindöld, vargöld, áðr veröld stepisk;
> mun eigi maðr öðrum þyrma.

> Brother fights brother, and both fall dead,
> Sisters' sons slay each other;
> Evil lies on earth, an age of whoredom,
> The slash of sharp swords, of shields breaking,
> Wind's age, wolf's age, till the world is wrecked.

The next purplish-white salvo took out Hagl and three of their other, enemy, selves. Adrenaline flared in Thorn's blood; no time to feel his brothers' deaths in this battle from which there could be no return, for it was Ragnarok. The survivors twisted and dived, as deadly lights slashed the blackness and they jockeyed to put their enemies where the satellites would impair their maneuverability and the star would ruin their vision.

Since this was his last battle, best make the most of it. Even though he heard Aesc whimper, heard him cry out, he roared with laughter until there was only silence in the comms. He and Kaon were paired now, and they took out one, then another of the enemy group before Kaon too vanished into blue-white vapor, leaving him to duel against the last ship.

He glanced at his fuel gauges. Not enough to make it back to the ship, but he had never expected to return alive. He didn't care. At the exact moment when he tried his last, suicidal, folly, the other ship fired—and exploded an instant later. Thorn's damage readouts burned crimson, showing critical failure in the power core, counting down seconds to the time when the ship would blow apart.

"Preparing to eject, Aesc," he spoke into the silent comm. The ship was yawing uncontrollably now on all three axes, and he fell against one bulkhead, then the boards. Ejection was all but a death sentence, but he had to try. He was simply sorry that Aesc would be left alone.

"Aesc?" Where was his brother?

"*AESC!*" he screamed as the ejectors blasted him free of his dying ship and toward the surface of the nearest world. His skull felt as if it would burst. Gravity clutched at his spine until the coolness of deepsleep hissed out and embraced him.

"He was hyped up during the fight," Pauli concluded, "and then drugged for entry into atmosphere. So he didn't have time to 'feel the deaths,' as he called it, until you helped him break out of the pod." She felt a kind of horrified pity for the Secess', who'd literally been hard-wired to his squad, to live or die. Her revulsion was . . . it was an actual pain. Then she was doubling over, and Pryor and Rafe were helping her to lie down.

"I told you I wouldn't have the baby until I knew," she panted. "Now I know. There's *two* ships out there, hunting one another. If we lie low, maybe they won't find us, even if we all have to hide up in the caves this season."

Rafe bathed Pauli's forehead, reminding her to breathe regularly.

"Cut power to the outlying fields," she ordered, then gasped as another contraction stitched itself across her belly.

"Not now, Pauli. Come on, like we practiced. Count with me," Rafe coaxed.

"Do it! Better we lose all the fields than get burned off!"

"I'll tell Dave," said Rafe, and Pauli could give herself up to the struggle within her own body. Even in the intervals between contractions she shuddered. Three seasons ago, she had given death. She had resented her assignment here, but when the winged Cynthians had been sighted—intelligent, flying beings—she had been as delighted as the other settlers. Communicating with them had reconciled her with Rafe.

"Steady, Pauli. Breathe in. There—"

At first, they had been grateful to find friends here. But then they had discovered the meter-long, segmented horror—the eaters. 'Cilla would always walk with a limp, the result of the eaters' digestive acid.

"Contractions about three minutes apart—no, make that two."

The first recon had been a failure, but the second had been disastrous. She'd been on it along with Rafe, ben Yehuda, and Borodin. Her captain. She whimpered, and Rafe seemed to materialize from somewhere and smooth back her hair. God, she was so tired.

"Not much longer," he soothed her.

"I'm trying," she panted.

She had always tried. She remembered the Cynthians hovering over their heads, diving at Captain Borodin as he tried to fly back to the settlement, she had tried to protect him . . . "trying . . ." she moaned.

"You're doing fine, love," Rafe's voice. "Just think about pushing."

She couldn't think about that. Even as she bore down, she remembered drawing on the Cynthian. "Does it matter what stage they're in when we kill them?" she'd screamed, seconds before a Cynthian brushed the captain with its venom.

"Falling . . ."

"Let it go, Pauli. Concentrate on *now*. On the baby."

"Couldn't even recover his ID tags . . ."

"Stop it! Now push!"

She glared at Pryor, then tried to concentrate on pushing. The decision to destroy the eaters had been hard, knowing what they were, willingly disrupting the Cynthian life cycle.

Genocide. She groaned. What made it worse was that

at the end, the Cynthians had understood. At least some of them had: Uriel and Ariel had tried to stop the nymphae from using the lethal paint, and, at the last, had died in despair.

How the fire had smelled when the last of the elder Cynthians had plunged into its heart! She gagged and sobbed.

"You're almost finished. Let it happen," Pryor whispered at her.

Her contractions were coming almost simultaneously now. Surely it couldn't be much longer. She had no choice now but to push. She had no choice then, either. Never any choice, she whimpered silently. The very caves where the settlers now hid had belonged to the Cynthians first. It hadn't been hard to create the poison that killed them; but as long as Pauli lived, she wouldn't be able to look at the sky without dreaming of the splendor of wings they had seen their first nights here.

"The children," she gasped.

"All fine."

The littlests: they'd tried to raise them free of their elders' taint of genocide. This child coming now—how would she explain?

Life-giver, Thorn had called her. The phrase had stung. But now it was going to be true. Please God, it was going to be true.

"I don't deserve this," she started to say, but Rafe's fingers brushed across her lips before catching her hands in a sustaining clasp.

The civs in the caves—they should report but—"One thing at a time, Pauli," Rafe told her.

The pains were like firing practice, targets coming at decreasing intervals, then all at once. She tried to get a fix on them . . . she was bearing down, she was panting, and she shouted triumphantly, tears rolling down her face, mingling with the sweat.

"Got him!" announced Alicia Pryor, and Pauli heard a thin wail that strengthened until, temporarily, it occupied all the world for her.

CHAPTER
14

"Ships, not one but two up there, the fields wide open to stobor, and now you tell me you've got a *what?*"

Ordering the civilians back to base was practically the first thing she did after the birth of . . . her son, hers and Rafe's. Serge was a healthy baby, she thought with sleepy contentment. Out of all this mess, something to rejoice about.

Their most recent argument about how best to dismantle the hydro tanks for transportation up to the caves had waked her. She sighed, and prepared to stand up, a slower process now that she'd given birth than she'd expected. She listened as the argument made the circular trajectory she had already predicted for it. As she expected, the news about Thorn Halgerd ended all argument about moving the tanks.

She waited a little longer. As someone mentioned "war crimes" for the first time, she walked outside, carrying Serge with her.

The sight of him silenced everyone. After a flurry of compliments (which a corner of Pauli's mind rejoiced in, understated though they were; thank God, her child was perfect), she seized her advantage.

"War crimes?" she asked, seating herself somewhat gingerly on a stool Rafe brought her. "And just which war criminals are we talking about?"

She patted her son's back, waiting for their murmuring to begin, then subside. She had orchestrated the questions she needed to ask before coming out here. Now she waited.

"I suppose you're waiting for us to ask what you

mean," someone in back commented sourly. *Beneatha, of course.*

Pauli shrugged. "I don't think I have to," she replied. "You know what we've done here. You know what that makes us. Does it matter that on Lohr's homeworld, the people that the Secess' killed looked like us, *were* some of us; and that on Cynthia, the people we killed had wings and scales? None of us is stupid or bigoted enough to say that all we did was exterminate a swarm of big, flying bugs."

She stroked her child's warm head, with its incredibly silky hair. "We knew what we were doing," she reminded them. "By rights, we should all be under arrest, if there were anyone here with the power to arrest us." Disturbed by her voice, the baby started to cry. Pauli comforted him, then passed him carefully to 'Cilla, who beamed as she held him.

"Some of us wanted no part of what was done with the Cynthians," cried a voice from the far side of the circle.

"You're alive because of it!" shouted Ari ben Yehuda.

"Ari, you're out of such order as we've got. As usual. I remember that some of you didn't want any part of what we did. But as I recall, you made no effort to stop it. I'm afraid that makes you accomplices."

Rafe broke in. "Let's say, for the sake of argument, that those people are not accomplices. In that case, what about it? Do *you* have the authority to set up a commission and conduct a war-crimes trial? Where's your mandate?"

The muttering grew. In a second, it might turn ugly. This was the danger point: while the settlers decided whether to turn vigilante or to maintain whatever law they had managed to preserve.

Pauli leaned back. "Sure, you can take matters into your own hands. No one will stop you. I'm damned if I'm turning weapons onto any of my own people. But if you do kill the prisoner, think what that makes you. And think what it'll cost the children once they learn."

People broke up into groups and started arguing

afresh. Talk, talk, talk, as Alicia had complained. But it was slowing them down. Suddenly the civilian tendency to talk matters to a slow death struck her as a blessed thing.

She glanced around. The perimeter guards were changing shift. One signalled thumbs-up at her. The weather had been fairly chilly for the past few days; this made the stobor torpid. But today was warmer; and she had the field generators deactivated. Stobor might be out.

"Well, what do we do with him?" The question she had most wanted to have asked drew her attention back from the fields.

"What do we do with him? Dr. Pryor has proposed an answer to that. Shall we let her explain it?" Pauli sighed, readjusted herself, and resigned herself for a long, long argument about whether Thorn Halgerd was a killer or a victim.

The dome housing the communications gear stood somewhat removed from the rest of the buildings. Pauli crouched nearby, waiting. Her macrobinoculars dangled from her neck. From time to time, she raised them and scanned the sky. Flashes of light told her that one ship had apparently forced the other to turn and fight.

People planted near the "infirmary" in which Thorn Halgerd was confined had carefully let slip the information that high overhead his old ship and its quarry had met.

If that doesn't lure him out, nothing will, Pryor had assured them.

It was logical that Thorn Halgerd would want to rejoin his ship, team back up with his one surviving groupmate and—to borrow one of his own slogans—serve his Republic by giving them information on this settlement.

"I still don't like the risk you've let yourself in for," she told Alicia Pryor for the tenth time that evening.

"He's conditioned not to hurt what he calls life-givers," the physician retorted. "Besides, I think he trusts me."

What was more to the point: Pryor, remembering

Halgerd, trusted his "son." Perhaps too much. Halgerd had been ruthless, but never cruel, however. So she thought that Thorn Halgerd would use his greater-than-Halgerd's strength and speed to subdue her, not harm her unless she struggled. Which, of course, she would not do. Not, she reminded Pauli, at her age.

Pauli had started to protest further—*arguing like a civ myself now!*—until Rafe had grabbed her arm. "She's trying to absolve herself," he hissed at her. Damned strange expiation, Pauli wanted to comment. If Pryor wanted to atone, she could do a better job practicing medicine, not putting her life on the line.

"*Damn you, Halgerd, move it!*" Hundreds of kilometers overhead, the warring Secess' ships feinted and fired. Inside the commhut, Pauli had only to access the computer to see the battle on screen. She was aching to do just that, and she could bet—had bet—lives on her guess that Halgerd couldn't resist it either.

"*We've freed up Alicia,*" Rafe's voice from her earplug alerted her. "*She's not hurt. Get ready, Pauli. He's on his way.*"

Ahhh, here he came. The tall, lean figure, bent almost double, slipped from the darkened infirmary's door, using every scrap of shadow for cover, and headed for the communications dome. Before Pauli could so much as stand up, he was inside.

Not that he could do any immediate harm in there. Ben Yehuda had reconfigured the comms. Now Thorn Halgerd could receive transmissions, but whatever he sent would only go to the infirmary where, by now, people would be listening in.

"Pilot Yeager . . . Captain?" the Secess' clone stated as she entered after him. "Should you even be up and around so soon?" His fingers caressed the commgear.

"I'm surprised at your concern," she remarked. "I trust you left my medical officer in one piece?"

He nodded. "I hope you're unarmed. I should regret injuring you."

"And yet," said Pauli, "you have no hesitation about telling your people—assuming they're still alive—where we are. Knowing what they'll do to us . . . what you've done to groups like ours."

"Ah!" Satisfaction rang in his voice as the coordinates of Cynthia space glowed on-screen. Two red blips dodged and fired across it at one another. Thorn punched in codes for identification, drew the transmitter toward him, and then, slowly, laid it down again. Doubt flickered in the gray eyes.

"What happens if your home ship is the one destroyed in that firefight?" Pauli asked. "Will you tell the other ship about us? After it killed your own?"

"I serve the Republic," Thorn recited absently, his eyes on the screen. One ship took a strong hit, and he flinched. His ship? The readouts he demanded didn't look good. That ship was probably venting air, sealing off the damaged compartments, never mind the crew who might be trapped. Or lost. For a treasonous moment, Pauli winced too at the death throes of a starship. Then she resumed her own attack.

"That ship killed your brothers! It turned on your Republic!"

"Quiet now—" he whispered, watching the silent, lethal barrage on the screen until the first ship went up in a tiny, brilliant sun that cast weird shadows on the dome's sloping walls.

Thorn punched up the survivor's identification code. With a growl of satisfaction, he reached for voice transmission.

"Thorn, Halgerd Group 6AA, to base ship. Aesc, are you there?"

"Are you sure he's alive?" Pauli asked. "You heard him cry out while the rest of your brothers were out getting zeroed. He sounded out of control to me. Don't they terminate you if you get that crazy?"

Halgerd increased volume on the receivers.

"They're short-staffed," he muttered half to himself.

"You hope!" Pauli snapped. She had to get him to argue if she were to try to turn him. If they couldn't turn him, win his allegiance, they'd have no choice but to kill him. The clone's hair glittered in the dim overhead lights, and she wondered what went on in his brilliant, starved mind.

"Another thing, Halgerd," she said, noting how he started and almost smiled at the name. "Assuming your people didn't kill him, what makes you think Aesc survived the deaths of the other four? You almost didn't. Do you know, though, Dr. Pryor thinks she's figured out why you lived?"

"*You're getting to him.*" Pryor's voice overrode the pounding of her own blood in her ears. "*Try to keep him talking. Make him realize that he's got no future with his old ship.*"

"Do you think they'll have you back?" Pauli needled.

"Shut up!"

"What if I don't? When I came in here, the first words out of your mouth were that you were worried I was moving about too soon after Serge's birth. Don't you see? That whole time you were turned loose in CompCenter, you and your groupmates differentiated yourselves from one another so much that the bond was strained. Then you hit your head, and your implant broke, dissolved, and was ultimately eliminated. That's why you survived."

"Aesc, please, Aesc, come in."

"Your Aesc is a stranger to you now," Pauli told Thorn's back. "You have nothing to go back to. A broken group? Sure, so they decant another Halgerd-clone. Another six-group. Do you think they'll let you and your Aesc join it as older models? Will they give you another implant? And even assuming all of that, what makes you think this new group would accept you—especially knowing all that you know?"

She leaned forward slightly, as if she held a knife and were going to slide it into the place between his hunched shoulders where the gray cloth had darkened with sweat. "You're contaminated, Thorn. That's how they'll look at you and Aesc."

"*Don't forget individuation, Pauli. Tell him they don't dare take him back; he'll poison all the groups,*" Alicia advised.

"You've *individuated*, that's what. You and Aesc, if he's still alive. Do you know what your genefather, as you call him, did with contaminated subjects?"

"My life or death doesn't matter," he mumbled.

"More chatter from your tapes? If you don't care, then why're you trying so hard to get to your ship?" Then revelation hit her. "Or is it Freki you're dreaming of? Look at what thinks it's human now—a cyborg clone!"

Thorn banged a fist down on the console. "Damn you, woman. Life-giver or not, if you don't shut up, I'll gag you!"

Rafe's voice broke in. "*Lohr what, Dave? Check the blasters . . . oh shit! Some security. Pauli, be careful. Lohr's managed to steal a weapon, and he's overheard . . . and heading straight for the comms.*"

Damn. She'd have to push Thorn even harder. But as she started to move toward him, the comm went live.

"Thorn . . . Thorn . . . can you hear me? I got a fix on your distress beacon. I tell you, he's alive. I'd have felt it if he died, you know I would. Please let me try to raise him . . ."

"Aesc . . ." Thorn's voice was hoarse with relief and longing. "Aesc, I'm here . . . at . . . wait, here are the coordinates." Again came the flurry of skilled fingers on the keyboards. "You were wrong!" he flung at Pauli.

It was only a matter of seconds, perhaps, before he realized that the comms had been tampered with. *Get over here!* she prayed silently, then shuddered to think that Lohr just might.

A different voice filtered through Aesc's pleas for contact.

"Told you . . . Halgerd AA's broken. The last pilot died, and the liaison didn't feel it. I think his implant's deranged. With respect, sir, I think he's too unstable to be worth keeping."

"Look at that ship, Thorn," Pauli whispered. "Listen to them; but look at the damage reports too."

"Thorn!" his groupmate's voice faded.

"Damage control!" Shouts of rage, distress, and fear blurred together, muffling the thud as Thorn's last brother fell forward onto his duty station. Then pure white flooded the screen, fading into a red-tinged haze. When it died, the screen was blank, the star system barren of ships.

Thorn Halgerd gagged and collapsed, but only for an instant. When he turned around, grief and anger battled in his pale eyes.

"He's dead."

"But you're not. Doesn't that prove what I said, Thorn? You're not just one of six anymore. You're unique. Alone!"

"Aesc—" it was a mournful whisper. Then Thorn tensed again and glanced back at the comm. "You rigged it—"

"We didn't dare let you contact the ship, Thorn. You trust Dr. Pryor, don't you? She said—"

"Lohr got away from us. He got a head start on Rafe and the others too."

Not now, for the love of God, Pauli raved silently. Not now, when I've almost got him. And if someone's going to shoot him, please, not Lohr, not after all we've done to turn him around too.

"Dr. Pryor explained about clone-groups and individuation to me, Thorn. I'm a pilot too . . . and it's not real easy for people like us to understand the medics, is it?" Pauli let her voice go gentle and warm, almost the way she spoke to her son. "Aesc never really had a chance, Thorn. I'm sorry. Really, I am. But don't you think he'd want you to live? You've got a chance now to be alive, not a fighting machine kept in a stass tank until they need you to die for them. You can *be* Thorn Halgerd, not one of six identical faces, tapes, and bodies; unique, valued for yourself alone. My God, man, don't you want it?"

"You're doing just fine, Pauli. I think he's ready to break."

Thorn Halgerd whimpered and sank into the chair by the comms.

"What you're feeling is grief, honest, human grief. Not something filtered through an implant. That's gone forever. But it was never all that you felt for Aesc."

Static from the comm crackled in the tiny dome. Thorn's shoulders heaved. Pauli could hear his strangled sobs. She took a deep breath to steady her nerves, then moved forward, her hand out, ready to lay it on his shoulder, to comfort and bring him back to the infirmary where Pryor could tend him and complete the change—

The door slid aside, and Lohr darted in, a blaster incongruously large and ugly in his thin hand. Pauli slapped the light panels to full strength. The semidarkness was too much like the burrows Lohr would never wholly forget. His eyes were all pupil, and he crouched as if he were hunting. Though he flinched instantly back at the bright lights, he didn't drop his weapon.

He blinked fiercely, but then his eyes adjusted, and Pauli saw in them all the fear and hatred of the feral child they had rescued, had tried to heal . . . would have healed already, if the man who slouched sobbing across the comms hadn't broken his fragile peace.

"Lohr," she said. "Please. Not you. Put the blaster away."

He glanced at her in dismay, then waved the weapon at Thorn Halgerd again, his dark, clever face intent on his prey. Yellow light shivered on the blaster's thick muzzle.

"I'm sorry, Captain. But when I heard he'd been at Wolf IV . . . I have to do this!" his voice scaled up. "For those of us who made it through the fire as well as the ones who died." He sobbed once, but then his voice cooled. "Get up, killer. Wolf IV was my home. Your boys used it as a target range for meteorites. And after you'd had your fun, you came in with lasers. Some of us lasted for months. But you're not going to. You ought to thank me for letting you die fast."

"Here's one way out," Halgerd muttered to himself. He sounded relieved.

Gauging Lohr's grip on the blaster, Pauli decided she probably couldn't deflect his aim without frying herself, but she started moving forward anyhow. *Why am I risking my life?* she asked herself. *Certainly not for Halgerd.*

No, not for Halgerd. For Lohr, who had protected and foraged for his little sister on Wolf IV when he might have left her to die. For a boy who had learned love and decency from the settlers, and who, despite his protests, was still one of the "littlests" whom they must try to preserve from the consequences of destroying the Cynthians. Genocides they might be, but their lives would not be wholly evil if they could remind such children that law and humanity still existed.

Pauli thumbed the transmitter wired to her collar.

"The damned fool's here, friends. I'm going to try to talk him out of killing our guest."

She turned to Lohr. "You're good enough at eavesdropping to know what we did to the Cynthians, and what we paid for it. Do you have to add to our burden by being no better than the rest of us . . . no better than *he*?"

Lohr's face twisted, but his hand never shook.

"All we want, Lohr, all we ever wanted was a place where you kids could be safe. Halgerd's given up, now, Lohr. You can kill him. But all of the littlests will learn about it, and they'll know that we failed to protect you from turning animal on us. Are you really going to steal their comfort from them? After they thought they were safe?"

Lohr's hand began to shake, and his face twisted.

Pauli's earplug whispered.

"Don't come in," she warned. Lohr was so unstable now he might fire on friends.

Thorn Halgerd looked over at her. "You stay out of range," he said. His voice was very bleak but resolved. "I accept execution."

"Lohr's just a boy. He's not going to execute anyone," Pauli snapped. Her nerves were jangling from this hateful mental warfare; and her breasts ached, a sure sign that Serge must be crying to be fed. "Lohr! You hand over that blaster!"

She was walking toward it, reaching for it, she almost had it . . .

"Stobor!" Shouts rang simultaneously outside the dome and in her earplug.

Pauli threw herself at the equipment.

"Not a life-giver!" she heard Thorn shout, and a hard shoulder hit her somewhere around the hips, sending her sprawling. Even as ozone stank in the dome, she punched up the field generator. At least she could stop any more stobor from getting through.

"Someone get ben Yehuda. His cub . . . down by the river . . . surrounded by them—"

Pauli started to crawl on knees and elbows toward the door. Even her teeth ached. Lohr was trembling violently, eyes on the blaster he had fired. It was only by the merest luck he hadn't wiped out Pauli, the equipment, or Halgerd, who levered himself up and balanced unsteadily, favoring his left leg, the one that had taken the burn that might have hit Pauli.

"Give me that thing!" Halgerd snarled. As light shrieked out again to score the dome's tough wall, his hand whipped out and slashed down across Lohr's wrist. He caught up the weapon, then stumbled forward, half running, half limping out of the dome at a speed amazing in anyone, let alone a man with a burned leg. Using Lohr as a prop, Pauli dragged herself to her feet.

"He break that wrist for you?"

"No, ma'am." After scaring the hell out of all of them, damned near frying her, and coming close to ruining irreplaceable equipment, now here he was, back to acting like one of the littlests again.

"Luckier than you deserve. He must not have been trying. Come on!"

Pauli started toward the perimeters, but walked straight into Pryor's outstretched arms. Lohr darted past them both toward the river.

"And where do you think you're going?" she asked.

"Fields. Halgerd's got the blaster now, but Lohr marked him first. I have to get there."

She noticed that Pryor's face sported a fine bruise; and she was still a little unsteady on her feet. "Want to try to stop me, Alicia, or do you want me to help you get there too?"

"You've got yourself a deal, Pauli. Let's move it!"

Ari had found himself a rock to climb on, and he was trying to beat off the stobor from there. He had a stunner, true enough; but its beam flickered, a sign its charge was all but dead. Stobor swarmed out of the river, which ruled out that means of escape for him.

The wrong kid had a weapon! Rafe thought, enraged. Here Lohr was, playing mad blasterman, while Ari, who could use a blaster to fight off stobor, and was as stable as they came, was making do with a stunner, if it held out, and a stick, if it didn't. Rafe headed toward the river too, alert for stobor himself. Around him, lances of fire flared out as people killed stobor. The air was foul with burning ground cover and charred eat . . . no, there were no eaters, anymore.

Rafe stopped beside three people who had their arms around David ben Yehuda.

"Let me through!" Dave screamed. His face ran with sweat and tears.

The beam from Ari's stunner faltered, then died altogether, leaving him in the dark. "All he's got now is a shovel!" Dave cried hoarsely. Rafe hefted his blaster. It wasn't weighted for throwing. He'd need to get in closer.

"Stay back, Dave," Rafe warned. "I'm going to try to throw the boy a blaster. That'll let him defend himself while we shoot through to him. He's a tough kid; we'll get him out."

Then they jerked their heads around as an accented voice shouted, "Move to the left, boy. I'm coming!"

Halgerd ran as if he outraced ten devils, one of which had already burned a chunk from his left leg, past the front line of stobor fighters, and toward the rock which the first wave of stobor were now beginning to surmount.

"Hold your fire!" screamed Rafe as Halgerd headed directly for the stobor. One good shock should warn him, he thought, though with that bad leg . . .

One shock was all it took. Halgerd grunted with surprise and pain, drew his legs under him, and leapt, a wide, shallow leap that brought him onto Ari's rock, where he flung one arm about the boy to steady himself, and began firing steadily, systematically at the creatures.

Pauli ran up beside Rafe, panting for breath. She braced herself against his shoulder and fired. Her aim was true.

Rafe pointed. Pauli swallowed. "Lohr marked him."

"He needs our help," Rafe said.

"He's got it."

Ahead of them, Halgerd wavered visibly, recovered, and kept on firing. "I think he's weakening," Pauli said. "How long can he hold out, after all he's been through? If he falls now, though, we stand to lose them both—"

"Here," Halgerd roared. "*Catch!*"

Snatching the stocky Ari in one arm, Thorn Halgerd flung him over the line of blaster fire. The boy landed on top of Rafe, and they both went down. Then Halgerd fell, his arms and legs thrashing wildly half-in, half-out of the water that churned with stobor. Then he lay still.

There had to be at least six stobor there, Rafe thought with a groan.

Lohr scooped up his blaster and started burning a path to the river. He was firing methodically and he pressed forward as quickly as he could.

He made it to the shore, had pulled Halgerd from the murky water, then flung himself down, head on the man's chest. "No!" the boy said. "No more deaders. Not if I can help it!"

He thumped the man's chest, listened again, and swore. He tilted Halgerd's head back to clear the air passage, meticulously adjusted his hands over the man's sternum, and began to press down rhythmically. His lips moved as he counted.

"Do you believe that?" Rafe asked as Alicia Pryor staggered to Lohr's side. Rafe followed her, gulping back his tears. Only as the adults took over resuscitation did the boy let himself collapse.

"I think we've turned two lives around tonight," Pauli said happily. She mopped at her eyes, and Rafe started to put an arm about her, but she coughed and swore that the smoke was choking her.

"Ari's fine. And he . . . Thorn's going to make it," Pryor announced. "Don't ask me how they augmented his circulatory system, but it's working."

"He's trying to talk," three people spoke at once.

Though Pryor began to hush him, Thorn Halgerd struggled onto one elbow, his eyes searching out Lohr. He licked his lips, then tried to speak again.

"Why?"

Pauli shoved Lohr forward to face the man. "Answer him, dammit!"

"I . . . Ari's my friend," he said, eyes downcast, one foot scuffing in the dirt. "Besides, when we first got here, well, my little sister limps 'cause there were these things, these eaters. They're all dead now, and they call it, call it genocide because the eaters grew up to be smart. To fly. It was wrong to kill them, but they did it to give us kids a chance to grow up straight. You . . . I know you did a wrong thing too, but you gave Ari a chance. Ari would have died!" Then his face contorted, and he twisted away, burrowing against David ben Yehuda's side.

"Don' . . . don't understan' . . ."

"You will," Alicia Pryor told him. "I promise that you will." Thorn's eyes filled with tears and the question he was too weak to ask.

"Why? Let's just say that I knew your father a long time ago." She smiled, and this time Halgerd smiled back. Then a spray hypo blanked the pain of his burnt leg, and sent him into sleep.

" 'To sleep, perchance to dream?' " Pauli heard the medical officer muse. "God, I hope not."

When Thorn Halgerd's leg healed, he announced that he planned to climb to the lost Cynthians' caves and live there by himself.

"If the caves housed your civilians, they'll do fine for

me," he'd told Pauli, Rafe, and Alicia, who had gathered to see him off. "In fact, they'll do better for me than for your people. I don't see the ghosts in them that you do." Thorn's nostrils flared as if he relished the air. The weather was cold for spring, and the sky shone the color of amber in which tiny plumes were scattered. His eyes scanned the horizon appreciatively, then went dark. "I have enough ghosts of my own."

"I wish you'd reconsider," Rafe said.

"You'd trust me? All of you? Even the civilians?"

"Lohr does. And we're all alone here," said Pauli. "You more so than most. If the scramble we watched is any indication, your Republic has all it can do fighting itself without checking out every one of the No Man's Worlds for settlements like ours."

How was her own side doing? It was pointless to ask. Now her "own side" was the humans on Cynthia. All of them.

"Look," said ben Yehuda. "Call this a test to destruction. You don't destroy easy. In fact, I'd say you passed a test that your . . . father didn't. You're definitely an improvement on the original."

Pryor stepped forward. "I have to agree with that. And you know," she said very softly. "We could probably turn around that sterility of yours."

Thorn froze. "Is that why you saved me . . . for the Halgerd genes?" At the look of sorrow on her face, his own face twisted, that eerie resemblance flickering between them again. Pryor shook her head.

Pauli opened her mouth to try, one last time, to persuade him to remain in the settlement.

"Let it be," he said, his voice gentle, almost wistful. "I have to get away. Look, let me try to explain. You say that everyone's alone. Well, I never was before. All my life, there have been voices inside my head. Others just like me. Then they were gone, and I was just one piece of a lost whole. That's not what you call alone. That's something else.

"I almost died of it. You saw. Sometimes I wish I still

could. Now, though, you tell me I'm unique, my own self, but it all still feels like having a brother killed inside my head. So I have to find out who 'myself' is; and I want to do it without a thousand voices clamoring at me.

"Besides, if I'm ever to live among you, I need to see those caves, to learn what price you paid to go on living. After all, I already know what price I—and my father—paid."

"And when you've learned what you have to?" Pryor asked.

He smiled at her. "Why then, I'll come back down, if you'll all still accept me. To take up the future you offered to an old friend's son." There was no irony in those words, Pauli thought. Already, Thorn was drawing comfort from the generous illusion of a past that Pryor had helped him create. Pauli remembered the poem she had quoted to herself the night Thorn reached Cynthia. "*Consequently I rejoice, having to construct something upon which to rejoice.*" Thorn would construct it quickly and well.

"You know," Pryor compelled herself into a shaky laugh, "you take after your father? You're just as stubborn."

Thorn shouldered the pack containing the food, the heatcube, the comm, and the few other things he had consented to accept from them, and started toward the foothills.

"Wait!" From around the curve of the nearest dome raced Lohr, a long bundle of struts and gleaming fabric bumping against his shoulder. His wings.

He came to a sliding stop and offered them to Halgerd. "They're a loan, see? You're a pilot; you'll know how to use them. So when you want to, you can come back down easier."

Thorn stared at the wings resting lightly on his hands. Gently he closed fingers around them. "I'll bring them back," he promised.

He turned. Without looking back, he walked toward the foothills, favoring his burnt leg, but only a little.

Silently they watched until all they could see was the sun glinting off his fair hair, and the metal of the wings he bore.

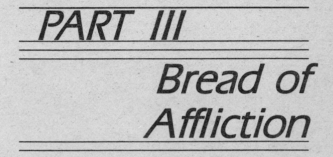

PART III

Bread of Affliction

Lo, this is the bread of affliction . . .
—Passover Ritual

As the wind sent the snow dancing in the counterpoint of light and shadow cast by two moons, Pauli paced, waiting for Alicia Pryor to emerge from the dome that served the settlers as a medical center.

Scared, by God, of a feast. I must be losing my grip, she berated herself. She stamped her feet and the glittering snow crunched underfoot . . . *like scales . . . Rafe and I climbed up to the caves where the moths laired, and their scales lay scattered everywhere until we stole enough to kill them.*

For an instant, the crisp snow and the white cloud of Pauli's breath reeked with the pheromones of moths, aroused for their mating dances in the thermals of the mountain passes.

Stop calling them moths, she corrected herself. *They were Cynthians. Moth,* Beneatha Angelou informed anyone who would listen, was a racist term. If you called the Cynthian natives moths, you created an excuse to think of them as less than human: bugs to be swatted out of the way as Pauli had ordered. But her order had wiped out intelligent creatures—*humans* in all but physical shape —and must not be softened by terms more suitable to pest control.

Wiped out. Had all the Cynthians been wiped out? One night Rafe had waked laughing from a dream of Cynthians swooping down from cliffs by a turbulent ocean. What about the other continents? he had asked. What if somewhere on this world (which they might never explore fully) Cynthians still flew, still built their pallid towers along the planet's magnetic lines, and still fled from their hideous young?

It was still genocide, Beneatha had declared when the subject of Rafe's dream came up. Just the attempt, just the thought, was enough to brand them: and they had succeeded too well as it was. *If that's how she feels, why invite me to this feast of hers?*

Pauli paced back and forth. Where *was* Pryor? Her feet were damp, damp on the frozen earth. *Not earth*, she reminded herself. *Earth is long lost to us; this is just soil.*

Whatever you called it, however much you escaped being Earthbound in speech and heritage, the ground was cold. Stupid field boots should have been proof against winter snows but they weren't. One of the techs was working on a way of replacing boots when their service issue wore out. Now that was a nice, satisfying task: you mended soles, stitched them, kept heels level, and considered the ways of making a better boot. You could do far worse on Cynthia than be a cordwainer.

For example, you could be a . . . a leader. Then you would have no chance to retreat to the comfort of physical work. Your task would be to make the decisions no one else wanted to make, to face—and keep on facing—issues those who followed you would have probably rather forgotten. Your tools were logistics, psychology, nerve, and will. Your products were the decisions you made, and had to live with, you and those you protected.

Boots would have been far easier. If you made them wrong, the most it would cost you was a blister.

"Waiting long?" came Alicia Pryor's voice, almost as clear as the air itself.

Pauli grunted. "What was it?"

"Tonsils," said the physician. "With all the screaming that the littlests have been doing, I'm not surprised. Sorry, though, to have kept you outside. I didn't want to resterilize."

Tonsils. No wonder, given all the children's screaming over what had occupied their attention for the past week: Beneatha's invitation to re-create Kwanzaa, a holiday honoring Earth traditions that she and her family had carried with them on every planet they'd touched. For the past week, 'Cilla had run about, her pale hands splotched with green, black, and red, while Lohr had made life hideous trying to force songs from a crude flute. Washington had made a total pest of himself by rehearsing his friends in Kiswahili; privately, Pauli thought that if he asked *habiri ganu*—"what's happening"—one more time, she might show him what was happening in no uncertain way.

But her irritations were not important. What was important was the children's delight in every facet of the holiday: its history, the seven symbols laid out on the *mkeka*, or mats ("they should be of cornhusks, but Kwanzaa calls for *kuumba* or creativity, so we'll improvise"), the whittling of a seven-branched *kinara* that had made David ben Yehuda stifle a smile, a frenzy of crafting, painting, and sewing of decorations and gifts.

Then there were the names. Many of the children, especially those of black ancestry, had chosen new names to mark Kwanzaa; so the Jamies, the Annes, the Johns, and the other names that the refugees had either remembered or been given once the relief squads had found them had given way to Toussaint, Mahairi, or Samory: "freedom names," Beneatha called them. 'Cilla had experimented with calling herself Kizzie, but "my name is Lohr," her brother had said; and that was that.

"Cold," muttered Pryor. "Hell with resterilizing; I shouldn't have left you standing out there." She stamped and breathed on too-thin fingers. The face she turned toward Pauli was tired, its meager flesh clinging too closely to the fine bones beneath. Violet circles underlay the physician's eyes, pale blue, but sparkling in the doubled moonlight.

Her anti-agathics were fading. The thought had occurred to her several times as the winter wore on. Anti-agathics had been plentiful enough for Pryor in her past career as a privileged researcher, but Cynthia colony had few such luxuries. Fear clutched at Pauli's belly until the odors of hot food, wafting toward her over the clear air, made it clench with hunger too. *How can I persuade her to divert enough resources to try synthesizing them? We can't risk losing her.*

Pryor walked more briskly toward the dome where yellowish lights shone and from which came laughter and singing. "Where's Rafe?"

Pauli grimaced. "Minding Serge. The *karamu*—that's the feast on the seventh day of this holiday—lasts all night; and he refuses to let me spell him."

Actually what Rafe had said was a lot closer to "You can't hide behind me all the time, Pauli love. You'll go, and—who knows?—you might enjoy it. Or are you scared?"

"You know it," Pauli had said. *A firefight would be easier. I know about firefights—or I did once.* Beneatha had fought her and Rafe every step along the way Cynthia colony had gone to insure its own survival. And now Beneatha was their hostess. It made for a certain amount of discomfort.

Pryor sniffed appreciatively at the dancing snow and, underlying the tang of the snow, the half-frozen river, and the smells of human habitation and production, the food that Beneatha and many of the botany/agronomy types had spent days preparing from their first harvest on Cynthia. If the eager clamor of the littlests . . . well, if they didn't help much, at least they no longer pilfered and got in the way.

It was good to see the children insisting on their own lives, their own joys. It was likely to be a good feast. The only problem was, that the woman hosting it had consistently opposed every one of Pauli's decisions: damned ambiguous hospitality.

She must have said that aloud, because Dr. Pryor laughed dryly.

"I don't think so," she said. "You know, I once heard a proverb that came—or so they told me—from Africa, the part of Earth that Beneatha's ancestors must once have lived in. 'Come into my home; sit at my table; then you will know me.'" She shrugged, and they walked in silence, their worn boots squeaking on the dry snow, which glistened like blue and green gems or scales from the moons and the sodium lamps that the life-science techs had set up about the domes they had appropriated.

Pauli sensed that the older woman was waiting for her to speak, and she determined to outwait her. Finally Pryor chuckled dryly. "Good for you, Pauli!" Then her voice turned almost hesitant. "Have you heard anything from Thorn?"

Pauli tilted her head up at the physician. "I thought that you'd be the one to hear from him." An incongruous bond linked them: aging aristocrat and renegade fighter cloned from cells of a man who had been Pryor's lover in a life no one on Cynthia could comprehend.

"I've tried," Pryor admitted. Her voice all but shook. "Can't raise him. Either the snowstorms block reception, or . . ." She shuddered.

Pauli stopped and looked at the woman. *He may be sick, or he might have fallen, be lying there now, alone. He grew up on ships: what can he know of planets and their winters?* No wonder Alicia's eyes were shadowed. "After this Kwanzaa business is over," she promised, "perhaps someone can go after him."

Go up into the hills, seek out the lair of the dead Cynthians to which the clone had exiled himself to assure themselves that a pilot who had helped devastate the homeworlds of a hundred children here hadn't broken his stiff neck? Right. But Pryor's face relaxed, losing lines and ten years in the process; and Pauli was glad of her words. Wasn't gift-giving connected with this holiday of Beneatha's? Then her promise was a small enough gift to the physician.

"They're here!" came a joyous cry from the dome at the end of the row. Three children erupted past the doors as they irised, and half ran, half slid in the packed snow toward them, grabbing hands, dragging them into a splendor of warmth and fragrances that made Pauli blink away tears.

Posters boldly drawn in red, black, and green hung from the drab walls like tapestries, while 'Cilla sat in a corner near the one empty wall space, painting frantically away at the poster that would fill it. She frowned, her tongue sticking out in concentration, her hands and face smeared with red and green as usual. Seeing Pauli, though, she leapt up with a grin, waving the poster to dry it.

Golden hooked crosses ("They're *ankhs*, and they mean everlasting life! Did you know that?") gleamed against the darkness outside. One table was heaped with the *zawadi*, or gifts, several others with food.

"Our first harvest from the fields, not just hydro," gestured a tech at heaping dishes of spiced yams and squashes, gourds and grains, mounds of rice glistening the same color as the ankhs, platters of fish and fowl (vat-cultured or not, they smelled wonderful), and huge, roughly woven baskets of bread. Pauli blinked again and set a name to him: Ramon Aquino, an ally of Beneatha's and, Pryor's subtle wink reminded her, her very constant companion these days.

Before them lay the woven mat, with its arrayed symbols: the candleholder with its red, black, and green candles still unlit; a sort of loving cup as roughly carved as the candleholder, fruits and vegetables, a gift or two, and rows of corn.

"*Habiri ganu?*" Washington cried at Pauli. Better schooled than she, Alicia Pryor replied promptly. "*Imani!* Faith, trust in our people, our parents, our teachers, and our leaders. Did I get it right, Beneatha?"

The xenobotanist turned from her careful arrangement of the corn ears.

"I expected *you* to listen," she said. "Now, about the *vibunzi*, the ears of corn: traditionally, each child in a family has an ear of corn; so that's one for little Serge, right, Captain?"

Beneatha handed Pauli the ear of corn with its dried husk and tassel, genetically engineered to be immune to the diseases of half a hundred worlds, its kernels shining red, green, and black, as if offering her a challenge. Pauli set it on the mat and sat back on her heels.

"And you, Doctor? Every household should have at least one ear in honor of the promise of children. Unless—do you have any children back . . ."

Pryor shut her eyes so quickly that Pauli almost imagined away the spasm of pain that twisted the fine, pale features. "Children?" she asked. "I have hundred of them. Most of them are here."

But there was another, outcast and cold in the Cynthians' caves. Pryor chose one ear, then another, and laid them down tenderly.

"But look at you!" she complimented Beneatha. Laying aside the usual drab bulk and dirt stains of field clothing, the xenobotanist had transformed herself. This evening she wore a tunic and overshawl richly patterned in red and black. Tiny braids looped beneath an intricately tied turban that set off her dark, fierce face. Almost all her friends and coworkers had dressed similarly: some in long dresses or robes, others in pullover tunics and loose trousers. Even in the least worn of her coveralls, Pauli felt drab and insignificant.

"Look how plain they are! Shall we decorate them too?" asked Ramon to a shriek of approval from the children.

Seconds later, Pauli faced a barrage of cloth, which two girls hung over her shoulders and twisted about her cropped hair. She saw Pryor transformed into some sort of tribal priestess—"too pale for a priestess!" cried the girl who now called herself Mahairi, then sat back patiently as another girl tucked the ends of Pauli's headscarf about and in to make a turban like Beneatha's. To Pauli's surprise, she felt herself laughing.

"Let's start the feast!" cried Washington, and led the children in bringing the dishes to the central *mkeka*, around which the invited guests sat or knelt.

"'Cilla!" cried Beneatha, "and who else? Who wants to light the candles?"

"I used to!" Ayelet cried. "Way back, before we left Ararat even—"

"These aren't the same," her brother interrupted, but

ben Yehuda raised a hand, silencing him. As the candles flickered to life, Dave's lips moved silently. Then Beneatha bent down and took up the ceremonial cup.

"Back on Earth, Maulana Karenga created Kwanzaa to help us remember our Motherland—and our struggles," for a moment her gaze was hot and intense on Pauli's face. "But it's also a time to celebrate our harvests, our community, and our children." Light flickered from the purplish contents of the cup and threw shimmering highlights on her face. "Dr. Pryor was right, you know. All of you children here, you should know by now that you *are* our children, just as surely as if we'd given birth to you."

"All of us at once?" cried Lohr, and the children laughed.

"Even you, bigmouth," 'Cilla hissed, pulling him back down beside her.

"It used to be that a *mzee*, a wise man or woman, would conduct this," Beneatha said. "I'm not very good at fancy speaking, so I'll be brief. We are a community here, and I asked you to come tonight to celebrate our harvests. First, the harvest of healthy children; second, the food you see all about you."

She raised the cup to her lips, drank, and passed it about the circle to cries of *"Harambee!"* and hands thrust up in salute as Pryor muttered something about communal cups spreading communal colds, then drank as joyously as everyone else.

To Pauli's horror, Beneatha was gesturing for attention. "It's also customary to introduce any elders or distinguished guests, like Dr. Pryor and Captain Yeager" —damn, would they stop calling her that! She hadn't prepared a thing to say—"before we ask for entertainment."

The xenobotanist grinned at her. *Don't worry, I won't force you to sing,* the grin said. Mischievous it might be, but it was kind. Pauli shook her head, and the woman beckoned to the first of many of the littlests lined up to perform.

'Cilla, with a picture for every guest. A chorus of

children; Washington and Samory turning cartwheels as Lohr played a new, carefully-carved flute. Pauli found herself laughing and clapping until Beneatha rose again.

"Now, we should have the remembrances of a man, a woman, and a child."

Must I speak? Pauli asked herself. *What can I say to these people?*

"Toussaint, will you speak?"

The boy rose like the black candle in the *kinara*, thin, straight, and shining. Except for the scar down one cheek, you couldn't tell him from a sheltered child from an inner system world. "I was hungry and afraid. Other children called me Scarface, when there was anyone else around at all, that is. Now I am not afraid—but I'm hungry!" he appealed to the adults, who laughed and promised "in a moment."

"But now I'm not Scarface anymore; I'm Toussaint, and I want you all to call me that. And this is my home."

"Will you speak, David?" asked Beneatha, and her dark eyes were unreadable.

"This is not my holiday, but yours," ben Yehuda said. "But both of them commemorate freedom and a long fight." He glanced down lovingly at the *kinara* with its brave candles: one black, three red, and three green. "What can I say, but that I'm glad to have been kept alive, sustained, and permitted to celebrate this joyous festival. May this be the first of many Kwanzaas we can share, all of us!"

Beneatha's eyes flicked to Pauli. "You're our guest, tonight, so I'll spare you a second time, Captain. I remember . . . sometimes it seems to me that I remember too much: every insult, every enemy, every anger, every sorrow. Tonight, with all of us gathered around for a feast, I hope that I will remember the good things too. Like this moment, with all of us in agreement for once."

"*Harambee!*" Pauli muttered, more loudly than she had planned. All around the room, people laughed, and laughed louder when she flushed and tried to apologize. She couldn't deny that Beneatha's remembering "the good things" would make her own life much easier.

She had little time for embarrassment, for the food was being passed. She heaped her plate with corn, with the candied yams and squashes, and fish. A basket of flat breads came her way, and she passed it on. "I can't eat all this!" she protested as she handed it back to Ramon, who promptly crunched his third crisp piece between white teeth, and handed the basket to Ari.

"You know what this looks like?" he asked his sister, who nodded. "Like Ararat, before we left. Only we had it in the spring." She grimaced, then ate the squash her father ladled onto her plate.

"Try the chicken, Pauli," Beneatha dropped down beside her. "It's got hot sauce on it, though." *That was two surprises. Beneatha had used her name, and had warned her about the spices.* The dish was hot enough to make her sweat, but delicious too. "You might have told me to bring something," Pauli complained.

"Next year." Her callused fingers toying with the leather ankh that hung around her neck, Beneatha glanced around the room and smiled broadly. "You know, I meant what I said."

Pauli nodded. "I know. I wish . . ." Her own memories, not just of actions but of nights spent mourning them, condemning them, rose up, and she shook her head. *If only we had had time to study the world before we landed! Perhaps we could have settled somewhere else . . . done something else . . .*

"It's rough on you, I know," Beneatha said. "I haven't made it any easier. No, I'm not going to apologize. I still think you were wrong. But what's done is done; and now we have to get on with things. Just believe me: I wouldn't want your job." She shook her head, firmed her lips as if to say "that's all," then rose and replenished the baskets of bread and vegetables.

What do you know? Pauli thought to herself. *A loyal opposition.* Rafe and Alicia had been right all along. *Not too dumb, are you, Yeager? In a century or so, you may have puzzled out this business of leadership.*

Long before the food stopped being passed, Pauli sat

back, and watched the others: 'Cilla limping over to sit beside her and hand Pauli a husk doll for the baby who was too young for such a late night; Lohr intent on his new wooden flute; Toussaint gnawing on a bone; Mahairi carefully refilling cups; Ari passing gifts to the younger children; Ramon leaning against a wall, a child asleep in his lap. Two women rose and stretched, one massaging the small of her back in a way Pauli remembered well. Their brightly patterned robes accented the graceful mounds of their bellies.

We're going to make it here, she told herself. *Just let it work out, that's all, so that there are still Cynthians on this world.* And what if moths, no, winged Cynthians . . . still flourished somewhere on the other continents. *Do you think that would absolve you, Pauli? Even if there were, if they were a danger* . . . she didn't want to think of it.

Resolutely she stared into the candle flames for what seemed like hours of feast, dancing, and songs. The colony was a going concern now. Even Beneatha had come around. She had been a fool to be afraid. She suppressed a yawn as much of relief as of satiation. Perhaps she could make her excuses and slip out to allow Rafe to have a turn at the feast. It wasn't right that he had no share in it beyond the wrapped parcels already set out for her to take for him.

Pryor glanced over at them too, then at a window where a clouded night sky shone purple and black. There were no such parcels, no such memories for Thorn—not yet, perhaps not ever.

Pauli caught her eye. "Remember how strong he is," she spoke without sound, an old trick of the service.

Resolutely Pryor smiled and turned her attention back to the children.

The sky was paling toward a snowy dawn; the party winding down into sleepy jokes and companionable huddles that made Pauli wish even more that Rafe had come with her, when Beneatha rose from her comfortable cushion by Ramon Aquino's side and again filled up the ceremonial cup for a *tambiko,* or libation.

"It's almost dawn," said Beneatha. "Pretty soon, we should all get up and go to work"—she grinned as moans rose from about the room—"or to sleep, whichever you can get away with. Before you go, there's one last part of the *karamu,* a farewell. I remember the first one I ever heard."

She shut her eyes, drawing the words out of memory: "Strive for discipline, dedication, and achievement in all that you do. Dare struggle and sacrifice, and gain the strength that comes from this. Build where you are, and dare leave a legacy that will last as long as the sun—"

"Oh God, I'm sick!" Ramon cried out. He rose so quickly that the child who had been drowsing in his lap scarcely had time to throw out his arms and save himself from a nasty fall.

"Dizzy!" he muttered. "So sick!" He was sweating profusely, and kept one hand pressed to his belly, kneading it almost the way that the pregnant woman had kneaded her back. "Sorry," he ducked his head at Beneatha, standing with the cup forgotten in her hands. "So sorry . . ."

He stumbled out into the night. Beneatha stood chagrined, the fine words of her speech forgotten.

"What was in that cup?" asked Pryor. "I didn't think he drank that much." Already she was rising, untwisting herself from the bright fabrics in which the children had swathed her, reaching for her heavy coat.

"Fruit juice," said Beneatha. "Ramon doesn't drink alcohol, anyhow. Maybe he has a virus and I ought to—"

From outside came a scream of pain and panic, and the cup dropped from her hand. Dark fruit juice spattered over the heaps of leftover food, soaking the bread, quenching out the candles and staining the mats as Aquino's full-throated bellow shattered what was left of the mood of the feast. Pauli's hand reached instinctively for the sidearm she'd politely left at home. All about her, children crouched, their eyes too bright, their hands seeking anything that might serve to protect them. Somewhere, horribly, one of them growled.

"Get away! I didn't want to kill you. I'm not going with you. Help me! There's a moth here, with black wings, and it's come to fly me down to hell!"

CHAPTER

16

"Someone get my assistants! Wake them up!" Alicia Pryor shouted. She had scrambled into her jacket as the door began to open. She set her shoulder to it and forced her way out into the night.

"Ramon!" she cried. *Drunk,* she had thought when Aquino first staggered to his feet. But Aquino didn't drink, Beneatha had said. The physician slipped on ice and went to her hands and one knee. It hurt to lever herself up; past sixty-five, your joints got stiff; and it didn't look like implants or more anti-agathics were anywhere in her future. Her breath panted after her in white streamers, and the cold slashed at her throat.

She wished for a hat. You lost at least half your body heat from your head; and she had to stay well now, she had to. She shuddered, but not from cold. If Ramon wasn't drunk, then her diagnoses were terrifyingly limited. He might have seizures, in which case, he wouldn't have qualified for the service. That left her two logical alternatives: food poisoning, or some virus that created a fever high enough to cause hallucinations.

And everyone in that dome had been exposed. Pryor swore in at least four languages and stopped long enough to snap some orders at the people who had trailed after her. "Get Rafe!" she ordered one of the children. Assume there was an epidemic—the stomach-gripping, icy fear every colonist faced and tried to forget. Her own staff would be on constant call trying to contain it. There would be little time for the type of investigation that would have to be done. *Damn all outpost medicine! what*

I'd give for the Santayana datanets! she thought. Since *she* had been exposed, someone else would have to know everything that she learned: Rafe was the likeliest candidate.

The child stood, almost blanking in terror. *These are our harvest too.* Pryor forced herself to stop, to speak calmly, gently, as if the girl had just been hunted from her lair on—where was Mahairi from? Didn't matter. "You trust us, don't you?" Pryor asked. "Yes, we're scared now, but we can take care of you. Listen to me. Get Rafe. Tell him to find me."

Thank God, relief flickered across the girl's face at having a task she could perform, and she ran off. *Fine. How's Rafe going to find you?* she asked herself.

Running about would only exhaust her. She forced herself to breathe regularly. What was that? When the rasp of her own breath subsided, she heard it again.

"Ramon?" she called. Not a scream this time, but whimpers and moans. She set off in the direction of the sound, amazed at how far the man had run despite cramps and nausea. She coughed, not from the cold, but from an odor that didn't belong in the night air. She sniffed cautiously. When they'd rescued some of the children, she had smelled mold, vermin, and urine; now she used that smell to track Ramon to where he lay, his knees drawn up, his fists clenched and twisting, his entire body arching as if to find relief from the cramps that twisted him.

"I've found him!" she cried, and knelt in the snow at his side. His face was pallid, despite his swarthiness, and his pupils were dilated. She laid careful fingers against his carotid pulse, and he jerked away. Pulse: very slow. His hands were freezing; and his breath came shallowly, foul with sickness and tinged with garlic. She stripped off her jacket to tuck it around the sick man: all he needed was hypothermia along with the food poisoning.

Or plague. The word insinuated itself into her subconscious, and forced a shameful tremor out of her. All the colonists had broad-spectrum immunization during basic training. But Cynthia had not—God knows—been fully surveyed; and the spectre of some new bug (terrible pun, that: ignore it, Doctor; let's have just the facts, please!) always haunted colonies, especially those as isolated as this one.

The ships could come and find only the ruins of domes, she thought. *We'd all be dead.* It had happened before.

Ramon's teeth were chattering. He glared at her, and she tried to soothe him. Before she could finish her first "there, there," he laughed hysterically, and thrust her aside, to run farther into the night. "The wings!" he shrieked. "Don't come after me, you death's-head, I didn't kill you!"

"The river!" Pryor screamed. Damn this getting old: she couldn't run fast enough to catch him. "Ramon, stay clear of the riv—"

Ice shattered beneath him, and a splash that had to be the coldest thing she had ever heard choked off his scream.

Even as Beneatha stood in the ruins of her feast, Ari ben Yehuda's eyes went wide with fear, and he lurched against his father, who flung his arms about the boy and eased him to the floor.

"I never meant . . . all I wanted . . ." Beneatha whispered.

Pauli reached up to pull off the colorful turban that laughing children had wound about her hair in what seemed like another life. Now her hair was damp with fear, and the children who had laughed as they dressed her like a puppet huddled against the walls. One of them growled. Several eyed the adults, clearly calculating whether they could scramble out the door after Dr. Pryor; Mahairi actually made it, and two more tried to follow.

"Lohr!" Pauli snapped. "Don't let the littlests run away."

The growling stopped. Lohr flung out one hand—still holding his flute—to bar the other children's flight into the cold. With gestures and whispers, he gathered them into a silent, watchful knot. 'Cilla clung to his leg, her eyes on Ari, Ayelet, and David ben Yehuda.

Pauli drew a deep breath. "Now," she said slowly, "no one's going to hurt anyone. Not on purpose, and not at all if I have anything to say about it."

One of the pregnant women (an agronomist turned social worker) suddenly whimpered and clutched her stomach in a spasm that made Pauli tremble with a guilty relief: *Serge wasn't exposed. Whatever it is, Serge is safe. For now.*

"Get all the sick ones over there," she gestured into a smaller room leading off the main one. "In the meantime I want someone to help the kids write down everything they ate last night. Everything." She forced a smile—the merest ghost of a cheery grin—at the tense youngsters. "That should take quite some time."

Their laughter was ragged, and lasted too long. A scuffle broke out behind Lohr, ending only when Lohr himself supported Toussaint to join Ari and the others. Sweat ran down over the younger boy's scar, and he wheezed for breath.

"Beneatha. Beneatha!" Pauli had practically to shout to draw the woman's attention. Stepping over the ruins of the feast, she drew the black woman's hands away from her cheeks. "We've all been exposed to something. Food poisoning, allergy, maybe something in the soil here. Do you have any ideas?"

"The food . . . I poisoned them," whispered the other woman. "Ramon . . ."

"You don't know that!" Pauli snapped.

"To think I condemned you. My own children, a second family for me, a second chance—I was so proud, and I may have—" Her voice keened upward, and her hands tensed into claws as Pauli held them.

"I meant to celebrate life!" she wailed. "Not end it!"

Sighing, Pauli tugged one hand free and slapped Beneatha sharply, then backhanded. "Someone get Rafe," she cried.

She tugged Beneatha over toward the other scientists,

who had begun to gather up the remains of the feast that could prove to be the end—not just of the people in the room, but of the entire settlement. *Dear God: who wasn't exposed?* she thought. *My chief medic, me, half the techs, my best engineer, and the kids.* The look of betrayal on Lohr's face struck her to the heart.

One man reached for the bundles of leftovers Pauli had planned to bring home, and she breathed a quick, guilty prayer of gratitude to Ramon, whose sickness had forestalled her. "Save those," she ordered. "We'll need them for samples." Her eyes went to the half-empty platters. "In fact, I want samples of every food here. Enough to test."

"Get s-s-samples of the uncooked food too," Beneatha said. That stammer was fear, not sickness, Pauli decided. No need to worry about wasting their winter stores: until someone discovered what caused Ramon, Ari, and a growing number of people to double over, dizzy and vomiting, they were all going to eat emergency rations . . . *and I just hope they last.*

All over the room people turned toward Pauli, and she stepped back until she could lean against a wall, fighting a surge of panic that threatened to bring her to her knees. A knot rose in her throat, and she could feel her pulse quicken. She took long, slow breaths. Someone here had to look calm . . . at least till Rafe got here, and then there would be two of them. She gestured, and someone turned off the light panels, allowing sunlight to slant in through the polarized skylights of the dome.

The pallid light was merciless. The bright colors of costumes, posters, and ornaments that had so delighted Pauli by candlelight and darkness seemed crumpled, tawdry, as out of place as dirty jokes at a funeral; food and juice stains gave the mats the aspect of a particularly grimy battlefield. The squashes and gourds had discolored, and their odor—

"Open the vents in here," Pauli ordered.

The dome stank: vomit, stale food, and some sort of moldy odor that was worse than the other smells combined. Glad of something to do, several techs passed out coats and blankets. Pauli went back to her study of the remaining food. If they were only lasers, or ship's plans! Not for the first time, she regretted the limits that wartime had set on her training: shiphandling, weapons, tactics—and that was that. But she had read something once about foods that could poison people if they weren't prepared properly, or from which nerve poisons could be derived. Gourds, or calabashes: something like that. She would have to remember to tell Rafe or Alicia. There was no telling what hunch or what stupid idea might provide an insight that could save their lives.

Running feet crunched in the snow, counterpointed by the gasps of a runner breathing cold air in through mouth and nose, then paused. Now Pauli heard other footsteps, heavier, measured.

"What's that?" came Rafe's voice, familiar, beloved, and as apprehensive as her own. It was all Pauli could do not to run out and fling herself at him.

"Alicia Pryor," said a low, hoarse voice she identified with difficulty as belonging to Alicia Pryor.

"When Ramon Aquino hallucinated, she went after him," Pauli said, "but he broke free and ran away . . . straight onto the river ice. It broke. Dr. Pryor tried to pull him out."

A muttered question. "No, we couldn't find the body. Must have slipped under the ice."

"Better get her inside and warmed up, then," Rafe said. "God knows, if we lose her too . . ."

Beneatha let out a low, hopeless moan, and Pauli gestured for one of her coworkers to take her aside. Rafe stomped into the dome, his eyes bright, his face flushed from the cold—and a look like death upon it.

One death already, Pauli thought. How many more would there be?

Pauli ignored the medic's headshake and swallowed another caffeine tab dry. She'd been exposed to whatever the contagion or poisoning was: she didn't dare use any stronger stimulant; nor could she afford to pass out. As the morning wore on, with its obscenely cheerful sunlight, she staggered and weaved from the research labs to the clinic.

"You don't get up until your medics say you can, Alicia!" she found herself shouting. "Now, you can either rest, or I'll have you sedated. Which will it be?"

Despite her exhaustion, she smiled to herself. Rather than use medication she might have a need for later on, Pryor would rest for several hours. "When they finish listing what everyone ate last night, I'll let you look at it," she promised the physician. "Maybe you can find some common factor."

As that day passed, and the sun rose on the next, her fear grew until she thought it could grow no worse. Now the hours passed a plateau of terror, an emotion so intense that Pauli might have collapsed from it, let alone the physical exhaustion of constant meetings, research updates, and her need to comfort those families whose children, or husbands, or wives lay shivering or screaming about moths with death's-heads, or winged skeletons until they were put under restraint.

As she darted from one meeting at which Alicia Pryor, her voice reduced to a coughing rasp, had reported that her rough and ready treatment of hallucinations seemed to work, except on those already weakened by convulsions or circulatory failure, she found herself confronted by two children, angry that the labs had appropriated research animals for tests—and that the beasts had all died.

Pauli straightened up, rubbing her back the way she'd done when she was pregnant. She forced gentleness back into a voice that had all but forgotten it. "I'm sorry about your pets," she said. "I truly am. Perhaps one day, we can get you others." As quickly as she could, she strode away toward life sciences. *Better them than you,* she thought, grateful, at least, that the children had not seen the maddened creatures shriek and thrust themselves at the researchers, their paralyzed hindquarters dragging behind them, as they tried to bite the researchers before they died.

She thought her fear could get no worse. But as the days passed, it only grew. Memories of lost colonies, lessons from the education she had cut short because of the war, pounced on her from ambush in the treacherous corridors of her memory, followed by even grislier stories of planets that had lost fifty or sixty percent of their population in the early years of their settlement. Would Cynthia colony be such a place? If, in years to come, the Alliance—or its successor—sent ships here to pick up the seedcorn they had stored, what would they find? Corpses, or madmen?

Time with her family might have comforted her. But she had not seen Serge at all; Rafe had barely time to tousle her hair and assure her that Serge and the children who had missed the *karamu* would be isolated from anyone—*themselves included*—who had been at the feast, or exposed to food from it.

Pauli strode toward the life-sciences dome, now turned into a quarantine ward which daily grew more and more crowded. She saw ben Yehuda stumble outside, and headed over to him.

"Ari?" she asked, laying a hand on her friend's arm. She was almost ashamed to meet his eyes; her son was healthy.

"Ayelet's with him now," he muttered and rubbed his hand over reddened eyes. "Have you got any kind of—thanks, Pauli." He took the foil packet of caffeine tabs, ripped one free with shaking fingers, and gulped it. "No, she hasn't come down with it. I can't understand; they ate practically the same things."

"The gourds!" Pauli cried. "Did Ayelet eat those squashes?"

Wearily Dave shook his head. "Good try, Pauli. You're thinking of breadfruits or taro, aren't you? Or the calabashes from which Earth aborigines made curare. I don't think so. They tested out normal."

A medic ran out. "Dave? You better get in here." Ben Yehuda froze, his eyes going blank in fear. Pauli grabbed his hand and held it hard.

"He's going into convulsions," the man told him.

"About five minutes ago he started to scream that the place was burning down, and we should all eject in the lifesupport pods. Maybe if you helped restrain him . . ."

"Restrain?" Dave's voice broke. "Restrain *my son* like some lunatic from the Dark Ages? Next thing, you'll tell me he's got a dybbuk in him and must be exorcised. Pauli—"

"Go on," she told him. "Ari's one of the strongest kids I've ever seen. He'll make it, Dave; he's just got to."

That day faded and her own strength faded with it. The caffeine tabs had worn off long ago. From the shivers that gripped her, Pauli realized that soon she would face only two choices: rest or the strong stimulants that, combined with whatever unknown food poison was turning healthy children and adults into raving, twitching maniacs, could be lethal. Surely everyone else in the tiny, jeopardized settlement must be equally worn out!

Rafe, at least, had had some rest. Now the tidy laboratory that had been his research domain was littered with food, cooked, raw, and whatever wrapped concentrates he snatched the time to gulp down. Beakers of something foul-looking called Ringer's solution stood next to half-emptied cups; he'd long ago passed the thoughtful stage of research and was now at the point where he muttered under his breath, clutched at his hair, and only noticed people around him if they shouted, then stood back quickly. Watching him was about the only thing that could make her smile: she dared not go near their son.

Leaving Rafe, she forced herself into a weary trot over toward the lifesupport domes. The sodium lights and the waning sun of late afternoon cast long shadows as the people who clustered outside the quarantine dome milled back and forth, unwilling to rest. Many—Pauli studied them—many had been at the disastrous feast, had been as exposed to as many of the foods under examination as she. None of the people lingering here showed any symptoms that she could notice.

Yet, why weren't they helping with the research, or

tending those who had already fallen ill? Instead, they wandered about, talking almost in a frenzy, and laughing when they did not talk. Their high-pitched, awkward laughter seemed forced, a fit accompaniment for the shadow-dance of their movements on the frozen ground.

"I have never had so much energy in my life," she heard one woman say. "I finished my research assignment, and now I am so worked up I can't sleep. Maybe when it gets dark . . ."

"Dark? That's when I like to work best. I think I'll talk with the medcrew. Perhaps they'll release me to other duties. This is pointless, this waiting around."

It all sounded very plausible; yet something was wrong. As Pauli walked past the speakers toward the dome, she found herself having to dodge long monologues delivered at high speed, or to answer questions that seemed never to have a point; she was shivering herself by the time she entered the dome.

'Cilla sat within, drawing; and Pauli's heart sank. Not this child too! She knelt beside the girl, and laid one hand on her shoulder. "Do they think you're sick too?" she asked the child. "You don't look it."

'Cilla greeted her with a dazzling smile. "I was dizzy, a few hours ago, so they made me come in here and lie down. But I had a dream, and had to get up and draw it. The colors! Ohhh, I've never seen such colors in my life! Golds and . . . and indigo, and spring greens, and purples you could practically eat! They shimmered like stars. And then *he* came . . ."

"He?"

"He had wings," 'Cilla went on in a low voice, "like one of the Cynthians, but a human face; and he was smiling like those angels the stories tell us about; and he picked me up and hugged me, and asked would I be his little girl. But I told him Lohr wouldn't like that, and—"

"And what, 'Cilla?" Pauli asked as gently as if she spoke to an infant.

"He put me down, and I woke up. See? Here's a picture of him. I just wish I had the colors."

To Pauli's surprise and relief, Dr. Pryor walked into

the main room at that moment. The door slid shut, but not before the screams rasped out, distracting everyone in the room but 'Cilla, who returned to her painting. Pryor walked carefully, probably still stiff from her attempt to rescue Ramon from the icy water. From time to time, if she felt that no one was watching, she coughed, her shoulders hunching up with the force she put into it.

"Any other deaths?" Pauli hated herself for asking.

"Thank God, no. Or not yet," Pryor answered. "We're likely to have some miscarriages, I think. At least I hope so: otherwise, I'm very much tempted to abort the women." She took a deep breath and held it, suppressing another spasm of coughing.

"This hits different people differently. 'Cilla, now, has a case of old-time religion: beyond that, I think she'll be all right. Ramon? you heard his hallucinations. A few others have had much the same visions—the moths, some skeletons with wings, the usual collection of serpents and green things that go squelch in the night: an addict's menagerie of them. They flash back, too. In general, what you see first is what you keep on seeing. I don't envy Dave, either, having to deal with a kid who thinks he's about to be cast into space in a pod."

She sighed, and pushed back limp hair that suddenly seemed more gray than blonde.

"Then there are the ones who are losing circulation in their extremities. If that goes on, we could have gangrenous limbs. I'm trying to stimulate circulation there."

"And for the ones hallucinating?"

Pryor sighed and shrugged. "I'm working on the assumption that there's some sort of alkaloid poisoning at work here and treating it accordingly. Eserine or acetylcholinesterase would be best, but, naturally, we don't have it. We don't even have any way to get medication directly into the brain. I tell you, Pauli, practicing outpost medicine is enough to drive you mad!"

Her outburst drew shocked laughter from both of

them. "I'm sorry," said the physician. "Where were we? I'm using epinephrine to stop the hallucinations."

"Won't that make them as frenzied as the ones outside?"

Pryor nodded despairingly. "For the older ones, or the ones who aren't in good condition, I combine the epinephrine with tranquilizers. Strong ones."

Pauli sighed. "I guess I'd better see what we're up against," she said.

Pryor turned and led her into one of the small quarantine units where a man twisted on his bed. His sheets were soaked with sweat, and from them rose a familiar, musty odor. Pryor lifted the brownish blanket that covered him, and pointed at the man's feet. They were slightly discolored now, as if bruised, the toes contorted, each entire foot drawn sharply downward. He twisted back and forth ceaselessly, unable to find rest or relief.

Only a scream from outside the dome saved Pauli from gagging, disgracing herself. She flung herself at the door, then out after the woman to whom she had spoken earlier, the one who had completed her work and now had nothing to do. "I'll make them use me, I'll make them!" she kept screaming, and flew at the nearest man, her hands clawing out to tear at his face. He caught her wrists and recoiled until two men came to secure her.

Pryor shook her head. "We're likely to have more and more of that. Frenzy, hysterical strength: God help us, we could be a village of maniacs by sundown. Rafe find anything yet?"

Pauli shook her head. "I had an idea," she spoke hesitantly, "but Dave told me that the squashes we had at the feast aren't the type that have to be cooked right, or they poison you." She sighed. "Dave says it's like going back to the Dark Ages." Abruptly she was as frustrated as Pryor had been by the limits of her powers.

"Damn! I keep thinking that I must be missing some piece of the puzzle."

Pryor nodded. "Why not sit down, then, and look at

another one? Maybe you can tell me what we've left out. I have the lists of everything the children ate. Not all of them ate the gourds, so that shoots your curare hypothesis, elegant as it was. And beyond that, there isn't a whole lot that all of them ate . . ."

Pauli rubbed her temples, a gesture copied by Pryor. Over in the corner, 'Cilla sat placidly sketching, an expression of almost angelic serenity on her mobile features.

"'Cilla?" asked Pauli. "Sorry to disturb you. But can you look at this list of what you ate last night, and tell me if it's complete?"

"Glad to," said the child and took the leaf of fax. Her lips moved as she muttered the words beneath her breath. Finally her head came up, and she looked puzzled.

"Does it matter if it was one of the special dishes, or what?" she asked.

"What do you mean?" asked Pryor, bending forward eagerly.

"Why you know: some things just go with a meal. Like glasses of water, or napkins, or . . ."

"Or bread?" asked Alicia.

"That's right. Those things don't really count. Lohr always said that whenever there were two foods, you always had to eat the solid, high-protein stuff first, because you might not have time to eat it second; and it's what really stays with you."

"Bread," mused Pryor. "Bread. Pauli, excuse me." She walked off with that rapid medcrew stride.

Pauli stared helplessly at 'Cilla. "Why isn't Lohr here with you?" she asked.

The little girl smiled as she always did at the thought of her splendid older brother, on whom even Captain Yeager relied. Her waxen skin almost glowed as if she were returning to normal health. Then she dropped her eyes—the faintly manic, dilated eyes of the poison victim—to her paper. "I sent him to talk to the others. They need him too."

Behind her rose Pryor's voice, not the gentle, controlled tones of the physician that the entire settlement had come to trust, but sharp, imperious, demanding to know how the bread had been baked for the Kwanzaa feast. She'd be wanting samples of the flour next, perhaps even the grain, Pauli was sure. She yawned and reached for a stimulant, then started to put it back in her pocket. Perhaps it might be a good idea to sleep now.

Realspace reeled about her, colors strobing, then fading to black as sounds dopplered past her range of hearing, only to explode in strident demands: PAULI DO SOMETHING! She did. She screamed, and Jump snatched the shriek from her lips. She could feel her throat rasp and vibrate with the scream, but she heard nothing. She looked down, and saw herself wavering in and out of existence; and facing her came a witches' star of enemy pilots, each with her own face as the RED ALERT lights and klaxons brayed . . .

Rafe's icy hand on her shoulder brought her fully awake. He leapt back just in time to avoid the counterattack some residue of her nightmare made her launch. She thrust clear of the covers that seemed to smother and imprison her and wiped a shaking hand across her brow. *Oh, God, sweating like Ari. Or Ramon. Why'd Rafe wake me?*

She looked up at him, appalled, and he bent to pick up a blanket and lay it about her shoulders. "You'll freeze like that, Pauli."

She gasped and sank back on the bed.

"Bad dream?" he asked, smoothing back her hair. Over her head, he breathed the words "in a minute!" but she intercepted them.

"What's 'in a minute'?" she mumbled. She was so tired; and her relief that she too was not about to convulse and hallucinate made her want to sleep even longer. But if Rafe was signalling "in a minute," something was wrong. She reached for her clothes, but couldn't find them in the dark. The LEDs on the chrono she hadn't turned off before collapsing into bed read 4:00.

"The lights won't work," Rafe told her. "There's been a power failure. One of the techs went crazy and tried to take apart computer interface with the generators. When we caught him, he started to scream that we were evil and had to be wiped out."

"Ohmigod," Pauli moaned, and it wasn't a prayer. Her feet, scuffling against the cold floor, kicked against her clothes and she bent to retrieve and tug them on. "Why'd you let me sleep?"

"Pryor's orders. Apparently you told her she could either rest or be sedated. She returned the compliment."

She swore, and knew that Rafe turned aside to hide an out-of-place grin. Stamping into her boots to settle cold feet in them, Pauli rose. "All right, Rafe. The lights are down because some maniac attacked the computer. *What else?*"

Rafe looked away. "We're on backups over at the lab. When the system crashed, it took most of the research database with it."

"*Shit,*" Pauli whispered, almost prayerfully.

"Yeah," said Rafe. "Now we have to start all over. And when you see the mess outside—Pauli, I don't know how much time we have left."

Shivering from the speed with which she had waked, Pauli strode outside and found half the crew who had been detached from the *Amherst* for duty here waiting for her. She also found catastrophe. Smeared across one of the central storage domes was a crude representation of a Cynthian, its huge wings daubed black, its jaws flowing a crimson that ran down to stain the snow like sacrificial debris before a bloody altar.

Smoke rose from the remnants of an outlying storehouse, adding an eerie cast to the deep gray sky. Much of the compound lay in darkness; rocks had shattered many of the greenish lights.

In the graveside glow of those remaining lay, writhed, or danced many people who clearly belonged in quarantine. Some should have been sedated or restrained. Some cried out in pain, their faces twisting horribly, while others tried to curl around on bellies as distended as those of women about to give birth. One or two people had bloodstained bandages swathing what should have been hands or feet.

Pauli pointed at them. "Those people should be cared for!" she declared, unable to keep the sick disgust from chilling her voice. "Have there been any deaths? What's happened?"

"Only two deaths so far," one of Alicia Pryor's assistants spoke up. "But a whole complex of new symptoms."

"Where's Dr. Pryor?" Pauli interrupted.

"Down with fever. No, it's not the madness. She caught it from that dive into the river. The rest of us . . . Captain, we've been working till we drop. We drafted as many able-bodied as we could, but then *that*"—he pointed at the twisting, grimacing figures—"started."

"What about the ones with the bandages?" asked Pauli. "What happened to their limbs?"

"Spontaneous amputation," said the assistant. "About twenty-four hours ago, each man complained of burning on his skin, and stabbing pains in the extremities, which turned black, gangrenous. Finally—you can see that there was very little bleeding. No infection, either." He seemed bemused by the cases.

Pauli stifled an insane impulse to spit, to turn her face away, to hide indoors until the last of this unholy settlement died, and she could die too. *One night's sleep,* she thought, *because they forced me to take it; and this is what happens!* "So, not only couldn't medcrew care for our sick," she made herself say, "but the rest of you couldn't protect vital installations."

"Ma'am!" interrupted one of the crewmembers. "These aren't poor sick people; they're mad—criminally insane, maybe. Only some of 'em scream and hop about. Others—you see that moth on the wall, don't you? They're crazy too: quiet, mean crazy, though. Some of them have taken the law into their own hands, and sentenced us all to die. Request permission to break out sidearms, ma'am."

"Permission denied," Pauli snapped. "I'm not having you use weapons on—"

"These civs are crazy!" shouted a crewwoman who wore security insignia and should have been more stable.

"They're not *civs,* damn you!" Pauli interrupted, her voice rising into a scream of rage that warmed her as nothing else could have done. "We don't have civs and crew here anymore. We have sick and well; sane and crazy—and right now I'm having trouble telling which is which. *Those people are your fellow settlers, lady: and you will damned well remember that!*"

The woman tried to meet Pauli's eyes, succeeded

bravely for an instant, then glanced down. "Yes, ma'am."

"All right, then. Now, I'm going to get the reports of the techs and scientists who've been working while the crew I thought I could trust plotted violence against their neighbors. And when I get back here, I want to see that . . . that artwork gone, and those people decently restrained and tended. Is that understood?"

The crew's "Yes, ma'ams" were roared so loudly that the people twitching under the sodium lamps whirled around to take notice. One of them laughed, the shrill, nerve-shattering laughter that Pauli had heard too often in the past days. Breathing hard, she strode over to the labs. For once, the tall Rafe had trouble keeping up with her.

"Didn't know you had it in you," he murmured. He didn't mean the fast pace, either.

"Neither did I." Now that she'd tongue-lashed her crew, guilt began to creep out from somewhere in her belly to chill the rest of her.

"Fine. Don't make a habit out of it."

Rafe slapped a hand against a palm lock bearing the signs of hasty installation, and the door irised. The first thing Pauli noticed was the computer. Its hum was stilled, and the lights of its drives were dark.

"We've asked for new supplies of all the food served at that damned feast of Beneatha's delivered here. Fortunately I took a lot of notes by hand," Rafe said.

Pauli sniffed. After the incredible luxury of uninterrupted sleep, her senses were as keen as the edge Dave ben Yehuda honed on a bush knife. "What's that I smell?" she asked. "It's sour."

"That's a new one," Rafe said. "Did more foods turn up while I was out?"

"Just that." The tech pointed at a sack from which spilled flour.

Pauli walked over to examine it, put out a finger to touch it, then drew it away and wiped it on her coverall. She was—it had been a settlement joke when they still had things to laugh about—barely an adequate cook, but even she knew that flour should be fine and powdery. This sample was discolored, and had an oily feel.

"Let's see the grain from which they make this flour," said Rafe. The assistant hoisted a sack onto the lab table and opened it. "It's a rye-wheat blend," he said. "The grains are modified for frontier use."

Rafe dug in a gloved hand and withdrew a handful, sniffed at it, then ordered, "Bring me a lab animal."

Pauli winced, knowing how the other beasts had died. Rafe shrugged helpless apology at her, opened the cage, and held out his hand. But when he offered the beast the flour and the grain, it backed away, its hackles up.

"It smells something bad," Pauli breathed. "But what?"

Rafe bent to examine the grain again. "This is . . . look at these seeds," he said.

Pauli leaned closer. "They're dark . . . rotten," she ventured.

"That's a fungus," Rafe told her. "Jared, try to find out if botany section has samples of these grains still on the stalk. Yes, you can tell Beneatha I think we're onto something. In the meantime," Rafe turned, automatically heading for the computer, and swore. He sighed. "How am I going to identify this fungus? I've gotten too damned dependent on the computer."

To be trapped, stymied, because the computer had failed! In that moment, she could understand Pryor's howl of rage at frontier conditions.

Beneatha ran in, stalks of grain in her trembling hands. Even to Pauli's untrained eyes, her skin had the waxiness she had noted in people entering the early stages of the madness, and her eyes were very bright.

"You should be in bed," she said. "Don't make me order you."

"Don't order me," Beneatha said, her voice reedy. She raised one hand to her throat as if she found breathing difficult. "I had one seizure, but the medcrew says I had it easy. I have to help," she added. "Please let me. You have to, or I think I'll go crazy again."

Rafe shook his head at Pauli and took the grain from

the woman. Delicately he reached for an ear of rye and examined it.

"It seems blighted," he observed. "Bent and oblong. And look at this color? What rye have you ever seen that's purple?"

Pauli watched as Rafe examined several more stalks of grain. Each, the rye especially, bore the marks he had noted: a distinguishing violet color, and the bent, oblong shape.

The xenobotanist shook her head. "I'd have noticed anything unusual," she stated.

"Then you'd better look at this," said Rafe. He tilted the bag onto the lab table, and Beneatha bent over it.

Almost half the stalks in that sack bore the violet taint of fungus.

"It wasn't like this when we harvested it," she said.

"It was rainy this summer," Rafe said. "And we've never tried these particular strains in Cynthian soil. But you're the xenobotanist. If this were a classroom—hell, Beneatha, if we were in a lab on Earth—what would you call this violet stuff?"

Beneatha shook her head. Her face ticced, then went calm as she thought. Instinctively she turned toward the nearest keyboard.

"Stop wishing for the computer!" Rafe said. "It's down, and I don't have time to reprogram it. Think, Beneatha! Once we all had memories, not hardware. We need your memory!"

"*Claviceps purpurea,*" she muttered. "That's what it looks like. And if this sack is any indication, then our entire grain supply—"

Rafe's eyes were very, very sad. "Our grain supply is contaminated with *claviceps purpurea.* Ergot. Now, I do remember about that ergot; there was a man in class with me who had a ghoulish fascination with it. A concentration of 0.05 percent of ergot is enough to produce symptoms of poisoning. And we have—what? Let's estimate that 40 percent of the grain in this sample is contaminated with it."

"So there's more than enough there," Pauli spoke

carefully, "to turn sane, hard-working people into screaming, dancing vandals." *I didn't eat any bread,* she remembered. *I'm not going to run crazy and abandon my people, my husband, my child. God, what a bitch I am to be relieved. Let's see, though. Who else at the feast didn't eat the bread? They can be released for duty right now.*

"That's right," said Rafe. "Here's the source of the madness. Ergot is very rich in alkaloids that paralyze the motor nerves of the sympathetic nervous system, and affects how the body uses adrenaline. Normally, when you're frightened, adrenaline makes your blood pressure rise. You have more energy for the short term, your nerves are sharper, and you can run or fight, if you have to.

"But if you have ergot in your system, then adrenaline expands the blood vessels, and blood pressure drops. Since the ergot also causes muscles to go into spasm—including the muscles of blood vessels—you can get thrombosis and every kind of cramps. Bloodflow slows to the extremities, which chill and look bruised. In some severe cases—like those poor bastards you saw—gangrene sets in."

"The summer was wet," Beneatha said. "No one thought anything of it, except to thank God we didn't have to irrigate. Ergot? That's stuff from the Dark Ages, when people danced before plaster saints. Why not ask me to believe in witch doctors?"

Rafe's voice was very gentle as he handed her back the grain. "There's something else," he told her. "Sometimes the ergot mutates. Then you have not just ergot, but lysergic acid, tasteless, colorless, and even more powerful. That's what's giving you the madness, the flashback hallucinations, even poor little 'Cilla's religious visions."

"Why didn't we find traces of it in their bodies?" Pauli asked.

"Because 95 percent of any dose is absorbed within five minutes after ingestion," Rafe told her. "The consequences, though . . ."

"Do people ever recover?"

"Instinctively Dr. Pryor used adrenaline—epine-phrine, she called it—to treat the hallucinations. But the adrenaline only intensified the symptoms of ergotism. It made the patients even wilder, and might even have caused them to burn out. But the tranquilizers calmed that. With luck, there won't be much permanent dam-age; though"—he shook his head—"I don't see much chance for the women who were pregnant to give birth to healthy children."

Beneatha hid her face in her hands.

"There's got to be some drug that's a specific antago-nist for lysergic acid. Thing is"—he shook his head—"since it's almost never used, I don't know what the drug is; and we can't ask Pryor. If only I had the database up . . ."

"I'll check the grain," Beneatha said, her thin voice a moan. "If it's contaminated, I'll burn it!" She dashed out of the lab.

Rafe shook his head. "She's probably right to do that."

"Does this mean we can never grow crops here?" asked Pauli. She had grown very still. If Rafe said "yes," it was their death sentence.

"No, only that after a wet summer, or a cold winter, we must examine them very carefully. If Beneatha says that the grain looked fine when she harvested it, I see no reason to doubt her word. But something—something in the soil, something in the grain itself, or our storage methods—caused it to turn bad.

"The problem is, we need the computer to find out."

Pauli paced back and forth. She felt as if she could smell the poison in the grain, which seemed so harmless. The violet of the fungus infection was even a rather attractive color. "Computer . . ." she mused. "Thorn! There's communications gear up in the caves. Didn't we have a terminal there too?"

Rafe leaned over the table to give her a hug. His arms felt so strong, so good, to Pauli. For a moment she clung to him, savoring the closeness. Then she pulled away.

"Then that's it," she said. "Someone has to climb up there and check the computer. It's funny: right before poor Beneatha's *karamu*, I promised to send someone to check on Halgerd. Now it looks like I'll have to go myself."

Rafe glared at her. "Don't argue," she said, holding up a hand. "I'm no good around a lab, but I have been up to the caves—"

"As have most of the people here, remember?"

"Yes, but can they fly back? Who else knows how to use Borodin's gliders? Are you going to send Lohr? Even if you trusted him around Halgerd, do you think he'd abandon the littlests? He's terrified for them. It's like the bad old times on Wolf IV have come back to snatch away the happiness they had just started to trust.

"No, Lohr's not going. And you're needed here. You know how to work with this . . . this ergot. What do I know, Rafe? I can climb, I can fly—and I can deal with Thorn Halgerd without wanting to shoot him where he stands." She held out her hands to her husband, who stood with his back half-turned on her.

"Rafe, you can keep order here as well as I. I'm the only one well enough trained but expendable right now to go up the mountain in winter, and you know it. But I can't do it if you're angry. Rafe, I need your support!"

Rafe crossed the table and held her close again. "You and your damned risks. I didn't want to love a pilot," he murmured. "I was so glad when you were stationed here. And now . . . you've found yourself a whole new set of dangers. You go, Pauli. But you'd just better come back safe. You see, you're right about every point except one: I can keep order. That much is true. But the only reason people listen to me is that I have you to back me."

Pauli trudged up toward the foothills, a pack laden with the dismantled wings of her glider awkward on her back. If she hurried, she could climb in daylight. Sealed into her flightsuit were copies of Rafe's research notes, anything that might help her use the computer they had left in the caves.

"Don't . . . don't forget Thorn," Pryor had said,

breaking off to cough. "You know how young he is . . . but the mind . . . potentially he's got the best brain on the planet . . ." Her blue eyes filled with tears, which Pauli didn't think the spasms of coughing had brought on.

"Tell him . . ."

"Captain, this is long enough," a medical tech warned Pauli. "Now, Doctor—" He slapped an antibiotic patch on her fragile throat.

"Reverse vampires," Pryor husked. "Damn, that stuff is scarce! Keep it till we need it!"

Pauli helped settle the older woman against the pillow that propped her to help her breathe, despite the fluid in her chest. "We need it now, Alicia," she said. "If you die of pneumonia, what will become of us?"

"You'll . . . think of something . . ."

"If you don't shut up," Pauli threatened, forcing a smile, "I'll tell Thorn Halgerd you're sick."

Pryor's sudden obedience turned the false smile real, and let her maintain it as she left the clinic. Rafe was waiting outside.

"I cached the pack at the camp perimeter," he told her.

"For God's sake, Rafe, tell them I'm sick, tell them I'm sleeping, or that I've gone to check on something—but don't tell people that I've left!" she asked. "I won't have time to see Serge before I leave, either. Will you kiss him for me?"

Rafe hugged her again. "Go now," he said. "We can't take any more of this."

She raised her eyes toward the distant, misty cliffs, tempted to fly instead of climbing up there. *Don't risk it,* she told herself. *Once you get some answers and transmit them, maybe you can fly back.*

What would she see up there? Pryor's fears for the Secess' renegade had affected her more than she wanted to admit. He might be sick, or dead up there *in which case, I'll give him a decent burial somehow,* she told herself. But if he was there, would he be an ally or an enemy? She hoped she wouldn't have to use the weapon heavy on her hip. Perhaps the weight Halgerd had placed on her—captain, a human born, not cloned as he had been, even the fact that she had given birth—would let her handle him.

He had gone up into the hills to be alone with himself for the first time in a short life every bit as deprived as those of the refugee children. The Secess' had made him a thing, a killing machine interfaced with other killing machines who looked like him, and whom he loved as much as any creature as starved for humanity could love anything. But they had died. Unaccountably, he had failed to die with them, failed to betray the enemies he found on Cynthia to the creators who had so abused him.

Pryor hoped to turn him, hoped that whatever had drawn his "father" to her side might serve to turn the cloned son from his exile back to humankind for the first time. Cloned from one of the most intractable minds ever to terrorize a research university, Halgerd was potentially a strong ally. If he could be turned. If he could be convinced that he too was human and had a stake in the dying settlement.

What if I tell him that Pryor is sick? At her age, people die of pneumonia. As Pryor knew, which was the only reason she consented to have the valuable antibiotics used on her. She knew her worth to Pauli and to the settlement. That was one tactic she could use. Another was the danger to the children, to Lohr who had had every reason to kill him, but who had saved his life.

What are these tactics? Pauli thought. *We're human, he's human. Let it go at that.* She quickened her pace, struggling up the slope, which grew increasingly rocky and increasingly steep. Soon she would be climbing, not hiking.

She brought up against a boulder so quickly that it forced a grunt out of her, then froze, listening. That scuffling crash, what was it? An animal? Her hand slipped down to her blaster, and she released the catch of the holster. There it came again. Not that she knew much about the habits of predators—other than humans—but she didn't think that a hunting beast would make that much noise. *Unless it was sick.*

She drew her weapon, and crept forward.

A spatter of pebbles fell, and something heavier with them. That was a human voice Pauli heard, crying out in pain and frustration. Who had seen her leave and been able to outpace her into the foothills? she wondered. And why would someone do that?

She set her weapon on low power and began to stalk whoever had cried out. It was hard to stalk noiselessly, while struggling not to fall on the scree, or to let boots scrape against the rocks. Fortunately, her quarry made even more noise than she. Up ahead now, Pauli girl . . . there . . . one last boulder . . .

A wail of pain and sorrow floated back to her and made her quicken her pace. Rounding the last boulder, Pauli saw Beneatha crouched at the base of a rock, her booted foot caught in a narrow crack. As the xenobotanist saw her, she laid her head down and wept.

"Why don't you ask what I'm doing here?" Beneatha demanded. Her dark face was coated with dust, except where tears and sweat had left clean black streaks.

Pauli glanced past the woman at the rocks. Another hundred or so meters ahead some of them were high enough to be classified as cliffs.

She sat down on her heels beside her old adversary. "Looks like I got here in time to stop you from doing it," she remarked, her voice calm as she'd trained it to be. "The river—I set a watch on the bank where Ramon . . ."

Beneatha turned her face away and laid it against the cold rock.

"I'm sorry," Pauli said firmly. "But if you're stupid enough to plan to join him, you had it coming."

"You know better than that." The woman's voice crackled with anger. She turned her head slowly, and Pauli was sure that she was gauging the distance between her hands and Pauli's blaster.

"Don't try it," she warned her, and holstered the weapon. "All right, so you don't want to throw yourself into the river where your friend died. But you certainly look like you were planning to throw yourself off one of these rocks until you got your foot caught."

Beneatha spat a series of words at her. "Good. Now you want to kill me, not yourself. That's a step in the right direction. Which, in case you'd forgotten, is back down toward that settlement. Where they need you."

"How can I go back there?" the xenobotanist cried. "I'm the one that's destroyed it."

"On purpose? You actually set out to spray that fungus on the fields? You wanted to strike half the population crazy? You tried to do that?"

"Don't overact, Yeager," snapped Beneatha. "You know what this place means to me. You know how hard I've worked to make it run, to help these children have a new life, to have one myself . . ."

Pauli raised an eyebrow and looked at the nearby cliffs.

Fresh tears streaked down Beneatha's face. "I can't forgive myself. I meant the Kwanzaa feast to celebrate our new future here—and look what it's done! How can I live with this?"

The sun was rising in the sky, and Pauli had a long climb ahead of her. She was conscious of a furious aggravation, and her back ached from squatting down.

"How do you think *I* handle it?" she demanded. "Something got by you, as it's done for centuries. But look what I did, what I planned. A whole race of people, wiped out! I planned it, and I'd do it again if I had to. You remember, you had plenty to say about the heartless, ruthless, racist military."

Beneatha's head drooped. "How do you handle it? I can't believe you don't care."

"That's the first sensible thing you've said since your feast turned sour!" Pauli declared. "I have to go up to the caves now to use the computer there. Which means I have to face a man I refused to kill. Then I have to come back. If I'm real lucky, I'll have something worth coming back to. You think I wouldn't rather join you in a nice quick jump off the nearest cliff?"

All the fear, all the uncertainty, and the months of

guilty frustration that Beneatha's principles inflicted on Pauli came bubbling up in an angry brew. "Dammit, you've been a thorn in my side long enough!" Pauli shouted. "You've fought at every point, you've been self-righteous, obstructive—and the minute you make a mistake, you want to take yourself out. I had you down for a pain, maybe an enemy, woman. I didn't have you pegged for a coward."

Beneatha glared murder at her. *Good. Just a little more.*

Pauli unholstered her sidearm, and began methodically to burn away at the rock that imprisoned Beneatha's foot.

"Don't jar my hand, or you won't be able to get as far as the cliffs," she said. The rock crumbled under the fine red beam. Despite the cold, she felt herself sweating. What if Beneatha brought a rock down on her skull and took the gun?

The last of the rock chipped away, freeing Beneatha's foot. The boot was scratched, but not punctured. "See if you can put weight on it."

Beneatha braced herself against a boulder, then, cautiously, stood free. "I can manage," she said stiffly.

"For how long?" Pauli asked the question flatly, with none of the anger and sarcasm she had used before. "Long enough to get to the cliffs? Or to get back home?"

Wearily she checked the blaster's charge, and slid it back into its holster. Beneatha was wearing her out, and the longer she stood here, the more formidable the climb to the cliffs looked. "You might want to think of something else," Pauli suggested. "If you really want to punish yourself, what's the worst thing you can do? Not kill yourself, certainly. But sentence yourself to life, life among the very people you injured. Do you want me to tell you that? Hell, I'll sentence you to live if you want," she took Beneatha by the shoulders and held her at arm's length.

"What do you think I've told myself?"

Beneatha bent and examined her foot again. "If I take the boot off, my foot will probably swell."

"Probably."

"I think I can hobble back to camp, though. They'll strap it for me there."

Pauli shut her eyes to hide tears of relief.

"I've got a comm, if you want to use it."

Beneatha shook her head. "Better not. Let 'em think I had a flashback, wandered off, and hurt myself. I'll say I blacked out, and when I came to, I limped on back. They'll put me under observation but"—she sighed—"it's better than admitting the truth."

Pauli held out a hand to the other woman.

"Don't think that this makes me approve of what you've done—or what you may do. Right now, I don't ever want to see your face again."

"I've never had your approval, so I won't miss it," Pauli said. "You can go right ahead and hate me all you want, Beneatha. You're not alone. But at least you'll be alive to do it."

The xenobotanist glared at her. "Why do I feel like I've been tricked?" she muttered.

Pauli sighed and adjusted her pack. It wasn't getting any lighter. "Do you really think I'm that smart?" she asked over her shoulder.

With any luck, that parting shot would keep Beneatha simmering with the fury and chagrin that would save her life all the way back to camp.

CHAPTER
18

Since the last time Pauli struggled up the rock chimney to the caves, the trip had grown no easier. Lit only by cracks in the jagged rock walls, and by faint light from where it opened near the Cynthians' caves, the rocky chute was dark by late afternoon. Ice made hand- and footholds treacherous; and if the rockfaces protected Pauli from much of the wind at these altitudes, an occasional frigid gust struck at just the right angle to draw wails and howls from rock, like breath hooting over an empty bottle.

Pauli cowered back into the nearest crack until the wind died and the howling subsided. In one such respite, she took out her light and hung it around her neck. In the next, she opened her pack and snatched out the first food she found, a high-energy sweet that hit the bloodstream with a rush of energy. Though she climbed more strongly after eating, she knew she'd have to pay later. Even in the icy cold of the rock chimney, exertion made her hair sweat and slide down her back before she had scrambled halfway up.

There were no moths to stop her now, she told herself. Even if there were, they'd all be dormant. And her worst fear, of a sudden attack of vertigo or madness while climbing, had vanished with the knowledge that she had not eaten any of the tainted bread. Ice and rock broke off in her hand, and her pulse rate spiked. *Adrenaline,* she reminded herself. *Good for rock climbing. Among other things.* She clung to the rock with both feet and one hand while seeking another grip. *Always stay anchored at three points,* her survival instructors had drilled her. At the time, she wondered why a ship's pilot needed to know such things. Now, she no longer wondered: she climbed, and she clung, and she thanked God for every sturdy rock outcropping.

The wind was working itself up into frenzy once more. She hunched her aching shoulders and pressed against the unyielding rock as the wind screamed into the shaft. It shook and boomed from its force until Pauli too wanted to howl. Then the wind died again. The quiet was unbearable.

"Thorn?" she called, her voice reedy and echoing as it rose into the still night air. "Thorn!"

That wouldn't do. She sounded like a scared girl. Maybe he hadn't heard. *If he's in the caves,* she realized mordantly, *he had to have heard it. Remember, he isn't just a clone. They augmented him.* Halgerd probably thought a climb like this was light exercise.

A grayish light told her that the lip of the chimney was almost within range. *Slowly now. Don't get cocky,* she warned herself in between sobbing gulps of air. That rock looked rotten; there was ice to her left. There! One foot secure. Now, try the other. Grip with the left hand, and with the right raise yourself until you can see over the rim, grab the nearest projection, test it, and lever yourself out!

She lay flat, panting, on the rock for long moments, almost too weak to fight the easy tears of exhaustion until she felt the sweat begin to cool all over her body. If she rested any longer, she'd put herself in danger. Like Pryor.

"Thorn?" she called again. But up ahead, the caves Rafe had plundered to kill the Cynthians were dark. She turned up her light, unsnapped the holster on her weapon—she was no match for Halgerd's speed, but she had to do the best she could—and advanced at a cautious, limping walk. Her muscles were beginning to ache from the long climb.

To her surprise, her left hand brushed across a rope. Someone had chipped and smoothed the rock here, and strung up handholds. She didn't think that the evacuees had had time, or heart, to make this place more than marginally habitable: so it had to have been Thorn.

The beam slanted across the cave as she entered. Her imagination turned the long shadows slanting up across the walls into the spectres of Cynthians dead seasons ago, dead and watching her. The caves still smelled faintly from their musk, and a few stray scales, somehow still preserved, glittered with reflected light.

Her light showed her traces of human habitation: neatly stacked cartons, scrubbed dishes, boxes of food. In the most sheltered alcove of the outermost cave she found tools, oiled and carefully wrapped, commgear, now deactivated, and—where was the computer? She edged farther into the caves, into the quarters that the settlers had marked out and hated. Immediately she recoiled.

Her light had glinted off shining wings.

At least she hadn't screamed. As soon as her urge to panic, to hurl herself out of the cave, and back toward home (such as it was now) subsided with her pulse rate, she remembered. Lohr had lent Thorn Halgerd his wings. To make it easier for the man to come back to them, once he permitted himself to believe he deserved companionship.

And Halgerd had hung them on the cave's wall right across from the neatly folded pile of foil blankets that he used as a bed. Nearby were a heatcube, a spare torch, and the computer. Halgerd's private quarters resembled nothing so much as a cell: just necessities, kept painfully tidy. Except, of course, for the wings, hung up in a place of honor, to remind him of what? that once he too had flown? or that once, someone had given him a gift?

Pauli shook her head and sighed. Slinging her pack from her shoulders, she set it down and approached the computer. Slowly, now. Tired is stupid. First, check with Rafe, if you can. She forced herself back to the mouth of the cave. As she suspected, the wind made transmission impossible.

If she couldn't provide the camp with an immediate answer, the least she could do was make certain that when she could talk to them, she'd have the right answer for them. Wearily she walked back to Halgerd's stark quarters, slapped POWER ON to set the heatcube radiating, then shuddered with relief as the warmth spread throughout the sheltered cavern. She switched on the light he kept here and wrapped herself in one of the light blankets. Then she tucked her hands in her armpits and strode up and down until her feet warmed too.

Settling down before the computer, she tugged her crumpled notes from her pack. So tired, she thought, yawning. And it was warm in here. She should eat something before she started work, she supposed, but it was warm here, out of the wind . . .

There was no point in trying now. Her eyes were blurring; she might just as easily erase data she needed as enter the facts she had. But she'd be damned if she'd curl up on the Secess' bed. She tugged another blanket from the pile, wrapped that around her too, and leaned against the rock wall, staring at Lohr's wings.

Should turn down the lights, she thought drowsily. But the light and warmth were good, so good; and it was quiet here. She caught herself slumping to one side. *Why not? It's not as if I'm going to wake up and see big, black moths hovering over me to bring me to trial.* After all, the Cynthians had wanted the human settlers to climb up to the caves. Uriel and Ariel had invited them. Now she was sheltered, just as they had intended her to be.

Lohr's wings glittered and blurred before her eyes, shifted into a shining haze like the nebulae on the Cynthians' wings as they danced in the high passes the way she'd seen them the last time she had climbed up here. Seen them, loved them—and been forced to destroy them.

No wonder some of the settlers had seen visions of black moths and death's-heads. If Pauli had eaten the ergot-ridden bread, she'd probably have seen them too—and deserved it. *Please let me make my peace with you,* she asked the silent, watchful caves.

Seeing visions? she asked herself, chuckled without much humor, then yawned again. God, she was tired.

"Who's there?"

The deep voice woke her. She uncurled herself and drew her sidearm. Halgerd must have seen the light and been just as reluctant as she to stride into the caves without warning. Now, finally, she heard footsteps on the rock.

"Who is it?" the man called again.

Pauli glanced at her weapon, shook her head, and holstered it. Halgerd had shown himself able to override the pain even of a blaster wound; either she killed him instantly, or not at all. And she had refused to kill him once, when he had been at her mercy. She saw no reason to change her mind.

"It's Yeager," she replied. Her voice came out very light against the echoes of his words, and she walked quietly into the outer cave, the silvery blankets dropping from her shoulders, her hands carefully idle at her sides.

She had forgotten how tall he was, how the light shone on his hair and the beard he had grown to protect his face from the cold. Despite the beard and the bulk of his worn coverall and jacket, he carried himself like an ambassador, the single time Pauli had seen one. An intimidating sight, especially since Pauli knew how fast he could be, could draw his own weapons if he had to . . . until she saw his eyes.

They were blue, as blue and as cool as Alicia Pryor's. But where Pryor's eyes could snap with aggravation or suddenly turn warm with compassion, Thorn's eyes were uncertain, even fearful, as he studied Pauli. She could almost watch the thoughts flicker behind them. *Why is she here? What incomprehensible, human reason has she for coming here?*

He was very young, Pauli knew. No more than twenty —and how much of that time had been spent in stass tanks? No doubt this period of exile was the longest interval he had ever remained conscious.

But he met her eyes steadily, as if it were a duty he owed her. Finally, tentatively, he smiled.

"Lonely!" he announced, and his voice came out uncertainly, as if he rarely used it. "Now that there is another person here, now I know that 'lonely' describes what I felt. What a wonder, to feel such things and recognize them for the first time."

He swung around slowly, in order not to alarm her. "When I saw your light, I dropped my pack outside. Allow me to go and get it. Then, perhaps, you will tell me what I can do for you."

He vanished into the cold. In what seemed like a remarkably short time, he stamped back inside, an enormous load weighing him down. He swung it from his back with an ease that astonished Pauli, then stripped off his jacket and stood watching her.

"Dr. Pryor hasn't heard from you," were the absurd first words out of her mouth. "She's been worrying about you."

He smiled as if someone had given him a gift. "I went back to the ruins of my emergency pod," he said. "To salvage. But I never thought my absence would cause her concern." Then he looked dismayed. "I still have so much to learn. How terrible if I have harmed her. Is she well?"

Pauli shook her head and stood aside to let him enter the caves he had made his own. "No, but that's not your doing," she said. "None of it's your doing. But none of us are well. There's sickness, madness, in the camp. Madness?" She sought for a referent that Thorn would understand. "Like losing one of your brothers."

His eyes never left her. Once again she watched the struggle he put up to comprehend the baffling morass of born-human emotions. "This sickness," he asked. "It is a plague? Or does it come from loneliness, as when one feels the death of a brother?"

Pauli lowered her head. "It comes from food. There was a fungus, a growth on the grain, and it made people sick. Some have even—" It had to be the warmth and her own exhaustion, but her voice was breaking, her eyes were filling in response to the innocent responsiveness in the tall man's eyes.

"Died?" he breathed. "This is too bad! And Dr. Pryor, who could help you, is sick." He glanced around the cave. "There is food here. I can help you carry it to your camp. But not now. We both have come a long way today, and it is cold. Still, your presence has warmed this place for me." He smiled, the disarming grin of a child. "How strange to come back to warmth and light! And despite your news, it is very pleasant. We will sit and eat, and I will learn what I can do to help."

His hand was on her shoulder before she could flinch away, and he steered her, as if she were something infinitely fragile, infinitely precious, back into the cave where Lohr's wings hung on the wall. "There!" he said, and opened out another blanket. "Now, we can both be warm. Are you hungry or thirsty?"

Let him play host. The same intuition that prompted Pauli to test the littlests, or goad Beneatha into a life-giving rage, awoke now, and she nodded, letting the man talk out his astonishment that someone would seek him out—and his fear. Gradually her own alarm in his presence faded too. The hot cup he handed her warmed her hands; its steam soothed her chapped face. As she sipped, she began to speak.

"The computer!" Halgerd exclaimed. "Of course you need the one your people left here. But you tell me you are *asking* me if you may use it? Why should you ask to use what is yours?" He activated the machine, and with a speed and deftness Pauli could not match, began to enter her information.

"Ha! this is a very old thing," he spoke as much to himself as to her. "I . . . Halgerd himself . . . knew of it, though, of course, it no longer existed on Freki. But on Earth, it was known for centuries throughout the European region. There is a list here: the Rhine, Paris, Lorraine, Flanders, Spain, even far to the north in

Sweden, where my . . . where Halgerd's people came from long ago. Thousands of people died. You say a dancing madness? Sleeplessness, visions, feelings of hot and cold, of limbs dropping away. And they prayed to their . . . their saints, but no one answered."

He looked up at her. He was actually pale, almost sick with distress. "It is hard, this living on planets," he murmured. "And your Dr. Pryor is sick too." He looked up at her with the perceptiveness of a child, or of his father. "What about *your* child?"

There had been a night when he had tried to betray the settlement to his masters, yet had stopped long enough to inquire if she should be out so soon after giving birth. Before she realized, she had laid a hand on his, to reassure and silence him. "Serge is fine. But many of the children are sick. Including Ari, the boy whose life you saved."

Halgerd rose so rapidly he upset his empty cup. "What can I do?" he asked.

"Let me use the machine," Pauli said. "Let me stay here tonight—no, this is your home now, and I am a guest. In the morning, I will call the settlement and tell them what I have found; and then I will return home."

"But I have food here, supplies, even the computer: things that you need. People should come and get them."

"And what will you do then?" she asked.

"Whatever I am ordered. It has been very long since I have had Orders."

"Thorn," Pauli leaned back to stare at him. "There's more to this business of being human than just following other humans' orders. These supplies here—we gave them to you. If you want to share them, I'll accept with thanks. But think, man. What will you do without them? Wait for me to tell you what to do again?"

"There are children down there. True-humans. If they need them . . ."

"Dammit, don't just transfer your stupid, mindless loyalty from your Republic to us! Think of yourself as 'true-human,' the son of a man with one of the finest brains ten star systems have ever seen. *Use* that mind you've got. Use it to figure out what you can do, if you want to help us, and how!"

"All I know," the pilot said slowly, "is ships. Fighting. Loyalty. And now, the new thing I learned when I first saw you here. That I had been lonely."

"I too know ships and fighting," Pauli said. "If you come down, you may not be lonely. Other things, yes. But not lonely. Will you try?"

He drew a deep breath and set his cup upright with shaking hands. "Would they . . ."

"Thorn, right now they'd welcome anything, if it gave them more of a chance! I can't promise that they'll all be glad you've come down. Hell, when you're dealing with people, I can't promise you anything. Except that I'll try. Dr. Pryor will try; and Thorn, she'll be very, very glad."

The tall man sighed and after a long time, he smiled. "She was my father's friend. I will come down."

He glanced up at the wings, then walked into the outer cave from which came the clatter and bustle of someone packing. She turned back to the computer, fed in the rest of her data, and waited for a hard-copy reply, which she tucked into her tunic. Again, the lack of survey data on Cynthia had harmed them. Ergotism usually appeared after a harsh winter, followed by a rainy summer. If they'd only known, they could have taken precautions. They could take them, though, from now on.

The crops would grow, and the settlement could recover. Most of the colonists were young and strong; they would heal, except for the people who had lost limbs, or their sight, or whose wits might wander for years yet. And even for them, surely there was much that could be done. There was hope yet.

Quietly, so that Thorn might not hear and be distressed, Pauli laid her head down beside the computer console, and wept.

"Captain?" came Thorn's voice, careful, respectful of her privacy—in his own quarters, for pity's sake!

Pauli scrubbed at her face and wiped her eyes. "What is it, Thorn?"

"I packed the food first," Thorn announced. "Perhaps we should sleep before we climb down." He entered the room and scooped up several blankets before he stopped, studied her carefully, and sat down on them. "You cannot sleep, either," he said. "We should still rest."

Pauli checked the precious data plaque in its sealed pocket, powered down the computer, and leaned back against the uneven, cold rock. Glancing at her for approval, Thorn turned down the light and smiled.

"Captain?" he asked.

"If you're going to live among us, Thorn, try calling me Pauli. Everyone else does—except maybe Beneatha when she's angry at me. Which is most of the time."

"I remember her," said Thorn. "She thought I should be executed. Will she still hate me?"

"Can't say, Thorn. I truly can't. Right now, though, I don't think she can hate anyone more than she hates herself. For the rest of it, though; it'll be what you make of it."

Thorn eased himself down comfortably on his blankets. "You know . . . Pauli, you cursed me for 'mindless loyalty.' I must tell you something, before we join the people . . ."

"The *rest* of the people," she corrected. Alicia would have been proud of her for that one.

"Yes. The other people. You know," he said, drowsily, "when my brothers and I fired on the planets like Wolf IV, I did what I was ordered to do. Orders were all that I had, and I didn't question if they were right or wrong. I didn't know that such a question existed. I wish, now, that I had. I think if I had known that there were people on those worlds, people like the boy Ari, and the other one, who fired at me, then gave me back my breath, I might not have obeyed. Then they would have killed me.

"But I'm alive now, and it hurts worse, even than feeling the deaths of my brothers, who died quickly and cleanly. Now, though . . . Pauli, is this hurt a way of making up for the deaths I caused? Can I ever do that?"

Pauli glanced up despite eyelids that weighed her down like a heavy pack. Halgerd's face was haggard, his eyes bright. But he did not weep. *Too young to weep yet,* she thought. *Too young to know how much he has to weep over.*

"I don't know, Thorn. I don't think people ever know." Her own eyes stung.

"Then what do they do, if they can't know?"

"They work as hard as they can. And when they can work no more, they try to sleep."

A change in the light woke Pauli, and she shifted under her blankets. She could not remember having wrapped so many of them about herself. Nearby sat Halgerd, who looked as if he had not moved since the night before. Had he watched over her all night? Half-embarrassed, half-touched, she sprang up and went to the cave's mouth. The day had dawned crisp and cold. "Good flying weather!" Thorn approved, and Pauli returned his grin.

"I think I can probably get through to the settlement now," she said, and activated the powerful transmitter they had left in the caves but which Thorn, thinking no one would care to hear from him, had never used.

For an eternity, static crackled, and then—"Pauli, is that you?"

"Rafe!" Abruptly the signal waned, then rose, disintegrating into howls and spatters of static.

"—emergency generator going! Yes, I'm here."

"Rafe, I've got the material we need. It's weather patterns! A cold winter, a wet summer, and you've got conditions under which you have to watch out for ergot. But the life-sciences people ought to be able to spray, and to select out an ergot-resistant strain! I'm coming down!"

Rafe's voice cut through her exultation. "That's fine, Pauli."

Over the static and the hum of transmission, Pauli heard other voices, sharp and dismayed. But she only heard sounds, not words, almost as if Rafe kept the speaker pressed against himself to drown out the messages.

"Not now," she heard him hiss.

"Rafe, what's wrong?" she demanded. "Have there been any more deaths?"

"Two miscarriages." She practically had to pull each word from him.

"It's not Dr. Pryor, is it? Rafe, damn you, if I'm worrying, how can I get back down there safely?"

"All right, Pauli. I'll tell you. Last night, there was a theft from the storage domes: food, heatcubes, blankets, and tools. Sometime in the night, the kids—all but the ones still actively sick and Dave's twins—sneaked out of the camp. I think Lohr decided that they'd have a better chance on their own, so he's taken them and gone to ground."

The pause dragged on so long that she almost didn't have to ask the next question. "Serge too?" she asked. In a moment more she would collapse, would draw herself into an aching knot and keen her loss. But not now. Not now, dammit!

"'Cilla's disappeared," Rafe said. "And you know how attached to Serge she is."

"I'm coming," Pauli forced the words out. "I'll fly down to you. Rafe, have you told me everything?"

The comm was silent for so long that Pauli was sure he had broken transmission.

"No," he said, his voice leaden. "When people discovered that the littlests had vanished, there was a riot. Somebody painted those black winged things all over the life-sciences' domes. Worse yet, in the confusion, one of the quiet crazies got loose again and wrecked some of our repairs. All the grain storage domes are without power now. Freezing cold. We've abandoned them for now."

"I'm on my way," Pauli ended transmission and stood up.

"The children are gone?" Thorn asked.

Pauli shook her head sorrowfully. "All of them. They couldn't trust us to take care of them. They couldn't even trust me to care for my own son!" It was Lohr, she knew. Lohr with his talents and his strength, his fears, his angers—and the trust the adults had betrayed: they had promised him protection, but been unable to protect those he protected from themselves.

"How far could they go without being spotted?" he demanded. All his earlier hesitancy and deference had vanished in what Pauli realized was his overwhelming relief that there was something he could do.

"Pauli, you fly back to the settlement. I'll take my wings—Lohr's wings—out and start a search pattern. One good thing about living up here alone. I probably know the land better than any survey map. Once you get the riot under control, you come fly patterns with me, or send someone else. Someone who can work with me and not see a murdering nonhuman bastard," he added.

"And if you see the children?"

"I'll signal you, then land and try to convince them to let me bring them back."

The words stuck in her throat. "If I know Lohr, they're armed. They've lived wild, Thorn, and they've killed before."

Thorn lifted Pauli's wings from her pack and began deftly to assemble the struts and the harness.

He looked up with a faint, bleak smile. "I don't think they'll kill me," he said. "For one thing, I'm faster than they. For another—look what a mess Lohr made of it the last time! When he's afraid, he turns angry. But he's lived among adults for too long. I think he'll be glad to hand over the responsibility for the other children—if not to me, then to someone he trusts. Someone he . . . loves."

He held out the wings to her, and she turned her back, allowing him to adjust them, before she fastened the harness. "Just fly straight," he told her. "I'll check in later."

How had she ever thought of him as young and vulnerable? What an ally he was going to be!

Pauli stepped to the edge of the cliff. The sky was pale,

with a drift of cirrus clouds, more fragile and lovely than any wings. She waited, choosing her moment, her gust of wind the way surfers chose their waves. There it came!— cold, fresh, swooping down to take her with it—

Pauli Yeager stepped off the cliff, extended her wings, and soared into long-awaited, exultant flight. The sun glinted off her wings, and she cried out a welcome.

CHAPTER

19

A tech's hand shook Rafe from a waking nightmare that somehow had turned into restless sleep. He leapt forward, his instincts screaming fight, then, as his eyes focused, he sank back. God, how his back ached! Once again, he had lain sprawled over his desk, his head buried in his arms among the clutter of notes he had scrawled longhand until he thought he never again would be able to uncurl his fingers. They still ached. His neck and back shifted and ground like tectonic plates, and when he spoke, only a rasp came out.

"Now what?" he muttered, and the tech bent confidentially close. The last time they'd waked him, it was to tell him that Beneatha Angelou had wandered away from the settlement with a relapse of her hallucinations. She had fallen, she told the medics, and when she recovered consciousness, she had staggered back home. He'd yawned. If that was what she wanted him to believe, well enough; better yet that she was still alive.

Perhaps in Beneatha's wanderings, she had seen the children on their way to whatever refuge Lohr thought he had found for them. (Rafe didn't think that the boy could get them all the way to the caves, which, at any rate, were occupied.) *Couldn't they even trust me to care for my own son?* Serge was gone, missing with all the children except Ari and Ayelet, whom David had taken home once his son's fever and sweating and nausea subsided.

Husky specimen that he was, Ari was out of danger, now. And waiting outside to talk with Rafe. Rafe called him in; and his sister came too. Perhaps one of them might have an answer for him.

Ari flushed and went silent. But Ayelet proved more talkative. Since she had not eaten any of the tainted bread, she had escaped the madness, though worry about her brother and her colony had set dark circles under her eyes and made her jump at any sudden movement.

"Why did you pass up the bread?" Rafe asked her.

"Lohr said I was too fat," the girl muttered, her eyes downcast, her full cheeks flushing awkwardly.

Rafe looked over at ben Yehuda, who shrugged, then took over the conversation.

"Sweetheart, did Lohr ever say anything to you that—"

"I've been trying to remember!" she cried. "You know Lohr: he's always quiet about what he thinks. Do you think you can bring him back, him and the littlests?"

Rafe covered his face, massaging temples with trembling fingers.

I'm not the one to ask. Rafe the weakling, with his smile for everyone, and his broken nerve. Look what happened: Pauli takes off for the cliffs, risking her neck because she knew I couldn't handle that mission. What happens here? She leaves me in charge, and the whole place falls to hell, or worse than hell. And now those mad bastard kids stole my son! Lohr, if I ever see you again . . .

Someone shook at him, and he leapt up, his hand grabbing for the weapon he always carried these days. "Oh, 's'you," he grunted, staring bleary-eyed at the tech who watched him from a wary distance this time. Last time he'd tried that, Rafe had caught him by the throat. "Wha's it now?" he grumbled.

"Someone's coming in!" cried the man. Someone? It had to be Pauli! Thank God. Tears came to his reddened eyes again. Rafe struggled out of his uncomfortable chair, stretched the worst aches from his spine, and hurried outside.

Noon light glinted off the reflective surfaces of canted

wings as his wife's glider banked and spiralled down toward the camp. Rafe started toward her, breaking into a shambling run as he anticipated her turns and her landing site. He was there as she touched down, staggered, and overbalanced into his arms.

For a moment, Pauli's face retained the exultant grin she wore whenever she managed flying time. Her body was taut, ready . . . poised, seemingly, for takeoff the moment she caught her breath.

Never love a pilot! he reminded himself. But the look on her face reminded him just how easy hc had found it to love her. But as he steadied her, pressing her against his body, the exultation went out of her; and she clung to him. Her grief flooded out from her hands and the skin of her cheek to engulf him.

"I've got answers for us," she whispered. "Thorn's flying search, and he should call in soon. He'll let us have the computer from the caves, and all the supplies we gave him."

Rafe straightened up, one moment past the brattish impulse that tempted him to sob out his failure in his wife's arms. How tiny she was—and how brave! And how terribly he had failed her when she had trusted him to keep order. Well, he'd kept some order, but he had not been able to prevent the children from fleeing, or the madmen from breaking loose. Smoke still wound up in greasy trails from some of the ruined domes; crudely painted black moths still dripped down the sides of many others.

Almost as bad as the ruined worlds, he thought, choking back tears. *No wonder the kids fled us. They'd had a bellyful of adult "protection."* His hands tightened on Pauli's narrow back and he drew on the strength that was the greatest thing about her.

After a long moment, she drew a shaky breath, and pushed free of him, her hands fumbling, despite long familiarity, with the glider's harness until the wings toppled from her back to the ground.

"Get everyone out here," she told him. "Everyone,

even the people who are sick—but not crazy enough to run wild if we take them outside. I'll speak to them outside the commhut."

Not a word of their child. Neither of them had ever been good with fine words: nor had they needed that many words between them. Now he could see grief bleeding her white, as it had bled him from the moment when he learned that Lohr preferred the wilderness to the adults who had murdered an entire race to protect them.

She stood waiting, the bright folds of her wings casting sparkles upon the grimy flightsuit that she had worn for the climb, as people walked, hobbled, or were carried toward the central area outside the commhut. Then, walking slowly so that everyone could see that she was still alive, still sane, still there for them, she joined them.

"I understand," she began in a clear, quiet voice, "that some of you have decided that we don't belong here. What I want to know is where you do think we belong? There aren't any ships, you know, to listen to us whine, and come take us away—unless, of course, you want to run the risk of the Secess' finding us.

"Have you thought of what might happen, though, if our own people find us? what they'll call us? how we're likely to be sentenced? Maybe some of you have, because some of you, I can see, think that the only thing left for us to do is die here."

She let the mumbling begin, rise, then peak in a few shouts of angry agreement. "How dare you?" she began in a breathless, angry voice that rose like wind blowing across stone: cold and unforgiving and dangerous. "How dare you suggest that we let ourselves die here? What sort of remembrance is that of the people we killed: to lose heart and die, and leave their world a desolation?

"I ask you, do you really think you deserve to die, and to forget what you've done—what we've all done? An entire species is dead, killed by us to protect our children. And now our children are missing"—her voice crackled with sarcasm—"and some of you are probably whining that we 'cannot interfere,' or that the kids—

children, all of them!—are smart enough to choose wisely.

"I told you when we killed the Cynthians: we have to make our own choices, and live with them. We . . . we the adults. That's what adults do. If we don't shoulder the burdens, no one else will. But we cannot choose death for our children, who've had so little of life."

"Where are they? Find them!" Pauli heard people in the crowd begin to cry.

"I've got a man looking into it," she assured the people. "Thorn Halgerd. He's giving us the supplies we gave him—bribed him with—to leave us alone. Giving them to us, because human children are lost, and he cannot bear that any child suffer pain if he has breath to stop it. He's coming down now. I don't expect you to love him. But I do expect you to make him decently welcome. Because his first thought, when he heard that our children were lost, was to think how best to help us. Not to scheme how he'd wait till we'd killed ourselves off, then contact the Secess'."

There was some grumbling at Halgerd's name but, "Dammit, when my son was trapped by stobor, Halgerd leapt in to save him and almost died himself! I'll make him welcome, if no one else will," ben Yehuda called. He would, Pauli thought. And Dr. Pryor—for Alicia, he was the son she never had—*at the Kwanzaa feast, she had taken two ears of corn,* Pauli remembered. *One was for the promise of children. But the other had been for Thorn.* And Beneatha was probably too guilt-ridden to protest at all. Useful for now, Pauli thought, and her humility would probably last for at least five minutes after any success they might have in pulling themselves together.

"I ask you: if we give up, what sort of a memorial do we leave for the Cynthians? What sort of life have we provided the children? And without them, what reason do we have to go on living?

"Now," Pauli went on, "those of you who weren't exposed to the tainted bread, half of you form up into search parties. That's right: count off right now! The rest of you, clean up that mess, and keep it clean! Get the people who are walking wounded to help. It'll relieve their muscle cramps, just the way dancing did in Earth's Dark Ages. And once this place is clean, you can all start acting like human beings, not scared animals!"

The trampled square swarmed with what looked like madness, but was far more purposeful.

"What about the grain supplies?" Beneatha's voice was a shadow of its usual hostile self. *Asking about the grain is a punishment she has passed on herself,* Pauli realized. She rose to her feet, starting to walk toward the woman who was still very ill. Her face was greenish, and she wavered perceptibly, even as she leaned on the arms of two of the life-sciences people. But when Beneatha waved Pauli back, she obeyed. *At least I can give her more dignity than she had up in the foothills.*

"The grain? We aren't the first community to lose a year's harvest," Pauli said. "But I'll bet you a year's pay it's the last we lose!" Beneatha refused to subside. She met Pauli's eyes, her chin up, her jaw truculent as ever.

Pauli nodded respect at her and gave her the brutal truth. "We'd best burn it, once everything else is taken care of. I'm sorry."

"Not half as sorry as I am," Beneatha murmured, turning away. "Not one-quarter. I'll have my people get torches ready."

"It can wait for now," said Pauli. But Beneatha had already left.

As the search parties set off, Pauli sank down on a bench, leaned back against the dome, and blew into hands chilled even through her gloves. "There's got to be something hot to drink," Rafe told her. "Probably from last night."

"It better be strong enough to fly by itself," she said. "Thanks." She pulled out communications gear, and shifted from frequency to frequency, sorting through the calls of one party. If getting hot food into her was the best he could do, he'd better go do it, he thought.

Legs coiled under her like a child, Pauli was still rapt over the commgear when he returned, with clean mugs steaming in his hands. Hard to believe that that fiercely scowling girl led an entire settlement, or planned to wipe out a winged race—or had loved him and borne a son *lost to them now!* The familiar grief twisted his guts again.

She glanced up and smiled at him, preoccupied, but trying to hide it.

"I'm trying to raise Halgerd," she said.

"Why him, rather than the others?" Rafe asked.

"Aside from the fact that he can cover more ground than the others? He's got Lohr's wings, remember? And his eyesight's naturally . . . no, that's not right; he's modified for keen sight and greater than normal strength. He can hold out the longest . . . wait a moment . . . holding out!"

She leapt to her feet. "Ayelet!" she shouted at the adolescent who was helping a woman whose hands were still shaking to wipe red smears of paint from a curved wall. "Get over here!"

Ayelet bounded over.

"Lohr took all the littlests, did he? *All* of them?"

"They're not here," the girl agreed.

"That's what I thought," said Pauli. She spoke into her comm. "Yeager here. Don't forget that the kids will be held to the speed of the slowest child among them, and they've got one with a bad limp."

"'Cilla!" gasped Ayelet.

"What about her?" asked Pauli.

"Lohr asked me once if anything . . . anything . . . ever happened to him, Ari and I should look after 'Cilla. We told him that our father would help too, but you know Lohr. He thinks we should do everything on our own."

"Did you promise?"

"'Course," said Ayelet. That was right, Pauli nodded to herself. She'd thought that Ayelet and Lohr showed some signs of pairing off. If it hadn't been for Ari, when Lohr lit out for a hiding place, Dave might well have had to tie down his daughter.

Interference crackled and hummed, shrieked up and down the scale as Pauli homed in on the one signal she had sought. "Thorn? Is that you?"

"Captain?"

Pauli shut her eyes with relief, and Rafe tried not to grit his teeth. His wife and the renegade were both pilots; small wonder they trusted one another . . . at least somewhat.

"Thorn," she acknowledged. "Remember that they've got very young children with them. One of them limps badly . . . and is holding a child. They can't travel that far, not burdened that way, and not with an undisciplined crew—"*Yes, but they disciplined themselves well enough to stay alive in the burrows of Wolf IV.*

"There's searchers out too," Pauli spoke into the comm. Another wail of static drowned out Thorn's answer, or perhaps the clone had planned it that way.

"No, don't worry about it. I've told them to expect that you'll be calling in."

Orders weren't enough for born-humans, the captain had told Thorn during a night that struck him now as unreal as any stass-tank dream. He had watched her as she slept, as he might have guarded one of his brothers. She could have had his life, could have his obedience, for a mere word; but she asked instead. Perhaps he could give her more than she asked for—perhaps even what she wanted: news of the children.

He scanned the ground below him, banking to investigate a stand of stubby trees in which a crew of children might have hidden if there were no more than five of them, and none of those five was more than four feet tall.

Orders weren't enough. But she—he could only call her Pauli when those clear, steady eyes of hers were on him, and it was disobedience to call her anything else—had ordered him: join the search parties, seek out the missing children.

Let me find them! he begged, and realized he had learned another word: prayer. He swooped still lower, the wind chilling his face even through the new beard he had grown, as he investigated a rockfield that began to slant upward toward the foothills. He wanted to find them: God, he yearned to find them, to bring the children, as a gift, back to the settlement and win a welcome he couldn't even imagine.

He had the food and the computer for them, though those things had belonged to them from the start. But the children! There was strength in Lohr, whom he remembered as a swarthy, too-thin youth, his eyes bleak with hatred and caution, his hand shaking on a gun far too large for any boy to use. He was still young enough to cry, as he'd done after he knew that Ari would live and—thanks to his own quick work—so would Thorn.

Thorn had never cried when he was Lohr's age. What good would it have done? He'd only have been sedated and tossed back into stass while officers pondered whether or not his tears betrayed some instability in his whole group.

There were younger children too: a frail girl who clung to Lohr whenever possible—his sister; and the captain's child too! Faces upon faces: it seemed hard to know that an entire city of faces awaited him—and not one was his brother.

But he had never failed in courage before. He banked again, and rose effortlessly on the thermals. Lohr was leading the children toward the hills, was he? The lad was no fool.

Thorn scanned the terrain, grateful as he always was in action for his augmented sight, his hearing that let him distinguish search party from search party, static from chatter, and messages from . . .

From music?

Thin and plaintively reedy, the sound of pipes floated up to Halgerd on the damp air. "Halgerd here," he spoke quickly, crisply, ignoring the one gasp of shock he heard. "Is any one of your runaways a musician?"

"Lohr has pipes," came the answer. There—he heard the music again, shrill, even infectious, coaxing the no-doubt exhausted children to struggle yet farther, up the slopes, into safe hiding behind their leader, who played to put new heart in them.

"Then I've got a fix on them!" Thorn called, and gave out coordinates.

He gained altitude and flew over them, trying to keep them in sight. Abruptly, however, the sun came out from behind Cynthia's heavy slate clouds, and his shadow flickered out over the runaways like a dark, elongated winged creature.

He hissed in aggravation. "They've spotted me!" he announced crisply, without apology (he didn't think that Captain Yeager had a stass tank to shut him into, much as he deserved it; and nerve induction was useless if you had no other brothers who would share the pain your blunder had earned). "I'm going to land."

"Wait for us!" came the deep voice Thorn remembered as belonging to David ben Yehuda. Interesting, he thought. That name came from Ararat. The Halgerd memories woke in him: Ararat was tough, and almost as proud a world—even making allowance for the fact that all the Alliance was rotten to the core—as Freki. Ben Yehuda . . . he was one of the crew who had brought Thorn in. Why was *he* so far from home?

"Thorn?" came Captain Yeager's voice, softer and more agitated than he had ever heard it.

"Do you see . . . a fair little girl, about your coloring, who walks with a definite limp? She might be carrying a child in her arms."

Her child. Thorn remembered when it had been born. He swooped lower, and watched as Lohr forbade his tiny army to flee. Instead, the boy turned and shook his fist at the departing glider and its pilot. *Damned good thing he didn't have a blaster this time,* Thorn thought. *This time, he probably wouldn't have tried to miss.*

Children down there . . . children of all sizes and all colors, though most were still too thin, their bodies marked with the struggle to survive. A black girl there; there an Oriental youth; two or three children with coloring much like his own . . . he scanned the crowd of tired children, his memories of the one child Pauli mentioned (and her own) as clear in his mind as a ship in the sights of the armscomp.

Even as he watched, the boy Lohr gestured the children to move again, ordering them, encouraging them, and as the ragged, weary line started uphill again, taking out his pipe and playing.

Thorn veered away from the children toward the search party that approached from the settlement. If he was wise, he would guide them from the air. But he was afraid he was not wise, not any longer; temptation burned strong to land and walk with the born-humans, as if he were one of them. If they would have him. He thumbed on his comm.

"Halgerd here again. I've located the children. Yes, they're fine. Tired, I think, but in good order. Sorry. Yes, they spotted me. Lohr shook his fist at me. But Cap . . . Pauli? I didn't see the little girl. Or your baby."

"'Cilla and Serge aren't with them," Pauli told Alicia Pryor, who lay propped up to help her breathe. *I'm not dying,* she had told the medcrew—and anyone else who came within range of her tongue, which was still scalpel-sharp, though her voice couldn't rise higher than a whisper. "Thorn will go in with the nearest search party."

"That's wise," Pryor said. "The kids will respond best to people they trust."

"Do they trust any of us now?"

"Pauli . . ." Pryor's blue-veined hand covered the younger woman's where it rested, clasped in Rafe's, on her blankets. "Of course they trust you! Why else punish you by running away?"

"Perhaps because they had enough of adult 'protection,'" said Rafe, his voice so bitter that Pauli soothed him with a gentle touch.

"Perhaps. But even if they run, they want to be found, assured they're loved, and brought back to safety."

"But 'Cilla," Pauli whispered.

"I couldn't quite believe that she could make it into those hills," Pryor mused, then began to cough.

"Lohr would never leave her behind. He adores her."

"And she adores him," said Pryor. "You remember when we evacuated everyone to the hills, she knew she had to stay behind. My guess is that this time she knew she couldn't march with the children.

"What a dilemma for a frightened little girl! If she stays with her brother, she risks slowing down every child, perhaps risking their lives. But if she remains . . . the camp is full of madness; and there is a baby whom she feels *she* should protect."

Pauli gasped. "Lohr may have suspected something. That's why he asked Ayelet to look after her."

Rafe unfolded himself from his chair. "Let's get Ayelet in here for a chat," he remarked too quietly.

One of Beneatha's techs (whom Pauli had last seen with her belly flaunted in the green and gold splendor of a long robe) stuck her head in through the door. "We're ready to burn the grain," she informed everyone.

"*No!*" cried Pryor. "Don't you dare! At least not yet!" She broke into spasms of coughing that made her sink back against her pillows. Gently Pauli wiped her lips.

"That's it! We were idiots. Pauli, help me get up. Now!"

The woman still had an aristocrat's haughtiness, Pauli thought. It was instinct to obey her, to ease her from her bed to stand on uncertain feet, then aid her to sit and to dress.

"You can't let them burn that grain now. It's 'Cilla," Pryor whispered shallowly, to avoid coughing again. "What if she's gone to ground there?"

"Be sensible, Alicia! The grain is contaminated. 'Cilla knows that."

"That child knows too damned much! She knows that we'll leave the grain alone. She also knows she cannot jeopardize the life of every child in the settlement by holding them back—and that her brother will insist that she do just that. But she is clever, with that innocent face of hers; she sits among adults day after day, and because she is quiet and she paints, they let her pass by unnoticed."

Pauli leapt to her feet, heedless of the tears streaking down her face. "And where she is . . ."

The life-sciences tech had sat down so quickly that Pryor reached for ammoniac spirits. "For God's sake, don't pass out on us!" the physician ordered acidly.

"Those domes are ice-cold," whispered the tech. "When the computer failed, we powered down the outlying storage areas. It's freezing cold there."

"We have to get there, before they torch the grain!" Pauli cried. She ran out of the clinic, her bootheels hammering first on the floor, then on the icy snow. She slipped and fell to one knee, recovering herself with an angry, impatient oath, then was up and racing toward the storage areas.

Beneatha and some of the life-sciences and bio techs approached. Each of them held a lit torch.

"There may be children in there!" screamed Pauli. "Hold off!"

Beneatha's unhealthy, jaundiced color shifted to an even grayer tone despite her umber skin. She hurled the torch to the ground, and ran for one of the domes.

'Cilla and Serge, God help them both, Pauli thought as Rafe came up and tried to ease Beneatha onto a bench, were hiding somewhere in those storage areas. She probably would not come out, not for any voice less loving than her brother's.

But they had to try.

For what felt like hours, they shouted and called, trying to keep the terror out of their voices as they approached. ("Get thermal blankets," Pryor whispered. "We've got hypothermia here . . . I hope.")

Pauli reached to strip the seal from the door, but Beneatha pushed her hand away. "I have to do it," she said.

"Flyer incoming!" someone shouted behind them.

Thorn Halgerd swooped down, banking and diving at angles that Pauli would not have dared to try. Even as he touched down, he braced himself, then leapt forward, running for the dome where he saw the most people gathered.

Dr. Pryor walked out to greet him, her hands going out, then dropping in the moment before he understood she wanted to touch him. Though his face was reddened with cold, and tense from the effort of hours aloft, he managed a smile that lit even his eyes, which had always been unaccustomed to smiling.

"We think that the little girl fled into one of the storage domes with the baby Serge," Pryor said; and that was all the greeting she gave him.

Thorn nodded, then pushed past Pauli, his wings clattering and falling from his back in long, orderly folds. Rafe moved as if to bar his way.

"No," said the pilot simply, "you shouldn't go in there, and the captain certainly should not. In case the news is bad, the.... the parents should be spared at least having to see it first. Please let me do this for you."

As the door irised slowly, unevenly, he edged inside. His feet scuffed on the dry floor. Then they heard grain sacks thud against the floor as he began a search that was as arduous as it was thorough until that sound, and then all other sounds, died away; and they remained outside the dome in silence.

A baby's cry rang out, like rain after a long drought. Pauli shivered with relief. Tears ran over Rafe's face.

But Halgerd's eyes were dry as he emerged from the storage area. He had two children in his arms, one a fiercely squalling Serge, hungry, dirty, furious—and totally beautiful. Pauli ran forward, laughing and crying, to seize her baby . . .

And stopped, even as she exulted at the weight of her son, grubby and smelly as he was, in her arms, at the way his arms clung and his head rubbed against her, seeking her warmth. Warmth, Pauli thought. The sunlight gleaming on Thorn's bright hair and forgotten harness suddenly broke into rainbows as tears welled in her eyes once more. For Thorn also held 'Cilla. Her skin was waxen, her eyes shut beneath heavy lids and her long, long eyelashes. She did not shiver; and she barely breathed.

"I was afraid of this," Dr. Pryor murmured. "Her body heat kept the baby warm until her temperature dropped . . ." She touched the child's wrist and shook her head. With a dreadful tenderness, she wrapped 'Cilla in blankets, then gestured at Thorn Halgerd to lift her once more and carry her toward the clinic where he had been restored to life.

He set off with those long strides, but stopped abruptly. Pauli ran forward. 'Cilla's blue eyes opened and she looked up at Thorn, with his hair the color of grain, and the silver of his flying harness and wings glistening where they folded and quivered over his back.

"I found you," she sighed. "Where did you and Mother go? We looked all over for you, Lohr and I. We were so"—she yawned deeply, then choked once—"not cold now, not scared."

"No, never again," said Thorn, his voice as hoarse as Pryor's.

The child gasped once again, and Thorn pressed her head against his shoulder with one big hand, then covered her from head to toe in the gleaming blankets like a blighted chrysalis.

"Sweet God, here comes the search party," whispered the physician. "And they've got the kids with them. Keep Lohr away!" Her voice broke, then failed altogether.

"That won't work," Thorn said. "When I lost my brothers . . . he too must feel the death for him to know that it's real." He handed 'Cilla over to Rafe, then walked slowly toward Lohr, unstrapping the flying harness as he approached the taut, grimy-faced boy.

Lohr gazed over at the tiny wrapped bundle with a kind of frenzied control, then looked at Thorn Halgerd, who held out the glider on the palms of both hands. "Here are the wings you lent me," he told the boy. "I wish I could give you back your sister too."

Man and boy stared at one another, the wings gleaming between them. Neither looked away, or wept. Neither, Pauli thought, was old enough to weep, really. The last time they had met, Lohr had saved Thorn's life, and had wept from relief and confusion. This time, Lohr was no longer a child, to cry freely, nor a man to weep (as Rafe was doing) for sorrow.

For that matter, neither was Thorn.

Finally, Lohr held out his hands, touched the wings lightly, then pushed them back. "You keep them."

"I lost five brothers," said Halgerd. "I still don't know which hurt worse, feeling nothing, or feeling the deaths."

Lohr nodded.

"I have supplies up in the caves. We'll need them down here," Thorn said, "to help make this place run smoothly again. Perhaps when the weather is warmer, you might come with me to help carry the things down. My own things, too. Would you?"

Lohr nodded, a mere jerk of his head.

"Then take back your wings," said Halgerd.

"I don't know if I ever want to fly again," Lohr whispered, looking down at his feet.

"You will," said Thorn. "I did."

He held out his hands again, so that the light could shimmer enticingly on the wings' struts and metallic cloth and this time Lohr's hands closed over them.

Ben Yehuda and his twins approached him at a run, but seeing the utter dignity of the boy, they slowed, then stopped, waiting for him to speak.

"You would have taken care of 'Cilla," he told them. "I know that." He walked over to Pauli as she stood, clutching her child, and gazed into its flushed face, wizened from screaming. "You must be my brother now, since my sister's dead," he told Thorn, then walked away from the children he had led. Thorn Halgerd followed. Man and boy headed toward the clinic. After several paces, they fell into step.

PART IV

Nemesis (ten years after Planetfall)

Because I do not hope to turn again
Let these words answer
For what is done, not to be done again
May the judgement not be too heavy upon us

Because these wings are no longer wings to fly
But merely vanes to beat the air
The air which is now thoroughly small and dry
Smaller and dryer than the will
Teach us to care and not to care
Teach us to sit still.

—T.S. Eliot, "Ash Wednesday"

Ayelet sat nursing her aching back and the comms again. It was boring, but comm duty was for the convalescent, the crippled, or—as Dr. Pryor had decreed—the pregnant, if she had any doubts at all about their health.

"Nothing's the matter with me!" Ayelet had argued. "I feel fine, except early in the morning, or when my back hurts. Nothing's wrong with me."

"Your age is against you," stated the doctor, whose own age was showing badly. The skin had fined back from the elegant lean bones of eyesockets and brows, had sagged in delicate folds on her slender neck. "Let alone the fact that you were malnourished during puberty. And besides, what do we know of Lohr's heredity? So you're at risk in this pregnancy. That means that you'll do light work, Ayelet, or so help me—"

So help her, Pryor was likely to have Ayelet tied down, or, weak as she herself was, tie the girl down herself unless Ayelet obeyed; and Ayelet, Lohr, and all their friends knew it. What was worse, Ayelet thought they'd probably help.

"When her mother was your age, she was in school," Ayelet's father had backed up the physician. "We hadn't even met. But when Ayelet and Ari . . . well, when she was pregnant, all the medics said how young she was."

Ayelet had seethed inside. Her mother (whom she remembered as a quick kiss on the hair and a breath of fragrance) was university-bred, much like Dr. Pryor; like her father, she had grown up with her eyes glued to a screen. Students bred, born, and trained like that tended to put off marriage, let alone childbearing. It was different, instinctively she knew it, it was totally different in a place like Cynthia and among people like those who had become brothers, sisters, yes, and a husband to her, people who had scrambled to early maturity while glancing over their shoulders lest a mortal enemy come up behind them. The urge to have something, someone, of your own or to leave some mark behind you—she had tried to explain that to her father before she and Lohr married. Tried and failed. Unlike her father, she hadn't the education to be clever with words.

Now, once again faced down by that superior, frustrating eloquence, she flushed. At least, when she was angry, she didn't feel like vomiting.

"Dave!" Ayelet cried angrily. "You all make me feel like a weakling or a fool."

"Never mind your 'Daves,'" her father had told her. "Just take care of yourself. You're not a weakling, but if you endanger yourself or my first grandson, you will be a fool."

Grandson? Ayelet thought with a quiet, secret smile. Her first child, hers and Lohr's, would be a girl. It had to be a girl they could name 'Cilla, after the little sister Lohr still woke in the night to call for and cry over.

"What sort of a name for a ben Yehuda is 'Cilla?" Washington had teased her once. Ari, who should have known better, joined in.

"We name after the dead," she had reminded him.

"You would never be permitted to name her that—if it's a girl, and I'm not saying it is!—on Ararat."

Ayelet had snorted. Ararat, her father's birthworld, was the second planet of which she had strong memories. Very strong. Pungent, even. Her father had married while studying off-planet; Ayelet and her brother had grown up in the cosmopolitan environment of a university world (if not as rarefied a place as Pryor's Santayana, New Trieste still was a child's wonderland). Not like Ararat, which she remembered chiefly for loud voices and unpleasant scenes.

Her mother had lasted a year or so there, then fled

back to New Trieste. "What do you mean?" she remembered her father shouting at a voice that belonged to an old man who lacked the courtesy even to show his face on the comms. "My kids aren't dirty; they don't need to be purified.

"Never mind!" ben Yehuda had shouted. "I'm not letting them be subjected to that stuff, not at school, and not from you. I'll take them offworld. Yes, I know it's exile. But we've usually been exiles, haven't we? Until, of course, we landed here and promptly became the oppressors we fled other places to avoid. Well, no thank you. My kids are tough, and I'm tough too. We'll manage just fine."

And so they had. Managed. Not lived, Ayelet thought. At first, she had missed her mother and her home. Later on, though, she and Ari had understood their own homelessness. Being children, they had had to be content to follow their father—their affable, splendidly competent father—from world to world. And then had come the war, years of enduring and wandering.

Until they came to Cynthia. This was her home now, hers and Ari's, even her father's. He was older now, heavier than he had ever been, oddly breathless and tired at times. Cynthia had taught them all a kind of patience. Lohr had taught her and Ari more: to fight, occasionally to rebel, and to use the rage she often felt but rarely dared express as a weapon in the struggle to endure the terrible days of Ari's sickness and the lean days thereafter, when Lohr stalked the camp as if his sanity had been buried along with his sister; and haunted Thorn Halgerd as if they had been born at one birth.

Those had been hard times for Halgerd too. Like the rest of them, he had grown very lean. Starving himself, Lohr shouted once, enraged at the man. Playing martyr.

"Are you trying to finish off the deaths, join your brothers?" he had snarled.

To Ayelet's horror, Halgerd's pale skin had flushed, his lean fists knotting. Halgerd wasn't just a clone; he had been augmented for speed and strength. If he struck

Lohr, he might crush his teeth or his jaw. If he was angry enough, just one blow might snap Lohr's spine; and Ayelet had already known she loved him.

But Thorn had unclenched his fists and turned away.

"That's the first time you've been angry at any of us," Lohr taunted him.

"The second. Your captain saw me the first time," Thorn had said, then turned away. Ayelet knew he had walked about the camp rashly, a willing target for anyone who wanted a scapegoat to strike down.

He and Lohr had been close those months, so close— "Don't you worry, *I'm* not one of his stupid brothers!" Lohr had snapped at her once with real venom. That friendship remained, even after Lohr and Ayelet married, and Ayelet conceived Lohr's child. Gradually she accepted the idea of Halgerd as a friend. She had always been patient: Halgerd was quiet, a gentle man who occupied much of his time teaching the littlests to fly, and the rest of it on designing the ultralights Beneatha called a risk to life and limb and a stupid waste of resources. (As Lohr said, *She would!*)

Why had Thorn never married? Ro Economus stared after him whenever he passed by. He was handsome and considerate, even shy, a combination that many women considered irresistible. Perhaps he had been alone too long. Perhaps the bond with his brothers had wrecked him for any other intimate ties. Besides, Lohr told her, Halgerd was still little older in actual waketime than they themselves.

Wake up! Ayelet ordered herself. She stretched laboriously, as did the child she bore. She patted her belly, exulting in the strength of her child's kicks. Patiently she rearranged herself in a chair that felt like it had grown even harder in the past five minutes and adjusted a cushion to support the small of her back.

She glanced at the monitors. As she expected, there was nothing doing out there in Cynthia system. No . . . there was something . . . teasing her, way on the edge of reception . . . she turned up the gain on the monitors.

Soon her watch would be over, and then even Dr.

Pryor couldn't refuse her a chance at light work in the fields. Just let her try, Ayelet promised herself.

That flicker of light again! She froze. It wasn't chatter. It *was* a signal. She turned up reception again, scanning all the usual bands, and most of the less common ones for good measure.

It *was* a signal. The last time they had suspected Secess' in-system—and got Thorn out of the deal—all but the eldest, the sickest, *and the pregnant, God damn-it!* were evacuated to the moths' caves. *We don't call them moths, not ever; they are Cynthians,* Ayelet corrected herself. None of the children was permitted to call the Cynthians moths; that was a racist term that reduced sapient beings to winged bugs. *We have to remember that they were people.* How often had the littlests been drilled in that?

Well, even a year after their deaths, the Cynthians' caves had reeked of musk and formic acid. By the end of the first few days of the evacuation, the stink of stale, terrified humans had been added to the brew. There wasn't much Ayelet wouldn't do to escape ever having to deal with that stink again.

Signal or no signal, she determined, lower lip outthrust and jaw squared in a brief rehearsal of the speech she planned to make, she wasn't leaving home again. This settlement, provincial as her father might find it, was *hers*; and she was staying put.

For she knew that Lohr wouldn't leave; and she wouldn't leave him.

The signal strengthened, grew focused, all chatter melding into one great beam of query directed straight at them.

That was when Ayelet heard the first recognition code.

Lohr, her father, and her brother could shove it, she told herself. She wasn't *that* pregnant (though she decided then and there that she'd exploit her pregnancy if she had to) that she couldn't climb up to the caves. But Cynthia colony was her home. She wasn't leaving. No matter what anyone said.

Anyone? What about these invaders?

Recognition codes . . . like all the littlests, the civilians, the officers, and the life-sciences people who were "none of the above," Ayelet had had the rec codes drilled into her.

Query? she asked when the ship's librarian came in with the data on Cynthia.

"Alliance ID codes," came the librarian's opinion.

"Alliance?" she asked the computer with the voice of a long-dead librarian.

"Yes, Lieutenant."

The panic button, red and taped down to the console, tempted her. She peeled away the tape.

Again the comms exploded into life with lines and lines of codes. That had to be a ship! Theirs or one of the Secess'? She ought to hit the panic button now, give the littlests a chance to evacuate.

But I'm *not leaving here,* she told herself, unusually truculent. *This is home.*

Again the signal rose. It was getting closer and closer, as if whatever tracked them scorned standard search patterns. That signal *knew* they were here. Which might mean that the war was over, and that the Alliance had come—with flourishes—to rescue its lost children. But that was a story not even the littlests would believe. Sure, the assured speed of the signal might mean an Alliance ship.

Or it could be betrayal: *that Becker!* Ayelet remembered him, all thoughts and plots as he watched the littlests like they were beasts who might suddenly go mad and leap for him. *He* might have changed sides; or someone who knew him might have been captured and traded the knowledge of Cynthia base for his life. Or her life.

This called for decisions Ayelet knew she couldn't make. She took out her commlink, blew into it, and spoke softly.

"Rafe, can you come to Comm Central?" she asked, sweating and ashamed because her voice shook.

* * *

David ben Yehuda shouted out the final order and stepped back. Rafe chuckled. Even from his hilltop vantagepoint, Rafe could see him frown, and he suspected that ben Yehuda was swearing under his breath. Just last year Dave would have shouted with rage if anyone suggested he take it easier. He was grizzled now, and chest pains meant that he had to ease up on heavy labor. The work crews drew breath (Rafe thought he could almost hear them suck in the air), leaned on their ropes, and lunged forward, straining for each step, struggling against each slide backward.

As they pulled the ropes taut, the great tents rose, soaring higher than any of the domes thrown up in the settlement's first seasons. That cluster had grown; in the past ten years, the settlement had almost earned the name of town; and thriving new families needed temporary quarters. The tents would serve until more permanent housing could be contrived.

Sunlight gleamed golden off the white, resistant surfaces of the tents, spiked and vaned like flying creatures yoked, just for now, to the land. They too were part of a harvest, just as surely as the fields that lay beyond, bordered by the brown river and the violent green of the ground scrub, ordered rows of amber and ochre, greens and golds, glistening violet all around their perimeter from the tiny repellors that protected their crops against stobor.

Even at this distance, Rafe could hear them, faint as the white noise generators that eased human ears on the starships he was well content never to see again. Or to think about. He shrugged off the memory, then rubbed his hands through hair thinning now at temples and brow.

A shout drew his attention. At this hour of the day, many Cynthians were working in the fields; Rafe saw Beneatha, thinner than she had been, her close-cropped curls graying at the temples, but her bony hands still emphatic as she directed her farmers. This year, her fields would yield three separate crops, spaced out over the growing season.

Rafe grimaced. It had taken months of research and a good deal of shouting to convince Beneatha that agroinfection of the crops with ice-minus posed no danger to vital insects and wildlife (including those ubiquitous, seasonal nuisances, the stobor). Their harvests had been leaner then. Now, however, they would never again have to suffer a lean season like the one they had endured the winter they had torched the ergot-infected grain.

All the settlers had gone short of food, the leaders shortest of all. The littlests' faces had hollowed out until they almost resembled the wild children Rafe had first seen on board the old *Jeffrey Amherst*. And despite Pauli's quips that it was definitely worthwhile to be pregnant, if only to be sure of full rations, he knew that she had been giving away her food. She had been gaunt by spring. When she miscarried, no one was really surprised. "I have other children to protect," she had said, and gone off by herself, as she had done more and more in the past years.

After that winter, the spring's planting had been as serious as any battle, Rafe thought as he stared out over the fields. His imagination transformed them to the fields of ten years past: much smaller and browner, new furrows gaping like wounds from which seeds and fertilizer seeped into the river every time it rained—and it usually rained that summer: so much so that once again they feared ergot and the madness it brought.

But the settlement had escaped. As if in celebration, in trust that the bad times were over that winter, at least four of the younger women—and Pauli once again—became pregnant. Rafe had been furious at her and more so at himself, but "she wants to replace her child," Dr. Pryor told him firmly. "It's her choice; and frankly, I think it will be good for her." Pryor too had worried about Pauli's long silences.

The colony thrived, what remained of it. Rafe glanced over at the graveyard, too large by far for his liking, yet thank God it was not larger yet. Many of the frailer settlers, those most gravely affected by the convulsions, madness, and tremors from the ergot, had died in the lean seasons before they could reap their next harvest. Some had been older people whose skills the colony could ill afford to lose; but too many of the others had been refugee children. Rafe blinked away angry tears, as he always did when he thought of them. Dammit, they hadn't had very much of a life, had they? He sighed. At least they had had some experience of trust and love to take with them into the dark. 'Cilla, bless her heart, had proved that. If she hadn't hidden with Rafe and Pauli's son, whom she had snatched to protect, she might still be alive today. Even during the worst shortages, her grave, and then those of others, had always been strewn with flowering plants.

The others? Pauli's voice floated up to him. High overhead, the sky was full of wings: the next generation of Cynthians, wheeling and banking (and escaping collisions by shrill cries and very narrow margins) as they practiced with the gliders. Rafe grinned; his own son Serge was up there, only a bit younger than Lohr had been the first times he had flown.

Lohr folded his wings and dived, straightening out in time to hear Pauli's indignant shouts. He landed, and she limped toward him with remarkable speed.

After she'd broken her leg in a gliding accident (who but Pauli would go aloft in high winds to shepherd a frightened child?), Dr. Pryor had warned her to stay off it until it healed. But that was the autumn the physician's pneumonia returned. For weeks she had been ill, and had never quite recovered, so Pauli promptly forgot her warnings. She had no time to lie, or sit idle, nor patience to delegate others to be hands and feet for her. At least, not for long.

She was up and prowling her settlement as soon as she could hobble; and now, she never would lose that limp.

Golden light glinted off the metal wings, and pooled at the horizon, where the sun was lowering. Fields and sky echoed with voices and songs. *These* Cynthians were alive, and they were making their world richer for their presence. *Please God, let this serve as our atonement,*

Rafe prayed, as he prayed every day for years. Not even Pauli knew he had started praying.

Certainly the past ten years seemed to prove that Cynthia had finally decreed that the past was past; and that the stubborn, guilty humans were the planet's children now. That, at least, was what some of the gentlest of the settlers thought—and what Rafe longed to believe.

At least, though, the children no longer looked down at the ground, following their elders' example. Many flew now, true to the heritage Pauli insisted that they remember. Farmers they were: that much was true. But Pauli forced them to remember an older truth: theirs had been a tradition of flight, of faring from star to star, whether any of them would ever see a starship again.

But this was a good life now, wasn't it? he pleaded at his memories. They had a fine life, now, purged of war, of vanities, or hunger, and full of productive work which enabled a man to see his own rewards. Even the feral children who had tried to run away had flourished into a unique harvest: Lohr was a capable aide to Pauli now, and an assistant to Thorn Halgerd, off by himself once again, testing the ultralight craft he hoped might let them cross the stormy Cynthian seas and explore other continents. He was happier alone, Lohr said, happiest of all while working on his designs for the ultralights. Ben Yehuda said his work was brilliant: unsurprising, if one reminded oneself of Thorn's real father—laureate, renegade, and their friend Alicia's old lover.

The alarm from Rafe's communicator buzzed imperiously, and Rafe started. It had been months since anyone had chosen that particular signal to summon him. He activated the device and heard Ayelet's husky voice. "Rafe, can you come to CommCentral? Bring Father . . . and the captain." Ayelet's voice was higher-pitched than usual, and Rafe didn't think he'd heard her call Dave "Father" or Pauli "captain" for years.

"What's the matter?" he asked, but knowledge began to turn his hands and belly chill. When the cold crept up to his heart, he would be wholly frozen, he suspected. But it was right. It was time. He started down the hill, Ayelet's plaintive voice floating in the clear air of his home.

"We've got ship signals."

Almost the same name as before, even. Gods. Ayelet thumbed communications to record the transmission, and held her breath to listen for the numbers and code series that must surely follow.

If the codes weren't right, they were all dead.

She thinned her lips and hit the panic button, then winced as she heard the sirens hoot across the settlement. *That* would ground the fliers, pull children from their play, adults from their duties or their rest, and send them seething into their evacuation groups by the numbers. The only people who would be spared the climb would be those too sick to walk. *And me,* Ayelet thought. *And me.*

The numbers flickered, then marched across her screens. So the war was really over? She'd believe it when Rafe and Pauli and her father confirmed it. And meanwhile, she'd give the settlement the time it needed to flee, just in case this was a trick.

Rubbing her lower back again, Ayelet settled in to wait. Adult that she was, wife that she was, and mother that she was about to be, nevertheless, she had called for help—fearful of a chancy universe, well taught from her years as a refugee.

The door irised to admit Pauli Yeager, running despite the limp that made her look older than her years. As its panels shrank back into place, an arm forced them apart, and Rafe thrust himself inside, followed by her father, and several others of the adults who really ran the colony. Ayelet shivered with relief, then forced herself (despite a back that ached more and more every day) to sit almost at attention. The last thing anyone needed was for her to cry.

(. . . "Don't cry, Ayelet, Ari. The captain knows what he's doing. We can outrun that ship . . . no, that salvo missed us, and in a minute or two, we'll Jump . . . remember, Jump is strange, but you can make it. Just one more time . . .")

Just one more time, Ayelet thought. One more time to summon her courage and the stolid silence that had lifelong proved to be her best defense. Her father had always told her, "You can make it just this once more," and he had always been right.

But even he had never faced *this.*

Still, years of love, security, trust . . . *yes, and continued survival* . . . made her smile at him.

"Just one more time," she shaped the words with dry lips. Even now, that won a twisted smile from her. *("Be my big girl. Don't show the littlests how scared you are.")* Damn, the old trick still worked!

The door ground back. Damage there, Ayelet thought, as the panels sagged, then forced themselves open again to admit Lohr, who supported Dr. Pryor.

"I relieve you, Ayelet," Pauli Yeager spoke formally, as she rarely did these days. Her voice returned Ayelet to the security of her brief childhood after the flight across hostile space to Cynthia. Once they were settled downworld, a word from Captain Yeager meant unquestioned reassurance. A small hand patted her shoulder, and "Good thinking" made her tingle with pride for an instant. The captain slid into the place she vacated and studied the record of transmissions.

"Message incoming," Ayelet warned, and watched the older woman nod. Her fingers tapped and she whistled under her breath while decrypt puzzled it out. "What *are* those damned codes?" she muttered. Then her brow cleared and her fingers blurred on the comm as she sent back recognition codes that surely must be ten years obsolete. Rafe leaned over her, one hand on her shoulder.

"I know, Rafe," the captain said hoarsely. "But look at the codes *they* sent. They don't just know someone's out here; they think it's us, or someone like us. One of their damned seedcorn dumps. And if they don't know the codes—" she shrugged.

Pauli muttered to herself, then, experimentally, tapped out a number sequence. Static erupted, faded, then solidified. She nodded to herself.

"Ayelet," asked Captain Yeager, "would you care to do the honors?"

Terror, buried all these years, bubbled to the surface and threatened to erupt in childish wails as, once again, comm lights flashed on her board. Though Pauli Yeager's words had been phrased as a question, Ayelet knew that they were an order. She drew a deep breath *("Yes, I am Father's brave girl, and yours . . . and my own, dammit!")* and punched for audio.

"Cynthia, is that you? This is *Amherst II . . .*"

Behind them, the door began to slide open again.

"Keep them out!" Rafe had a sudden vision of yelling children, though *these* children, even now, were likelier by far to go silent and prepare to fight to the death.

Pauli looked up at him, her eyes so bright that Rafe raised work-stained fingers to brush something shiny from her cheek.

"I remember that voice," she announced in a harsh voice. "It's Becker. *Becker*. The marshal. Remember him?"

"He left us here," Rafe nodded. "Lousy survey, barely enough equipment, and a ship's bay full of kids—and he left us here with fine words about our maybe being the last generations of humans to survive with their genes intact. Let me get my hands on him, and his genes may be the only thing of his that I'll leave intact. And that won't be for lack of trying."

"The war's over, he says," Pauli breathed. "And now he's come—"

"To fetch us?" Pryor whispered, then coughed, and bent double coughing harder. Lohr tore himself from the green-lit comm screens long enough to fetch her a cup of water.

"You're good at making *us* take our medicine," Ayelet heard him say. "You should take your own advice." Pryor muttered something rueful and profane back at him, and, despite the time and place, Ayelet grinned.

"That, or bring others to join us. Secess' types, maybe. Look at this!" Pauli cried. "The *Amherst II*'s crew. The roster lists their homeworlds: equal parts Alliance, Secess'—and Earth."

She looked up, and for a moment Ayelet saw the young, eager Pauli Yeager who had visited the refugees on board the old *Amherst* so many years ago: the hot pilot, enraged by the sacrifice of a ship, who took the time to speak kindly with the littlests even when they sensed how angry she was that anyone could abandon people like that. It made them like her, talk about her, dream about being like her, even now. But no one, not even the captain, ever had dreamed of contact with Earth again.

Pauli bent over the computers, punching up a course, running her hands through her hair, close-cropped for practicality though she rarely wore a helmet or any type of headgear now, and muttering to herself in a pilot's trance of calculation as she saw trajectories form and flatten on the screens.

"Can't land there," she told the screen. Her fingers danced, and the trajectories curved again, and the machines beeped to indicate a course locked in.

"We'll be in voice contact within minutes," she said. "Best get everyone out of the way."

"Do we evacuate?" Rafe asked, low-voiced. "The groups are ready to move."

Pauli shook her head. "They need to be here to see," she told him. "You remember, love. We discussed it. There can be *no* extenuating circumstances. No exceptions. I'll clear the landing area."

She punched the panic button. Once again, the siren shrieked like the very throat of hell, then was replaced by Pauli's calm voice.

"Cancel evacuation, but clear the area. I repeat, clear

the area. We have a ship incoming. Duty crews should stand by with fire extinguishers and await my orders."

She rose and limped out the door before it had struggled halfway open, and Rafe followed her.

That damned ground scrub! and they had fields to protect. Had Ayelet been in the captain's place, she would have forgotten the fires that a landing might spark. How would she, Ari, and Lohr ever remember all the details that Pauli had mastered? *Be patient,* Ayelet told herself and glanced at Lohr.

But for once he neither smiled nor looked at her. He had on the expression that Ayelet privately called his "scenting danger" look, a blend of fear, instinct, and cunning raised to the level of tactical planning. He had one arm about the doctor, who sagged against him and looked older than Ayelet had ever seen her. She blinked, shook her head irritably, then seemed to twitch, all except her left hand.

"I'll be all right," said the physician, but her speech was slurred.

Lohr stared at her, his dark eyes cynical.

"I have to be there for them," she insisted. "Lohr, don't make me beg—"

"We'll all go," said Ayelet, shutting down the comm. No need to stand a watch against landing ships now. After a lifetime of running and hiding, for once, she intended to stand her ground.

The *Amherst II* descended in a wildness of light and sound, a wreathing of smoke, against which masked settlers rushed with fire extinguishers to protect their land—if not their skins. The ship's sides had been sleek once, but now showed scars and the too-worn contours of a ship better suited now for salvage than starflight. Its markings were strange: the sigil of Earth superimposed over what looked like the emblem of the Alliance. Smoke and foam wreathed about that too-rakish hull. Then the settlers stood back, a ramp slid down—

And out walked the Security Marshal Becker who Ayelet remembered: older, slower, but just as watchful as she remembered from the days before they landed on Cynthia. Following him was a strange, wiry brown man who wore a blue uniform that she had never seen before. Then came many other crewmembers, dressed in a patched assortment of flightsuits that could be called uniforms only because they bore the same insignia worn by the brown man, modified by various emblems that Ayelet understood meant various ranks and specialties. She almost thought she remembered which were which.

Despite the fear that clawed at her, how wonderful it was to see new faces, faces from a hundred worlds, Secess' and Alliance together. Ayelet's eyes filled. The war was over. Crew from Alliance and Secess' alike wore those new markings over their old uniforms. It gave them a type of kinship. What was that line from one of her father's old plays? *"O brave new world, that hath such people in't."*

Were they the brave new world, though, or were the newcomers? Their expressions didn't seem to match Ayelet's exultation, now that her fear had turned to joy. Gradually that joy cooled. She had been right about the kinship among the newcomers; wrong, however, in attributing it to their uniforms. What really made them look akin was their expression, the strained look of veterans forced to the limits of their understanding: that and the well-kept weapons they held trained on the settlement.

Ayelet turned instinctively to look for her settlement's leaders. Surely the captain would shout an order, and this stranger-crew would lay its weapons aside; or Rafe would smile, and say something tactful. But even as Ayelet watched, Rafe and Pauli approached the ship and its tense, heavily armed crew. Limping slightly, Pauli Yeager lagged behind her taller husband, who turned to wait for her.

They had changed into their flightsuits. Even those durable synthetics were faded and much creased after the many years they had been folded away from bugs, vermin, fresh air, and light. After the many years of sparse rations and sparser leisure, the old uniforms sagged. Neither of them wore weapons but Pauli carried what looked like a recorder tucked beneath one arm.

As Marshal Becker and the brown man walked down the ramp, Pauli drew herself up and saluted. Tears ran down her cheeks.

CHAPTER
21

"They know you. So you go first," the thin, brown man, whose three names, Amory Eliot Neave, lettered across his chest betrayed lineage as much as the sigil he wore, told the Alliance marshal. Nodding brusque thanks, Becker strode down the *Amherst's* ramp before the smoke from ground cover ignited by the ship's landing could spin away to nothing. The woman behind Neave himself, a tall, pale virago from Abendstern, hissed under her breath as Neave gave him the precedence. But she was as well trained as the other Secess' in the mixed crew, and neither fidgeted nor protested, not by so much as an indignant, choked-off "Sir!"

Even the smoky air was better than that on board ship, Neave thought as he watched Becker blink through the thinning smoke. He was probably trying to recognize in the small, shabby crowd circling the ship the people he had left here: Project Seedcorn. The Secess' woman's eyes bored into his back as they had for the entire trip.

Only the Secess' training—and the Alliance's—had kept former enemies from tearing apart the ship they now shared. The Secess' had emphasized military virtues. And the Alliance, of necessity, had stressed discipline. Both sides had succeeded far too well. That was why the damned war had dragged on for so long, slagging planets, and gutting stations, and exiling Earth from her own.

Only exhaustion had finally allowed Earth forces to break through the blockade and regain an ascendancy that was as much moral as military. Remembering the first coded messages that announced Earth's release, Neave blinked hard once. If need be, he would blame it on the smoke.

Earth had seen the end of the blockade as freedom, but it had quickly turned to care. With production lines in place, a population undiminished by a war that relied as much on attrition as planet-slagging, Earth was in a position to dictate terms to the exhausted combatants, who—after many years of rebellion—turned back to the mother world with a relief that they fought not to show. *As if they were runaway children, relieved at the approach of adults. What,* Neave asked himself, *would they think if they knew how scared we were when we saw what they had done?*

Imperceptibly he tried to shift his shoulders, to ease the ache in them. His spine felt as if some demon interrogator had beaten each separate vertebra with a particularly hard club. *I am too old to hop from world to world, dammit.*

What could Earth do for these returning prodigals?

Never mind Earth. What can I do? It wasn't for a strong spine or iron nerves that he had been included on this mission, a fifty-year-old smiling public man who was neither that smiling nor that public, if the truth be known. A Franklin party member in philosophy as well as in politics, Neave had helped argue for a speedy reintegration of both sides into a systems-wide government. *God help us all,* he thought as he had thought every day since accepting this assignment. *A pragmatist with a sense of ethics.* Pragmatist that he was, he could understand why such a person might be valuable. The only problem was that he was the only such person of sufficient tact and seniority, and that he himself must bring the news to worlds isolated (some lacking ships with Jump capability, others actually—it was hard to believe—planet-locked) by a generation of combat without being killed as the messengers of ill fortune by militant holdouts. Still, it had been his duty; and he had agreed—just as they had known that he would.

And then, Becker had revealed his doomsday plan, this Operation Seedcorn.

Unlike many of the strategies he'd heard of, this one had even held a demented sort of promise. For one thing, it was nonviolent; and part of the Franklin party's political agenda was a highly pragmatic pacifism. You didn't fight, not from some lofty principle of nonviolence, but because you'd already lost more than you could bear. Earth . . . Earth was weary, drained after a generation of what amounted to siege. As for the groups that called themselves Alliance and Republic . . . *perhaps our pacifism goes deeper than common sense,* Neave had thought the first time his ship stood off from one of the slagged worlds.

He had insisted on an orbital flight: someone, he declared, had to witness. Had they gone closer to investigate, he learned, the entire crew would have had to undergo the painful, humiliating rituals of decontam.

And he had enough trouble with that crew already. Politics and safety decreed a mixed crew for Becker's pickup mission: and a very mixed crew it was, intimidated by vague threats to believe that not even God would help anyone from the Alliance who picked a fight with a citizen of the former Republic, or hoped to, by calling them Secess'.

It had not been an easy trip for Neave. The others were regular military, veterans with the strongest possible opinions on shiphandling and tactics, and who barely controlled those opinions when Neave ordered the weapons systems disabled. But it was hard on the regulars too, who were forced to live and stand watches with the very people whom they had tried to kill before the Armistice.

Now it was going to be hard on the marshal who found himself faced with people he had marooned and given the command: "Live and be human." After all, he had told them to be human, and humans weren't all that forgiving, now were they? It remained to be seen whether this group would welcome Neave or throw rocks at him.

"You must remember, ladies and gentlemen." In the

best Franklin style, Neave had harangued the ill-assorted, ill-at-ease crew on board *Amherst II* each time someone quarrelled. "We must all hang together, or assuredly we will all hang separately."

Now, he would have to bring the glad tidings to yet another group.

It had been a hard trip, always waiting for the other shoe to drop, or the other crewmember to swing, or the other ship to shoot. He hadn't felt especially noble, the way people who used passive resistance were supposed to. In fact, he had been conscious of a furious irritation. He—and Earth—were being used, he suspected, by factions whose weapons had scared them into temporary cooperation. So, for now, they would try it his way. Then, once their fear subsided, they would probably revert.

As a Franklin, he wasn't averse to fighting, much though he preferred negotiations; it was just that it hadn't worked during the blockade . . . and he had been assigned to this ship. In order to survive, most citizens of Earth had submitted themselves to the type of discipline that allowed a man like Neave to walk unarmed among warring parties: it created a moral, rather than a military, ascendancy. Or so he hoped.

Before he had been pried from his university with the damnable direct commission that put him in charge of veteran officers and a scar-sided ship, he had been a scholar whose passion for military, political, and legal history made him the perfect victim when his superiors looked for someone dispassionate to draft for this assignment.

"Anyone who wants this job deserves to get it!" he had protested, and been told that his reluctance only indicated how well suited he was to his new role as commissioner. Wonderful: he had used that line himself to inveigle people onto university committees, and never had realized how obnoxious it was.

He missed his university, his library, his peace. A generation living under blockade had been a generation turned inward: when Neave thought of exploration, he thought to explore the mind and spirit, not a galaxy barred to him by armed ships . . . yet here he was, commanding just such a ship. Others would fly it, and fire—better yet, *not* fire—the weapons; Neave's job was to weld a fragile accord into a lasting peace, reconciling Alliance and Secessionist into one human—and one humane—government before there was nothing left to govern, and before the only peace that could be expected was the silence of slagged and wasted planets.

Accordingly, the woman behind him, seniormost of his Secess' staff, would not push forward, indignant that a man of the Alliance had been granted precedence. Nor would the Alliance marshal take advantage of it. If Earth had been appalled by the war, so had the worlds who fought it. That was Neave's only hope: that former enemies would prefer Earth rule, Earth protection, to the desert they had made for themselves. It seemed to work for now.

So far, so good, thought Amory Neave, who had learned to be thankful for small mercies. He started down the ramp himself, slowly, so he might examine the thin, wary people who made up Becker's Operation Seedcorn on this world.

For civilians and refugees who had farmed, not fought, during the last suicidal war years, they weren't much, Neave thought. They looked as much like veterans as his crew. Many of the adults were still of an age to be in the service, though all but the man and woman heading toward Becker wore drab civilian gear.

But the eyes on them, especially the youngest! They glittered, flat, unreadable, almost ophidian. Barely out of their teens, many of the settlers watched the ship, not with the excitement or relief Neave had hoped for—*here are your rescuers!*—but with suspicion. Their hands twitched near belts bare, thank God, of sidearms.

Neave caught the eye of a thin, dark man, barely more than a youth. As soon as the boy perceived himself observed, he jerked up his chin and looked away. *Don't trust us, do you?* he asked silently. *If I had been dropped here on Marshal Becker's bare word, I doubt I'd trust us either.*

"Lieutenant Yeager?" he heard the marshal greet the woman in uniform, a worn, sagging outfit she must have saved for years against just such an occasion. Small and alert, and browned from years of weathering, her eyes gazed at the ship with such longing that *she must have been a pilot,* Neave concluded. With really remarkable discipline, she turned from her loving scrutiny of the ship's lines to Marshal Becker.

"Where is Captain Borodin?"

"The captain . . . he died our first season here," said the woman. Her voice went hoarse, and she glanced up at the man at her side. He nodded encouragement, and she smiled faintly.

She's still young! Neave realized, and sighed at the weariness that her voice and glance betrayed. She limped forward, and her eyes flicked over him in a brief, shrewd examination. Then, again, she turned her attention back to Becker. He, at least, was someone she remembered.

Interesting, Neave noted, that she looked at nothing for very long, least of all at the newcomers. He tried to catch her eye again, and noted how she flushed and looked away, as if frightened or ashamed. Two children ran up to her and the man beside her, clutching them by the legs. Gently the woman disengaged their grips and nodded at a heavily pregnant woman little more than a girl herself to take them away.

Bless you, child, I'm not your enemy, he thought at her earnestly.

"Since I was next in chain of command," the woman said, "I took over . . . as best I could. I have the captain's log here for your examination. May I present Rafe Adams, lieutenant, Life Sciences? You may remember him," said Lieutenant—no, better call her Captain— Yeager. It was always better, Neave thought, to assign a higher rank to a stranger. And this thin, strained woman would require gentle handling.

"Indeed, I do. You've all done well," said Becker.

Had they? Though many of the adults and all of the

many children (who had constantly to be kept away from the ship, the skin of which was still burning hot from deceleration and landing) looked fit and hale, there were others—two or three looked notably weak. One man with enormous shoulders balanced on crutches; he was missing a foot. And there was even one elderly woman, leaning on the arm of the angry, dark young man whose gaze had challenged him. Neave could already sense the restlessness of his medcrew, who would probably put her in sick bay's intensive care unit as soon as they got their sterile hands on her.

The settlement bore signs of fresh construction. One point in their favor. Acres of thriving fields stretched out behind it down to and along the riverbank—another point. But then there was a brown stretch of fallow ground heavily dotted with crude markers and flowers. Neave counted the graves and tightened his lips. *"I had not thought death had undone so many,"* a line from an old verse flickered across his memory in ironic comfort. Too many dead for the colony whose records Becker had showed him, with its complement of young adults and children. This world of theirs looked friendly, even kind. Yet the graveyard was full. What had happened here?

But the Yeager woman was speaking again, shaking her head against Becker's words. "Begging the marshal's pardon, but we have not done well. We have merely done the best we could." She took a deep breath. "I have added to Captain Borodin's log. And kept records of my own. An inquiry, you could call them. Here they are."

The tall man, Rafe Adams, gasped. "Pauli, you never told me . . ."

She hushed him with a glance that told Neave that these two were very close. "My husband, Raiford Adams," she said, explaining.

"Secrets, Rafe? Command responsibility." Her voice took on the singsong of memorization. "'Upon the receipt of charges or information that a member of his command has committed an offense punishable by the code, the commander exercising immediate jurisdiction over the accused will make, or cause to be made, a preliminary inquiry into the charges or the suspected offenses sufficient to enable him to make an intelligent disposition of them . . .'"

"Pauli, for God's sake!" the man called Rafe blurted. She hushed him with a hand that, though callused and scarred, was very small.

The people behind began to mutter, and Becker gestured more quickly, more urgently, than any subordinate should to his commander. Neave hastened the rest of the way down the ramp.

"Commissioner Neave," said Becker. "May I present Lieutenant—or is it Captain?—Pauli Yeager?"

"Sir," the woman drew herself up and saluted. At Neave's gesture—he still was ill-at-ease among the spit and polish of military rituals—she relaxed into the slightly crooked stance enforced by the fact that one of her legs was shorter than the other, probably from a badly healed break.

Then her glance fell on the insignia he wore. "Earth," she breathed. "Then the blockade's down."

Neave nodded, answering the question she left unasked. "We survived the war intact, and now—"

"And now you've come to take us all back into the fold, have you?" To Neave's astonishment, the plain, brown woman's eyes kindled, and her hands tightened on the records she had offered Becker. "Reunite the human race now, and clean up, is that it?"

"Pauli, don't lose it now," said Rafe.

"I'm not going to, Rafe. So much for your seedcorn, Marshal Becker. You didn't really need us, did you?"

Becker shrugged. "At the time, we saw no other options."

The fight went out of the woman, and she held out the documents, not to Becker, but to Neave.

"Then I take it, sir, that you represent authority here. Accordingly, I must present the results of my investigation to you and to your legal officer."

He was not a soldier, had never been a soldier; and he

knew he was missing something. "Why the legal officer?" he asked. "I should think that you might need medical officers more right now." He gestured at the frail woman who staggered toward them, supported by the young man.

"She *was* my chief medical officer," Pauli Yeager murmured, distracted. "Her anti-agathics gave out. If you could help her . . . but don't distract me, sir. I need your legal officer because"—again came the tone of rote learning—"'no charge shall be referred to a general court-martial for trial until it has been referred for consideration and advice to the staff judge advocate or legal officer of the convening authority.'"

Neave looked around quickly. Some of the settlers had started forward, their hands raised. Neave's own guards hastened down the ramp, sidearms drawn to protect him.

"It's not fair!" shouted the man on crutches, who lurched in his haste to draw closer. An Earth officer blocked his path. "Becker, you dropped us on a world where survey had done a half-assed job, assuming it looked at Cynthia at all, with limited supplies, and no transportation. 'Fend for yourself,' you told us. 'Keep alive; you're our only hope,' you said. How could we know . . ."

"Know what?" Becker yelled back, goaded into anger in front of his commander and his former enemies.

"That Cynthia was inhabited!"

"*Was* inhabited," gasped the medical officer who waved aside offers of help from her own people and Neave's staff to stagger between Pauli Yeager and Rafe Adams, whose grip, when she would have fallen, aided her to her knees.

"You're a perceptive man, Commissioner," she gasped in a voice that would have been cultivated if there had been any life to it at all. "You recognize anger. They have a right. You see, we were left here, told to be human, remain human—and now, along you come . . . the war's over, you say. We'll unite humanity"—she gasped for breath, her pale face turning whiter than Neave thought anyone could turn and still live—"but not us," she bent her head. "Not us."

"Get her inside," the Yeager woman snapped the order at the young man and the heavily built, pregnant woman who stood close beside him.

But when they tried to lift her, she fluttered one hand at them, warning them off. "Have to . . . stay," she gasped.

If this went on much longer, Amory Neave truly thought that they might need another marker in that too-large graveyard. *I haven't come all this way to die of curiosity,* he told himself. *Mutiny, assassination, or war, perhaps. But not curiosity.*

He stared at the woman standing in front of him, proffering whatever records she had compiled and kept secret even from her husband. "A general court-martial, Captain?" he asked. If he achieved a properly military tone of voice, perhaps it would help her to speak.

"Quiet, everyone!" She turned and held up her hands at the settlers. "You know it has to be done. Now shut up and let me say it.

"Begging the commissioner's pardon," she turned back to him, formality set at maximum. "These are the charges. Violation of the Genocide Treaty. Genocide. Conspiracy to commit genocide. Direct and public incitement to commit genocide. An attempt to commit genocide, and complicity in its commission against the native Cynthian race. Effective immediately, I place myself under arrest."

The shouting match that followed was the worst in Neave's memory; and he had had a lifetime of experience with faculty meetings, political negotiations, and a large, turbulent family. Hardly were Captain Yeager's accusations out of her mouth than her husband was demanding to be arrested, while half the colony either wanted to join them or to protest any action taken against them, then and there.

For all of his experience, he was afraid he would have to let them shout themselves hoarse. Becker tried bellowing into the crowd and was silenced wretchedly when a thin, intense black woman stalked up to him with a list of errors in the initial survey report. He could promise her a decent survey; he had a crew full of junior officers who would probably ambush one another to win seats on such a mission—and thank God, it took his mind off the self-accusation Yeager and Adams had made. Genocides. And they looked so . . . so human and normal. Somehow, naive though it was, Neave expected genocides to bear some Cain's mark, some taint of bestial fury that set them apart from humanity.

The young man who had escorted the aged medical officer and who now knelt beside her raised his head. *Satisfied?* his lifted eyebrows seemed to ask. For a moment his face was hard, unforgiving. Then the woman he supported raised a hand, and his face gentled.

"Ayelet?" she asked.

"She's over with Dave, Alicia," said the young man. Neave followed his glance and saw a barrel-chested man, his hair grizzled, standing away from the crowd, while the pregnant woman who was probably this boy's wife held his hands and tried to comfort him.

"Good," breathed the medical officer. "I want . . . want to see Pauli and Rafe . . . through this one, but—" abruptly her lips went blue, twisting in a sudden spasm of pain.

"Get a doctor!" Lohr cried as he eased the woman down. Her hands clutched then, with appalling quickness, relaxed, palms upward, white against the vivid ground scrub. Where shouting failed, that movement silenced the colonists.

"Dead?" breathed Pauli Yeager.

A medical officer from Neave's ship pushed past her, scanners ready. "No," he said, but the reassurance slipped out of his voice.

Lohr rose to his feet. "I'm calling in Thorn," he said.

"No . . ." it was the merest thread of voice, but it stopped him in his tracks.

"Alicia, don't you want to see him?" asked the girl named Ayelet. "He's like your son."

"He . . . *is* my son. Keep him . . . keep him away . . ."

"He's got the right to choose what risks he takes," muttered Lohr. "I think he'll take this one." He loped off, and the people circling the dying medical officer hushed her.

Finally Pauli Yeager knelt beside her too, her log and whatever preposterous report she had prepared during years of isolation still clutched in her arms. "Lohr's right, Alicia," she said, her voice wonderfully gentle. "Thorn's got to know it all. He's got a *right*."

The older woman sighed and closed her eyes. "Get her inside," Yeager told Neave's physician, ignoring such niceties as chain of command, and the fact that she had recently placed herself under arrest.

Lohr came running back. "I reached Thorn!" he shouted.

Tears seeped out from under Alicia's eyelids.

"He's coming in, of course. On one of the newest fliers. He says they work fine." He bent over the physician as she was being carried away.

"I wanted . . . him safe . . ."

"You can't protect him from this," Lohr said. "He's a man now, not a rehab case. And what's he going to do? Hide till these people go away?" Abruptly his face twisted, and he looked like a much younger, wilder person. "I wish to hell they had never come!"

"Thank God they did," Pauli Yeager told him. "If they hadn't, it would have meant that there was nothing left . . . up there." She gestured at the sky. "That Becker was right, and we had to be seedcorn for the humanity that was no longer there."

"But what's going to happen to you and Rafe . . ."

"And David and all the others?"

"Pauli . . . Captain," Becker cut in, "you've spent the past years in isolation; your people are angry about inadequate reporting of alien life. I honor your wish to be scrupulous, but aren't you confusing self-defense with . . ."

"It was genocide!" Pauli snarled at him. "We had to kill the Cynthians to protect ourselves, but that makes no difference. If we'd had ships, we could have picked up and moved, but you took the ships. You grounded us. So we had to kill them."

Becker's hands and lips moved as he tried to silence the woman. Neave observed how the Secess' officers had moved in and were listening avidly.

"Now you're here, the war's over, and everything is going to be wonderful: is that it? You've all been scared, and so now you're huddling together. The last thing you want is a trial for war crimes. It might open too many old wounds. But damn you, Becker, you dropped us on this world to *be* human for you. We haven't been, not since we killed the Cynthians. Do you expect us to like that?

"I want to fulfill my mission. I want to be human again. If that means a trial, all right, then. You cannot do worse to me than anything that's happened, that we've done to ourselves since you left."

Her husband laid his hands on her shoulders. She leaned her cheek against one of them.

"I know. The children. All of them, not just ours. I've been happy despite what . . . the Cynthians, but I always feared that this day would come. That's why I prepared that report. We were put here to be human; and humans cannot do what we did and hope to escape the consequences."

She limped slowly toward Amory Neave, holding out her reports and log almost pleadingly. "The laws were written on Earth," she told him. " 'Persons charged with genocide or any of the other acts . . . conspiracy, incitement, attempt . . . shall be tried by a competent tribunal of the State in the territory of which the act was committed, or by such international penal tribunal as may have jurisdiction.' You've got them all here, sir. Alliance, Secess', even Earth, after all these years."

Neave found himself shaking his head. *The war is over. Let the dead be dead. Let yourself be welcomed back into a common humanity, like the crew of my ship,* he implored her silently.

"I was put here to be human," she repeated. "I can't let this go unnoticed and unpunished. I want to be clean again." Her voice trembled uncontrollably.

Neave sighed. Because he had no other choice left, he took the documents from her hands.

The same lines of text had glowed on Neave's terminal so long that by now he thought they could have been burnt onto a less advanced model. With a keystroke, he could erase those words. With a second one, he could stop anyone from recovering them. He could do that, he could. And then he could burn the hard copy, crossed out and, in many places, written over in the scrawl of someone who wrote as seldom as possible, who found the act painful. If he did that—erased the records, destroyed the paper—that would be the end of the report that Pauli Yeager called her "investigation" and had thrust into his hands, along with the responsibility to act on it.

There would remain only her word. And his. He could, for example, allege that she was overstressed. Or he could deny ever seeing such a report.

To destroy it was one possible action. But what he, unlike the innocent system that hummed and glowed in the privacy of his quarters, could not do was forget that such a report ever existed. He was a Franklin, therefore —he hoped—a reasonable man. He might erase the report, then the personnel file, of Pauli Yeager, but he could not unmake facts. He had met her. She had written the report that condemned herself, her husband, and their closest friends as genocides. And she had all but demanded to be arrested.

To deny any of that was solipsism; and he had seen too much, since the blockade lifted, of what happened when people tried to make the universe over in their own images and—worse yet—their own theories even to toy with the idea. Franklin had lived in an age of reason and had helped to build a nation. He, Neave, surviving an age of war, must turn his longing for an age of reason into an attempt to re-create it.

But he had also lived in an age of survivors; and the people whom he faced here, on whom—if they were allowed to have their stubborn way—he would have to sit in judgment, were survivors.

What a waste. If Neave had had a moment to waste, he would have sworn. But that was a waste of words. He turned with a sigh back to "Captain" Yeager's report.

The report was long and not especially well-written. A pilot who had turned, reluctantly, to administration of a colony, she had turned even more reluctantly to the task of self-accusation. Her words were awkward, choppy—yet sometimes, the silences spoke more achingly than the ideas she actually managed to set down. Neave bent over the awkward text once more. She had collected evidence and precedents for years, it seemed, but she had no more idea of how to organize it into a damning case than he had of piloting.

To do her justice, she didn't need to know the organizational tricks. Neave, steeped in the history of Earth, need not even access his records to remember the examples that Pauli Yeager had so laboriously culled from the colony's inadequate computer system . . . probably in the loneliest watch of the night, when the system was not running at capacity, or in the scant moments she spared herself from her duties as commanding officer. No, it was not a well-organized document. But it was remarkable that it existed at all.

Shaking his head, he scrolled back and forward in the text. Here were the words of a man who had been guard and officer at one such trial: "The Nuremberg Tribunal established for once and for all what had never been established before—that a person who committed an unlawful criminal act, even if he had done so while occupying an official position, was still responsible personally for what he had done."

How must she have felt upon reading that line? There was no denying that Yeager and her associates felt personally responsible for the elimination of the Cynthians. He could hear that hoarse, matter-of-fact voice raised in outrage. "Elimination, Commissioner? That's a fine euphemism for murder, isn't it?"

He could dismiss this entire case as irregular. God knows, it was, and God knew even better, he wanted to. Or he could cast about to find extenuating circumstances, including the one Yeager and her colleagues had dismissed: they had been charged with the protection of a colony.

"What about it?" she had asked. "It doesn't matter that I must protect people, or that as an officer, my job is to obey orders. All lawful orders. I was a pilot, Commissioner. In a scramble, I could have taken out a . . . Secess' pilot," Yeager paused, her eyes suddenly pained . . . "assuming I was fast enough. That would have been all in a day's work. But there is a difference between that and exterminating the Cynthians. I *know* the difference. That's what makes me guilty."

Had all the Cynthians been wiped out? The survey of this world was flawed—God knows, with every report Neave read, he realized that more and more fully. Already he had detached some of his younger crew to explore the continents that the colonists had lacked aircraft to visit. Would that matter?

"What if some Cynthians survive?" He had asked Pauli Yeager that when he visited her in the dome that she and Rafe Adams lived in, and that was now their "prison." A prison including children, friends, visitors —and accomplices.

For a moment, hope flickered in Yeager's eyes, then subsided.

"We cannot know that," she told him.

"In any case, does that matter?" countered the grizzled, barrel-chested man Neave had seen earlier talking with his daughter. "If we didn't kill them all, it was by the grace of God. Because we were desperate, and we might have tried. Probably would have tried.

Besides, can you imagine looking at a Cynthian now, and knowing what we had done?"

"When we first planned the idea, when we first thought of it . . ." Rafe let his words trail off, and Pauli had shaken her head emphatically.

"We can never be free of it," she said. "But I would like to"—she shrugged—"be *clean* again, if I can. To pay. To finish payment." She shook her head. "After the last Cynthians died, I wanted to die too. I'm sorry, Rafe, but I did. It had nothing to do with you. But I didn't think I deserved to die, so I sentenced myself to life. Worse than that, I had to stay alive in such a way that the kids, all of them, would think of me as someone to admire. But it's over now, Commissioner. You-'re here, and I will not submit to this charade a moment longer."

Here it was in her report, that same awareness of guilt that made a genocide hanged centuries ago declare, "It will take Germany one thousand years to repay its guilt."

"It will take us forever," Yeager had written in dark capital letters across the margin, "but is that any reason to avoid repayment or whine about its terms?"

Neave buried his head in his hands. He had not wanted authority, much less authority over a case that, if referred back to Earth as some damnable regulation or other must surely demand, could shred the fragile accord between Alliance and Secessionists—very well, they called themselves the Republic—as easily as he could shred Yeager's report. He had only to watch the faces of his crewmembers. Becker walked small these days, his desire to bury the whole wretched matter obvious to anyone who had ever sat in on negotiations. He had, Neave knew, a career to rehabilitate.

Just how far would *he* go to bury it? Neave wondered idly. There was no silence like the grave. And he knew Becker had a more pragmatic, therefore less ethical, bent than he.

He massaged his temples with long, well-cared for fingers so unlike those of the woman who had produced this damnable mess. Becker probably wouldn't go that far, but Neave had a legal—hell, he had an ethical—responsibility to make certain. Yeager and her friends were guarded by Earth crew, men and women he had chosen and could trust. Factions. Neave shook his head at his own action. Factions led to secrecy, to dissension; they *were* dissension. He schemed where he feared to persuade.

Becker wasn't the only one among his staff he didn't trust. There was also the woman from Abendstern, Elisabeth von Bulow. She had been some sort of minor governor there and had been chill in her criticisms of the colony. "Wallowing in sentimental guilt" and "democracy verging on the anarchic" were some of her milder observations.

What would von Bulow have made of some of the "governed" on Cynthia? Like the man ben Yehuda, a civilian engineer who had violently refused repatriation to his native Ararat just that afternoon. "I left Ararat because I felt angry and disgraced when it refused to accept my family. It seemed to me that I, not Ararat, was true to its reasons for existing. Now you ask me to return and ask them to accept me, a criminal? A genocide—on Ararat? Better they think we died in the war." His eyes had been red and swollen, and he had covered them with his hands.

Have him watched, Pauli Yeager had mouthed at Amory Neave. Prisoner and commander their roles might be, but he had obeyed.

And then there was the xenobotanist, Beneatha Angelou, who had shouted at Becker. "I'm not going to accuse myself," she told him forthrightly. "I opposed killing the Cynthians. You can say that since I'm alive, I'm an accomplice; and I'll reply that that's unjust." A minute afterward, her face softened remarkably. "I've got to say though, that if you try me with them, I'd be in good company. I've never known any better. Surely you have to take that into consideration too?"

All of them agreed, however: the children had to be shielded from the consequences of their elders' acts.

Granted, it was hard to see in the set jaws and angry eyes of people like Lohr and Ayelet the starved, feral "littlests" described in the colony's records, but . . . but . . . the children's welfare had remained the colony's chief concern.

Neave cast further for ways out of this maze. What about a statute of limitations? The oldest Earth law on the books declared that there was no statute of limitations on genocide charges. The crime carried the death penalty. Now, that opened up possibilities. According to the rules governing courts-martial (at least as far as Neave's hasty study of them could confirm), all sentences involving the death penalty had to be referred offworld. To avoid the embarrassment of a trial, Neave could simply refuse to refer the case offworld. That would protect the fragile union that Earth, Alliance, and Secess' now enjoyed. It would be logical, simple—but would it be just?

He had a good idea of how Yeager would react to the idea.

He sighed and had turned back to her report again when his desk communicator buzzed. With relief, he slapped the circuit open. It was his chief medical officer, temporarily stationed in the colony's crude medcenter.

"Commissioner, you'd better get over here."

"Dr. Pryor's dying, is that it?" The physician had reported that the colonists' medical officer had collapsed from a massive stroke, the last of several, all of which had been complicated by age and overwork.

"She's *been* dying since we made planetfall here," the physician said. "It's remarkable that she hung on this long. That's not what you have to see, though. It's about that 'Thorn' that they called in."

"Her son," Neave agreed. He prided himself on his memory for detail.

"Some son!" A commotion rose from the other end of the line. When the physician spoke again, his voice was hushed and chastened. "Only by adoption. His name is Halgerd, Thorn Halgerd. It sounded Frekan to me. So I consulted von Bulow, who turned white, then told me to mind my own goddamned business . . ."

Neave's door annunciator blared into a demand for attention, admission, action—"I think she just came to tell me herself," said Neave.

"Well, I don't envy you, sir. Apparently, this Halgerd is Secess' . . ."

"Republic," corrected Neave.

"And Marshal Becker thinks he's probably a war criminal."

Neave suppressed an impulse to groan. There seemed to be entirely too many people on Cynthia who could be shoved into that category already.

"But this is what's odd, Commissioner."

What was odd? Aside, of course, from how long his annunciator could continue at full blare without something breaking—aside, of course, from Neave's head. "Go on, Doctor," he said, resigned.

"Von Bulow's just as eager as Becker to have the man killed."

It was full dark when Amory Neave started down the ramp of his ship again. Outside milled any of his crew who were off-duty, and many members of Cynthia colony, most of them young. Among them were the former "littlests" Lohr and Ayelet, whom the others consulted as authorities.

"Ayelet, you were on comm duty. What did Thorn say?" The woman speaking was tall, black-haired, and possibly fifteen years older than the woman who answered her.

"Lohr was the one who called him in when Dr. Pryor took such a downturn," Ayelet said. "Lohr, did Thorn say anything else to you but that he'd come back as quickly as he could?"

Lohr shook his head, then raised macrobinoculars.

"You know how fast he flies," said the dark-haired woman. "If she dies before he gets here, I'm afraid he won't forgive himself."

"There . . . I've spotted him!" Lohr cried.

Around him, the *Amherst II*'s crew suddenly tensed. What did they know about Halgerd that he didn't?

"For one thing, he's a pilot," a crewmember told him. 'A Secess' . . ."

"Republic," snapped Elisabeth von Bulow.

"Pilot," the man finished. "We always heard in the Alliance that they were married to their ships, or hard-wired, or something."

"Rumors," said von Bulow. "Pilots' rumors, designed to save face."

Neave held up one hand. That type of argument could get out of hand so quickly that he forbade it whenever possible. He had seen classified reports on the Republic's pilots, who were, apparently, successful applications of now-proscribed cloning technology. Publicly, of course, officials like von Bulow disavowed such reports.

Now he found considerable interest in observing the Abendsterner. Her pale face acquired two splotches of color high upon her cheekbones. "On Freki, they did manage to clone a few pilots," she conceded. Her voice was chill, dissociating herself from such goings-on. "How can you expect a clone to observe the protocols of war? The Frekan pilots were unstable. Those who didn't die in combat suicided, most of them."

What protocols are those? Neave stifled the question before it could escape him.

Lohr whistled in admiration. "Just look at him!"

Neave gestured imperiously for young Lohr to hand over the macros. Yes . . . here came the controversial Thorn, in what looked like an ultralight construction halfway between a glider and an aircraft. He flew magnificently, flamboyantly, swooping, banking, and dipping with superb disdain for the laws of gravity, if not those of wind currents.

He gasped as the man took one particularly risky dive, then caught himself and rose on an updraft. The moons' light glinted off his aircraft, sparkles of silver and violet, and he had a sudden, poignant recollection of one of the holos in Yeager's report: Cynthians with ten-meter wing-spans dancing on the night winds, the galaxies on their wings glowing in the moonlight. No wonder the colonists clung to their gliders, unwilling to give up the beauty of flight, as well as its use.

"Shoot him *now!*" hissed von Bulow. He gestured her to silence and watched in admiration as the man touched down, leapt from his craft, and dashed toward the dome that housed medcenter.

"Get him!" the woman cried and started forward.

"Thorn, move it!" Lohr shouted, and threw himself at the Abendsterner. Ayelet, moving far more slowly, stepped into what would have been the crewmembers' line of fire. No one obeyed von Bulow.

"My God, look at that man run," one man muttered.

"He's a filthy construct!" spat von Bulow. "Cloned, augmented . . . Freki never scrupled to use proscribed technology."

At another time, Neave might have enjoyed the irony of an official criticizing the successful work of her alleged allies. Now, he found himself hypnotized by the man he had seen, taller than most pilots, his hair, flightsuit, and pale skin all gleaming in the metallic colors of the moonlight. He was almost inhumanly fast and graceful.

For an instant, he turned his face toward Lohr, and Neave was struck both by the regular features and the anguish that twisted them.

Lohr launched himself after Thorn, and Neave, shamelessly, eavesdropped.

"She didn't want to see me, is that it?" Halgerd wasn't even winded by his flight and his run.

"She wants to protect you, idiot!" Lohr snapped. "Didn't you see the ship when you touched down? Apparently the war's over, and now the place is crawling with guns and bureaucrats."

"Oh, shut up, will you!" Ayelet interrupted, her voice almost stifled. "Thorn, if you want to see Alicia alive—"

"But be careful!" the tall, dark-haired woman hissed, one hand almost touching Thorn Halgerd's shoulder. "The woman over there, the pale one. She's from Abendstern and says you ought to be shot."

Thorn had been halfway inside the medcenter when the warning came. He turned around, again with that incredible speed of his, and flashed a glance across von Bulow, the crew, and Neave himself, his pale eyes flickering as if his gaze could not just record each of them, but evaluate them. Neave had never felt such a strong urge to drop his eyes. Thorn Halgerd might, as von Bulow argued, be a construct, but he had undeniable presence.

Then he straightened and turned his attention back to the Abendsterner. *Quite a family resemblance,* thought Neave.

"Quick, Thorn!" whispered Ayelet.

The man turned, but not before he had sketched a tiny, contemptuous salute at von Bulow. Letting her seethe, Neave followed Thorn Halgerd, ignoring the colonists' glares, and slipping inside just as the door irised closed.

The *Amherst*'s chief medical officer stood against the worn, sloping ivory plastic of the dome's wall. His hands were idle, his mouth set. As he saw Neave, he shook his head. Halgerd registered the headshake and hunched his shoulders as if warding off a blow. He shook his head, bewilderment blurring his too-regular features.

"Go on!" Lohr gave him a push toward the screened alcove where Dr. Alicia Pryor lay.

"Is . . . she conscious?" Thorn's voice almost begged the medical officer to say "no."

He shook his head. "You can't hurt her, son. She's been waiting for you. You're all she's been waiting for."

Thorn shook visibly, then disappeared around the screen. "My dear son!" Neave heard the joyous murmur, hardly more than a ragged breath, and blinked hard, just once. There was no shame in admitting emotion, just in permitting it to blind you.

Someone touched Neave's arm, and he jumped, bitterly ashamed of his role as eavesdropper.

"Commissioner?" It was Ayelet. "Could you tell someone to ask Rafe and Pauli, I mean the captain, to come over? She and Dr. Pryor were awfully close." Another woman might have tried to look at him appealingly, or to coax, but Ayelet's very lack of such arts moved Neave more.

"Bless you, child, this is their colony, not mine. Their arrest is only voluntary."

"Only?" Ayelet's head tilted as she listened to the murmur of voices from Alicia Pryor's cubicle. She gestured Neave to stand farther off, leaving the dying woman her privacy. "Commissioner, Pauli has decided she's under arrest. That means she'll stay put unless you say otherwise. I know it would mean a lot if you sent for her." Abruptly Ayelet's brown eyes flashed. "And I'd say she has it coming."

The monumental, childlike integrity of this girl!

"And if I went myself, you'd be rid of an outsider, is that it?"

Her blush and wide smile cast a wildrose prettiness over her heavy features, and Neave understood what it was that the mercurial Lohr had seen in her. That, and the decency, the stability, she must have learned from her father, now under suicide watch, and the woman for whom she pleaded.

"Never mind," Neave said gently. "I'm not insulting you. I'll bring them myself. You go on back in." And then, because, commissioner or not, he had children of his own, he offered Ayelet what comfort he could. "Your husband and this Thorn—they'll need you with them."

"Come in, Commissioner." Yeager and Adams sat close together, but rose as he entered. The silence in their quarters was palpable, almost restful. Neave glanced around at the simple furnishings, a blend of prefab and local workmanship, one or two fine pieces, including a woven hanging bright in colors of crimson, green, black, and gold. There were even a few printed books.

"Is it Alicia?" Rafe Adams asked, his hand dropping protectively on his wife's shoulder.

"Her son flew in a few minutes ago. He's with her now."

Pauli lowered her eyes.

"Your Ayelet sent me to fetch you."

Rafe's bark of laughter surprised them all. "That's Ayelet. Doesn't know the meaning of tact, or rank."

"She said you wouldn't leave here unless you were ordered. I volunteered to bring you. Figured they were better off without me. And I wanted to talk with you."

His eyes fell on a tattered paper book. Plato, for a wonder. Pauli saw his surprise. "Alicia let me have it," she said in a low voice. "I'm not particularly well educated, Commissioner. Not like Alicia. Or you. Would you believe that this is the first time I've had to read, or just think, since we landed here?"

Neave raised an eyebrow to ask permission and picked up the book. The ragged pages fell open to the "Crito." Passages were heavily underscored and noted in the crude, round hand with which he was now familiar.

Again, the sense that he was eavesdropping made Neave flush, and he laid down the book. "Let's go," he said. "I want to warn you, though. About Thorn. One of my staff thinks he ought to be shot."

"That would be the Abendsterner," Pauli said, her back toward him as she reached for her jacket. Rafe took it from her and laid it gently over her shoulders. "She knows what he is, a successful experiment in proscribed cloning technology. So do we. Pryor spotted it in an instant. He'd ejected from his ship, and we brought him in, almost dead from the loss of the others in his group. Beneatha . . . some of the others wanted to try him for war crimes. That's a laugh, isn't it? Who's the more guilty, him or us?"

She shrugged into the jacket. "Ask Lohr. They're friends, he and Thorn, yet we're pretty sure that Thorn was part of the fleet that slagged his homeworld. Thorn and Alicia sort of adopted one another; she'd known his . . . genetic father back before the war. We think he's been happy with us. Do the Secess' want him back?"

"He landed here after we . . . killed the Cynthians," Rafe added hastily.

It was the law, wasn't it? Neave asked himself as he ushered Rafe and Pauli out the door. Even years before the discovery of Jump, Earth agreements stated that astronauts, as they'd been called then, were regarded "as envoys of mankind in outer space" and should have "all possible assistance in the event of accident, distress, or emergency landing on the territory of another state." The same agreement called for them to "be safely and promptly returned to the state of registry of their space vehicle."

Halgerd was as much an embarrassment to the people who created him as was Pauli Yeager's insistence on a genocide trial.

Neave had expected Ayelet to be waiting for them outside the medcenter, but found Lohr pacing there instead. His hands were hooked into his belt to stop them from trembling.

"Quick," he said, and his voice was hard. "Thank you for bringing them." The words came hard, but forced a small, tight smile from Pauli Yeager.

Laying an arm over Lohr's shoulder, Rafe brought him inside with them. The screen had been pushed away, and Neave stifled a gasp at how flat the white covers lay over Dr. Pryor's body. Thorn Halgerd knelt hunched beside her, his face inhumanly calm, his hands resting on the bed.

"Alicia," Pauli breathed and went over to her dying friend.

"Sorry . . ."

Pauli shook her head. "That you couldn't see us through this one? I only wish we could have spared you all of it." She bent and kissed the aged woman's forehead. "You thought you helped Thorn grow up. Look what you did for me! 'Licia, I couldn't have managed without you. It's all finished now. Rest easy."

She bent lower to catch. "What's that? I'll keep Thorn safe. I promise."

Muttering an apology, Neave headed for the door and almost lurched into it. It would have been indecent to remain; he wasn't certain he could forgive himself for staying as long as he had.

He stumbled outside into a night blessedly free of the taints of antiseptic and death.

Footsteps clattered behind him. He heard a quick, urgent gasp.

"Mother!" Thorn Halgerd cried out sharply.

The door irised shut on his unpracticed sobs. Neave wished that he had not heard.

Slowly Pauli Yeager and Rafe Adams left the medcenter dome, their arms around Thorn Halgerd. Though he towered over the woman, he leaned heavily on her as well as Adams. As he passed Neave, he averted his face. The others also refused to meet Neave's eyes. The tall, dark-haired woman whom Neave had noted before hovered protectively close to him, while Lohr and Ayelet fanned out sideways in what Neave recognized as a flanking maneuver to protect their friends.

"I had to see her," Thorn said. "You know I had to come back."

"I know," said Rafe. "Just like we had to turn ourselves in."

"Construct!" came von Bulow's voice. "That's right, you!" The blond man turned toward her—*that obedience was a reflex!* Neave thought—and drew himself to attention.

"You don't have to!" Pauli hissed. "It's not a matter of orders and born-humans anymore, Thorn. You're ours! You broke that conditioning."

"Did I?" Halgerd's eyes seemed to go blank. One hand clasped and unclasped as if trying to hold himself back from the pull of orders he had been conditioned to obey.

"Yes, you did. Remember? And besides, you can't obey those Orders. You know what they'd mean for you. And Alicia made me promise to keep you safe."

But von Bulow was advancing on the newcomer, who took one step back, then recollected himself and tried to make a stand. He was taller than she and, as Neave knew from Yeager's report, far stronger and faster; but he seemed to cower before her.

"The law," Elisabeth von Bulow stated, "requires that people of one state party shall render all possible assistance to the astronauts of other state parties, *then return them safely and promptly . . .*"

Pauli edged out from under Thorn's arm and stalked over to stand before the Abendsterner. ". . . to the state of registry of their space vehicle. I know the old precedents from Earth too. I've had ten years to study them. That treaty also states that we should have been notified of phenomena discovered in outer space which could constitute a danger to the life or health of astronauts. You see how well it was enforced."

"The Republic has a legal right to the return of . . .

"Thorn Halgerd—"

"Halgerd AA-prime—" Pauli and Thorn spoke simultaneously.

"The Republic," Pauli mimicked coldly, one eye on Neave to see how far she could go, "unless we are all being deceived, no longer exists. However, the planet Freki has a right to the return of one of its citizens. Should Freki request it, and the *citizen* consent." She darted a quick glance at Thorn, his cue if he was able to take it.

"He's not a citizen!" snapped von Bulow.

"I note," Pauli observed, her voice low, sly even, "that even you call him 'he.'"

"No," agreed Thorn Halgerd. "I wasn't a citizen. I was what you called me. A construct. Forced to obey orders, even if they meant my death . . . or my brothers'. Damn you all, you made a thing of me and of my brothers! And then your people sent us out to kill men who might have been us. Who *were* us, cloned from the same genefather. I can't forget them either, the men they were, for we *were* men, even deprived of a normal life by the tanks and your damned conditioning. Ever since these people took me in, it's been worse. Now I can't forgive you for killing the men my brothers should have been with my friends to help them. All that promise, and you killed them. At least I had a chance to hear Aesc before he died.

"If you return me to the Republic, they'll probably terminate and dissect me. Not 'kill.' You *kill* humans, not property. Things like me." He turned to Pauli, who clasped his arm with both hands, then to Neave.

"Commissioner, these people shared their humanity with me. As long as I'm alive, I'm not leaving them. I claim asylum."

Neave turned his head in time to catch Pauli Yeager's imperceptible nod.

"What about his crimes against humanity?" asked the Abendsterner.

"For slagging *my* homeworld?" Lohr cried. "He didn't know what he was doing. Your people did. Besides, what's that to you? You gave the orders. You wanted that done. And when it was done, when *he* did it, you threw him away. For thanks, you would have killed him. Well, we caught him, and we're going to keep him."

Pauli walked forward. "The poor commissioner," she laughed sharply, ironically, and held out a hand to Neave. "He's been looking for technicalities since he landed here, and we've been too stubborn to give him any. Relax, Commissioner. Just this once, here's a technicality for you. Thorn doesn't need asylum; he's got citizenship. Thorn Halgerd's the son of an Alliance national." She raised her chin at von Bulow, mischief gleaming in her eyes. "The late Dr. Alicia Pryor adopted him legally. I've had it on file for years. Lohr's right. You threw him away, and we took him in. You have no claim on him now."

"Citizenship can be revoked," von Bulow insisted. "There are precedents: people accused of war crimes can be stripped of citizenship, extradited . . ."

"You tell *me* of the war-crimes trials?" Pauli Yeager asked, her voice breathless, hard. "Me? In the name of God, do you think that a day's gone by when I don't think of them?"

Or identify with judge and criminal both, Neave thought. Not a woman easy to like, this Yeager, with her damnable guilt that spared neither herself nor anyone around her; but von Bulow was no charming specimen either.

Neave withdrew his attention from the fray to the way that the light generated by the repellors edging the fields shimmered in a violet haze above the river. It reminded him of night mists on the farm his family had owned. He had loved it, had visited it every year until the spring it was sold to pay for his education. Since then, his only home had been Earth itself: no one place, unless it was any place where the truth, the sanctity of facts, counted more than people's whims or prejudices.

By that standard, I could call Cynthia home, he thought, and shuddered.

I'm not well educated, Yeager had said of herself. Yet she had neatly stymied Becker, von Bulow, and Neave himself since the moment that they had set foot on this world. He wished he had never seen it.

Shadows wandered and merged in the moons' light, and he heard voices . . . "don't trust . . ."

"You never do."

"Shut up!" A woman's voice hissed, and Neave strained to pick up the whispers that followed. A breeze stirred the ground scrub, flapped in the sag of the huge tent nearby, and he felt like cursing it.

"Do you think he'll hear? Do you think he'd care if we got them away? You saw. He wants a way out."

"I say we get them away, Pauli and Rafe. Thorn too."

"Do you think he'll go?"

"We'll make him!"

"Lohr, you're crazy. Thorn's stronger than any of us; we can't *make* him do anything."

"Then I'll talk him into it. What about Dave, Ari?"

"They've got some medtech watching him all the time. Can't get him away, and frankly, I wouldn't want to try."

"Don't cry, Ayelet. At least this Neave's saved Dad for us."

"Commissioner." Yeager had walked over to him and laid a hand on his arm. "My husband and I will return to our quarters now. I have one request."

With difficulty, he drew himself back from the plot whispered in the shadows. "Name it, Captain."

"You'll have enough officers, I think, from the combined services of Earth, Alliance, and Secess' . . . I mean, the Republic . . . to convene a general court-martial. May I ask, please, that you do not name Elisabeth von Bulow to the board? In light of what has just happened, I do not think she could render a fair judgment."

Von Bulow sputtered, and Neave allowed himself a thin smile at her discomfiture. "A point well taken. Captain Yeager, you have my word."

She inclined her head with an odd formality, as if his word alone would guarantee her what she sought. A woman of formidable honor herself, thought Neave.

I do not want to have to try these people. I do not want to condemn them.

What choice do I have?

Much later that night, Neave was still ignoring his messager and the barrage of files and personal requests that no doubt awaited on board ship. Instead, he wandered about the colony, slipping from the misty circles of light into shadow, from clusters of domes out toward the open fields.

"Commissioner?" called one of the omnipresent "littlests," now adults ready to start families of their own. "Don't go beyond the repellors. There might be stobor. One will give you a nasty shock, and if you stumble into a bunch of them, it could kill you."

This planet could kill, Neave thought. Had killed. When his own exploration teams returned, he would know the full extent of its powers and potentialities: the mountain barriers and storms that had prevented the colonists from moving out of the Cynthian natives' path; the land, possible crops and resources—the report that Becker's Project Seedcorn should have had, but did not.

He wanted to leave it. That desire was an ache in his

gut: to leave Cynthia and its stubborn, naive moralists; to return to the libraries of an Earth that hoped that this time, it could declare itself dedicated to peace, and be right, for a change. He wanted to talk—God, did he want to say a few things—to the people who had saddled him with this assignment and confront them with the irony he now perceived. He had protested his lack of qualifications for the job, but now—who *is* qualified to conduct a genocide trial? he asked himself.

It ran in his family, they had told him. By now, very little else did: land, artwork, and other property having long ago been sold to help Earth weather the blockade and educate the last Neave with suitable rigor. Independently Yeager's awkward research had unearthed the very trials at which one of his ancestors served. Neave remembered that one. Like himself, he had been legally trained; unlike himself, he was a military man (though, in his case a direct commission had taken care of that problem).

What was it his ancestor had written? "I felt I had come to speak for the dead. The tribunal itself would be the voice of the civilized world."

Had his ancestor been, like Neave himself, reluctant to act, even more reluctant to judge? He didn't think so. It had been a time for soldiers with strong loyalties to regions and factions, none of which Neave himself possessed. What would such a man have done if the criminals in that case had insisted on their "rights" to arrest, trial, and execution? Who were "the dead" that he must speak for? The native Cynthians? The settlement's first commander, dead because of sloppy information? The refugees and children in the settlement's too-large cemetery? And what was "the civilized world"? The people who had made and now demanded to unmake Thorn Halgerd, or Becker with his plots and excuses? What about himself? "Looking for a technicality," Yeager had described him. He would have thanked every god in any pantheon he'd studied for the opportunity to play Pilate: wash his hands of this world's seismic moral quandaries, and flee. What about the children for whom the settlers had killed? They were plotting now to help their leaders break their arrest: a crime, by all laws, and yet love drove them to it too.

Perhaps they were the ones who were civilized.

His boots crunched in the ground scrub, and he stumbled over something, swore, then saw what he'd tripped over. "Forgive me," he muttered to the grave marker that had almost brought him down. Ramon Aquino, it read; and someone had etched an ankh into the stone with a blaster. He traced the circled cross's outline and noted the date—the outbreak of ergotism that had turned the settlement into a colony of maniacs. Neave turned and walked back the way he came. Wandering in graveyards: God knows, the next thing he'd be writing poetry, and he was a philosopher, a governor, not a poet.

Abruptly he strode toward the dome where the colony's leaders had confined themselves.

"Lohr's been unnaturally well behaved for the past weeks, I'd say, wouldn't you, Pauli?" Rafe told Neave.

She nodded. "I should have expected some sort of outbreak from him by now. I suppose this sudden burst of chivalry, I suppose you would call it, is reasonable. Do you want us to stop it, Commissioner?"

Rafe laughed. "I think that the commissioner would be just as well pleased if we agreed to it, love. He has a classic case of ambivalence. What about it, sir? We let Lohr and his friends spirit us away, maybe to the caves or to the base Thorn established with those new gliders of his; and the case falls apart. David ben Yehuda's too sick to stand trial; Thorn's claimed asylum—and Commissioner Neave is off the hook."

Neave forced a chuckle, wondering which was harder to take: Yeager's nerves or her husband's urbanity? Ambivalent was barely the half of it.

Pauli looked at Neave, then picked up a book he remembered. "I told you I wasn't particularly well educated, Commissioner. But I've managed to puzzle out this much." She handed Dr. Pryor's copy of Plato to him, and the "Crito" was clearly marked:

Moreover, you might have in the course of the trial, if you had liked, have fixed the penalty at banishment; the state which refuses to let you go now would have let you go then. But you pretended that you preferred death to exile, and that you were not unwilling to die. And now you have forgotten those fine sentiments, and pay no respect to us the laws, of whom you are the destroyer; and are doing what only a miserable slave would do, running away and turning your back upon the compacts and agreements which you made as a citizen."

"Tell me, Commissioner, what happened to the man who said that?"

Neave coughed. "He died in prison. By his own hand. But he was innocent."

"Still, innocent as he was, he was sentenced and he died. How much more should we . . ."

His judicious, rational calm finally punctured, Neave erupted from his battered chair.

"Damn you, woman, how can I try you? You're *human*, and you killed aliens and call it genocide."

"Which it is." Yeager's voice was inexorable.

"Say that it is, then. You know what you did. I know what you did. Do you think, though, that you're going to get a fair trial? Do you think that anyone can judge you?"

Again, Adams laughed hollowly. "Let he who is without sin among you cast the first stone?"

"Man, can't you talk sense into your wife?"

Rafe's eyebrows rose, and he snorted.

"Me, get Pauli to change course? I haven't managed it

once in fifteen years. *You* try it," Rafe answered. "Look, Commissioner, I opened contact with the Cynthians. They were human, all right. Intelligent. Kind. They liked us; and we betrayed them. Convene your trial, Commissioner. Do it the best you can and the fastest you can. I'm bone tired. Alicia was the lucky one; she's out of it now. It will be good to rest."

It will be good to rest. Neave's eyes hadn't burned like that since he was a graduate student in the last frenzied days before his qualifying examinations held despite the war. He sighed, and pulled out the lustrous, blackish-green plaque that held the exploration preliminary report from one of the exploration teams. It glistened, luring him back to the fascinating topic of a fresh new planet—*Earth was old and tired, drained from the blockade; the worlds of the Secess' and Alliance, those not slagged or glowing, were in even worse shape.* Once his crew conducted a proper survey, Cynthia could be opened up to immigrants who would have all the advantages of the settlers' experience and full backing. Apparently the team had inspected Halgerd's designs for ultralight craft and begun to test them in storm conditions like they might find over the seas here.

Neave sighed. Once he knew who the construct's "father" had been, he would have been surprised if Halgerd's designs had not been brilliant. The test results tempted him with distraction. So what if it was an adventure? It was his responsibility, therefore his duty to study it. Rationalization lured, but he turned his attention away from the plaque and the way it caught and focused the light in his cabin, and resolutely chose another plaque.

The LEDs of his screen danced, wavered, and reformed. His back felt like someone had set fire to his spine as he reviewed the rules of evidence: writings, official writings, letters, reports—Gods. Then there were the rules relating to witnesses. *An accused person who voluntarily testifies as a witness becomes subject to cross-examination upon the issues concerning which he has testified and upon the question of his credibility . . . When the accused voluntarily testifies about an offense for which he is being tried, as when he voluntarily testifies in denial or explanation of such offense, he thereby, with respect to cross-examination of such offense, waives the privilege against self-incrimination, and any matter relevant to the issue of his guilt or innocence of such offense is properly the subject of cross-examination.*

He had no doubts on that subject. Yeager and Adams had pleaded guilty. They would testify against themselves. The only problem would be "explanation of such offense." He already knew that they did not consider any explanation relevant.

His door annunciator buzzed. "Yes?"

"David ben Yehuda, sir."

"Come in."

The door slid aside and ben Yehuda entered. The weeks since the *Amherst II* had touched down had stripped weight and vigor from the man. His hair was almost totally gray now, and he walked as if uncertain of each step, as if the ground might open and swallow him. He stood before Neave, clasping and unclasping his big, competent hands, and blinked when he was asked to sit down.

"I think I had better stand for this," he said.

"As you wish." Neave angled his screen away from the man and punched up his records. *Depressed.* Well, he knew that. Yeager had as much as ordered him to put her old friend on suicide watch. And, judging from the conversation Neave had overheard, his children concurred in that decision. He was a civilian. If Neave waived jurisdiction over him, he would have to be extradited for trial. *As well shoot him here, and far kinder,* thought Neave.

"I have a request to make," ben Yehuda said.

Neave tilted his head and raised an eyebrow.

"Try me with my friends. Please. I assisted the military governor to make and implement her decision. I've held a reserve commission; you could activate it and try me too."

"Will you sit *down,* man?" demanded Neave, his patience fraying. "I dislike being towered over. Now, sit down and explain to me this passion everyone on this benighted world seems to have for self-incrimination."

Ben Yehuda seated himself on the edge of the nearest chair. "I told you, I'm from Ararat. One generation removed from Earth. Does the commissioner know anything about Ararat?"

"The commissioner—dammit, man, you're not on trial yet, so speak like a normal person!—assumes that Ararat is a planet settled by members of one minority group. Since Mount Ararat was where, allegedly, the Ark touched down after the Flood—"

"That's right, sir. I'm Jewish. Not observant: never was. And when the courts on Ararat denied my wife and kids full citizenship, I left. I won't deny I was angry. But that's not an excuse. The thing is, as a citizen of Ararat, I should have died rather than conspire at . . . at what I did. As I saw it, I had a choice to make: my kids' lives as opposed to the lives of the Cynthians.

"So"—he held out his hands—"I made my decision and knew I'd pay for it all the rest of my life. But the others, Commissioner. There were plenty of people here who opposed the decision to poison the Cynthians. They shouldn't suf—"

The annunciator rang again, and both men jumped.

"Were you expecting anyone?" Neave asked ben Yehuda, more to see his face than anything else.

"My watchdog is outside. I wish you'd remove him. I'm not going to kill myself."

"Your son thinks otherwise . . ."

"My son's a protective idiot. Takes after his father."

Again the annunciator rang, louder this time, and repeated, a strident, insistent pattern of notes.

"Come in," Neave said, on a sigh.

The woman who entered was thin, her black skin taut and unwrinkled about dark eyes that flashed with indignation. Her hair was silvered, and seemed to wreathe her face as much from the angry electricity that informed each of her movements as from natural curl.

"I thought you'd be here doing something stupid, Dave," she greeted the engineer. "Beneatha Angelou, Life Sciences," she introduced herself curtly to Neave, who had risen and begun a courteous speech about remembering her. Indeed, he wasn't likely to forget her last outbreak.

"What are you here to do?" ben Yehuda asked. They were old enemies, those two, Neave observed; good enemies, a relationship rich and mature with many years and conflicts.

Despite herself, Beneatha grinned. "Certainly not to turn myself in. You know I opposed a military government on Cynthia from the start, and I certainly opposed the annihilation of the Cynthians—"

"I remember, Beneatha. You asked me how *I* could personally consent to such a decision. It was a good question."

She nodded and made a "humph" of dissatisfaction. Then she looked for a chair, waved Neave off as he offered to place it for her, and turned it, to rest her arms and chin across its headrest.

"I need to tell you something," she informed Neave.

Politely he steepled his fingers.

"Aside from the fact that I think that Dave here is being inflammatory, I want to state for the record that I'm damned if I'm going to turn myself in. Maybe I did wrong in not stopping these people; God knows, I argued myself blue in the face trying. But, Commissioner, what you've got to know is how hard they tried to keep the colony going. During the epidemic of ergot, I think we all would have died without them. Is there some way I can have that put into the record?"

Neave smiled at her. "I'll have one of my officers take

your deposition," he said. Suddenly he liked the caustic woman enormously. "Is that all you came to say?"

"Not quite all. Thorn wasn't at fault. And please," her eyes suddenly filled with tears, "don't blame the kids, though some of them are blaming themselves right now. They were too young. We tried to protect them, give them some semblance of the normal life they never had. And we did just fine! Commissioner, you just look at our kids. We brought them up *clean!* It doesn't explain anything, or excuse anything, but if we were set down here as seedcorn, I think we did a pretty good job."

She rose as quickly as she had seated herself, and was halfway out the door before she turned.

"Thanks," she said. "You've been handed a lousy situation. I think you'll do your best too."

The door slid closed behind her. Neave sank back into his chair and saw that ben Yehuda had steepled his fingers against his lips to hide a smile.

"Usually she's even more emphatic," ben Yehuda said. He rose to leave too. "If you try me as a civilian, you'll have to extradite me, won't you?"

Neave lowered his eyes. "Not to Ararat, I promise you."

"That's all I ask. Thanks."

The door whispered open, then closed.

Damn. I like these people. How am I going to try them?

He flipped back to the manual on courts-martial. Subsection: general court-martial. Direct examination. Cross-examination. Redirect. Recross . . . the labyrinth of precedent, tradition, and—he had to believe it— justice. The trial counsel had been making heavy weather of Captain Borodin's log, Yeager's continuations, the colony's records, and the "investigation" Yeager had prepared.

Heavy weather. How *had* Halgerd's ultralights withstood the ocean storms? Looking guiltily at the vacant walls in case they showed signs of reproaching him, Neave fed in the exploration team's report and scrolled rapidly to the end, his eyes flicking with the phenomenal speed of an experienced skim reader. He hissed under his breath. "Await subsequent reports" indeed! So much for distraction.

He could find no way around it. He would try the Cynthian leaders; and after he tried them, and convicted them—for so the evidence led—he would have to order them executed.

CHAPTER

24

Painstakingly groomed in their ancient uniforms, uneasy in the wardroom set aside for the court-martial, Pauli Yeager and Rafe Adams sat on the very edge of their chairs. After so many years away from starships, being aboard one again was a matter for wonder and discomfort. After one incredulous look about that room with its bright enamels and unscratched surfaces, they had sat quietly, their eyes turned toward Neave. Flanking them were their defense counsel and his assistant. Two spruce young men for whom Cynthia was their first planetfall outside Earth's system, they were the articulate, flexible best that Neave could find.

And, he thought as he called the court to order with a faintly apologetic cough, they were a damned sight more comfortable seatmates than the three officers who sat to either side of him, each wearing the official face that masked distrust of Neave (whose direct commission made him ranking officer) with self-conscious professionalism. He had seen more animation in museum exhibits.

His subordinates were correct on one issue: any one of them had more practice conducting courts-martial than Neave. And were welcome to every bit of practice that they had: he wished he could have turned this one over to them, too. He sat back as the trial counsel seized his moment to take over. Neave heard himself mentioned in the appointing orders, and blanked out briefly. Then, the TC's announcement, "The prosecution is ready to proceed with the trial in the case of the Government of Earth against," slapped him back to awareness.

I am twenty years too old, he thought, *to want to set a moral precedent. I'd rather go home and leave these people to build their own homes in peace.*

"The tribunal," his ancestor had written so many centuries ago, "would be the voice of the civilized world." Or worlds. It hardly seemed fair to array all that power against the shabby, painfully earnest pair sitting opposite him, who would willingly have waived the whole ponderous fanfare.

The TC reverted to the drone of ritual, swearing in the court reporter, announcing his own qualifications, then those of the defense counsel. Neave grimaced, as he had each time he thought of that. In all the preparations for this mission, no one had thought to provide enough lawyers for a general court-martial. The spruce young men who served as defense counsel had nowhere near the experience of the TC, who promptly announced that for the record, while the youngsters flushed pink to their ears and wanted to thrust the TC out an airlock, if Neave was any judge. Unlike him, they were young enough, ambitious enough, to want in on this trial. They still had theories of justice, blind-eyed, absolute, and removed from humanity. Better say "intelligent life" instead of "humanity," Neave cautioned himself.

"No member of the defense present has equivalent legal qualifications. You have the right to be represented by counsel who has such qualifications," he informed Yeager and Adams, who listened attentively. "Unless you expressly request that you be represented by the defense counsel who is now present, the court will adjourn pending procurement of defense counsel who is so qualified. Do you expressly request that you be represented by the defense counsel who is now present?"

"I do not," said Pauli Yeager, even as Rafe laid a hand on the assistant counsel's shoulder. Neave would have sworn that Adams' gesture was fatherly, comforting him despite his wife's rejection of his professional services.

Neave sat upright. If Yeager wished, she could use the

lack of qualified defense counsel as a way to force the court to adjourn. The young man at her side had his mouth open to suggest that, but the TC ground on inexorably.

"Do you also wish the services of counsel who has legal qualifications equivalent to those of the member of the prosecution mentioned?"

"I do not," Yeager said, then held up one hand to forestall the next questions. "I do not desire the regularly appointed defense counsel and assistant defense counsel to act in this case. In fact, we"—her hand went out to touch her husband in a gesture of which, Neave thought, she was completely unaware, though her voice betrayed her at the last with a faint quaver—"we waive counsel."

She tilted her head slightly, wryly at Neave. *Play out your charade, Commissioner. I will not stop you.*

He sighed and excused both young men, who saluted and left the room as slowly as military protocol might allow. The monitor before Neave on the desk flashed, green against the gray of the plastic into which it was set, courtesy of the military to the civilian in their midst. That was his cue to speak.

"Proceed to convene the court," he ordered. Seeing no way around it, he asked Yeager and Adams to rise. "You, Captain Yeager, and you—"

"Lieutenant will do just fine," Adams supplied. "Sir."

"Lieutenant Adams, do swear that you will faithfully perform the duties of trial counsel and will not divulge the findings or sentence of the court to any but the proper authority till they shall be duly disclosed. So help you God."

"I do." After their oath, they looked at one another, and Pauli even smiled faintly.

The spruce young defense counsels they had refused would have tried—as Neave knew perfectly well—all manner of challenges, conniving at a postponement or adjournment that would thrust judgment offworld where it might be safely forgotten. Meanwhile, the TC droned toward the arraignment.

The accused, he informed them, had the right to waive

the actual reading of the charges and specifications against them. Yeager looked up at her husband, who shook his head.

Carefully as the judges themselves, they listened while the charges were read out in the TC's most impressive voice. Genocide. Intent to commit genocide. Conspiracy to commit genocide. Stares by the other members of the board must have seared like lasers, but the pair sat imperturbably, until Pauli nodded, as if to confirm that the TC had listed all the charges correctly.

For God's sake, Neave wanted to shout at them, *how can you stand hearing what you're being accused of?*

We did it, he knew they would answer. Involuntarily he shook his head. Why would they put themselves through this? You had only to speak to them to know how passionate their remorse was. They had spent every day for the past fifteen years atoning. Wasn't that enough?

That was what the court had been assembled to judge. Then Neave remembered. Operation Seedcorn. The settlers had been left on Cynthia as part of an attempt to hide human survivors from what many feared would be the devastation of all known worlds. Yeager still took those orders seriously. To be human. To preserve human lives and human values—among which was this formality of a trial. "I want to be human again," Captain Yeager had told him, over and over again. "I want to be clean."

Not just for herself, but for the colony she had condemned herself to protect. Even more than Neave himself, these people were Franklins in the old sense of the word. Farmers. Plain husbandmen and -women who had raised their crops despite tremendous odds and now sought to lay down their burden. Even if their actions cost them their lives.

Do you want *to hang together?* Neave thought at them. *Would you rather hang together than live separately?* Throughout the hours and hours of interrogation and deposition, he had been unable to shake any of them in the slightest from their pleas of guilty.

I wish I did not respect these people. I wish I did not like them.

"Before receiving your pleas," the trial counsel warned them, "I advise you that any motions to dismiss any charge or to grant other relief should be made at this time."

Yeager and Adams simply shook their heads. "The defense has no motions to be made," she said. Her husband rose to enter their pleas. She rose with him, clasping his hand in a gesture that Neave thought was instinctive. No doubt, had they been aware of it, they would have deprived themselves of its comfort.

"The accused, Raiford Adams . . ."

"And Pauli Yeager . . ." her voice finally husked and trembled, and Adams squeezed her fingers.

"To all specifications and charges, we plead guilty."

There was no statute of limitations on genocide, so that line of argument was out. With as much of a shrug as the impassive TC could manage, he looked at Neave. *It's in your hands now.*

Neave looked down. On his monitor, the proper words, the ancient words, glowed, reminding him of his role. *Why must you do this?* He had demanded that, and they had answered, until they were all hoarse and the question began to imply, *Why do you force me to judge you?*

"I'm tired," Rafe had told him. "It will be good to rest."

"You have pleaded guilty," Neave stated as impressively as he could. His voice echoed in the room, barren of all decoration except the green and blue sigil of Earth, emblazoned on a field of stars. Despite the white noise generators, he heard muffled footsteps and voices outside the sealed, guarded doors.

"By so doing, you have admitted every act or omission charged and every element of that offense. Your plea subjects you to a finding of guilty without further proof of that offense, in which event you may be sentenced by the court to the maximum punishment authorized for it. You are legally entitled to plead not guilty and place the burden upon the prosecution of proving your guilt of that offense. Your plea will not be accepted unless you understand its meaning and effect. Do you understand?"

Make us prove your guilt. Make us prove what is human and what is not, he wished them. But they were already, predictably, nodding.

"Yes, sir."

The footsteps outside grew louder, were approaching the room, and the rumble of voices rose to a shout.

Neave raised his voice to be heard over the uproar. If this went on, he would instruct the door guards to silence the corridor. "Understanding this, do you persist in your plea of guilty?"

"Yes, sir." He could barely hear their reply over the cheers outside. Dammit, they deserved better than to have a riot outside. He just hoped that it was a riot, and not a mob. "I want that noise shut down," he instructed the guards acidly. "If it means putting half the crew on report, do it."

Instead of the impassive "yes, sir," he expected, he heard one of the guards erupt into a wild yell. An instant later, the doors burst open. The officers seated on the bench with him rose, outraged, as five men and women in grimy flightsuits rushed down the hall.

"What is it?" Neave had to ask.

"Their team made it across the ocean," one of the guards yelled, jubilant. "And they found moths!"

A military man might have arrested the whole jubilant, unruly lot of them for contempt of court, or any number of other charges. The TC was already on his feet, shouting something about "outrage."

Yeager and Adams had sunk back into their chairs. Their faces were flushed; for an instant, their huge, incredulous smiles gave Neave a vivid picture of two young, reckless, and—in their way—innocent officers who had spent youth, innocence, and even human decency out here in the No Man's World. Then their smiles faded, and they wept.

Rafe hugged Pauli close and drew her toward the ramp that led to the open sky where several children banked and swooped in victory rolls. In a community this size, of course, the news could have spread at the speed of light; somehow, Neave could not blame the survey team for spreading the news that a colony of native Cynthians survived. A cheer went up as Yeager and Adams walked down the ramp, blinking through their tears, their steps as uncertain as any invalid's.

Neave drew close, eager to overhear anything they might say.

They shook their heads as they watched the settlers laugh, hug one another, and cheer. Then, as always, they turned to one another. Neave's shadow fell across their path, and Rafe turned to look at him.

"You understand, of course," Pauli Yeager said.

He nodded. "Of course. This doesn't change anything."

Yeager almost smiled. "I thought that we could trust you to see it that way. Good enough.

"At least they're happy," she looked out to see a tall woman with cropped dark hair swung into a joyous dance by a taller, blond man—Halgerd, his face transfigured by a grin. Rafe pointed at the sky, and Pauli looked up, her eyes following a small, thin boy whose victory rolls were the most flamboyant. "I'm glad for them. Their skies won't be empty."

"There was a while there," Rafe explained, "when we couldn't bear to look up. Then we saw the kids copying us, and we realized that our children might grow up with their eyes fixed on the mud, not the stars. But it was hard."

"It still is," said Pauli Yeager. "Commissioner, the fact that your people found living Cynthians is wonderful, but it doesn't make up for our having killed the ones on this continent. You don't have to succeed to be . . . what we are. That's the law. We thought we were killing all of them. We tried to." Her face twisted then, like a much younger, gentler woman's, and she hid it against her husband's shoulder. "But, O God, I'm glad we failed."

* * *

Rafe strode toward the survey team. The newcomers to Cynthia were tired, muddy, but their grins—the last time he'd seen a grin like that was after the first time his son Serge had grounded his flier without sliding two meters on his backside to do it. *Do they really think this changes things for us?* he wondered as one of the young men flung an arm about his shoulder.

"I've got the tapes of the last . . . contact," he said. "I assume you'll want to communicate with the Cynthians on the southern continent. Let me get the tapes, and I'll see what else I remember."

A flourish of fair hair, a slim, upright figure flickered across his awareness, and, for a sickening moment, he thought it was Alicia Pryor before the anti-agathics betrayed her to sickness and age. "Commissioner!" Damn. The von Bulow woman again. Her resemblance to the dead physician—that was another good reason to hate her guts; her conduct with Thorn had been the first.

"Yes?" Give Neave that, he barely raised an eyebrow at the Secess' tone.

"These two . . . officers are under arrest. A person in the status of arrest cannot be required to perform his full military duty, and if he is placed—by the authority who placed him in arrest or by superior authority—on duty inconsistent with such status his arrest is thereby terminated."

Neave achieved a mild glare. "Thank you," he said blandly.

"For God's sake!" Pauli spat. "You've got a chance to meet an intelligent, friendly alien race, and you want to play this by the book? Who knows more about the Cynthians than the man who made the first contact?" She flushed, and her voice trailed off awkwardly.

"We aren't asking to take command," Rafe put in quickly. "Just to serve in an advisory capacity. That doesn't have to be 'military duty,' is it, Commissioner?"

Taking Neave's look of relief for consent, "Come on," Rafe repeated. "Let's dust off those tapes."

* * *

As no one had had the heart to do for many years, he darkened a dome's wall. Once again, the great swooping Cynthian elders Pauli had called Uriel and Ariel darted across the night sky, whorls and comets gleaming along their wings, the scales of their bodies shimmering and the eerie glow of their compound eyes catching the light of both moons.

"We can't hear them 'speak,'" Rafe had long since deteriorated into lecture mode. "But the computer breaks the frequencies down into the analogical constructions typical of their thought processes . . ."

He could feel eyes on his back. *How could you kill creatures this beautiful?*

How? Deliberately Rafe skipped forward to the mercifully brief footage of the hatching towers, arrayed across the world's magnetic lines, and the one or two shots of the meter-long larvae they had called "eaters." He heard Pauli gasp, and himself gagged at his memories: Borodin falling into a field that teemed with the larvae; Pauli's "I hope he died before he hit the ground"; the awful stink of acid and ozone as they trained their blasters on creatures they had only begun to realize would metamorphose into winged splendor . . . *a shot of a young adult, wings unnaturally bright from the pigments we gave them; the last elder dying once they answered his question "Why?"*

"Shut it *down*, Rafe," Pauli muttered desperately.

He brought the lights up and stared bleakly about the crowded room.

"Those are Cynthians," he said. "Tell me, what did you see?"

"Well, sir," said the senior man of the survey team—about Lohr's age, Rafe judged, "we crossed the ocean and did some tests. Your man Halgerd ought to be really proud; the composites he's been working out for his gliders would definitely survive the storms we ran into. We picked up definite seismic activity, one or two dormant volcanoes, and a number of extinct ones. Apparently there's a chain of them. Well, in one of the largest caldera . . .

"We were getting readings on infrared. Life readings. So we dived to check . . ."

And saw the wings, the gleaming wings, Rafe thought. The catch of breath, the wonder, the ache at the back of the throat at all that beauty . . . *at least some are still alive! I hope they prosper.*

"They didn't seem to have any fear of our craft, Captain," came a reply to Neave's question.

"No, they never did fear . . . except their own children," Pauli muttered.

Winged, beautiful, and you killed them. How could you bring yourself to kill them? Neave, his mind full of the glory that they had thought—and thought wrongfully— had existed only on tape.

"You have no idea just how *big* this crater was. Down below was a sort of lava flat, but the crater itself was . . . it was carpeted with ground scrub like you have here, but wilder, lusher. We saw some of those towers like you showed us."

Hatching season, Rafe thought. The pale, fragile towers would split as the larvae woke to whatever ravenous instinct passed for awareness in them, and they ate. He shuddered, and realized that Neave was watching him. Carefully he drew himself erect and still.

"The tapes," he husked. "Take them. If I can help you, don't hesitate to let me know. I'm not going anywhere."

For the first time since she broke her leg, Pauli had consented to swallow a sedative. Rafe sat by their bed until she fell into uneasy sleep, then left the darkened room to look in on their children. One decent thing about house arrest: they had left them Serge and 'Cilla to care for.

But how long could that continue? Rafe stared down at his children. They were fearful now, afraid as he had once sworn no Cynthian child must ever be. Though years ago Serge had demanded the dignity of his own tiny room, tonight he and his younger sister huddled close together. Rafe bent over them, straightening their covers, easing twisted arms and legs that might ache tomorrow if he didn't move them now. 'Cilla whimpered a little, then sighed into peaceful dreams.

Two children were a heavy burden to lay on Lohr and Ayelet; perhaps David ben Yehuda . . . but if David too were sentenced . . . Rafe tried to ward off panic by thinking. Who would take the children? Thorn, perhaps: if all went well, in his grief for Alicia, he might turn toward a woman who had wanted him for years. It didn't matter. There were many children on Cynthia who had no parents. Lohr, for example: though these days he called himself ben Yehuda.

The settlers would look after Serge and little 'Cilla. It might be better that way. Others would be coming: farmers, refugees, scientists, teachers. What sort of life would his children have if the newcomers learned their parents had been the genocides who had tried to wipe out the native culture? No: the nights when Rafe could wander into his children's rooms just to observe them were fast running out.

The thought made him feel old and tired. Life on Cynthia aged a person. Hard as it seemed, those glossy young lawyers Neave had assigned him and Pauli were about their age; yet they were unlined, unscarred . . . innocent. Rafe chuckled sardonically.

A low, desperate cry made him whirl and run back toward the room he and Pauli shared. Like their children, she had twisted herself into a tight knot of fear, almost a fetal ball. He laid a hand on his wife's shoulder.

"Pauli, Pauli, come out of it," he murmured. Unaccustomed as she was to sedatives, she must be reacting to this one. Shadows still underlay her eyes; the sedative had brought her unconsciousness, but no rest.

She moaned and curled herself even tighter, rejecting the waking world. "No," she whimpered. "Don't . . . don't want to face them . . . it's cracking . . . oh, God, they're going to break free!"

Her cry woke her, and she hurled herself into a seated position. For a moment her eyes were blank with terror.

Then they focused on Rafe. Warmth and sanity returned to them.

He laid fingers on his lips, stepped to the door, and listened. No, Serge and 'Cilla hadn't been disturbed by their mother's nightmare. Reassured, he sat on the edge of the bed and held out his arms. She threw herself into them and clung to him as he wiped her forehead and eyes, then stroked the sweat-damp short curls—beginning to gray now—at the nape of her neck back into some order.

"Easy, love," he whispered. "It's almost over now."

"Tonight, when you showed the old tapes . . ."

"Hush, Pauli. They needed to know for the people who will come here after we're gone. And it's all evidence. Now quiet, rest now. Lean back . . ."

He eased her back down onto the bed and lay beside her, propped on an elbow to look at her while she molded herself against his side. So many years now they had been together, years when she had led, and he had followed until her strength was gone. Then it was he who would hold her, sustain her until that magnificent, dogged nerve of hers returned and she could fight once more.

For the last time, my love. Take my strength too, he wished at her and drew her close. She sighed and smiled, already more than half asleep again.

"Don't want to face them . . ." Long after Pauli slept, Rafe lay holding her, pondering her words. Face whom? There was only one possible answer to that. Pauli feared the eaters.

Scarcely daring to breathe lest he wake her, Rafe slid his arm out from beneath her head, lay still while listening to her even, shallow breathing, occasionally broken by little sobbing whimpers. Then, finally, he rose from their bed, and went into their living quarters.

Pauli wasn't the only one who could study law on the sly. He typed in a brief search. *Genocide . . . Extradition.* The screen flickered a few times, then cleared as letters formed on it. "Genocide . . . shall not be considered as political crimes for the purpose of extradition. The Contracting Parties pledge themselves in such cases to grant extradition in accordance with their laws and the treaties in force."

Neave, who seemed to subscribe to some weird variant on an ethic of nonviolence, was just looking for an out; and here it was—the thing that Pauli feared most of all: to be turned over to the Cynthians.

Rafe's breath came fast. Despite the chill in their quarters, he was sweating. Neave's exploration teams had sighted hatching towers. And he had seen one crack open, seen one of the meter-long larvae fasten its mandibles in a child's foot, smelled the acid, and heard her scream. Poor 'Cilla. She had survived that attack, but the lamed foot it left her with had ultimately killed her.

Borodin—until she was dragged back, Pauli had tried to blast her way through to his body, or whatever the eaters had left of it. Rafe still prayed that the old captain had been dead or unconscious, never to feel the bite of chitin or the burn of acid.

He and Pauli . . . bile gushed into his mouth. To be given to the eaters while still conscious, aware. "O God, help," he whispered.

If that were their sentence—Rafe shuddered. Through a haze of tears, he rummaged in a chest until he found his old kit and sighed with relief. People never questioned a xenobiologist's need for unpleasant chemicals: aromatics, or caustics, or even poisons. He caught up a glass pipette, dipped it into one such vial, then sealed it in a tiny tube which he secreted in an inner pocket of his jacket.

He yawned as the day's emotions finally registered on his nerves and body and headed back to bed. Gently he drew Pauli into his arms until she sighed in her sleep and curled against him, her head pillowed on his shoulder. So many years they had lain like that; the first time seemed like only a day or so ago. Soothed by the rhythm of his heartbeat, her breathing softened and steadied.

Such a fierce spirit in such a tiny frame. He knew that

Pauli had submitted herself to justice and would never evade her sentence by suicide. But as long as Rafe had that tiny pipette with its heavy dose of quick, lethal, and painless venom, she would not suffer. A flick of the thumb to open the tube, a quick scratch; and Pauli would have the peace she yearned for.

In that much, at least, he could protect her. Pauli wasn't the only one in the family to have secrets. *Don't let me lose my nerve*, he prayed.

He buried his face in Pauli's hair, which smelled of mown grass and sunlight. Her warmth lulled him, and within moments, he was asleep.

CHAPTER
25

The moons had set, and the night sky had not even begun to turn gray when the summons came. The people who had sat with them all that night started, then forced faces and bodies to stillness—all except Lohr. Like a much younger boy, Lohr flung himself first into Pauli's arms, then Rafe's. Ayelet embraced them slowly, as cautious of her pregnancy as Pryor (rest her soul) could have wanted.

"It kicked!" Pauli breathed.

"Pauli or Paul: not 'it,'" Ayelet corrected gravely. "I have always wanted . . ." she gulped, then went on, "a big family."

Rafe bent and kissed her cheek, cast a longing glance at the closed door of the room where Serge and 'Cilla slept.

"We mustn't keep them waiting," he spoke quickly. "Come on." His hand on Pauli's arm was warm, familiar, and it shook only slightly.

Only Amory Neave, his pilot, and two of the huskier survey personnel waited outside. Pauli looked them over ironically. *He cannot believe we need to be restrained. Not after all this time.* They had chosen the time well. Most restless of the settlers, Thorn Halgerd (finally accompanied by Ro Economus, thank God!), had joined some of the ship's crew in more flight tests of his ultralights; and at this hour, anyone else in the settlement was asleep, too tired to notice that their leaders had gone on . . . been sent on . . . ahead.

"Let's go quickly," she said. "If you'd wanted to draw a crowd, you could have let us sleep in."

Her bravado contrasted poorly with her pale face and dark-circled eyes. Still, for an instant, it was she who led the way toward the waiting scoutship. Her feet rang on the landing ramp. Once on board, she strapped herself into the padded seat, a movement still instinctive even after all these years. *One last flight*, she thought. *At least, I'll have that.*

She wished they would have permitted her to pilot the ship that would take her and Rafe across the ocean: an exercise in futility, seeing that her licenses must have expired years ago. But still, a last request . . . they had not asked her what her last request was, an attempt to preserve the illusion that she and Rafe were being taken to the eastern continent to help the survey team already camped there to speak with the Cynthians.

Weight pressed Pauli against the seat, which tilted as the ship rose into the air. Vibration built up, rose into a hum, then a whine: the ship quivered in a downdraft, then righted itself and gained altitude.

Rafe lay with his eyes closed, but opened them even as she watched. He brought one hand up to brush the breast pocket of his workjacket, then smiled at her.

The ship trembled again, then steadied. Trade winds? Pauli thought. A sort of slipstream? The surveyors working with Thorn Halgerd to build ultralights able to cross this world's oceans would need to know that. She would remember . . .

She would not have that chance. That, and the task of encouraging, leading, and loving the one small human settlement on Cynthia, would pass to cleaner hands today. It was good that Thorn and the crewmembers got along so well; it augured well for the day when Earth and its allies would send more settlers to Cynthia. Perhaps, she mused, it would be better if the newcomers built towns of their own, and didn't try to live among people who had all but forgotten that faces other than their own existed in the cosmos. They might like and respect the older settlers, but they could never, never understand.

From the moment when the exploration team disrupted her court-martial with shouts that they had spotted winged Cynthians, she had known Neave would extradite her and Rafe.

It was like him to have broken it gently. He had seen the Cynthians, she knew. There had been days when he had . . . vanished. "I am sorry, the commissioner is unable to see you . . ." Oh, she knew what that translated into. Neave would study the Cynthian survivors, would pity them as any decent person must; and when he returned, Pauli would finally see in his eyes the chill disgust with which decent men and women must regard her, regardless of her protests. The Cynthians had been winged, free, and beautiful; and she had killed them. The commissioner could not help but be revolted by the thing into which she had turned herself.

"They want to see you," he had told them.

"Do they understand what we did?"

"I tried to make them," he said. "I don't know how well I succeeded. You may have to explain the rest of it."

Somehow, Pauli doubted that. As a scholar and politician, Neave had proved too adept at the game of constructing verbal analogies that, raised from the level of human voices into the high frequencies of Cynthian communications, enabled humans and Cynthians to speak together. He would have made them understand. Still, if they wanted to hear her own admission of guilt, she had confessed once already; a second time wouldn't alter anything. And it would be good to see winged Cynthians again, she thought . . . *Uriel and Ariel dancing on the thermals . . . then, pallid, febrile, their wings shedding brightness, trying to restrain the younger Cynthians . . . folded wings plummeting into the flame* . . . She whimpered at the memory, then glanced about.

No one had heard. Not even Rafe had noticed. The whining of the ship's engines rose in pitch as it gained speed. Pauli shut her eyes, remembering the fantasy that had stayed with her from the first time she flew: that her nerves and muscles were keyed in with the fuselage, her arms extended with the aircraft's wings as it balanced and swooped—*like her son and his glider, or a Cynthian swooping down the airstreams.* Not a day had passed that she didn't yearn for that sight.

Likely, it would be one of her last. How could the Cynthians fail to condemn her and her husband? Loyalty to species—to Pauli's shock, even Elisabeth von Bulow had dragged out species loyalty as a reason not to extradite her.

"Do you call human having arms and legs, a pale skin like yours?" Beneatha had demanded. "Then why did you call Halgerd a construct? What about Armand over there, who lost a foot? And then there's me, of course."

Rafe lifted an eyebrow. "What are you thinking?"

"Of the way Beneatha set up Elisabeth von Bulow," Pauli said softly. Rafe chuckled, the low, rich sound Pauli loved. "Next thing she knew, she was protesting that humans didn't have to have pale skins, that she wasn't a racist . . ."

"'Then why,'" Rafe drew Beneatha's words out of his own recollections, "'do you argue against extradition in this case? Because they don't look like people? Because they're just bugs, and you don't need to worry about the rights of a bunch of *moths?*'" Deliberately she had used an epithet for which she had punished a generation of children on Cynthia. "'What's Thorn, then, but a moth with arms and legs? What's to stop you from thinking of me as just a moth with black skin? Oh, you claim that your people *made* him? Show me the building blocks you used: egg, sperm; human, down to the last chromosome. He looks like you, but call him a moth too. Easier to kill him that way, isn't it?

"'Racism, shape-prejudice—damned if I know which is uglier. Maybe this is. After all, you don't enslave moths; you just kill 'em. Look, I've met Cynthians. You haven't. They're human all right, a lot more human than some I could mention.'"

That was when Beneatha realized that she had just argued successfully to turn her own friendly old enemies over to the Cynthians. Intelligent they were, human by the extended moral definition she had proposed. But they were *alien.* What sort of punishment would they mete out? Pauli had never seen Beneatha flee the site of a victorious argument before. And she had only heard her weep once.

She sighed. What other punishment could there be? If only Rafe thought she was a restless sleeper, not every night, she waked sweating from a vision of him staked out on a plain that writhed with newly hatched, ravenous Cynthians while, overhead, their elders watched to see a grisly justice done.

Better not to think of it now. Concentrate on the flying. Considerately, Neave had ordered the pilot not to opaque the ports as the ship arced up to where the sky was perpetually dark. *The condemned woman gets one last request: to fly again. But what is Rafe's request?* Then, sunlight exploded over the arc of the terminator, slashing across land and cloud-frosted water alike, shimmering in the haze of atmosphere; and Pauli shivered with delight.

Just for this moment, the ship was hers. She could imagine herself and Rafe hurtling free of the constraints of Cynthia's air and Cynthia's gravity and Cynthia's burdens, speeding clear of the system and then, in one triumphant Jump, leaving it behind them forever. Then the ship changed attitude. The arc of its climb began to level out, and the whine of its engines hushed to the whisper of hypersonic travel.

Of course, they could not break free. Beneath the stars and indigo of true space, so like the whorls on a Cynthian's wings, the horizon glowed crimson and yellow; and they sped toward it, the air in the tiny ship vibrating with the speed of their passage. Moments later, the ship arced downward. The sharp contrasts of dawn and deep space diminished and blurred as the ship reentered atmosphere over the eastern ocean. As it slowed and slashed downward, it quivered, buffeted by the fierce ocean winds. Lashings of rain vanished into steam as they neared the ship, its skin superheated by the speed of deceleration. Curdled white and gray, pierced by an occasional flash of lightning, enveloped them.

In the half-light, Neave's mouth was pursed into a thin

line, and his skin was greenish. Rafe kept his eyes shut, retreating into that calm fastness that had sustained them both for all these years. Pauli swallowed hard and prayed that she didn't disgrace her former career by heaving up her last meal all over the bulkhead. It truly had been too long since she had flown. She was truly truly earthbound now. Perhaps that was part of her punishment.

"The ocean," Neave nodded toward the viewports. Star pilot turned landswoman, turned Franklin, what could she know about seas? A tossing immensity of waves, capped with white like the clouds through which they had passed, a violence of motion and color that held her enthralled—the ship leveled off. For the first time she felt a sensation not of acceleration, but of speed. They were hastening toward a blur on the horizon that resolved, even as she gazed, into a barrier range of rock cliffs that the ship gained height to surmount. Again rain and wind buffeted them; and once again they descended.

"Must be a barrier range," Rafe murmured. "We're beyond it now."

Sun shone through the clear ports now, drying the beads of rain that still slanted across them.

"Sensors report life," the pilot announced.

Instinctively Rafe and Pauli sat upright. That would be the Cynthians.

"Careful," Neave ordered. "They may not know to evade us."

After all, it would hardly do if the very ship that carried Pauli and Rafe to justice inadvertently shredded the judges.

"I'm running the warn-off tape," announced the pilot, and Neave nodded approval.

"There they are!" Rafe cried, turning in his straps to point at a blur of sunlight on wings far feebler, but more wonderful than the ship's wings which had lured them too close. The ship slowed and lost altitude with such speed that Neave swallowed convulsively.

The Cynthians withdrew to a safer distance. Seeing them bank and wheel, Pauli sighed once, then subsided.

These Cynthians were not hers to marvel at; she was theirs to judge and, most probably, execute. She gulped against the sick fear that flowed up from her belly at what means they might choose.

"Caldera below," announced the pilot's voice, filtered from controls. The ship banked, then descended so steeply that the passenger restraints tightened and the seats shifted into full landing position. Below them yawned an enormous crater. Whatever volcano had created it must have lain dormant for hundreds of years. Now a lake glistened like a sapphire in a setting of red gold . . . and emerald, since the rest of the basin was thick with lush ground cover above which only a few skeletal trees projected.

At a safe distance, the Cynthians followed them down.

The ship touched down. Pauli released the seat restraints and stood. With the vibration of the engines and the wind no longer coursing through the ship and up into her own body, she felt abruptly weak. The ship itself seemed like a dead thing—unlike the glowing creatures that poised nearby the instant the landing ramp extended.

Their antennae and palpae quivered back and forth so quickly that they were practically a luminous blur.

"That's a lively conversation they're having about us," Rafe commented as he helped the survey team set up the translators.

"Were *your* Cynthians always so curious?" asked Neave.

"Always," Rafe said, low-voiced. "The young adults especially. They would try to snag things with their winghooks and pull them over to where their claws could get a grip on them. The elders stopped them every time they could."

"This group seems fascinated by us," remarked a woman from survey. "Each time we land, more and more Cynthians come to meet us."

"It isn't just you," Pauli told her. "Look."

Not a hundred meters away rose the first of a series of

pale towers. She knew that if she checked, she would see that on this continent too, the Cynthians' instinct had led them to build their incubators along the "lines" spun out by their world's magnetic poles.

"They build those towers to hold their eggs," Rafe said. "So they come to check on the hatching. See those fissures? It won't be long now."

He moved to stand beside Pauli. He had one hand pressed against his chest, and alarm stabbed through her: he had never complained of chest pains, never suffered shortness of breath. With his free arm, he hugged her to him. Her head came to the top of his shoulder. She rubbed her cheek against his arm, even as her nostrils flared at what she couldn't help thinking of as "moth-spoor": the musty, musky smell of excited creatures, combined now with a hint of something acrid, which must be the larvae before they hatched.

Her hand clutched for the sidearm she had surrendered weeks past, and she knew that Neavc had seen the move.

"You couldn't judge me before," she told him. "So don't try to on this. You can't imagine what the eaters look like. Or smell like."

Once the first larva touched her, how long would it be till she fainted from shock and agony? Even now, she could remember Captain Borodin's surprised, agonized bellow as an adult's venom touched him. She drew a shuddering breath and moved out from the circle of Rafe's arm. Three or four of the largest adults mantled their wings, lifted easily into the air, and let themselves drift toward the humans, landing with a clap of wings that quite evidently called the meeting to order. Bright scales drifted from their wings to settle on Pauli's face and hair. How like Uriel and Ariel they were.

"Let's get this over with," she said.

The translators glowed, their screens taking on the green glow she remembered so well, and the Cynthians, antennae shivering in anticipation, drew nearer.

* * *

"The cracks in those towers are getting wider," Pauli warned Neave and his crew. "If they should split, head for the ship and take off!"

The sun had long since turned the amber of late afternoon, and a wind had picked up: exciting weather, if you had wings or a glider to fly with. Many of the Cynthians circled aloft, though their gemlike compound eyes always returned to the translators and the humans that clustered about them.

"What about the Cynthians?"

"They're just as scared of their young as you'll be. *Believe me*, you'll be scared." She forced herself not to shudder just this once and hoped that her comment hadn't sounded like a rationalization of her crime.

"They're not moving," Neave pointed out. "Let's go through it one more time."

Pauli sighed. So far, this business of getting sentenced to death was more tedious than frightening. She nodded at Rafe, who crouched beside the translators, only one or two meters away from the largest Cynthian of all. If he stretched out a hand, he could probably touch him.

That reminded her. "Rafe," she warned in a low voice. "Don't stay so close. Remember, the horns below the palpae—they secrete a nerve toxin." Just one touch of it had been enough to send Captain Borodin screaming out of control and to his death in a field full of eaters.

The translator's screen flickered, then lit.

"Here it goes," Rafe said. His hands were shaking from the strain. After one or two errors that made him hiss, clear his screens, and begin again, he produced the first of the analogies that he had constructed to explain to these Cynthians what happened to their sibs far to the west.

Adult Cynthian/larvae; human adult/human children.

One of the elders flicked out a wing toward the nearest tower in an almost human gesture. Rafe nodded, then thought better of it, and keyed in the signal both groups had agreed upon for affirmative. As the larvae were to the Cynthian adults, those small, two-legged creatures curled up on the screen were to the human adults.

Well enough.

Now for the next one.

Cynthian larvae/ground scrub; human children/ground scrub.

Actually, that stretched the truth. Humans didn't really eat the ground scrub, but they needed the land it covered in order to grow their own food.

The Cynthian elders waited, antennae and palpae rigid, wings motionless.

Sighing, Rafe keyed in the next analogy.

Larvae/human children; human children/sign of prone figure or dead body.

The larvae needed the same food as the human children and would destroy them if they could.

Abruptly Rafe became angry. He keyed in a new analogy.

Larvae/Cynthian adult, one wing broken, lying on the ground; larger larvae/blank space. Surely it had happened that an injured Cynthian could not flee the hatchlings and lay in their path, to be devoured along with everything else. The elders quivered, a quick flash of splendor as their wings shook, then reverted to their previous stillness.

"Tell them, Rafe. For God's sake, let's make an end!" Pauli muttered.

Humans/adult Cynthians; humans/adult Cynthians lying dead.

There it was in so many words: humans had killed Cynthians.

Humans/larvae; humans/blank space.

Humans had eliminated the Cynthians' larvae. On one continent, at least, there had been no next generation for bright winged elders and rash nymphae to guard, then flee from. An instant later, all the Cynthians had thrust themselves into flight, as if terrified of the humans.

The screen went blank, and red lights flashed on the translators as the Cynthians' agitation burned out one of the boards.

Behind him, he heard one of the survey team ask Commissioner Neave in an unhappy, low voice, "Sir, are we really going to leave these people to be eaten by grubs? Doesn't seem decent."

Neave glared at the man. "Well, it doesn't!" he muttered, then turned back to the translator, opening its back and replacing the board. The fissures in the hatching towers seemed to have widened. Rafe checked his breast pocket, gauging the distances between the towers and him, between him and Pauli. He would have time to grab the hypodermic and spare his wife before the larvae overran them. She would never scream like 'Cilla when the acid and the mandibles attacked her foot; she would never know what killed her. Reassured, he waited for repairs to be finished.

The elders' antennae flared, whipped into immobility, then fluttered more slowly. Good. They'd reached agreement on what they wanted to ask.

Larvae/ground scrub; humans/ground scrub.

That was a restatement. Rafe signed "affirmative."

A new message formed on the screen, and he took so long to puzzle it out that the screen blanked, and he had to signal for the Cynthians to send it again.

Yes, that was a tower, a hatching tower forming pixel by pixel on the screen. A tower encircled . . . by what? A crater like the one in which they stood.

Well enough. *Hatching tower/crater; human children/ interrogative?*

"They want to know whether the Cynthians we killed built their towers in craters like this one!" Rafe said.

"What difference does it make?" Pauli asked.

"Just answer the question," Neave said.

Rafe's hands trembled as he typed out his answer:

Cynthian larvae/open plain; human settlement/open plain.

Not only did the larvae and the humans require the same food sources, and the same land, the larvae, like the humans, roved unchecked upon it.

The elders opened their wings. One pointed with its winghooks at the humans. *Wings/Cynthians; wingless arms/humans.*

Winged Cynthian/mountains; wingless human/beneath mountains.

"I think they understand we had no place to go," Rafe whispered. "They don't seem to realize . . ." He wanted to crawl off and throw up, or weep because so far, these Cynthians did not regard him as a monster.

"Do you see that, Neave?" Pauli demanded. "You tell that to von Bulow, and you ask her, which of us is more human. *They* don't have the slightest idea what genocide is."

A scream of sound and light blanked the translators and nearly shorted out the entire communications system. Most of the Cynthians circled aloft, agitation in every movement of their tiny grasping claws and their wings. Several even showed the everted horns, bright drops of poison glinting on them, indicating extraordinary distress.

"I think that that really upset them, sir," said the woman from survey. "By their definition, civilized people keep their kids . . . their larvae . . . in check."

Finally, insistently, one signal appeared on the screen. *Larvae/towers; towers/crater.* Over and over again.

"Let them know we understand!" Neave ordered.

Rafe signalled agreement. "I think that this is what we've got so far. *Civilized* Cynthians understand that their larvae are a menace, so they build the hatching towers in craters like this, where the ground scrub is thick enough to sustain them until they hibernate and can emerge as nymphae, to fly out of the crater. I assume that once they've metamorphosed, the others take them in charge, just like they do . . . they did . . . back home. Anything else seems unthinkable to them."

"As if," Neave spoke half to himself, "aliens had landed on Earth among headhunters or cannibals, and we had to explain *them.*"

"What difference does it make?" Pauli asked. " 'Civilized' or not, they're still *people!*"

Rafe sealed his breast pocket and strode over toward her. "Are you truly that determined to die?" he asked.

"They think it may make a difference." He gestured at the towers. "Pauli, for the love of God . . ."

"Getting another signal."

Rafe drew Pauli with him as he went to study it.

Five human figures/ship; interrogative/many ships.

"Yes," Rafe muttered. "There will be more ships, more people . . ." His fingers flew on the keyboard and the screen filled: *many humans/many ships.*

Clearly the Cynthians wanted something of the people who had placed themselves in their power.

Cynthians/interrogative; many humans/many ships.

"What happens to you when those humans come?"

That was quite a question. It was only a matter of time, months perhaps, until Neave's report drew the homeless or the adventurous to Cynthia to settle there. He was a man of Earth; he knew his world's history, one in which technologically sophisticated cultures drove out and destroyed less advanced ones.

Neave stepped forward. This was definitely something he could understand. "We hang together, or we all hang separately," he muttered. "You tell them, Rafe. You tell them that when those humans come, they will be protected."

Pauli grimaced at him. "Like the Indians or the Tasmanians? We went through those rationalizations years ago."

Neave smiled. For the first time since he had touched down on this planet, he knew his course. "But we've got two things that the Indians and the Tasmanians never had."

"What?"

"First, the determination never to allow that to happen again. I know, we've heard that before. But now, we have you and your descendants, to make certain that no one tries it. To stop anyone who dares."

Rafe blinked hard. When they returned to the settlement, he would destroy the poisoned needle. He shook and drew Pauli close to him. They would have years yet. They would not be easy years; he foresaw a day when settlers would outgrow the west, and demand to explore this continent, to strip it of its resources, and drive its inhabitants off their home. Not while he lived, they wouldn't. And not while his children lived either.

"You know," Neave told the two of them, "some people used to think that the worst punishment for a genocide was to be forced to live in the midst of people he had tried to kill. You . . . you can never forget, you know. And you must pass the knowledge on to your children. You will be truly set apart, for all time."

"Signal again!"

This time the screen showed *Tower, falling on its side/larvae; humans/ship.*

"The hatcheries are beginning to break up!" Rafe pointed. In a few moments the ground would swarm with eaters. Already the adult Cynthians had all taken to the air.

Neave turned toward the Cynthian elders and nodded with real respect. "We've been warned," he said. "So long as we leave them in peace, they want nothing more: no punishment, no vengeance."

"I told you how gentle they were," Pauli said. "There was only one time when they fought; and that was to protect their young."

"Speaking of which—"

Collecting their equipment, they raced for the boarding ramp as a crash from behind them warned that the first of the hatching towers had fallen. The stink of acid grew strong in the clear, cool air of the dying afternoon.

"Take off as soon as you can. We don't want to catch any of the larvae in our backwash," Neave said.

Rafe strapped in quickly, averting his face. Let them get off the ground quickly! He didn't think he could see one Cynthian larva, let alone a crater full of them, without wanting to burn them out of existence. But he had the rest of his life to conceal that feeling and to insure that his children grew up without it. There were Cynthians to guard. There would always be—thank God—Cynthians to guard.

"Each generation," Pauli muttered as acceleration pinned them into their seats. "Each generation will have to decide all over again not to kill, not to exploit."

"But there will be caretakers to remind them of the price to them as well as their intended victims," Rafe said. "Us, and our children."

The ship arced up through the clouds and into the stillness of the night sky, sprinkled with stars in whorls more wonderful than the patterns on a Cynthian's wings. Above them were the stars that they would never reach again, though their children or grandchildren might, if all went well, soar among them once again. Before them lay the atonement that would encompass their entire lives. It might not be—was not—enough; but it was all that they had to give. Behind them lay the memory of a splendor of wings.